A Black British Canon?

A Black British Canon?

Edited by

Gail Low

and

Marion Wynne-Davies

First published 2006 by
PALGRAVE MACMILLAN
Houndmills, Basingstoke, Hampshire RG21 6XS and
175 Fifth Avenue, New York, N.Y. 10010
Companies and representatives throughout the world

PALGRAVE MACMILLAN is the global academic imprint of the Palgrave
Macmillan division of St. Martin's Press, LLC and of Palgrave Macmillan Ltd.
Macmillan® is a registered trademark in the United States, United Kingdom
and other countries. Palgrave is a registered trademark in the European
Union and other countries.

ISBN-13: 978–1–4039–4268–5
ISBN-10: 1–4039–4268–4

This book is printed on paper suitable for recycling and made from fully
managed and sustained forest sources.

A catalogue record for this book is available from the British Library

A catalogue record for this book is available from the Library of Congress

10   9   8   7   6   5   4   3   2   1
15   14   13   12   11   10   09   08   07   06

Printed and bound in Great Britain by
Antony Rowe Ltd, Chippenham and Eastbourne

For our children
Sian, Richard and Robbie

Contents

PART III   GENEALOGIES AND INTERVENTIONS

List of Illustrations

Acknowledgements

We owe a debt of gratitude to many colleagues for their invaluable advice. Primarily, the participants and contributors to two conferences at the University of Dundee, *A Black British Canon?* (2001) and *Black British* (2004), helped formulate, develop and consolidate ideas for this book. We would also like to thank several individuals for their continued commitment to this project, in particular Peter Easingwood, Jane Goldman, Peter Kitson, E.A. Markham, Susheila Nasta, Caryl Phillips, Gordon Spark, John Thieme, Aliki Varvogli and Geoff Ward. We have received invaluable financial support from the University of Dundee, the Dundee Contemporary Arts and the Scottish Arts Council. Our thanks are also due to the editorial staff at Palgrave Macmillan, Helen Craine, Paula Kennedy and Emily Rosser, who have been very, very patient. Finally, we wish to thank our families for their good humour, in particular our three children who have tried hard to understand exactly what we were writing and why we were doing it.

GAIL LOW
MARION WYNNE-DAVIES

Notes on the Contributors

Sandra Courtman is Senior Lecturer at the Institute of Education, University of Sheffield. She has edited *Beyond the Blood, the Beach and the Banana: New Perspectives in Caribbean Studies* (2004) and Joyce Gladwell's *Brown Face Big Master* for the Macmillan Caribbean Classics Series (2003). Her research activities and publications are particularly concerned with recovering 'lost' and occluded Caribbean women's writing from the 1960s and 1970s.

Alison Donnell is Senior Lecturer in Postcolonial Literatures at Nottingham Trent University. She has edited *Companion to Contemporary Black British Culture* (2002) and co-edited *The Routledge Reader in Caribbean Literature* (1996) and *Representing Lives: Women and Autobiography* (2000). Her forthcoming works include: *Working on Critical Moments: Rereading Twentieth Century Caribbean Literature, Una Marson and Louise Bennett* and *Una Marson: Selected Poems*. She also co-edits *Interventions*.

Femi Folorunso is an Arts Development Officer at the Scottish Arts Council, Edinburgh, where he has shared responsibility for cultural diversity and equality policies. Before joining the Arts Council, he was co-director of the Scottish Universities International Summer School. He has taught dramatic literature and cultural studies at various universities in the UK and in Nigeria, and his research interests encompass post-colonial drama and theatre of the Black diaspora. He is currently working on a book on the cultural sociology of modern Scottish drama.

Gail Low teaches contemporary anglophone writing at the University of Dundee. She has published essays in *New Formations, Women: A Cultural Review, Research into African Literatures, Kunapipi* and *Journal of Commonwealth Literature*. She is the author of *White Skins/Black Masks: Representation and Colonialism* (1996) and is currently working on the institutional history of the rise of literatures in English in the UK, 1950–68.

John McLeod is Senior Lecturer in English at the University of Leeds, where he teaches postcolonial literatures. He is the author of *Beginning Postcolonialism* (2000) and *Postcolonial London: Rewriting the Metropolis* (2004), and is co-editor (with David Rogers) of *The Revision of Englishness*

(2004). His forthcoming work includes *The Routledge Companion to Postcolonial Studies*.

Michael McMillan is a British-born writer of Vincentian parentage. His plays and performance pieces have been produced in the UK and Holland and include: *The School Leaver, Hard Time Pressure* (Royal Court Theatre); *On Duty* (Channel 4); *God Don't Like Ugly* (DNA Amsterdam); *Invisible* (based on Ralph Ellison's novel *Invisible Man*; Double Edge Theatre and The King's Head Theatre); *Brother 2 Brother* (Talawa Theatre, 1998); and *Blood for Britain* (Radio 4). Books include: *Living Proof: Views of World Living with HIV/AIDS; The Black Boy Pub & Other Stories; If I Could Fly; Growing Up is Hard to Do.* He has also had essays in: *Lets get it On: The Politics of Black Performance (1995); Black British Culture & Society* (2000); *Theatre and Empowerment: World Drama on Stage* (2002); *Black Theatre: Ritual Performance in the African Diaspora* (2002).

Mike Phillips is an academic, writer, broadcaster and journalist, critic and award-winning crime writer. His novels include *Blood Rights* (1989), *The Late Candidate* (1990), *Point of Darkness* (1994), *An Image to Die For* (1995), *The Dancing Face* (1997) and *A Shadow of Myself* (2000). He has co-produced and co-written the television series and book, *Windrush: The Irresistible Rise of Multi-Racial Britain* (1998). *London Crossings* (2001), a 'biography' of black Britain, is his most recent book. He is currently Royal Literary Fund Fellow at the London Institute (LCC), and is writing the second of his Central European trilogy of novels, a volume of essays on British identity in the 21st century with Continuum, and preparing six virtual exhibitions on Slavery and the Making of the Caribbean, and Black Europeans, for the British Library website. He is also the Cross-Cultural Curator at the Tate Gallery, London.

James Procter is Senior Lecturer in English at the University of Newcastle upon Tyne. He is the author of *Stuart Hall* (2004) and *Dwelling Places* (2003), and editor of *Writing Black Britain 1948–1998* (2000). He was also an editorial advisor for Routledge's *Companion to Contemporary Black British Culture* (2002).

Leon Wainwright is Lecturer in History of Art at Manchester Metropolitan University. His publications include contributions to *Wadabagei* (Fall, 2000), *Companion to Contemporary Black British Culture* (2002), *Visual Culture in Britain at the End of Empire* (2004), *Black Arts in Postwar Britain* (2004), *African Artists in the UK* (2005), *SALIDAA: South Asian Art and*

Literature in the Diaspora, and exhibitions at the British Council (New Delhi, India) and Gallery Momo (Johannesburg, South Africa). He is currently completing a book entitled *Diaspora Presence*.

Andy Wood is completing his doctoral dissertation on Black British culture at the University of Dundee. He has contributed to *Wasafiri* and was part of the editorial team of the *Companion to Contemporary Black British Culture* (2002), writing entries on music and musicians.

Marion Wynne-Davies teaches in the English Department at the University of Dundee. She has published essays on postcolonial writing, Australian and New Zealand film and Canadian women's poetry. She has also edited several collections of essays including, *Much Ado About Nothing and The Taming of the Shrew* (2001) and, with S.P. Cerasano, *Gloriana's Face: Women, Public and Private in the English Renaissance* (1992).

Introduction

Gail Low and Marion Wynne-Davies

The 1980s and 1990s saw the emergence and consolidation of an important body of creative writing, visual and performing arts that circulates under the sign of 'Black British'. Despite the problems associated with, what Kobena Mercer has called, an 'authenticating myth of origins' in the history of black representation, the enormous productivity of the 1980s represents a kind of creative watershed in black expressive cultures.[1] It has certainly led to the current eminent stature of some black artists and to an intense critical interest in their work. Significantly, a number of important creative writing anthologies appeared in this decade, notably, *News from Babylon* (1984), *A Dangerous Knowing: Four Black Women Poets* (1984), *Let it be Told: Black Women Writers in Britain* (1987), *Watchers and Seekers* (1987), *Charting the Journey: Writings by Black and Third World Women* (1988), *Storms of the Heart: An Anthology of Black Arts and Culture* (1988), and *Hinterland* (1989).[2] The 1980s was also book-ended by the publication of one of the earliest critical and literary guides to black British writing, David Dabydeen and N. Wilson-Tagoe's *A Reader's Guide to West Indian and Black British Literature* (1988).[3] The sheer quality and quantity of black writing that emerged in the 1980s was consolidated in the 1990s with novelists such as Caryl Phillips, Hanif Kureshi and David Dabydeen, and poets like Linton Kwesi Johnson, Fred D'Aguiar, Grace Nichols and Jackie Kay, who moved beyond national recognition to international acclaim.[4]

At the same time, the emergence of independent film and video workshops in the 1980s generated a lively self-reflexive aesthetic debate that was to have important repercussions on black British culture as a whole. Both art house and more popular films, such as *Burning an Illusion* (1981), *My Beautiful Laundrette* (1985), *Territories* (1986), *Passion of Remembrance* (1986), *Handsworth Songs* (1986), *Looking for Langston Hughes* (1986) and *Sammy and Rosie Get Laid* (1987), were screened to critical acclaim. If no single black

1

British director (or scriptwriter) has quite achieved the fame of figures like John Singleton or Spike Lee in the USA, there is now a significant cluster of black filmmakers and scriptwriters (John Akomfrah, Issac Julien, Julien Henriques, Meera Syal, Ayub Khan-Din, Udayan Prasad and Gurinda Chadha among others) with a credible body of work to their credit.[5]

In the adjacent area of cultural and artistic production, the Blk Art Group, the Black Art Gallery, the ICA, Ikon, the work of the MAAS (the Minority Arts Advisory Service) and the publication of *Artrage* have all served to make the names of black British artists, like Lubaina Himid, Sonia Boyce, Keith Piper, Maud Sulter, Ingrid Pollard, Eddie Chambers and Rasheed Araeen familiar to a wider public.[6] For example, Araeen curated *The Other Story*, an exhibition of work by Asian, African and Caribbean artists in Britain at the Hayward Gallery in 1989.[7] Despite the controversy generated around the category 'black art', and the refusal of some well-known artists to take part in the event, *The Other Story* is recognized as a key moment in the mainstream public recognition of black artists. Since then, Chris Offili and Steve McQueen have both won the prestigious Turner prize, while Issac Julien was shortlisted in 2001.

The black presence in music, theatre and other performing arts has an equally active if longer and more diffuse history. The 1970s reggae scene, which encompassed groups like ASWAD and Steel Pulse, gave expression to black urban youth culture, and had its counterpart in the 'dub' poetry of the 1970s and 1980s, with poets like Linton Kwesi Johnson. And with Soul II Soul came the popularization of specifically black British urban dance music.[8] Subsequently, groups like Temba, Talawa Theatre Company and Tara Arts, which began forming from the mid-1970s onwards, contributed performances throughout the 1980s and 1990s that worked towards reinterpreting classic canonical literary works with an eye for, and awareness of, cultural difference; they have also brought new performing traditions to British theatre.[9]

It is not surprising, therefore, that academic interest in black British culture should have begun to respond to these 1980s developments and is now seen to be rapidly expanding. Key scholarly texts began appearing as early as 1996, but 2000 saw a flush of publications, including Kwesi Owusu's *Black British Culture and Society*, James Procter's *Writing Black Britain*, Gen Doy's *Black Visual Culture* and Courttia Newland and Kadija George Sesay's *IC3: The Penguin Book of New Black Writing in Britain*.[10] In 2002, the launch of the *Routledge Companion to Contemporary Black British Culture* marked the consolidation of a discipline.[11] Moreover, new academic monographs and collections of essays are appearing all the time; for example, Mark Stein's *Black British Literature* and Kadija Sesay's *Write Black Write British: From Post Colonial to Black British Literature* are the most recent examples.[12]

Yet, the questions about who or what is black British and what kind of artistic practices and material culture is signified by the appellation, have mutated and modified throughout this period of academic interest, and are currently the subject of much debate. Taking the long view, late-1960s political activism in Britain drew inspiration from the Civil Rights campaign in the United States, with its protests against racism and its demands for equal justice and citizenship rights. Subsequently, the politicization of black identity gained force with new social movements, such as Black Power, which crossed the Atlantic, and Rastafarianism, which came via the Caribbean. In Britain there were specific campaigns for educational reform (the Black Parents Movement) and anti-racism in policing (particularly towards the repeal of the 'sus' or stop-and-search laws).[13] Black British, as a political collectivity, gained discursive currency with organizations that campaigned jointly, such as, the Race Today collective, the Organization of Women of Asian and African Descent (OWAAD) and Southhall Black Sisters. But what 'black' referred to or the use of 'black British' did not always fit into an identikit. For example, James Berry, in the introduction to his seminal poetry anthology *News from Babylon*, writes of a black aesthetics and a black diaspora that resulted from an Afro-centric history and legacy of slavery, though he does not employ the term black British.[14] In contrast, Rhonda Cobham writes of a 'Black female identity' and 'Black British speech rhythms' in her preface to *Watchers and Seekers*, while also including writers of South Asian and Chinese descent.[15] Prabhu Guptara's *Black British Literature: An Annotated Bibliography* defines 'black British' as 'those people of non-European origin who are now or were in the past, entitled to hold a British passport and displayed a substantial commitment to Britain, for example by living a large part of their lives here.'[16] Both Gilane Tawadros, in her forward to the *Mirage: Enigmas of Race, Difference and Desire* exhibition in 1995, and Doy in *Black Visual Culture*, write of the difficulties of settling on an agreed nomenclature for what 'black' signifies. For example, the use of upper or lower case 'b' in the term denotes different groups, with the lower case signifying non-white communities that have suffered a history of racism, and the upper case 'B' referring to an assertion of a chosen Afro-centric cultural identity.[17] By the late 1980s critics favoured an anti-essentialist critique of identity that provided a conceptual and philosophical underpinning for a collectivity of black peoples with shared histories and experiences of racism. More famously, Stuart Hall's 'new ethnicities' stemmed from a reworked politics of representation that would reveal the 'extraordinary diversity of subjective positions, social experiences, and cultural identities which compose the category "Black"'.[18] As Kobena Mercer remarks, various cultural groupings of Asian, African and Caribbean descent 'interpellated themselves and each other as "black" ... predicated on political and not biological simi-larities' in order to engender an inclusive and 'pluralistic sense of an imagined community'.[19]

The strain of this inclusive agenda has led other critics to bemoan the dangers of homogenization. Tariq Modood's critique was not atypical; he argued against the race relations' orthodoxy, which decreed that there was a 'common positive identity behind the idea of "black"', asserting, instead, that the racism Asians and blacks suffer is a 'negative condition' and not how communities should 'understand and value ... [themselves] to be'.[20] In the 1990s, the fracturing of political alliances across cultural and ethnic groups has led to a more restricted use of the term 'black British'. Hall acknowledges as much when he observes, somewhat regretfully, that following the 'individualist cast' of the post-Thatcher period, the differ-ences and internal divides within black British identity mean that Afro-Caribbeans and Asians can no longer be 'subsumed and mobilised under a single political category.'[21] State-instituted policies of multiculturalism and equal opportunities, coupled with shrinking resources, have encouraged further fragmentation. As Ambalavaner Sivanadan remarks, instead of banding together in resistance, communities are encouraged to battle each other 'over position and power ... [for] a place under the ethnic sun'.[22]

There are, however, some exceptions to this fragmentation. For example, even as late as 2000, Doy's study of black visual culture uses the term, 'black British', in an inclusive fashion, attempting 'to preserve the resonances of collective perception and response to social oppression on the grounds of "race"'.[23] The increased utilisation of separate categories, such as 'British Asian', 'Asian British' or, more importantly, the politicized constructions of a religious and ethnic identity such as, 'British Muslims', has begun to mark a new phase in the politics of culture and the culture of politics.

The contestation over the name 'black British' and what it signifies, is an important reminder of the need to resist the naturalizing of race as skin colour, particularly through common usage. The inclusion of a shared history and cultural politics of race across a range of disciplinary fronts may be necessary to guard against a whitened version of Britishness, thereby, to rephrase Gilroy, putting black back in the Union Jack.[24] But, at the same time, we should be wary of glossing over debates about black aesthetics and a black British canon, ignoring disputes in favour of a smooth and seamless history. It is precisely this form of ghettoization that Fred D'Aguiar argues against in 'Against Black British Literature', where he rejects the 'skin deep' blind herding of black people into a special category, empha-sizing that this denies the 'will and dynamisim' of black people in their endeavours.[25] It is essential, therefore, that contestations over the meaning of the terms, 'British' and 'black British,' should not be swept aside, since they foreground the ideological and discursive imprint of key political signs.

In many ways, these conflicts call attention to the performative function of the identitarian terms as signifiers of political mobilization and representation, leading to questions such as, who calls such a collectivity 'black', for what ends, and to what effect? Given such contestations, and the urgency of the subject area in terms of cultural analysis across institutions of higher education and schools, it is important that the concept of black British and the terms of its cultural productions are re-examined. Black British writing has a long history, beginning with the slave narratives of Olaudah Equiano and Ignatius Sancho, through the work of 1930s Caribbean writers such as C.L.R. James and Una Marson, to the Windrush generation of authors and artists including Claudia Jones, George Lamming, Sam Selvon, John La Rose, Kamau Braithwaite, V.S. Naipaul, Wilson Harris and Aubrey Williams.[26] These writers demonstrate an acute awareness of being black in Britain, but their work simultaneously figures as a substantial contribution to British culture and politics. This book sets out, not to trace a history or highlight areas of productivity, but to challenge the way in which black British writers and practitioners are being seamlessly incorporated into the academic canon, and to problematize the consequent disciplinary institutionalization.

A Black British Canon? excavates the wider possible significations of 'black British' by exploring the term in specific relation to visual, textual and performative traditions, thus providing a multidisciplinary and multi-generic overview. The book also seeks to historicize the emergence of key writers, intellectuals, artists and texts against a moving backdrop of a black British textual and political history. Essays in the collection invoke a broadly materialist approach by addressing social and cultural movements, and by examining the institutional, funding and publishing networks that support black British culture. As opposed to ascribing biblical status (sacred value) to a body of texts or writers, all essayists are concerned with both the politics and the processes of canon formation. Some take issue with expectations that black British texts must exhibit identifiable and characteristic traits, preferring instead to interrogate those responses. Others debate the use and abuse of canonization, asking what is included or excluded from its domain and arguing for a perpetually renewable canon.[27] Others look specifically at the critical, historical and paradigmatic challenges that black British offer. Given such diasporic allegiances combined with interdisciplinary and generic cross-fertilizations, the relentless border crossings represented by the essays in this collection call out for a new language of criticism – one that is sensitive to specific intersections between national and transnational modalities and adroit in its handling of the complexities of aesthetic modes. This volume as a whole asserts that we need greater self-reflexivity with regard to the choices we all make as we select, read and recommend texts within, what Gayatri Spivak has called, the 'Teaching Machine' by examining the institutional histories and politics of that making and unmaking.[28] For the process of commemoration and canonization, the negotiations surrounding its cultural and political claims, the occupation of specific institutional positions are all crucial questions that inform anyone engaged in the task of teaching, disseminating and reading multicultural texts.

A Black British Canon? comprises an introductory essay, three separate but interlinked Parts entitled, 'Interrogating the Canon', 'New Languages of Criticism', and 'Genealogies and Interventions', with a concluding overview. Mike Phillips' introductory essay, 'Migration, Modernity and English Writing: Reflections on Migrant Identity and Canon Formation', discusses the concept of black British identity and interrogates what it means to be a 'black British writer' both from personal experience and through a tracing of historical, literary and political contexts. He questions the way in which the political arena of late 1990s engendered the term 'multiculturalism' as a New-Labour emblem celebrating cultural diversity, tracing instead the realities of marginalization and a 'benign cultural apartheid'.[29] But Phillips also expands the questioning of ideologically laden political tropes through an analysis of migration, from the Enlightenment, through Modernism, to the present-day. In so doing, he demonstrates the way in which migration has been used to define boundaries, both of nationhood and the self, as well as to construct borders between exclusion and inclusion. In concluding, Phillips brings the notions of multiculturalism and migration together, through a sense of personal experience, to show the ways in which the concept of black British challenges and alters boundaries, positions itself at the centre of the current political debate on nationhood, and finally demands that the academy breaks out of its 'multiculturalist prison'.[30] In many ways, the subsequent essays in this collection attempt to rise to that challenge, to question its premises, or to explore further the issues raised by Phillips.

Part I consists of three essays grouped under the title 'Interrogating the Canon'. For all their pedagogical practicalities, canons, as Phillips suggests, must always be open to revision, contestation and interrogation, and, consequently, cultural critics should always be self-aware of their supposed purposes in their investigations. The essays in this section address specific problems associated with the use and abuse of canon formation, from the status of popular forms to exclusionary practices.

James Procter's, essay, ' "The Ghost of Other Stories": Salman Rushdie and a Black British Canon?', looks at the question of canonicity in terms of value and evaluation, in relation to Rushie's writings and to his constructed role within the canon. As such, Procter discusses Rushie's work and its uncertain relationship with black British writing in order to explore 'the "principles" of canon formation'.[31] Moreover, like Phillips' exploration of multiculturalism, Procter questions the seemingly benign nature of transnationalism and uses Rushie's writing as a way to uncover fissures and divisions within such categorization. At the same time, Procter advocates retaining 'black British' as a concept, since, 'it seems to disrupt rather than enshrine certain canonical orthodoxies.'[32] In the following essay, 'Not Good Enough or Not Man Enough? Beryl Gilroy as the Anomaly in the Evolving "Black British Canon"', Sandra Courtman looks at the critical reception of Beryl Gilroy's *Black Teacher* and *Sunlight on Sweet Water* and explores the reasons why they remain on the margins of the black British literary canon. Courtman contrasts the critical rise and fall of E. R. Braithwaite's *To Sir With Love* with that of *Black Teacher* and argues that their canonization or lack of canonization can be tracked against readerly expectations that they should variously conform to popular entertainment, literariness, socio-educational reforms and the politics of multicultural education. Courtman explores why Gilroy's 'contribution of black literature remains obscure and questionable, whilst her contribution to multi-racial education [is] universally acknowledged', by examining the text's transgression of the generic norms and its anomalous refusal to be cast in the role of a representative black feminist text.[33] As such, Courtman also evades the commonly accepted labels of canonization, pointing out that the reception of Gilroy's work makes for 'uncomfortable reading for both black and white.'[34] The final piece in this section, 'Questioning Cultural Diversity and the Role of National Institutions and Strategies', takes the form of an interview with Femi Folorunso of the Scottish Arts Council. Rather than focus upon the way in which individual authors, such as Rushdie and Gilroy, challenge the formation of a black British canon, Folorunso interrogates the 'Britishness' in black British and argues for a radical re-examination of regional identities that have been occluded in the narrativization of black British. Folorunso begins by examining the formation of the Arts Council in terms of the historical and political implications for migrant populations within Britain. Subsequently, he looks specifically at the case of Scotland, and the way in which black British cultural studies have still not fully engaged with diverse regional identities. As Folorunso points out, such startling gaps exist not only at the level of the academy, but also have serious implications for funding bodies such as the Arts Council. As this final piece suggests, canon formation must be interrogated, not only from within academe, but also in relation to the impact that funding bodies have on what is valued and upheld as representative cultural forms, since the issue of canonisation 'is, more often that not, mired in the complexities of everyday language ... of economics, and of the possible one-dimensional construction of national identity'.[35]

The two essays in Part II, 'New Languages of Criticism', address the paradigmatic challenges that surround black British and assess the strengths and weaknesses of existing critical vocabularies. From a self-aware recognition of current disciplinary practices, this section looks to the past and to the future, focusing specifically upon recent debates concerning 'transnationalism' and the radical insurgence of black cultural production, which together have brought about not only new kinds of writing but also new publishing conditions and new audiences. Like Folorunso, John McLeod, in 'Fantasy Relationships: Black British Canons in a Transnational World', interrogates the notion of 'British' in the appellation 'black British'. He analyses the anthologies that appeared at the anniversary of the *SS Empire Windrush*, the ship that in 1948 brought the first large group of west Indian immigrants to the UK, and argues that this chronological 'gathering' of texts and writers implies a tradition or model of generational influence that might be misleading if it limits us to mainly 'national, rather than transnational, fields of influence'.[36] McLeod argues, from a consideration of Kwame Dawes, Bernadine Evaristo, Jackie Kay and Caryl Phillips, that black British writers not only straddle different locations and audiences, but that their work is informed by differing and varied aesthetic traditions. Unlike, the contributions to Part I, McLeod's analysis sees no disjuncture between national and diasporic consciousness, rather, demanding a re-evaluation of the new critical languages that have developed to explore and explicate black British cultural production. In the following essay, ' "New Forms": Towards a Critical Dialogue with Black British "Popular" Fictions', Andy Wood, like McLeod, makes a case for a new and distinctive language of criticism. Wood is concerned with popular culture, in this instance with popular music. Taking Linton Kwesi Johnson's work as the focus of his argument, Wood explores the development of musical forms that grew out of the imported 'materials' of a Jamaican reggae tradition, and which have subsequently been transformed into the urban rhythms of dub poetry and the popular music of street culture. He tracks the ways in which Johnson and others have created and sustained distinctively black British forms that have influenced writers and performers by encouraging cultural productions that balance local concerns with diasporic influences. Above all, the two essays in this section emphasize the need to develop critical languages that are not only capable of dealing with works which do not fit into preconceived ideas of what a black writer should write about, but also one that can deal adequately with border crossings between high and low, specific national and diasporic intersections, and across aesthetic and generic modalities.

The essays in Part III, 'Genealogies and Interventions', offer a self-reflexive map of the debates that accompany a range of texts in art, film, theatre and literature, which have been interpellated by, or interpellate, the sign of black British. Michael Macmillan, in 'Texts of Cultural Practice: Black Theatre and Performance in the UK', sketches a less well-known, but much needed, history of black theatre and live arts in Britain, and looks at some of its key generational and paradigmatic developments. Calling attention to the distinctiveness of black performance art, which has been generated from the mixed media of music, dance, digital, filmic and representational forms, Macmillan argues that these hybrid 'aesthetic representations signify a reinvention and re-imagining of self in a cultural political context where identities are continually fragmented and hybridised'.[37] In parallel, Leon Wainwright, in 'Canon Questions: Art in "black Britain"', explores the 'critical, institutional and historiographic project of canonising the work of diaspora artists in Britain'.[38] He traces a history of black British art from the 1980s to the present day, evaluating the formative ideas and showing how these are related to current artistic practice. Wainwright also analyses the way in which art institutions, galleries and public funding bodies have offered increased support to black British artists, but also warns that the consequent canonization of black art in Britain has led to a degree of 'circumspection and fixity'.[39] Gail Low, in 'Shaping Connections: From West Indian to Black British', plots a further genealogy within the history of black British culture through an analysis of some key moments in its self-representation. Low begins by exploring and challenging the way in which the development of the 'transnational, migratory and diasporic consciousness across cultures', has tended to ignore the discursive aspects of black British culture.[40] Instead, she posits the question, 'black British for whom?' in order to explore the way in which 'West Indian' was transformed into 'black British', while simultaneously retaining transnational discursive connections. In order to historicize and evidence these questions, Low focuses on three areas, newspapers, poetry anthologies and polemical journals. She concludes with a questioning of canon formation that draws upon the history of migrancy and settlement in order to show the interpellation of readers within complex and often discomforting transnational discourses. Together, the essays in Part III undertake a materialist understanding of canonization as a politics of cultural production across a range of individual, activist, corporate publishing and exhibitionary institutions.

Alison Donnell's concluding, 'Afterword: In Praise of a Black British Canon and the Possibilities of Representing the Nation "Otherwise"', returns us to the all-important question, what might be at stake in proposing a black British canon, and reminds us that the value of texts are tied to the political and historic choices we have made 'in a certain context and at a certain time' and must be open to inspection and revision.[41] Rather than offering a general genealogical and cultural political framework of black British history, the afterword opens up questions about canonicity and key critical debates. In doing so, Donnell interrogates ethical and aesthetic investments in relation to the changing nature of political struggles and rights' discourses from the postwar period to the present day. Donnell argues powerfully that a teleological trajectory should not be mapped onto a generational shift in emphasis or onto the politics of cultural forms, rather than the cultural forms of politics wherein black is assumed to be integrated into the Union Jack. In the current climate of fortress Europe and the media 'hysteria over refugees and asylum seekers', the discourse of rights and the contestation over nation – signified by the black in black Britishness – is now more urgent than ever.[42] The conclusion of this collection does not aim, therefore, to summarize, but rather offers a polemical intervention into the debate about the black British canon, highlighting current interventions and posing questions for the future.

As Donnell reminds us, a canon is what we produce as we make those choices about what we read or write about.[43] All the more crucial then is the demand, not only that we know what we have chosen, but how we have chosen it. This implies a self-reflexive attitude to the processes and histories of canon formation, the negotiations surrounding its cultural and political claims, and the occupation of specific institutional positions. Such concerns are crucial to cultural critics engaged in the task of teaching and disseminating multicultural productions, as well as to those who read, view and study those works. And this is what unites the essays in this collection: recognition that the issues and problems surrounding canonicity are not simply academic, they involve, of necessity, a series of wide-ranging and constantly shifting cultural dialogues that have a significant impact upon contemporary society.

Notes

1. Kobena Mercer, *Welcome to the Jungle: New Positions in Black Cultural Studies* (London and New York: Routledge, 1994), p. 14.

2. James Berry (ed.), *News For Babylon: The Chatto Book of Westindian-British Poetry* (London: Chatto and Windus, and the Hogarth Press, 1984); Barbara Burford, Jackie Kay, Grace Nichols and G. Pearse (eds), *A Dangerous Knowing: Four Black Women Poets* (London: Women's Press, 1984); Lauretta Ngcobo (ed.), *Let it be Told: Black Women Writers in Britain* (London: Virago Press, 1987); Rhonda Cobham and Merle Collins (eds), *Watchers and Seekers: Creative Writing by Black Women in Britain* (London: Women's Press, 1987); Jackie Kay, Liliane Landor, Gail Lewis, Pratibha Parmar, *et al.* (eds), *Charting the Journey: Writings by Black and Third World Women* (London: Sheba Feminist Publishers, 1988); Kwesi Owusu (ed.), *Storms of the Heart: An Anthology of Black Arts and Culture* (London: Camden Press, 1988); and E.A.Markham (ed.), *Hinterland* (Newcastle upon Tyne: Bloodaxe Books, 1989).
3. David Dabydeen and N Wilson-Tagoe (eds), *A Reader's Guide to West Indian and Black British Literature* (Coventry, UK: Dangaroo Press,1988).
4. Caryl Phillips, Hanif Kureshi and David Dabydeen, and poets like Linton Kwesi Johnson, Fred D'Aguiar, Grace Nichols, Jackie Kay.
5. For a discussion and description of black British films see: Stephen Bourne, *Black in the British Frame: Black People in British Film and Television 1896–1996* (London: Cassell, 1998); Kobena Mercer (ed.), *Black Film/ British Cinema*, ICA Document 7 (London: Institute of Contemporary Arts, 1988); and Michael T. Martin, *Cinemas of the Black Diaspora* (Detroit, Michigan: Wayne State University Press, 1995).
6. For a parallel discussion and description of black British art see Rasheed Araeen, *The Other Story: Afro-Asian Artists in Postwar Britain* (London: Hayward Gallery, South Bank Centre: 1989); Gilane Tawadeos (ed.) *Mirage: Enigmas of Race, Difference and Desire* (London: Institute of Contemporary Arts, 1995); Gen Doy, *Black Visual Culture* (London: I. B. Tauris, 2000); and Leon Wainwright's essay in this collection (see below pp. 143–67).
7. Rashreed Araeen, *op. cit.* See also Doy, *op. cit.* pp. 11–12.
8. For a discussion of black British music from the 1970s to date see Paul Gilroy, *There Aint't No Black in the Union Jack* (London: Hutchinson, 1987); and Andy Wood's essay in this collection (below, pp. 105–25).
9. For a discussion of black British theatre see Michael McMillan's essay in this collection (below, pp. 129–42).
10. Kwesi Owusu (ed.), *Black British Culture and Society. A Text Reader* (London and New York: Routledge, 2000); James Procter (ed.), *Writing Black Britain* (Manchester: Manchester University Press, 2000); Doy, *op. cit.* and Courttia Newland and Kadija George Sessay (eds), *IC3: The Penguin Book of New Black Writing in Britain* (London: Hamish Hamilton, 2000).
11. Alison Donnell (ed.), *Routledge Companion to Contemporary Black British Culture* (London and New York: Routledge, 2002).
12. Mark Stein, *Black British Literature: Novels of Transformation* (Columbus, Ohio: Ohio State University Press, 2004). Kadija Sesay, *Write Black Write British: From Post Colonial to Black British Literature* (Hartford: Hansib, 2005).
13. For a political and social history of black British, see Mike and Trevor Phillips, *Windrush: The Irresistible Rise of Multi-Racial Britain* (London: HarperCollins, 1999); Dilip Hiro, *Black British, White British* (London: Grafton Books, 1991); and Ron Ramdin, *Reimaging Britain: 500 years of Black and Asian history* (London: Pluto, 1999).
14. Berry, *op. cit.* pp. xii–xxvii.

15. Cobham, *op. cit.* pp. 7 and 9.
16. Prabhu Guptara, *Black British Literature: An Annotated Bibliography* (Sydney: Dangaroo Press, 1986), p. 16.
17. Gilane Tawadros, *Mirage: Enigmas of Race, Difference and Desire* (London: Institute of Contemporary Arts, 1995), p. 13; Doy, *op. cit.* p. 9.
18. Stuart Hall, 'New Ethnicities', in Houston Baker (ed.), *Black British Cultural Studies* (Chicago and London: The University of Chicago Press, 1996), p. 166.
19. Mercer, *op. cit.* pp. 291–2.
20. Tariq Madood, *Not Easy being British: Colour, Culture and Citizenship* (Stoke on Trent: Runnymede Trust and Trentham Books, 1992), p. 29.
21. Stuart Hall, 'Frontline and Backyards: The Terms of Change', in Owusu, *op. cit.* p. 126.
22. Kwesi Owusu, 'The Struggle for a Radical Black Political Culture: An Interview with Ambalavaner Sivanadan', in Owusu, *op. cit.* p. 422.
23. Doy, *op. cit.* p. 9.
24. Gilroy, *op. cit.*
25. Fred D'Aguiar, 'Against Black British Literature', in Maggie Butcher (ed.), *Tibisiri: Caribbean Writers and Critics* (Sydney: Dangaroo Press, 1988), p. 110.
26. For a recent and comprehensive account of black British writing see: C.l. Innes, *A History of Black and Asian Writing in Britain 1700–2000* (Cambridge: Cambridge University Press, 2002).
27. Alison Donnell, see below pp. 201–2.
28. Gayatri Spivak, *Teaching Machine* (London: Routledge, 1993).
29. See below pp. 22 and 30.
30. See below p. 37.
31. See below p. 37.
32. See below p. 44.
33. See below p. 53.
34. See below p. 70.
35. See below pp. 88–9.
36. See below p. 98
37. See below p. 140.
38. See below p. 156.
39. See below p. 154.
40. See below p. 168.
41. See below p. 191.
42. See below p. 198.
43. See below pp. 201–2.

1

Foreword: Migration, Modernity and English Writing – Reflections on Migrant Identity and Canon Formation

Mike Phillips

My name is Mike Phillips and I'm a novelist among other things. You may not know that I am a United Kingdom citizen, and you may not know that I do not think of myself as a Caribbean writer, or an African writer, or an African American writer, or a diasporic writer, or even as a writer with an ambiguous stance somewhere in the middle of the Atlantic. No such luck. I think of myself as an English writer, and all of this seems simple enough, except that I also think of myself (and I often describe myself) as a black British writer. In this last persona, however, I am perpetually and consistently confronted by a specific difficulty, which is to do with a perceived disjunction between who I am and my identity as a writer. I want to point to the nature of the difficulty by quoting you an email I received recently from a woman, who described herself as being of Jamaican/Scottish parentage, and who was writing a PhD, which she described as

> largely devoted to a discussion of issues for mixed race people in this country not least the historic invisibility, and the pressure to identify as a single, specific race that tends to come from people outside of the experience of being racially mixed.

She went on to say:

> The self-identification is important here, as mixed race people so often have their identities decided for them by others, and are so rarely allowed to self-identify without a fight.[1]

This put me mind of several similar discussions I have had in the past with my eldest son, whose other parent is white, and it also put me in

13

mind of the fact that I shared the same sense that my identity as a writer was perpetually under attack.

When I published my first novel in the second half of the 1980s the concept of a black British writer was not on the radar of most critics.[2] By and large it was a term they would have applied as a racial or ethnic categorization rather than a cultural one. In any case 'Black British' was a contentious and highly contested ascription, until about halfway through the 1990s, for reasons I'll describe later. But over the last ten years, as the label took on new meanings, it started to become a useful way of commanding attention in the cultural marketplace. Of course, a great deal of work which carried that label came out of the old postcolonial syllabus and was neatly repackaged as 'black British'.

That was one strand which was harmless enough, except that it meant critics couldn't understand or explore the context in which the work they were studying was created. On the other side of the coin, some critics hurried to locate an identity within the African American experience and to describe the black British as a sort of subset of black America. At the same time, it became apparent that, to an alarming extent, the imagination of academic and other critics seemed to confine black British work to critiques which privileged notions of the outsider, the alien, the exile, and described its struggles to define an emerging identity almost exclusively in terms of a network of assumptions about cultural 'resistance'. On top of all this, our work is labelled as 'black British', not because of its content, or style, or mood or tone or because it has a British landscape or says anything about Britain, but because the author has a dark skin and conveniently happened to spend some time in this country. What's important about this is that these are elements which establish a trope that ignores the actual experience and the dynamic developments which brought the term black British into view and made it an essential and useful statement of identity. When you come to consider the process of canon formation the results are more or less self-evident.

For example, take a recent and highly praised book describing the work of black and Asian writers about London, Sukhdev Sandhu's *London Calling*.[3] The book begins with the writing of former African slaves in the eighteenth century and moves through the next two centuries to the present day. Its dominant imagery renders blacks and Asians as outsiders – travellers, exiles, migrants – and, after analysing the work of the mid-century Caribbean writers, the author simply recycles these postcolonial familiar themes. As a result, the book ignores the period which followed Caribbean migration in the middle of the twentieth century. This was a time when the establishment of a black strand in the British population and the ensuing conflicts became a central issue of political and social life in Britain, triggering a number of important changes – in the constitution, in the institutions of central and local government, in the arrangements for urban planning, housing, policing, and a great deal more besides. These were changes which the post migrant generations of black writers often found themselves tracking, not as spectators, but as conscious agents in the restructuring of the city's self-image.

Arguably, therefore, the most important black writing to take London as its focus over the last two decades has been about a network of slippery transitions between public and private concerns – identity, community, citizenship and nationality. But *London Calling*'s insistence on rendering black writers as migrants and exiles means that the latter half of the book ignores the elements which govern this transformation. One consequence is that Sandhu's reading can't make the appropriate distinctions between the social experiences of black and Asian writers, or assess the influence of class and ethnic status, or discuss different responses to the environment of different decades. He compares, for instance, Caryl Phillips's characters' arrival in London during the 1950s, with the excitement of Hanif Kureishi's suburban heroes' journey to the metropolis in the 1960s, but he can only describe the differences in the most banal terms – Phillips, he says, is 'gloomy' while Kureishi is cheerful.[4]

Another consequence of this approach is that writers who describe London from inside a complex interaction with its structures and changes are ignored by Sandhu's account or shoehorned into his version of the migrant saga. This leaves out any detailed consideration of Andrea Levy, Ferdinand Dennis, or myself.[5] Typically, Sandhu bookmarks me as a novelist 'of distinction', quotes liberally from my non-fiction work about migration, but ignores the fiction set in London. Novels set in the world of local and central government or London's art galleries clearly don't fit the preconceptions of the book. Similarly, there is no consideration of the writers who experience London as part of family life or childhood. No Courttia Newland, or the rash of Brixton boys like Alex Wheatle, Anton Marks *et al.* No mention either of the black writers who create characters from inside the enclaves of English professional life, like Mike Gayle's (un)black London teacher, or Nicola Willams' black and female South London barrister.[6]

Descriptions of this kind place black and Asian writers in an a-historical arena, where their most important common feature is the colour of their skins. The critic Tabish Khair argues that one effect of this view has been to foster the emergence of a swathe of contemporary writing which 'seeks to cast the reader in a passive and celebratory role'.[7] Khair has labelled this trend 'the death of the reader', and he illustrates it by reference to 'slippages' in some recent iconic 'multi-cultural' texts. Beginning with Zadie Smith's *White Teeth*, he writes:

> if one reads it from outside the celebratory space of multicultural Britain, one notices intriguing gaps and silences. The one that I still remember relates to Samad Miah Iqbal who claims to be and is portrayed by the text as the great-grandson of Mangal Pande, the Indian sepoy who fired the first shot of the 1857 revolt. Samad is a fireband – if not fundamentalist – Muslim much of the time and the sceptical reader in me could not reconcile this fact with the name of his historically authentic great-grandfather. For Mangal Pande is not just a Hindu name, it is a twice-born, pure-as-snow Brahmin one. It is difficult to imagine the descendants of the Mangal Pandes of India converting to Islam, let alone a firebrand version of it, and that too after the snuffing of the last symbols of Muslim glory in 1857.
>
> Of course this is not life; this is a novel. But if this is a novel, there ought to be a story around this spectacular conversion. The story is never narrated, or not visibly enough...
>
> A similar problem confronts the sceptical reader in another celebrated novel, Yann Martel's *Life of Pi*, which – in spite of its solid adherence to certain textual and mainstream definitions of religions (particularly 'Hinduism') – is rather shaky in the field of names. Take, for instance, this extract: 'He was a Sufi, a Muslim mystic ... His name was Satish Kumar. These are common names in Tamil Nadu.' It could be that, in the years I have been way from India, Tamil Nadu (in South India) has been invaded and colonised by people from North India so that North and West Indian names like Satish Kumar have become common there. I am willing to allow for that possibility. But I still find it difficult to imagine a pious Muslim, even a Sufi, with a Hindu name – for Satish and Kumar are both Hindu names.
>
> One wonders what such omissions signify?[8]

What these omissions signify, according to Khair, is the absence of 'textual traces ... that enable the reader to fill the gaps, smoothen the rough patches, justify the "errors", "authenticise" the fiction.' In other words, to open a space for the reader to interpret, accomplish, and be active. Khair goes on, however, to note:

> But if this space is foreclosed – not just in the text, which leaves unexplained and uncontextualised gaps, but also in criticism, which refuses to note these gaps – if this space of active reading is foreclosed, then all

one can have is a kind of celebratory echoing of dominant whims. The author might or might not be dead, but the reader is surely expected not to think much for herself – not to read in other words.

Khair concludes the argument by quoting an anecdote from his own recent experience:

> I had just finished reading *Brick Lane* while waiting for the airport authorities to let me know whether I could board a plane to Heathrow in order to catch a connecting flight from there. In the past this would not have been a problem. But, unknown to me, the rules had been changed in London a few days back and now some passport holders were required to have a valid visa even to catch a connecting flight from the same airport in England. While I waited, I read the last pages of *Brick Lane*, where the main protagonist approaches a skating rink wearing a sari. But you cannot skate wearing a sari, her friend says. 'This is England', the protagonist replies, 'You can do whatever you like.' Perhaps. Perhaps.
> I know that I laughed hysterically for about three minutes when I was informed that, in spite of many visits to England, in spite of a letter of invitation and valid tickets to my destination, I would not be allowed to board my plane. I wished I could be a protagonist in Ali's novel. My history, regardless of Barthes, did not set me free either as a reader or a person. I was bound to notice names, for my name is always noticeable. I was liable to be kept from boarding the double-decker of even multicultural Britain. I could not do what I liked. I could not even do what I had paid for.[9]

While reading Khair's essay my own list of slippages began to assemble itself, notably an extravagantly inaccurate reference to the Notting Hill riots in Diran Adebayo's novel *Some Kind of Black*.[10] This eschewed the social, political or economic context, and served up the events as an other-wise inexplicable eruption of racial hostility – a violent clash between ethnic cultures. As a result, one of the novel's central metaphors (the riots) manoeuvres its characters neatly into an internal parallel with the now established multi-culturalist narrative, where migrants move, 'from a tranquil, though limited "traditional" (ordered) space through a jour-ney of much conflict and upheaval to the safe domain of a more com-plete and fulfilling Western multiculturalism'.[11] There are a number of indications that the process of canon formation which is now in train has become one of the boundaries outlining this a-historical multicultural space, where migrants are confined within an circular (and endless) rigmarole of celebration.

In the circumstances the temptation for someone in my position is to engage in what Gayatri Spivak calls 'retrospective hallucination'.[12] She argues that the ruling elites in the Third World, along with professionals and intellectuals who have their origins in Africa and Asia, reconstruct their own history or, to put it another way, re-invent their roots, which they claim spring from a historical world of uninterrupted ethnicity and nationhood, that existed before the takeover of imperialist and colonial culture. This re-invention becomes a rhetorical trope, which locates such people in a traditional stereotype where cultures are fixed and separated in history, partly because this particular view of culture has been, in our time, the official gateway to the transnational academic and business world in Europe and the USA. I think of the Trinidadian novelist V.S. Naipaul, who resurrected his role in an Indian caste system which his family had abandoned when they went to the Caribbean, and who, consistent to the end, has recently been supporting the attempts of Hindu nationalists to link themselves with a pure pre-Muslim Hindu culture.[13] But the history of postcolonial and migrant intellectual effort is layered with this kind of affirmation, and the rhetoric, during the last couple of decades, has also begun to conflate a reconstructed nationhood with the historical roots of migrant identity. Franz Fanon, Aimé Césaire, the poets of Negritude, all wrote within a specific historical context and they are part of our history, but partly as a result of this history, the spokesmen and women of migration now tend to trace migrant identity to a pre-colonial and autonomous ethnicity, an autonomous nationhood, an ancient paradise, from which the migrants have been, somehow, exiled – and of course, migrant academics, writers and artists, for understandable reasons, have not been slow to identify themselves with this overarching popular narrative.[14]

We are also forced, I would say, into this position by a framework of popular racism which calls on us to trace the history of cultures through a kind of arena of separate development, as if cultures existed in a series of boxes, distinct from each other, and distinct from the world in which they exist. The result of this tradition of retrospection is that, for the migrants, their assertion of dignity, self respect or even humanity is supposed to be a constant recall of an imagined cultural tradition, an instant recollection of exclusive cultural roots, as if there was no other way of convincing society about their worth.

But as a black writer with a migrant background, now a citizen of a European country, Britain, I have to be conscious that my actual experience offers a continual challenge to this rhetoric of retrospection. For instance, English is my native language. Like most Caribbeans and many Africans I grew up speaking both standard English and a *dialect* of standard English. In the retrospective tradition it has become fashionable to interrogate our Atlantic dialects for African survivals, but it is equally possible and rather more obvious to trace the dominant influence of Elizabethan English, the language of Shakespeare and the King James Bible, along with a number of archaic regional dialects, notably from the seafaring southwestern coast of England. The point, however, is that, as a reader and writer, my experience of language located me in a tradition where such figures as Chaucer, Shakespeare and Dickens figured largely, and drawing upon the richness and complexity of my own language involved my entering and exploring a culture which had evolved at some distance from the circumstances in which I had grown up. According to the arguments of postcolonial retrospection this is transgressive behaviour, a rejection of the task of reconstructing one or the other nativist tradition. But as every genuine artist knows, creativity is a matter of grappling with the landscape in which you find yourself; and it seemed to me when I began to write fiction, as it does now, that resurrecting an imagined utopia in order to describe my identity would be a sterile approach, an intellectual cul-de-sac, whose likely consequence might have been to shut me off from my environment rather than liberating me for constructive engagement with my fellows.

The study of migration has also been dominated by certain major lines of sociological enquiry, which place the phenomenon of migration – the act of people moving across borders to settle in different places – in the context of social conflict and political anxiety: and it seems to me that this sociological thematization has had the effect of persistently distorting both our understanding of cultures and of the cultural consequences of migration. In Britain we've become very good at this. We know for instance, that migrants and the children of migrants have been excluded from certain occupations, and that our system of public education has allowed a shameful proportion of migrants and of migrant children to emerge without useful qualifications. We know that recruitment of migrants and their children into the police force, the Civil Service and so on has been blocked by discrimination. We know also many of the mechanisms, which control this situation. The real problem, however, is to find solutions – and after two decades of revelation, discussion and retraining there is now a growing realization that, if there is any answer to the problems we face, it lies in an understanding and a remodelling of the political and social culture we inhabit.

This is a difficult matter. Britain began to tackle the issue earlier than its continental neighbours, partly because our colonialist history created conditions in which migration became a central political issue during the mid-twentieth century, and partly because our cities and a number of our institutions had already begun to be reshaped by the fact of migration. This also led to an early realization that a purely sociological approach to these issues was not entirely useful. It became apparent, therefore, that culture was the only medium which could provide a framework for the solutions which had to be sought.

The product of this understanding was, in Britain, the concept of multi-culturalism. I've already hinted at some of the difficulties, but I want here to discuss the term within specific historical circumstances and to outline specific consequences which flow from its use, because, although multi-culturalism was a term already in use in various settings, in Britain it achieved popular status as a response to specific conditions. It is crucial to note that the term entered our popular vocabulary during a specific period (in the second half of the decade of the 1990s) and within a specific context. When we – we, that is to say my brother Trevor and myself – began working on a TV programme and a book about the Windrush at the end of 1996, it seemed to us that 'multi-cultural' was a term which was making claims about British society which were more or less false. So we used the title, *The Irresistible Rise of Multi-racial Britain*.[15] But in-between the conception and the actual anniversary of the Windrush landing a number of things happened. First, there was the murder of Stephen Lawrence and the subsequent McPherson enquiry which characterized a number of British institutions and authorities as 'institutionally racist'. This was a drama which played itself out in front of the TV cameras and in the daily headlines of tabloid newspapers. Secondly, Labour won the General Election and ushered in the first age of New Labour. Thirdly, there was a campaign for the mayor's office in London which was won by Ken Livingston, the man who had originally set out to create a species of electoral rainbow coalitions to support the GLC.

In hindsight the political and social anxiety of the Stephen Lawrence affair, the re-branding instincts of New Labour and the political opportunism of the mayoral campaign were all gathered up and reflected in the long aftermath of Windrush; and it was also obvious that we needed a new brand name to describe what was happening to the British population, especially in our major cities. Up to that point, 'multi-racial' had been a more or less acceptable code word for the changing population in our cities, and the eclipse of the term is instructive. Multi-racialism was rather too closely associated with Afro-Caribbeans, and a number of ethnic groups were uncomfortable with the term. In any case, *multi-racialism* served as a persistent reminder of conflict and oppression, the sort of thing the politicians in particular wanted us to forget. For example, our Minister of Culture, Chris Smith was deeply committed to a cultural diversity, which would feature the inclusion of homosexuals, language groups and so on. So *multi-culturalism* emerged from this background as an emblem of a diversity which had an official imprimatur, or to put it another way, had become part of an official strategy for containing the implications of a social and political crisis.

But multi-culturalism offered different meanings to different people. It was more or less devoid of challenging content, since the phrase merely referred to the existence of different cultures in the same place, while at the same time it was, for a number of people, symbolic of elements they hoped to embrace – equality, tolerance and so on. Ironically, even the right-wing and racist parties, deadly opponents of multi-racialism or what they might have described as race-mixing, recognized the advantages of a multi-cultural arrangement in which each 'culture' could maintain its exclusivity behind various social barriers.

The problem has been that, on the one hand, multi-culturalism uttered a rhetoric about the co-existence of cultures from all over the world, and we demonstrated that by supporting Hindu religious festivals and the Notting Hill Carnival among other things. We had a high visibility of black and Asian people especially in popular entertainment and music. Overall, politicians and public figures paid an obligatory respect to the idea that there were several different cultures in Britain which enjoyed equal status.

The reality of life in the multi-cultural state was, however, very different. Multi-culturalism had its shareholders, of course. The rubric had made life easier for a number of institutions and authorities, who were able to retreat or delay such issues as equal opportunity recruitment by putting in place a multi-cultural policy which devoted relatively insignificant funding to supporting religious festivals and oral reminiscing. Multi-national corporations and local enterprises also benefited hugely from the commodification of identity which was implicit in the operation of multi-cultural. On the other side of the equation were a relatively small number of artists, entertainers, entrepreneurs and administrators, from the ethnic minorities, whose task it was to execute the strategy. These duly entered the lists of the great and the good and were duly rewarded with various honours and decorations.

At the same time we had a developing tradition of discrimination and marginalisation towards those people who came from the cultures we were celebrating. The idea of cultural diversity also started to become a useful tool for maintaining the barriers originally put in place by racial discrimination. To put it crudely the argument said: 'you have a culture which we will support and praise, but that implies that we don't have to make room in our culture for you'. So multi-culturalism, instead of being a process which made connections between social, political and economic conditions, became a sort of bridge which allowed various people to step lightly from one phase of history to another imaginary phase without having to dabble in these dangerous waters of cultural conflict.

Now you can see the potential in this for a kind of benign cultural apartheid, which is precisely why the organising principle of my own writing is concerned with trying to understand how migration fits into a framework of theoretical argument about the development of art and letters in the English language, rather than trying to recover notions of ethnic or cultural purity. The exploitative potential of the multi-cultural concept is precisely to do with its reading of cultures as autonomous and isolated from each other in history, but it is true that migration and its cultural effects can be read in entirely different ways; and it's also true that the trends associated with migration have begun to set in motion decisive changes in the way that we understand cultures, their relationship and their interaction.

The first thing is to identify what we're talking about. Migration is not, of course, a twentieth-century phenomenon. People were moving across borders before there were borders. The populations of every continent owe their origins to various kinds of migration, and they haven't stopped moving since. So, I'm not going to argue the virtues of migration, if only because the thing was self-evident (even before we ever heard of famous migrants like Arnold Schwarzenegger, arguably Austria's most successful migrant). Migration, on the other hand, has nearly always been associated with a species of dramatic intervention in the social, cultural and political forms of one location or the other.

We habitually speak of these movements of peoples in terms of conquest or invasion – imperialist ideology fostered the idea that when two cultures met the superior culture inevitably destroyed or drove out its inferior. So, we also talked about civilization as a matter of ownership in which the conquerors imposed their culture or took over the cultures they found. Imperialist Europe and its emigrants even believed that they introduced the idea of culture to territories in which such notions didn't exist. I think here about Joseph Conrad, and his novel, *Heart of Darkness*, a title which became part of the English language in describing Africa, and in a sense we see these notions persisting in the attitudes that Edward Said, the Palestinian academic, described as 'Orientalism'.[16] So, the themes which run through the development of the nation state were concerned, not only with who belonged to the nation and why, but also with where the boundaries lay between inclusion and exclusion.

But while there is no doubt that the ideology of race and nation which policed these boundaries pervades the practice of European artists and writers in the modern period, there were also other interesting ways of talking about nationhood, rooted in other kinds of reality, and it can be argued that artists and writers have also persistently chosen other paths through which they have opened up an avenue of escape from the strait-jacket of nation and nationality, and from the limitations of race and ethnicity. This is a practice which challenges the notion that, in the world of ideas, migration represents a sudden and alien incursion into the ecology of the arts in Europe. Instead, the effects of migration are part of how modernity and modernization have shaped our world, and, in particular shaped the world of the arts and culture. So in this process I can't talk about migration as if it were merely an aspect of race and racism – not because those things don't deserve a focus, but because the issues of migration go well-beyond anxieties about the colour of people's skins; and I can't talk about migration without discussing modernity because modernity offers us new insights into migration. For instance, there is a moment in Europe, the start of the Enlightenment and the extraordinary movements of the eighteenth century where the nation state emerges to dominate the rhetoric of identity, and to define the boundaries between inclusion and exclusion.

One product of Enlightenment thinking, which went along with the development of the nation state, was a secularisation which encouraged Europeans to question the religious rubric in which the soul and its relationship with the City of God was the index of the individual. The result of this questioning was a state of mind in which the self could be identified with idea of nation. You can collect a bundle of characteristics, assemble them into a single personality and offer this individual up as a synonym for the nation. The nation itself could be thought of, or described, as an individual – so the French Marianne, the American Uncle Sam, the English John Bull and so on – were all products of this junction between individuals and the symbolism of the nation.

But as we pass through the nineteenth century, our ideas about what constituted the individual self change radically. In Freud, we see the argument that we aren't born as ourselves, we acquire a self which is already stressed and divided by internal conflict, fractured into ego, superego and unconscious, and we hold these things together by entering into a symbolic order of language and culture.[17] So we arrive at the end-point of the European Enlightenment, already in a condition of serious doubt about the status of the individual self, and this is a climax which brings on industrialism, control of information and centralization of its distribution, capitalism and military power. Hand in hand with this is modernism: aesthetic self-consciousness; interest in language; rejection of realism in favour of 'the real'; abandonment of linearity in favour of montage and simultaneity; Romanticism or emphasis on the value of aesthetic experience; depth and universal mytho-poetic meaning; privileging fragmentation; and the valuing of avant garde culture.

Modernist poets like T.S. Eliot provide us with illuminating descriptions of these states of mind. At the beginning of 'The Lovesong of J. Alfred Prufrock' you can read this divided consciousness, this new awareness of a divided and fragmented identity:

> Let us go then, you and I,
> When the evening is spread out against the sky
> Like a patient etherised upon a table;
> Let us go, through certain half-deserted streets,
> The muttering retreats
> Of restless nights in one-night cheap hotels
> And sawdust restaurants with oyster-shells.[18]

In true modernist style, poets like Eliot reflected on the unreliability of words themselves, how they crack and break down into imprecision, and how they serve as a metaphor for the way that identity in modern times could never hold a single irreducible form. As W.B. Yeats, Eliot's contemporary, wrote, 'Things fall apart; the centre cannot hold.'[19] Joyce goes further in highlighting the nature of language as a reflection of fragmented identity: parodies of advertising, journalism, literature, science, colloquial speech and classical analogies all get tossed in to focus on the tools we use to construct meaning. What emerges in *Finnegans Wake* is what he calls 'the waters of babalog', in which meaning breaks down and flows into the shape of the narrative – the waters recreating and creating new meanings, contradictory statements.[20]

This brings us back to our particular tranche of modernity, the migration which has been going on while all this history has been in process. In the eighteenth century the Enlightenment had already brought the concepts associated with non-Christian, non-representational, pre-industrial art into the Western canon. The Cubists and their cohorts, after all, imported ideas about 'the Primitive' to justify their disdain for neoclassical and realist modes, and so on. What's new, then? As we know the transcultural has been walking among us for a very long time. What is important however, is the notion that the migrations which alter cultural perspectives in the twentieth century do not emerge from isolated moments of inspiration or compulsion. Instead, they are the resolution of processes which were set in motion during preceding centuries by the operations of the most powerful nation states. After all, what did the empires of the nineteenth century give their subjects? Well they gave them modernity in the shape of speed, industrialization, the irresistible export of capital, instantaneous communication, centralized authority, universal surveillance, and a culture of quasi-liberal despotism.

As such, one difficulty for the imperial mission was reconciling the political liberalism of the Enlightenment with its most important achievement, the nation state, within the framework of a rapidly expanding transnational capitalism. The logic of the nation was to impose cultural barriers between itself and the others which existed in the outer darkness. At the same time, the corporate needs of trade and military dominance drove its members outwards to engage with those others, but rationality itself created social and cultural stresses which could only be resolved by a political rhetoric which justified despotism of one kind or the other. Modernity provided an arena in which all these different elements operated. So now, as a result of the movements of the last three centuries or so, we have in the twentieth century a globalized space in which the movements of migrants into regions like Europe provoke a ferment of debate about cultural ownership, about identity and about the nature of the self.

In effect, migration in the twentieth century, has had an extraordinary impact which forced the realization that we lived in the middle of a peculiar break with the past. That we were moving towards a new aesthetic where the boundaries between art and culture were to be blurred, where culture and commerce couldn't easily be distinguished one from the other, where art and everyday life could be the same, and where the constant flow of signs and images turned in a perpetual conversation about meaning. Ironically, the practice of a modernist aesthetic co-existed comfortably with a traditional view about the ownership of cultures. Joyce himself, in *A Portrait of the Artist as a Young Man* has Stephen Daedalus say, (after a conversation with an Englishman), 'the language in which we are speaking is his before it is mine ... His language, so familiar and so foreign, will always be for me an acquired speech. I have not made or accepted its words.'[21] What stands out here is the sheer oddity of the sentiment, coming from one of the premier exponents of the English language, someone who shaped the way we speak and understand its idioms, and this apparent contradiction is a demonstration of the way that the traditional view of culture could survive hand in hand with modernist practice.

This brings me back to the meaning of black British identity and its potential in the process of canon formation. Artists are called upon to occupy a particular role in the business of arranging and fixing identity, because the pursuit of any kind of artistic endeavour is a public statement. Art and artists emerge from history, and at the same time recreate a history of their own activities. So in talking about the relationship between black British artists, black British identity and some of the dilemmas I've been discussing, I need to discuss what it means to be black British, because, although we use the label continuously nowadays, it is largely the practice of artists which has called this label into being, and what they've done goes beyond a cosmetic multiculturalism and begins the reconfiguration of identity. In fact, we needed this term to describe a particular shift in awareness, which was not only to do with ourselves, but also to do with what was happening inside the United Kingdom.

We know a great deal about the constitutional and legal framework within which British citizenship has evolved over the last fifty years. This was a political struggle, which went on over the space of fifty years and which opened up new categories of British identity, and made a new statement about citizenship in Britain. It is also clear that the process is not at an end. It has made possible a constitutional statement about our citizenship which does not depend on ethnicity or racial origins. But, at the same time, this political formula does not account for the way that individuals perceive themselves. My passport tells me where I can go, for instance, and even what I am able to do in certain cases. It does not tell me who I am. This 'who I am', however, goes to the heart of a fundamental issue: the problem of how our notions of self are constructed.

Many postcolonial writers tended to suggest that an individual's identity was an autonomous entity – an *a priori* characteristic of skin colour or geographical location, something to do with the individual's relationship to a particular ethnic group or a particular place, a particular piece of territory. They were, accordingly, concerned with mapping the outlines of an authentic self which sprang out of a specific historical continuity, and whose health could be determined by the extent to which it resisted the invasion of alien elements and cultural dominance. It is this background which makes the phrase 'black British' a necessary, and a challenging one, because, in the circumstances, it constituted a new argument about identity, which altered certain boundaries and created new possibilities.

For instance, the conventional way of talking about migration in Britain almost always focuses on the 'moment of arrival' because there is always a demand that ethnic minorities should be framed within this 'moment of arrival' – a moment which appears to value and privilege the arrival but which also, much more powerfully, is an argument that defines cultures as separate and alien to each other and extends that definition into the past.

But this moment of arrival is an imaginary moment, because there were lots of black people in Britain before then. We have begun to discover that the history of the black British community truly begins, not with the moment of arrival, but with a routine daily negotiation about crossing boundaries and barriers, about expanding limits. At the heart of this routine negotiation is a reshaping of the self, and in the process what emerges is a divided, fragmentary, contradictory consciousness, which we are obliged to take for granted.

Now I would argue that any individual consciousness is determined or over-determined by compulsory relationships and external processes. No one is a simple and autonomous unit. This is the point at which we all emerged from the long transformation of the post-Enlightenment world. In the case of the black British, we were obliged to be conscious (aware) of the sense in which our selves were characterized by compulsory relationships with the people and the environment we found in the United Kingdom. This environment was composed of any number of different things; it was comprised of a bundle of economic and social features, forming a horizontal market place of cultures, coercive pressures, and a set of narratives about identity, about what people were.

So our reshaping of identity was determined by a continuing negotiation about the nature of language, about the meanings of behaviour, about things that were said, about how to learn, what we learned and what we taught. It was determined also by the internal play between a specific and singular history, that is the history of our own families, the history of the group to which that family belonged, and the historical circumstances which dominate the lived experience of a person or persons in this arena. For instance, we associate the coming into being of the whole concept of black Britishness a number of historical crises which are very important in the life of our communities: for example, the Notting Hill riots, the struggle against 'sus', the New Cross fire, the death of Stephen Lawrence and so on. These historical circumstances frame the way we see ourselves and the way that vision of ourselves develops. All these elements and more go to make up the identity of any individual. What makes the narrative British is that these things took place within specific geographical and cultural limits and are determined by the conditions and processes operating within the limits of these particular boundaries. So, the development of the concept black British is complex, it takes place over time, and it exists in a creative tension with a modernist conception of self-hood and a particular concept of individuality – and it takes this reconstituted individual out of the private realm into the public arena – a shift which immediately creates an argument about the recasting of national identity.

But black artists in Britain work within the framework of race-thinking. Audiences and people in general look at our work with the question in mind, 'What is he saying about us? Does he like us? Is he attacking us? Is he condemning us?', rather than asking: 'What is he saying?' If I say that we live in a framework where racial divisions determine our view of almost everything I'm not making an accusation, merely stating a class of fact which accounts for many things. It accounts, for instance, for the fact that the inventiveness and creativity of black British artists have traditionally been submerged in a narrative about race, so that the productions of Caribbean, or African American, or Asian, or African artists are somehow perceived as offering the same view of the world as that of a black British artist. This is a consequence of a framework of ideas dominated by race – dominated also by generations of 'retrospective hallucination', as Spivak puts it.[22]

Most black British artists, however, come from a peasant or semi-rural, working-class background which on the ground never completely shared in the nationalist post-colonial reconstruction of Third World history. The reality in which their work is grounded happens to be this routine renegotiation of identity in their new homes, where the historic formation of diasporic blackness, as well as universalist notions about an 'uncorrupted' identity, or about unbroken connections with black roots, have no actual connection with their day-to-day experience. On the contrary, the authentic identity of many migrant communities begins with the tension of operating several different selves at the same time. You'll see this most clearly if you live through, with some of the new East European migrants, the process of operating a new language, new religious ideas and new manners. The consequence of this tension is that, as migrant artists, the choices we make are often transgressive or at least unrecognizable within a context which demands from us an unambiguous black outline, 'black' that is, in terms of a rigidly stereotyped conception of culture.

Typically, until very recently, the general context in which black British writers work has tended to regard us as another group of blacks who simply happened to be where we were, only notable for the colour of our skins; and the demand from us was to reproduce the 'drama of race.' In the present day, it is possible to see an equivalent being created, where the drama which is demanded from East Europeans is the drama of difference – a drama rooted in the distinction between rich and poor. I'm suggesting here, that, typically, as artists, our major struggle is not so much with dramatic manifestations of racism, although we struggle with those too, but is fundamentally concerned with the routine daily endeavour of representing who we think we are within our specific circumstances, with unlocking and exploring the specific history from which we emerge, and with finding outlets for that enterprise.

By contrast, in the past, black artists in the United Kingdom were, traditionally, more rigidly confined behind the barriers of ethnicity, where we were required to sketch out a picture of an alien identity. On the other hand, the necessity of breaking out of these limits, in order to talk about the changes which were occurring in our own lives and about our relationship with our new environment, is precisely what gives the work of black British artists its radical tenor, and the potential for radicalising our nation's view of culture and what it means.

Again, I want to distinguish this enterprise from the post-colonial process in which artists are concerned with a very different view of identity. Instead of reclaiming and reconstituting historical identities, our history has delivered us into a process of reshaping, becoming a different kind of individual self; and this is a process which takes place in a sustained dialogue or conversation with all the elements which go to make up this new self. This signals the emergence of a new consciousness, springing from the time and place which contains it, and linked to various other narratives about migration, about urban experience, about tensions between nationality and citizenship. So, what you are reading when you read my books, for instance, is a part of the mechanism by which the concept of the black British came into being, a reconfiguration of selfhood, which is a necessary precondition of the transcultural process.

On the other side of the equation all this has had a specific and interesting effect on the culture and identity of the United Kingdom. We, the British, recognized this fact in what I describe as the cosmetic rhetoric of British multiculturalism, but this is precisely why the term and the concept has had to be challenged. The rhetoric of inclusion conceals the fierceness and intensity of the struggle we are presently waging over cultural territory and over the identity of the state. At this moment in Britain, we face a long constitutional argument associated with Celtic nationalism. The establishment of regional governments in Scotland and Wales are only the beginning of a debate about the retention or dissolution of the British union, and in the last few years another argument has emerged – what does it mean to be English? That is, someone who, whether or not they were born there, lives in and identifies with the country, England, as opposed to any other constituent country of the British Union.

If we use that definition, a substantial part of the English population now has fairly recent origins in Ireland, Scotland, Wales, Central and Eastern Europe, Africa, Asia and the Caribbean. This fact is rapidly rendering archaic the old view of Englishness as an ethnic club, and we now begin to recognize that we are in the middle of a cultural struggle to reinterpret exactly what Englishness and Britishness mean, to re-interpret who has the right to say who we are, and towards what we should be sympathetic. This struggle is partly the result of a sort of sympathetic vibration provoked by the significance of the changes going on in the body of migrants.

Black British and Asian writing is within the epicentre of this vibration and central to the recognition that a new debate has begun to organize categories of identity, opening up a new landscape. Within this land-scape, we begin to go beyond the pre-existing, the *a priori* definition of our nationhood which I heard my fellow citizens outline as I grew up. They used to say: 'We know what we are, because that is what we are. And if you have to talk about it, you are not one of us.' British writing of every kind now has begun, with a certain tentativeness, to take advan-tage of the opportunities opened up by this new debate where people are *not* saying, 'We know what we are.' *Instead they're saying*, 'We don't know what we are and we have to decide.' I speak now about the writers of migra-tion, rather than about migrant writers, because in this new atmosphere, it becomes the task of writers from any and every part of the population to understand and explore new meanings.

At the same time, there are major features which the black British experience and its literature makes explicit: the phenomenon of migra-tion, movement and mobility, the renegotiation of selfhood, the histori-cising of new identities and the reconstitution of a dominant culture to reflect again new identities which are often in conflict. All these things together can flow, separate, join up in the same space, and co-exist. And not only co-exist, but actually offer the possibility of recreating a single culture with very different facets.[23]

So the meanings associated with this experience, seem to me to offer a defining vision around which a canon may be assembled, given that these are meanings which offer the potential of releasing both writers and crit-ics from ethnicity and skin colour. The extent to which the British acad-emy can meet this challenge will itself define whether it possesses the ability to resist the commodification of the cultural markets, whether it has the capacity to engage creatively with its own history, and whether it can locate a viable pathway out of the multiculturalist prison.

Notes

1. Email correspondence with Angeline Morrison.
2. Mike Phillips, *Blood Rights* (London: Michael Joseph, 1989).

3. Sukhdev Sandhu, *London Calling: Descriptions of the English Metropolis by African, Caribbean and South Asian Writers, 1772–1998* (Oxford: Oxford University Press, 1998).

4. Sandhu, *op. cit.,* p. 301. For example of Phillips' and Kureishi's work see Caryl Phillips, *The Final Passage* (London: Faber, 1984), and Hanif Kureishi, *The Budda of Surburbia* (London: Faber, 1990) and *My beautiful Laundrette* (London: Faber, 1984).

5. Reference to some of Mike Phillips' works may be seen in the authors' biographical notes (see above p. xii). Among Andrea Levy's writings are *Every Light in the House Burnin'* (London: Headline Review, 1994) and *Fruit of the Lemon* (London: Headline Review, 1999). Among Ferdinand Dennis works are: *The Sleepless Summer* (London: Hodder & Stoughton, 1989) and *Duppy Conqueror* (London: Flamingo, 1998).

6. Works from these authors for further reading might include: Courttia Newland, *The Scholar: A West Side Story* (London: Abacus, 1998); Alex Wheatle, *Brixton Rock* (London: BlackAmber Books, 1999) and *East of Acre Lane* (London: HarperCollins, 2002); Anton Marks, *Bushman* (London: The X Press, 2004); Mike Gayle, *My Legendary Girlfriend* (London: Flame, 1998) and *Turning Thirty* (London: Flame, 2000); and Nicola Williams *Without Prejudice* (London: St Martin's Press, 1998).

7. Tabish Khair, 'Laeserens foedsel – og doed,' *Information,* 25 November 2004, p. 12. The quotations in English are taken from Khair's English manuscript version of the essay, 'The Death of the Reader'.

8. *Ibid.*

9. *Ibid.*

10. Diran Adebayo, *Some Kind of Black* (London: Virago, 1996), p. 47.

11. Tabish Khair, *op. cit.*

12. Gayatri Spivak, 'Who Claims Alterity?,' in Barbara Kruger and Phil Mariana (eds), *Remaking History* (Seattle: Bay Press, 1989), pp. 269–92; p. 275.

13. For a discussion of V.S. Naipaul, see Bruce King, *V.S. Naipaul* (Basingstoke: Palgrave Macmillan, 1993).

14. See Bruce King, 'The Internationalization of English Literature', *The Oxford English Literary History,* Vol. 13, 1948–2000. pp. 125–40.

15. Mike Phillips and Trevor Phillips, *Windrush: The Irrestistible Rise of Multi-Racial Britain* (London: HarperCollins, 1998).

16. Joseph Conrad, *The Heart of Darkness* (London: Dent & Sons Ltd, 1902). Edward Said, *Orientalism* (London: Routledge & Kegan Paul, 1978).

17. Henk de Berg, *Freud's Theory and its Uses in Literary and Cultural Studies: An Introduction* (Rochester, NY: Camden House, 2003).

18. T.S. Eliot, 'The Lovesong of J Alfred Prufrock', in *Collected Poems 1909–1962* (London: Faber, 1974), p. 13.

19. W.B. Yeats, 'The Second Coming', in *Selected Poetry* (London: Macmillan, 1974), p. 99.

20. James Joyce, *Finnegan's Wake* (London: Faber, 1939), p. 103.

21. James Joyce, *A Portrait of the Artist as a Young Man* (St Albans: Triad Books, 1977), p. 172.

22. Spivak, *op. cit.,* p. 275.

23. See, for example, the recent BBC TV series, *Who Do We Think We Are,* in which British celebrities trace their origins to Africa, Asia, the Caribbean and Eastern Europe.

Part I
Interrogating the Canon

2

'The Ghost of Other Stories': Salman Rushdie and the Question of Canonicity?

James Procter

In a piece first published in the *New Statesman* in 1990, Paul Gilroy compares the diverging fortunes of two heavyweights of the British media during the late 1980s: Salman Rushdie and Frank Bruno. Gilroy argues that, at the time of his first World Championship fight against Mike Tyson, Bruno became a potent symbol 'of the future of blacks in this country', while Rushdie and the 'Affair' that surrounded him came to symbolize the foreignness of Muslim settlers. What Gilroy calls the 'canonization' of 'our Frank' was contemporaneous with the marginalization of British Asians, who found themselves construed as utterly and irredeemably different:

> For a while, Frank's muscular black English masculinity became a counterpart to the esoteric and scholastic image of Rushdie – the middle-class intellectual *immigrant* – so remote from the world of ordinary folk that he was able to misjudge it so tragically.
>
> For two weeks the stories were articulated directly together. They fed off each other, echoing, replying and re-working the same range of visceral themes: belonging and exclusion, sameness and assimilation ... The image of each man stood as a convenient emblem for one of Britain's black settler communities, marking out their respective rates of progress towards integration. Each image increased its symbolic power through implicit references to the other – its precise inversion.[1]

Entitled 'Frank Bruno or Salman Rushdie?', Gilroy's essay asks why the kind of antiphonal relationship articulated above has been overlooked in contemporary critical commentary. He goes on to implicate left-liberal thinking and its adherence to the conventional canonical distinctions between high and popular culture:'[a]longside the lofty principles and abstract aesthetic excellence invoked by Rushdie's supporters in the nation's literary elite, Frank's triumph must appear trivial and base'.[2] Gilroy's provocative and unexpected articulation of Rushdie and Bruno in the late 1980s provides a productive cue for a more extended dialogue between Rushdie and black British canon formation below. Most notably perhaps, it encourages a departure from some of the canonical boundaries between Asian and black, working-class and middle-class, the avant-garde and the everyday, high and popular culture, that bisect black British canon formation.[3]

However, in other ways 'Frank Bruno or Salman Rushdie?' seems to reinstall the very divisions it so deftly disrupts. It remains unclear, for example, whether Gilroy's aside about Rushdie as a 'middle-class intellectual *immigrant* – so remote from the world of ordinary folk that he was able to misjudge it so tragically' represents the critic's own position, or that of the media. This is because, while Gilroy provides a nuanced analysis of Bruno in a way that defamiliarizes and detaches him from media imagery and stereotype, no similar analysis is offered of Rushdie. As a result, the left-liberal perspective on Rushdie goes unchallenged, while Bruno is rendered a complex, progressive signifier. The residual populism of this approach prematurely forecloses further consideration of Rushdie's relationship to black British cultural formations in a way that risks reproducing the canonical distinctions between high and popular culture the essay so productively breaks with in other ways.

More generally, Rushdie seems destined to share a decidedly uncertain relationship to the question of a black British canon. It would appear Rushdie is too posh, too abstractly aesthetic, too lofty and detached to be worthy of consideration within the provincial, popular context of black British everyday life. At best, he represents a partially acknowledged, shadowy figure in available black cultural criticism. He comes into view at certain pivotal moments, during the Rushdie Affair for instance, but for the main remains virtually absent from accounts of black British culture and politics. Aijaz Ahmad's influential critique of Rushdie in *In Theory* is instructive within this context because it encapsulates a number of more general assumptions about Rushdie's writing to emerge during the 1990s. His reading of *Shame* in that text opens with a lengthy sentence on canon formation:

> The axiomatic fact about any canon formation, even when it initially takes shape as a counter-canon, is that when a period is defined and homogenized, or the desired literary typology is constructed, the canonizing agency selects certain kinds of authors, texts, styles, and criteria

of classification and judgement, privileging them over others which may also belong in the same period, arising out of the same space of production, but which manifestly fall outside the principles of inclusion enunciated by that selfsame agency; in other words, a certain kind of dominance is asserted and fought for, and is in turn defined as the essential and the dominant.[4]

The question of canonicity is foregrounded by Ahmad because Rushdie 'occupies a distinguished place at the very apex' of postcolonial, or 'Third World' literature (an issue we shall return to at the end of this essay).[5] Among other things, Ahmad suggests Rushdie's canonical status is founded upon, while serving to conceal, his privileged class position and his avant-garde, highly aestheticized, postmodern fiction of migrancy. For Ahmad, Rushdie's ideological moorings in high modernism and his deployment of (post)modernist narrative forms amount to an abandonment of 'the social condition of the Third World migrant', illuminating the writer's real 'conditions of production' as part of a wealthy and privileged metropolitan exile.[6]

While I share Ahmad's concern that Rushdie's migrant condition is ultimately universalized 'as an ontological condition of all human beings', this essay questions the view that we can read off class straightforwardly in Rushdie's writing as a rigid determinant of politics, as if class privilege alone forecloses political action.[7] There is a paradoxical danger that Ahmad's account reifies Rushdie's writing, removing it one step further from the conditions of production that have helped shape it. Ahmad's dismissal of Rushdie depends on a materialist critique of figurative and aesthetic dislocation with which he is, in fact, complicit in terms of his own dislocation of Rushdie from a black British milieu. In a spirit that is ultimately unfaithful to Ahmad's opening sentence on canonicity above, this essay will suggest that Rushdie 'belong[s] in the same period, aris[es] out of the same space of production' as a nascent black British canon in the 1980s. At the same time his fiction has tended to 'fall outside the principles of inclusion enunciated by' various canonizing agencies. This essay is *not* striving to 'open up' the black British canon to Rushdie, a strategy that would merely repeat the familiar, if redundant inclusion/exclusion binary of canon theory.[8] Rather it is interested in what the vexed relationship between Rushdie and black British tells us about the 'principles' of canon formation in this area and how it might inform future formulations of black British canonicity.

Rushdie's rise to prominence during the 1980s is contemporary with the emergence of black British as a canonical organizing category.[9] Yet, in Ahmad's analysis, and in available criticism more generally, it can feel as if novels like *Midnight's Children* (1981) and *Shame* (1983) 'came from nowhere' (as Rushdie himself put it recently).[10] It is worth remembering in this context that both these novels appeared at critical moments of 'race' rioting and writing in Britain. During these years Rushdie was involved in voluntary work in race-relations organizations, he was chairman of the Camden Community Relations Council and lobbied against the Nationality Act of 1981 that led to the urban riots of the same year. He spoke out on events such as the demonstrations in Southall, police violence, immigrant housing and institutional racism. He wrote against Britain's imperialist nostalgia in the early 1980s around the period of the Falklands Crisis, criticizing the rash of Raj films on British television that included *The Far Pavilions* (1984) *The Jewel in the Crown* (1984) and *A Passage to India* (1984).[11] In the late 1980s he provoked a significant debate on the evaluation of black British cinema.[12]

Such biographical information is not offered here to persuade the reader of Rushdie's 'real' or radical political intentions: the always vexed question of intentionality is particularly problematic with a writer like Rushdie who has written so excessively and influentially on his own work. I would argue from this perspective that, if anything, Rushdie's intentions have been granted too much authority, serving to fix or stabilize the meaning or significance of his writing, as if its political content can be decided in advance. Nevertheless, viewed provisionally and critically, such biographical 'background' information does suggest an important, alternative location for re-reading Rushdie's fiction of the 1980s and a means of questioning notions of prescribed political content. Here I am interested in developing a line of argument first suggested by Syed Manzurul Islam in his compelling essay 'Writing the postcolonial event: Salman Rushdie's August 15th, 1947':

> Let us not forget London, 1981. For a migrant that was a time in a hell hole when, still reeling under the ominous clouds of Thatcher's 'swamping' speech, he or she faced the terror in the streets in the hands of skin-headed-Paki-bashers, and with the gaze of a British bobby looking at him or her as if he or she were a mugger or an illegal immigrant. But there was more in store: worse houses, worse jobs if there were any going at all, virginity tests at the airport, and everywhere the echoing sound of Pakis-Darkis-Wogs-Go-Home. It was in the face of the long shadows of these spectres that Salman Rushdie published his celebrated booker of bookers – *Midnight's Children*. Critics – prone to hasty fabulation – hailed it as 'a continent finding its voice', but I would say that it was a migrant's event.[13]

Where, for Ahmad, Rushdie occupies an essentially rhetorical space of privilege and (post)modern excess, Islam locates him in a socially defined place and time: babylonian London, 1981.[14] It is by focusing our attention on 'London, 1981' that Islam makes available an important location of production, generally overlooked in relation to Rushdie's writing.[15]

In his essay, 'Imaginary Homelands', Rushdie suggests the unreliable narration of *Midnight's Children* is not so much an Indian disease, as the result of his own location within the British nation-state: '[w]riting my book in North London, looking out through my window on to a city totally unlike the one I was imagining on paper, I was constantly plagued by this problem, until I felt obliged to face it in the text'.[16] To read *Midnight's Children* in the spirit of the 'double perspective' or 'stereoscopic vision' Rushdie advocates in his essay, 'Imaginary Homelands', is to bring into sight a supplementary narrative in which the emergency and communal tensions of the Indian nation-state appear alongside a peculiarly British emergency.[17] As Rushdie suggests later in the essay, something is lost, but also gained, in translating India from his migrant location within London. So what is gained? Or what might be gained in reading Rushdie's notoriously nebulous notion of hybridity in conjunction with the authoritarian homogeneity of Thatcherism; his heterogeneous crowds alongside London's riotous black population; Mrs Ghandhi alongside Mrs Thatcher? A book about memory and forgetting, the preservation and repression of the past, *Midnight's Children* makes a peculiarly apposite allegory of amnesiac Britain in the early 1980s, as the trauma following the aftermath of empire set in. In the novel, the cold comforts and reassurances of imperialist nostalgia – of Falklands conflicts and Raj remakes – are displaced by the uncertainties and contradictions of Saleem's flawed memory.[18] It is significant that the Braganza pickles, which form the ultimate repository for Saleem's memories, are not merely consumed in India, but also in England.

In Rushdie's next novel, *Shame*, black Britain is more than an absence that potentially supplements the text, it erupts into the otherwise enclosed narrative of Pakistan. Central to this narrative is the character, Suyifa – who operates as the embodiment of shame in the novel. Born with red cheeks, Sufiya is the carrier of her mother's shame at not having mothered a son, and more generally of the various and violent sexual and political repressions that dominate the text. Her 'stinky blushes', we are told, are 'like petrol fires' (her very name, Su-fiya, registers this incendiary image), and smell of burning, blistering those who try to kiss her. At the close of the novel, Sufiya's repressed shame ignites, and 'the fireball of her burning' reeks havoc in the form of frenzied, inflammatory serial killings across Pakistan.[19] Yet, it is not just Pakistan, but Britain that represents the source of shame in the novel. Sufiya is the ghost of another story with an 'entirely unghostly' setting: Proper London. She grows 'out of the corpse' of Anahita Muhammed of East London, a girl murdered by her father for dating a white boy. She is also the ghost of an unnamed British Asian girl, attacked by a group of white youths on a late-night train. Most strikingly, perhaps, she is the embodiment of the British/Brixton riots of the early 1980s that the authorial narrator watches on television:

> Looking at smoking cities on my television screen, I see groups of young people running through the streets, the shame burning on their brows and setting fire to shops, police shields, cars. They remind me of my anonymous girl. Humiliate people for long enough and a wildness bursts out of them. Afterwards, surveying the wreckage of their rage, they look bewildered, uncomprehending, young. Did we do such things? Us? But we're just ordinary kids, nice people, we didn't know we could ... then, slowly, pride dawns on them, pride in their power, in having learned to hit back.[20]

This image of incandescent rage and of smoking English cities that so graphically haunts the petrol fire blushes of Pakistan's Sufiya Zinobia, appears fuelled by canonical black British imagery from the 1980s. Incendiary imagery, tropes of fire, and of burning, rage through black British writing of the 1980s.[21] For example, in Linton Kwesi Johnson's 'New Craas Massakah', which refers to the fire in New Cross that killed 13 black youths, and which fuelled the Brixton riots of 1981, we are told how 'di whole a black Britn tun a fiery red ... red wid rage like the flames af di fyah'.[22] There are striking intertextual parallels here between Johnson's 'fyah' and Rushdie's Sufiya: fire operates in both texts to denote riotous activity and to connote displaced psychosomatic fury, anger, and the return of the repressed.

Incendiary imagery is also central to Rushdie's next novel, *The Satanic Verses* (1988).[23] Interestingly Rushdie has said of this book's notorious title that it strives for 'the sort of affirmation that, in the United States, transformed the word black from the standard term of racist abuse into a "beautiful" expression of cultural pride', a process of transformation pivotal to the translation of black into the British context in the 1970s.[24] The novel contains clear references to black power in Britain and to the riots of the early 1980s, while the narrative self-consciously inserts itself within a canonical black British literary tradition through its allusions to Mary Seacole, Olaudah Equiano and Linton Kwesi Johnson. Less obviously, but more pervasively, the book strategically adopts black British cinematic forms and devices from the 1980s, notably those deployed in the controversial, avant-garde production of the Black Audio Film Collective, *Handsworth Songs* (1987).

Handsworth Songs was screened a year before the publication of *The Satanic Verses*. The film takes mainstream documentary footage focusing on civil unrest and rioting in London and Birmingham in the 1980s, and re-edits it to draw attention the limits of the documentary tradition and its 'ways of seeing' the black British community. It does this by, for example, using dissonant music and sounds, by using out cuts that focus on the acts of mediation (cameras filming, or taking pictures, the use of recording equipment, the activities of the reporters behind the scenes) rather than on the events they seek to mediate. In doing this, *Handsworth Songs* (like the 1984 film, *Territories*, which also influences this film and, perhaps, *The Satanic Verses*), defamiliarises the dominant regimes of representation used by the white media, signaling its limits, and questioning the documentary's implicit claim to present the facts transparently, truthfully or objectively.[25]

It is precisely these techniques that Rushdie adopts in his literary evocation of the same riots in the imaginary location of Brickhall in *The Satanic Verses*:

> - Cut. - A man lit by a sun-gun speaks rapidly into a microphone. Behind him there is a disorderment of shadows. But between the reporter and the disordered shadow-lands there stands a wall: men in riot helmets, carrying shields. The reporter speaks gravely; petrolbombs plasticbullets police injuries water-cannon looting, confining himself, of course, to facts. But the camera sees what he does not say. A camera is a thing easily broken or purloined; its fragility makes it fastidious. A camera requires law, order, the thin blue line. Seeking to preserve itself, it remains behind the shielding wall, observing the shadow-lands from afar, and of course from above: that is, it chooses sides.
> - Cut.- [26]

Like *Handsworth Songs*, the narrative here lingers on documentary processes and equipment (the camera, the reporter, the microphone) rather than on the riots themselves, in order to denaturalize the event and deny the truth claims of documentary footage. It reproduces the fragmentary form of the film through strategic use of punctuation and repetition of the word 'cut'. It repeats the disjunctions between what is heard and what is seen in *Handsworth Songs*, through reference to the camera 'which sees what he does not say'. It echoes the questioning of commonsense understandings of riots in the film through its ironic reference to the reporter who, we are told, confines himself, 'of course', to the facts.

At stake here are more than conventional issues of copying or even influence. *Handsworth Songs* was the subject of a negative review by Salman Rushdie in January 1987, which itself informed a key debate regarding canonicity among black British intellectuals in the late 1980s.[27] In his review Rushdie says 'There's a line that *Handsworth Songs* wants us to learn. "There are no stories in the riots", it repeats, "only the ghosts of other stories." The trouble is, we aren't told the other stories. What we get is what we know from TV.'[28] Rushdie arguably gets it wrong here, in terms of the film's careful disruption of what we know from television. However, it's worth noting what Rushdie does not, which is that the line: 'There are no stories in the riots only the ghosts of other stories' is itself a ghostly echo of Rushdie's line in *Shame*: 'All stories are haunted by the ghosts of stories they might have been.'[29]

Such dialogic echoes recall the kind of antiphonal relationship between Bruno and Rushdie described by Paul Gilroy in 'Frank Bruno or Salman Rushdie?' The complex interplay between, for example, Rushdie's literary fiction, black British cinema and the poetry of Linton Kwesi Johnson, raises interesting questions about the relationship between genre, form and a black British canon. For Ahmad, it is ultimately Rushdie's abandonment of realism in favour of (post)modernism that results in political impotency. It is this choice that prevents Rushdie from offering plausible political alternatives, from 'includ[ing] regenerative possibilities [or] producing resistance to oppression, solidarity and integrity in human conduct, or any sort of human community.'[30] Where for modernism, dislocation was experienced as a loss 'what postmodernism has done is to validate precisely the pleasures of such unbelonging, which is rehearsed now as utopia, so that belonging nowhere is nevertheless construed as the perennial pleasure of belonging everywhere.'[31] While I find this line of argument persuasive in various ways, Ahmad's hasty equation of Rushdie's magic realist fabulation and utopian excess with nowhere is, ultimately, too easy. Fredric Jameson's commitment to utopia is instructive here. Where Marxism has traditionally been critical of utopian thinking and its 'diversion of revolutionary energy', Jameson argues for a reassessment of utopia in the present: 'now it is practical thinking which everywhere stands as a testimony to the power of that system to transform even its adversaries into its own mirror image. The utopian idea, on the contrary, keeps alive the possibility of a world qualitatively distinct from this one.'[32] If Rushdie's utopian poetics of unbelonging are, on one level, marked by bourgeois detachment, then they also need to be understood in conjunction with Thatcherism and its insistence on certain 'practical', commonsense racialized forms of national belonging in the 1980s. Rushdie's aesthetics of detachment and transnational mobility do not inevitably correspond to political detachment, but might be said to imagine alternative, utopian forms of attachment in the face of an increasingly insular Britishness around the time of the Nationality Act (1981).

The literary uses of utopia in Rushdie's fiction seem particularly significant when located in terms of Thatcherism's 'pragmatic' approach to the arts in the 1980s, and more specifically, the attempt to incorporate black British artists through 'minority' and multiculturalist discourses. As Hazel Carby records in an essay on 'Multicultural Fictions', published a year before *Midnight's Children*, multicultural discourses placed a particular pressure on black British fiction from the late 1970s to be representative and to reflect the realities of the immigrant experience.[33] During the 1980s Rushdie spoke scathingly on numerous occasions about the rise of multiculturalism in Britain. Meanwhile, in 'Imaginary Homelands', he argued that the biggest pitfall facing black British writers is 'the adoption of a ghetto mentality. To forget that there is a world beyond the community we belong, to confine ourselves within narrowly defined cultural frontiers, would be, I believe, to go voluntarily into that form of internal exile which in South Africa is called the "homeland" '.[34] In many ways, this statement characterises what Ahmad would call Rushdie's privileged detachment, his aloofness from the everyday politics of the black community. Yet contradictory expressions of communal belonging ('we belong ... ourselves') are present, if subordinate, here. More importantly, viewed from the perspective of prevailing discourses of black British multiculturalism, we might legitimately ask to what extent the excessive anti-realism, or magic realism, of Rushdie's 1980s fiction was both informed by, and formulated as, a reaction to some of the more earnest forms of documentary realism being urged by Thatcherism's state apparatus.[35] It is worth noting in this context that magic realism does not necessarily represent an easy aesthetic departure from, or debunking of, the real. Since it developed historically in interwar Germany, magic realism has also been understood as a symptom of the artist's endeavour to reconcile the present reality with an alternative (sometimes utopian) version of that reality.

The discrepancy between Rushdie's commonsense canonical status in postcolonial studies and his uneasy or unsettling 'black British' status party comes about because the transnational rhetoric of contemporary postcolonial criticism and theory has been able to play a much more powerful and pervasive role than the comparatively unfashionable label 'black British' in shaping a canon of diasporic writers and writings in the UK. One of the reasons I think black British is worth persisting with is precisely because it seems to disrupt rather than enshrine certain canonical orthodoxies associated with transnational postcolonialism.[36] Rushdie's rise and rise during the 1980s and 1990s was contemporary with the rise of postcolonial criticism and theory.[37] It was not simply that Rushdie's canonical status was assured by the susceptibility of his writing to the discrete conceptual frameworks of postcolonialism that were subsequently applied to his work. Rather, and more fundamentally, his writing played an extraordinary and unparalleled constitutive role in the very formation of postcolonial theory, whose vocabularies of hybridity and migration register the taint of his presence. The current fall of Rushdie from the literary firmament, following the publication of *Fury*, is itself interesting when viewed from this perspective.[38] The postcolonial recovery from what Vijay Mishra has called 'Rushdieitis' arguably has as much to do with the current turn from culturalism to materialism as it does with intrinsic literary value. Where Rushdie was once embraced for his excessive aesthetics of postcolonial diasporic hybridity, he is now more frequently accused by postcolonial critics of being too aesthetic, of privileging poetics at the expense of politics in a manner that is deemed inappropriate to the new, historicist agendas of postcolonialism. As Revathi Krishnaswamy notes in an essay that extends some of the arguments in Ahmad's chapter, 'Rushdie de-materializes the migrant into an abstract idea'.[39]

While it has not been my intention in this essay to absolve Rushdie from these recent critical assessments, which have played a valuable role in highlighting some of the limits of a culturalist agenda, it does seem odd to charge an artist with being too aesthetic. If theories of canonicity have taught us anything, it is to be suspicious of spurious notions of intrinsic literary value. As critics we need to acknowledge our own part in the evaluation and subsequent devaluing of Rushdie's aesthetic of diasporic hybridity. Rather than writing off Rushdie in the present moment, I want to suggest it is our responsibility to make his aesthetic do more work than the current fashions within postcolonial studies are making it do. Rather than looking for progressive political content, as if it is somehow embedded within individual literary texts, we need to pay more attention to the ways in which we articulate, or connect them to contemporary political concerns.

If Rushdie was overvalued in the 1980s and 1990s, then it is not enough to ask him simply to step aside in the 2000s. His work deserves to be re-read in relation to alternative, frameworks, contexts and canons, including a black British canon. This might involve reading along different grains, as well as against the grain. As Peter Widdowson argues, to regard certain texts as critically 'canonic' is to illuminate their manufactured status and thereby provide a position from which to defamiliarize them by detaching them from the secure cultural meanings they have accumulated. He goes on:

> such works can also be re-read in ways which release them from their own canonic status ... little bits of 'great' literary works become familiar quotations – so familiar, indeed, that we cease to think of what they might mean inside or outside their original textual location.[40]

Krishnaswamy's important point that Rushdie 'dematerializes' the migrant into an abstract idea needs to be countered by a recognition that Rushdie himself has become a de-materialized, canonical abstraction. Rushdie's contradictory political imagination, with all its potentially progressive and reactionary elements, has been rendered overly coherent in the struggle to expose the limits and excesses of his migrant vision.

Notes

1. Paul Gilroy, 'Frank Bruno or Salman Rushdie?' in *Small Acts* (London: Serpent's Tail, 1993), pp. 86–94; pp. 87, 88–9.
2. *Ibid.*, p. 88. Gilroy's essay goes on to identify two other causes. First, he blames common-sense contemporary racism and its exploitation and exaggeration of differences internal to the black British communities. Gilroy refers to this process in terms of the 'Goldilocks-and-the-three-bears theory of racial culture and identity' where 'animal blacks enjoy an excess of brute physicality and wily oriental gentlemen conversely display a surfeit of cerebral power, while only the authentic Anglo-Brit is able to luxuriate in the perfect equilibrium of body and mind' (p. 89). Second, Gilroy points to the abandonment of black as a term that articulates African Caribbean and Asian experience:

   > Some of what were once black communities are now happily shrugging off that label. The precarious political grouping, which for a brief, precious moment during the late 1970s allowed settlers from all the corners of the Empire to find some meaning in an open definition of the term 'black', has been all but destroyed. Today, polite 'anti-racist' orthodoxies demand an alternative formulation – 'black and Asian'. This involves the sacrifice of significant political advantages but is presented as a step forward, a means to remind ourselves that by invoking the term 'black', we are not 'Africanizing' our struggles or declaring everybody to be the same. (p. 93)

Gilroy proceeds cautiously here. He does not advocate a nostalgic return to older forms of black identification of the 1970s. On the contrary, his essay is motivated by a desire to take Bruno's canonization seriously, as a significant development at a time when 'racism regularly constructed blackness and Britishness as mutually exclusive social and cultural categories' (p. 87). Nevertheless, the essay closes by insisting the break up of traditional alliances across Britain's black communities 'cannot conceal a new political problem. What do we say when the political and cultural gains of the emergent black Brits go hand in hand with the further marginalization of "Asians" in general and Muslims in particular?' (p. 94). In my view Gilroy's point remains a moot one.

3. See Gilroy's comments on the break up of 'black British' in note 2 (above).
4. Aijaz Ahmad, 'Salman Rushdie's *Shame*: Postmodern Migrancy and the Representation of Women', in *In Theory: Classes, Nations, Literatures* (London: Verso, 1992), pp. 123–58; p. 123.
5. *Ibid.*, p. 125.
6. *Ibid.*, p. 127.
7. *Ibid.*, p. 127.
8. In his ground-breaking study, *Cultural Capital: The Problem of Literary Canon Formation* (1995), John Guillory argues that the commonsense debates currently governing debates on the canon, and which centre on the inclusion and exclusion of certain writers and texts, are 'misconceived from the start' (vii). While he does not dispute the fact that changes to the canon are desirable, he questions the way in which the inclusion/exclusion binary grants literature a *representative* status that is problematic:

> Clearly a 'representative' canon does not redress the effects of social exclusion, or lack of representation, either within or without the university; nor would the project of canonical revision need to make this claim in order to justify the necessity of curricular revision. But in construing the process of canon formation as an exclusionary process essentially the same as the exclusion of socially defined minorities from power, the strategy of opening the canon aims to reconstruct it as a true image (a true representation) of social diversity. (p. 8)

Although Guillory's study seeks to shift our attention from the contents of individual texts to the institution itself, it also has valuable things to say about how our reception and interpretation of those texts are premised on a mistaken notion of representation in terms of what he calls 'imaginary politics'. By imaginary politics, Guillory does not mean the opposite of 'real politics' but 'the reduction of the political to the instance of representation, and of representation to the image'. In short, debates on the inclusionary/exclusionary canon are premised on the (problematic) assumption that literature is a reflection, or mirror of the real, an assumption this essay will also suggest has informed the negative reception of Rushdie's work.

Guillory also suggests that the idea of a separatist canon inserts 'minority' or 'multicultural' literature within a regime of value that privileges 'transgressive, subversive, antihegemonic' (20) expression. Evidence that this is currently the case in black British literary criticism can be found in the critical legitimation of brilliantly 'subversive' novels like Selvon's *The Lonely Londoners*, and the critical silence surrounding more 'conservative' texts such as E.R Braithwaite's

To Sir, With Love (1959). It perhaps explains our critical preoccupation with the 'revalueshanary' poems of Linton Kwesi Johnson at the expense of love poems like 'Lorraine'; the early Kureishi of *My Beautiful Laundrette* and *The Buddha of Suburbia* over this later work in which race and ethnicity are not part of the explicit content.

9. Though it had been used in a British context since the 1970s, 'black British' did not become conspicuous within a literary context until the years 1986–88. Even so, its usage has been inconsistent and patchy. Prahbu Guptara's *Black British Literature: An Annotated Bibliography* (Sydney: Dangaroo Press, 1986) makes assertive claims for the term as an index for African, Asian and Caribbean writing. In collections like Merle Collins and Rhonda Cobham (eds), *Watchers and Seekers* (London: The Women's Press, 1987) and Lauretta Ngcobo (ed.), *Let it Be Told* (London: Pluto Press 1987) the editors appear to register a more cautious acceptance of the relationship between black and British through their respective subtitles: *'Black Women in Britain'* and *'Black Writers in Britain'*. *Watchers and Seekers* draws together writers of African, Caribbean, South Asian and Chinese descent, while *Let it Be Told* is an African Caribbean collection, apart from the inclusion of Agnes Sam (a South African of Indian descent). Early anthologists like James Berry use 'Westindian British' (see *Bluefoot Traveller*, London: Limestone Publications 1976 and 1981, and *News from Babylon*, London: Chatto 1984) rather than black British, while E.A. Markham speaks of 'Caribbean poetry from the West Indies and Britain' Caribbean' in *Hinterland* (Newcastle-Upon Tyne: Bloodaxe Books, 1989). The first sustained study of black British writing, David Dabydeen and Nana Wilson-Tagoe's important but critically neglected *A Reader's Guide to West Indian and Black British Literature* (Mundelstrup: Dangroo Press, 1987) notes that 'Black British is even more problematic' than the term West Indian (p. 10). The authors go on to say ' "Black British" literature refers to that created and published in Britain, largely for a British audience, by black writers either in Britain or who have spent a major portion of their lives in Britain' (p. 10). The vagueness of this definition, along with the fact that 'black British' appears in scare quotes suggests a certain unease with the category and what it includes/excludes. Dabydeen and Wilson-Tagoe ask a number of valuable questions, that nevertheless go unanswered: is 'black' an aesthetic or a racial category; what is 'British', and is it sufficient to group writers under such a heading? Although they limit their own discussion to West Indian black British production they hint that, had they more space, Asian writing might also have been included. Nevertheless, its absence is telling.

10. Rushdie made this comment in an interview with Hari Kunzru in 2003 available at http://www.harikunzru.com/hari/rushdie.htm (last accessed 11 February 2005). Salman Rushdie, *Midnight's Children* (London: Picador, [1981] 1982), and *Shame* (London: Picador, [1983] 1984).

11. Salman Rushdie, 'Outside the whale' in *Imaginary Homelands: Essays and Criticism, 1981–91* (London: Granta Books, 1992), pp. 87–101.

12. See James Procter (ed.), *Writing Black Britain 1948-1998: An Interdisciplinary Anthology* (Manchester University Press: Manchester, 2000), pp. 261–5.

13. Syed Manzurul Islam, 'Writing the Postcolonial Event: Salman Rushdie's August 15th, 1947', *Textual Practice*, 13:1 (1999), pp. 119–35; p. 119.

14. Once again, it is interesting how class operates surreptitiously here to secure alternative political readings of Rushdie. If for Ahmad, Rushdie's wealthy

background affords him special insight into the ruling elite of Pakistan, for Islam Rushdie's writing is informed by a very different kind of subaltern migrant consciousness associated with unemployment, poverty and homelessness. The *various* class positions that Rushdie both takes up and disavows in his writing, and which register a profound ambivalence for the 'minority groups' he describes, are arguably smoothed over by both critics.

15. For example, Ahmad says that *Shame* is a novel set almost exclusively in Pakistan 'although a couple of episodes do take place in India' (Ahmad, *op. cit.* p. 139) in a way that seems to neglect London's part in the novel's latent and manifest content.

16. Rushdie, *op. cit.* (1992), p. 10.

17. To read Rushdie as a supplementary to a black British canon (that is, not as something incidental, but something unfolding within), is to acknowledge an oppositional politics in Rushdie's work that critics have refused. In the late 1970s and early 1980s the New Racism placed the migrant on the other side of the national frontier. One wonders whether part of the spectacular success of *Midnight's Children* had to do with its handling of empire at a safe distance, beyond the boundaries of the nation-state, in a period of heightened Raj nostalgia.

18. Rushdie's anti-Thatcherism suggests a significant affinity with black British cultural production of the 1980s.

19. Rushdie, *op. cit.* (1983), pp. 136, 121, 286 and 317.

20. *Ibid.*, pp. 116–17.

21. See for example, John McLeod, *Postcolonial London: Rewriting the Metropolis* (London: Routledge, 2004).

22. Linton Kwesi Johnson, *Mi Revalueshanary Fren: Selected Poems* (London: Penguin, 2002), pp. 55–60. The second syllable of Sufiya's Asian name comes to register an intriguing West Indian/black British lilt here, when read alongside Johnson's 'fyah'.

23. Salman Rushdie, *The Satanic Verses* (London: Viking, 1988).

24. Rushdie, *op. cit.* (1991), p. 403.

25. Sankofa, *Territories* (1984).

26. Rushdie, *op. cit.* (1988), pp. 454–5.

27. For Rushdie's review and the response it provoked, see James Procter (ed.), *Writing Black Britain 1948–1998: An Interdisciplinary Anthology* (Manchester University Press: Manchester, 2000), pp. 261–5.

28. *Ibid.*, p. 262.

29. Rushdie, *op. cit.* (1983), p. 116.

30. Ahmad, *op. cit.* p. 151.

31. *Ibid.*, p.157.

32. Fredric Jameson, *Marxism and Forms: Twentieth Century Dialectical Theories of Literature* (Princeton: Princeton University Press, 1971), p. 111.

33. Hazel Carby, 'Multicultural Fictions' (Birmingham: Centre for Contemporary Cultural Studies, Paper no. 58, 1979).

34. Rushdie, *op. cit.* (1991), p. 19.

35. Such a reading does not just have implications for an internal evaluation of the work of Salman Rushdie, but for a black British canon more generally. Rushdie's writing has typically been valued (and as we have seen, devalued) for its avant-garde experimentation and magic realist abstraction. In contrast,

realism was the prevailing discourse of black British literature for much of the 1980s. Rushdie's avant-garde aesthetics need to be articulated with the black British realisms to which they are in part a reaction, rather than being seen as discrete opposites. Beyond the more obvious issue of influence and those antecedents, such as Hanif Kureishi and Zadie Smith who in different ways draw upon Rushdie, it is perhaps significant that the black British literary scene of the late 1970s and early 1980s had almost abandoned the novel form in favour of poetry and the short story. However, the elephantic text of *Midnight's Children* appears to have stimulated a return to the novel as the dominant black British genre, whose presence may be detected in the big novels associated with the likes of Zadie Smith and Monica Ali today.

36. If, as John McLeod has rightly argued, a transnational focus allows us to attend to the canonical constrictions of black British (see 'Some Problems with "British" in "a Black British Canon" ', *Wasafiri*, 36, Summer 2002, pp. 56–59), this essay has argued black British may also help us locate and negotiate (rather than a resolve) what I take to be some of the canonical constrictions and slippages of 'transnational', and its tendency to smooth over, or simply not linger for long enough, on local/national formations.

37. *The Empire Writes Back* (1989), the first and the most influential textbook of post-colonial studies, takes its name from a quotation from Salman Rushdie that is prominently displayed on the back cover of the first edition: 'the empire writes back to the Centre'. It is particularly interesting within the context of this chapter that if Rushdie's phrase is conventionally regarded as a play on the *Star Wars* film, then it also has a more local, black British inter-text in the Birmingham Centre for Contemporary Cultural Studies text, Paul Gilroy *et al.* (eds), *The Empire Strikes Back* (London: Hutchinson, 1982).

38. Salman Rushdie, *Fury* (New York: Random House, 2001).

39. Revathi Krishnaswamy (1995) 'Mythologies of Migrancy: Postcolonialism, Postmodernism and the Politics of (Dis)location', *Ariel*, 26:1 (1995), pp. 125–46; p. 132.

40. Peter Widdowson, *Literature* (London: Routledge, 1999), p. 23.

3
Not Good Enough or Not Man Enough? Beryl Gilroy as the Anomaly in the Evolving 'Black British Canon'

Sandra Courtman

> By absolute values, a true writer can never be other than what he is. But in our imperfect world his living light will only shine among men if it appears at precisely the right time.[1]

As a Guyanese writer, Beryl Gilroy may be considered anomalous because, during the period of the 1960s and 1970s when she first began to seek publication, black women writers were largely invisible both in Britain and in her native Caribbean. The 'Anomaly' in the title of this essay is a descriptive term used by Joanna Russ in *How to Suppress Women's Writing* to explain the forces which 'work against women writers who dare to write'.[2] In this chapter, I shall be arguing that Beryl Gilroy's work has suffered because of what Russ describes as the, 'isolation of the work from the tradition to which it belongs and its consequent presentation as anomalous'.[3] The tradition from which Gilroy appears to be isolated was a significant body of work that was published in Britain by anglophone Caribbean writers, almost exclusively male, who made their reputations in the 1950s and 1960s. This blossoming corpus would lead Sam Selvon, in 1994, to comment on, 'the wonderment and accolade that greeted the boom of Caribbean literature and art in Britain in the early fifties'.[4] Writers, like Sam Selvon, George Lamming, Andrew Salkey, V.S. Naipaul and Edward Kamau Braithwaite arguably defined a tradition of Anglo-Caribbean-British literature for themselves and for the generations of writers who followed.

These male writers and their works are central to debates about the processes of canonization and the implications of being subsumed within a supposed 'black British' homogeneity, arguments that are fully engaged with elsewhere in this volume. However, in considering Gilroy's reputation as a writer, it is not possible to place her in these debates without acknowledging her invisibility. If she were beginning her writing career now, she would find the market for her work much changed. It is the sheer presence and volume, now taken for granted, of contemporary black women's writing in Britain that enables John McLeod to pose the question of their labelling in his article 'Some Problems with "British" in a "Black British Canon" ':

> How wise would it be to declare Evaristo's book [*Lara*] as 'black British'? What would happen if one were to include it as part of a 'black British canon'? These terms emphasise inclusion and particularity on the grounds of a race or nation, yet *Lara* cheerfully fragments such homogenising fictions.[5]

However, as Gilroy's work has rarely attracted British literary-critical attention, it is difficult to say whether she has suffered, or benefited, from 'inclusion and particularity on the grounds of race or nation'. In mainstream British academia, she is rarely acknowledged as important in any of the literary rubrics which might locate her – as a woman writer, a black woman writer, a black British writer or a Caribbean writer. She remains the little-known and un-theorized precursor to the talented Evaristo. Her reputation as a pioneering writer and cultural analyst bears no relation to that of her famous son Paul Gilroy. So much so, that in a special tribute following Beryl Gilroy's death on 4 April 2001, Carole Boyce Davies felt bound to add:

> Many people in the academy express shock when they learn that she was the unidentified mother of Paul Gilroy, author of *The Black Atlantic* (1994). Proud of his accomplishments, confident about his skills, she had many questions about his practices. Many in London whom I have interviewed go as far as to state that she – more than her son – was the (under)recognised expert on Black British culture and Afro-Caribbean experience in London. This point is important as it once more illustrates the way in which the intellectual and creative work of Black women is often undervalued.[6]

Here, Boyce Davies is gesturing towards the rather different treatment that Beryl Gilroy received in comparison to her male contemporaries and even to that of her son. That women's work was considered trivial in comparison to the male equivalents was the norm for Gilroy's generation. As Russ writes: 'I believe that the anomalousness of the woman writer – produced by the double standard of content [unworthy of the male-dominated canon] and the writer's isolation from the female tradition – is the final means of ensuring permanent marginality'.[7] There were notable exceptions, of course, such as Andrew Salkey who, as writer in residence at the BBC in the 1950s, was especially supportive of Gilroy and other women writers.

Given the gate-keeping gender politics of the 1950s and 1960s, my argument is much less concerned with the wisdom of defining who should and should not be included in the impossibly fluid and contestable category of 'black British'. Indeed, the contradictions implicit in such a label cause Mike Phillips to make a sharp comparison with a famous white writer:

> Unfortunately the bulk of knowledge and research in this [black British] field has very little to do with black Britain and everything to do with a tradition of colonial or postcolonial studies ... To get a feel for the thing, imagine the work of Graham Greene being described as African, or South American or Vietnamese literature because he happened to have set books in those places. When blackness enters the frame rationality goes out of the window.[8]

Rather, for this chapter, I have researched a specific history of a black woman's desire to be included in the wider category of *writers*. Unlike Evaristo, Gilroy was a Caribbean woman writer working in an almost complete literary void.[9] Also, she worked with styles, and in genres, that would render her work an anomaly in any potential listing in the British literary scene of the 1950s, 1960s and 1970s. Fred D'Aguiar's comment that '[c]reativity itself cannot be contained for long in any fashion or vice-hold which the process of naming and compartmentalising seeks to promote' is undoubtedly true, and it is for that reason that Gilroy's work exists at all.[10] Yet, inspite of women's uncontainable creativity and the blossoming corpus of Caribbean literature, there are virtually no black Caribbean women publishing in Britain in the years between the 1950s and early 1980s.[11] The reasons for this absence are both historically and politically complex. However, Gilroy's experience as a writer may help us to understand how women's invisibility is bound up as much as with gender politics, as with market-place whims and the vagaries of academic literary taste.

The paradox of Gilroy's literary marginality is sharpened and exacerbated by the honours bestowed upon her in her later years by British academic institutions. She is often cited as a pioneering black Caribbean woman. In this essay, I will explore Beryl Gilroy's reputation and her battles to be taken seriously as a writer. With Gilroy's best-known autobiography as a case-study, I shall consider its problematics of form and content that may have played a part in her neglect, against the backdrop of West Indian patriarchy, which made her work anomalous in an early and evolving black British canon. Focusing in particular on *Black Teacher*, the essay will discuss whether or not its form had a direct bearing upon its being under-valued as literature, or whether it has suffered from the type of isolation and misrecognition that Joanna Russ explicates so clearly in *How to Suppress Women's Writing*.

Published life writing by a black woman is undoubtedly a rare achieve-ment in the early British postwar period, especially that depicting West Indian women's experience of migration and liminality. Gilroy's work merits attention for it enables one to make connections between gender and genre in the context of debates about the formation of an early, male-dominated, black British canon. This essay will explore why Gilroy's literary contributions to black literature remain obscure and questionable, whilst her contribution to multi-racial education is universally acknow-ledged. Why is it that *Black Teacher* has received little literary-critical atten-tion, remaining on the margins of (what is arguably defined as) a black British literary canon? We need to understand Peter Fraser's enigmatic remarks in Gilroy's obituary that 'Her qualities as a writer were more slowly appreciated by critics than readers.'[12]

A question of literary value

Beryl Agatha Gilroy was born in Springlands, British Guiana in 1924, and in 1951 made the long journey to London to continue her professional development as a gifted teacher. Like most young women from the West Indian colonies, she travelled hopefully but I doubt that she had, at that time, even secret aspirations towards becoming a professional writer. Between 1951 and 1976, the year that *Black Teacher* was published, she became known as a writer of radical children's readers. By the late 1960s, she had had both her 'final passage' novel and her Guyanese reminiscences rejected by publishers.[13] Therefore, *Black Teacher* was her first major publi-cation for adults. For a black woman to publish an autobiography in 1976 is a phenomenon worth exploring in the context of a postwar lacunae in Caribbean women's' literary history. We might now read *Black Teacher* as life writing which confronts the thorny construct of a colonial identity and the contradictions presented by a metropolitan identity quest. But *Black Teacher* was published, not for its contribution to this now well-developed strand of postcolonial enquiry, but for its usefulness to 1970s debates on Britain's failure to provide a culturally-fair education. It appeared at 'precisely the right time', and because it was considered politically apposite *Black Teacher* was appropriated for its usefulness as a sociological and educational text. We know that texts are appropriated by different groups of readers and read in different ways, but in this case the text, from the outset, seems to have been situated within discourses of education and sociology – a positioning that would limit its audience and prevent its wider appreciation as life writing.

Since I began my research on Gilroy in 1994, she has been increasingly eulogized and anthologized; presently, she would be considered a serious omission from any postwar account of black British writing and experience.[14] It would be misleading to suggest that her achievements are always downplayed; since her death, her reputation may be argued to be overinflated. A recent website on Guyanese writers in England, which includes entries on Wilson Harris, Roy Heath, David Dabydeen, Pauline Melville and John Agard, states that: 'Beryl Gilroy is, or was, a significant figure in the literature of the UK diaspora'.[15] However, it is difficult to find her work studied in British universities or criticized in British journals of literary criticism, and so the evidence for this significance is questionable. In the USA, her recent novels tend to attract more scholarly attention, sometimes of a celebratory kind. For example, she was honoured for her fiction by The Association of Caribbean Women Writers and Scholars in 1996, at Florida International University. The fact that she is feted in the USA and on global websites does little to help us understand her neglect by British critics.

Clearly, Gilroy did have supportive networks in Britain, such as the Caribbean Women Writers Alliance at Goldsmiths College in London. For example, she was due to deliver the keynote address to the 4th Annual Caribbean Women Writers Alliance a few days after her sudden death in 2001. However, Gilroy was under no illusion about the lack of detailed critical attention paid to her work in Britain. Even when publicly honoured, she recognized that her literary reception was unequal. In an otherwise upbeat interview with Roxann Bradshaw for *Callaloo*, she remarks:

> Without even this positive talk, you get things that are amazing, like when they invited me to become a Fellow of the Institute [of Education, University of London]. Normally, they don't give black women fellowships ... Well I was at the presentation, I was with Donald Woods, you know *Cry Freedom*; they knew everything about that man, but they knew very little about my work. I said 'Why did you do this?' And they said 'Well we didn't have time to study your work', and that is what I call subliminal racism. It is there but they wouldn't acknowledge it, because it is not so important; but they knew everything about Donald because he is one of them [a white male].[16]

Thus it remains a paradox that, whilst she has been honoured by such academic institutions in Britain, her work rarely received any sustained critical attention. Her work and her achievements may be represented, extracted and reduced, but they also rarely elicit comment.

Perhaps this lack of commentary indicates that whilst she is recognized as a pioneering figure in the evolving black British landscape, the literary quality of her written work does little to merit critical attention. This would be the most readily available explanation and in this respect she joins the greater majority of writers who are not validated by the academy. In the course of my research I have tried to unravel by whom, and by what absolute literary standards of excellence, she is deemed not 'good enough' as a writer. As practitioners, we know that a disproportionately small number of writers and their works continue to be circulated within the academy. The critical practices that shore up this selectivity are hidden, yet robust. As scholars, we often question how is it that certain writers and their works are canonized whilst others are dismissed. We attend to the general processes of canonical flux and try to understand how cultural forces' shifts in taste move writers in and out of the literary canon. We sometimes attempt to influence these changes by bringing 'lost' writers back into print.[17] However, it is rare to find a critic who engages directly with his or her own notion of critical value and where it might derive from.

Roger Sale engages with the idea of literary reputations in his book, *On Not Being Good Enough: Writings of a Working Critic*, where he reflects on his role in the circuit of publishing, reviewing and academic criticism.[18] Literary reputations are, in his view, unnecessarily inflated to the detriment of many unknown novelists. In the course of his book, Sale states that 'one third of novels [produced in a year] are hopelessly bad'; but he asserts this without letting us in on his criteria, and thus unquestioningly subscribes to the very value-system that he is intent on revealing. Pierre Bourdieu, in *Distinction: A Social Critique of the Judgement of Taste*, tells us that the business of aesthetic appreciation entails 'a detachment and disinterestedness which aesthetic theory regards as the only way of recognising the work of art for what it is, i.e. autonomous'.[19] Bourdieu reveals how a traditional literary critic relies on apolitical and asocial 'disinterested' standards that underwrite his objectivity and enable him to select from all those 'hopelessly bad 'works to find the ones which are important and original. Bourdieu attempts to explain how critics, such as Sale, and any reader or reviewer does this:

> This historical culture functions as a principle of pertinence which enables one to identify, among the elements offered to the gaze, all

the distinctive features and only these, by referring to them consciously or unconsciously, to the universe of possible alternatives. This mastery is, for the most part, acquired simply by contact with works of art – that is, through an implicit learning analogous to that which makes it possible to identify styles, i.e. modes of expression characteristic of a period, a civilisation or a school without having to distinguish clearly, or state explicitly, the features which constitute their originality. Everything seems to suggest that even amongst professional valuers, the criteria which define the stylistic properties of the 'typical works' on which all of their judgements are based usually remain implicit.[20]

The 'pure gaze' of the disinterested critic, then, is learned by distinguishing the new work in relation to a body of existing canonical work. The evaluation and the consequent exercise of taste are, therefore, inextricably bound to what has been learned and discarded by a privileged race, class and educational apprenticeship. We can only speculate on how Gilroy's earliest manuscripts (*In Praise of Love and Children* and *Sunlight on Sweet Water*) might have been received in terms of the dominant literary and publishing apparatus. At this time, the tradition of Caribbean Literature was just being recuperated and established through a body of new work and, as such, few British publishers would have been able to place the texts, even experimentally, within the standard 'modes of expression characteristic of a period, a civilisation or a school'. Gilroy herself describes how much of an outsider she felt when she tried to introduce her work to British publishing houses in the 1950s:

> The publishers, editors and other occupants of the inner publishing sanctum had been raised on the stereotype, preserved them and could not see beyond them. Talking with some about my writing brought the discussion to a dark and barren place. Their class-education had not prepared them for encounters with colonial minds.[21]

This is not surprising given that British publishing houses in the1960s were dominated by white males of a certain class and education. But Gilroy also threatened newly acquired masculine power relations in that publishers tended to employ male West Indian writers to read 'niche' manuscripts that might be considered 'foreign' to the British tradition. She explains how her work might see to threaten the status quo:

> When my work was sent to the male writers from the West Indies to be read, these men, in order to be as erudite as they were expected to

be, turned to the idiosyncratic and the fastidious. My work, they said, was too psychological, strange, way-out, difficult to categorise.[22]

It is the very separation of aesthetics from social history that gave rise to the apolitical critical practice of a Western academy; therefore I find arguments that lay the blame for the neglect of Gilroy's writing squarely on its supposed lack of literary-aesthetic value are necessarily circular. I choose instead to confront the critical silence that envelops *Black Teacher* through the book's history and politics. It is helpful to leave the question of the literary value aside, and instead trace the historical conditions that gave rise to the autobiography. I am interested, for example, in some of the critical responses to the first edition of *Black Teacher*, and how these might have affected its subsequent reception. Finally, I should like to argue that *Black Teacher* is much more than a useful account of Gilroy's radical educational practice. It is radical autobiographical practice too, and more to the point in danger of becoming, to borrow Leela Gandhi's words, 'the forgotten content of postcoloniality'.[23]

Black teacher, black writer

We might begin by comparing *Black Teacher*'s promotion and reception to that surrounding E.R.Braithwaite's *To Sir, With Love*. Gilroy's book is recognizably a woman's version – it covers similar autobiographical territory and shares something of Braithwaite's pedantry and style. However, Braithwaite's book was promoted as a *story*: 'The best-selling *story* of a negro teacher in a tough school in London's East End.'[24] *Black Teacher* is most usually ignored as narrative. In so far as I have been able to discover, Guptara is the only critic to compare Gilroy's and Brathwaite's autobiographies and to consider their content in relation to literature. He suggests the following:

> Surely, the distinction between literature and sociology is precisely that literature offers us the experience of what it feels like to be an individual or a member of a certain group, while sociology concerns itself with cognitive knowledge or with people in the mass.[25]

Black Teacher, then, should be recuperated as an example of women's *literary* expression: as literature which offers, not sociology, but an imaginative experience of what it felt like to be a black woman in Britain in the 1950s and 1960s. To understand why it is that the text has been consistently overlooked as an example of Caribbean *writing*, the circumstances

which determined its content and form – and which prompted its publication – need to be examined.

Black Teacher was not regarded as the material for popular entertainment. It is not that *To Sir, With Love* was necessarily better written, but
primarily because the infant-school settings of *Black Teacher* do not provide for the frisson which undercuts Braithwaite's mastery of his pubes-
cent class (embodied cinematically in Sidney Poitier's erotically charged
performance in the 1967 film of the book). The reason why Gilroy's text,
which deals with racial confrontation in the setting of the workplace, would
be claimed for socio-educational purposes is, therefore, easily imagined.
As possible 'literature', its central concerns – a young teacher's quest to
fight racial discrimination whilst finding ways of managing her infant
class – might have been regarded at the time of its publication as having
only specialist appeal.

To Sir, With Love was written and published in the late 1950s, before
'the problem' of multiculturalism had been forced on to the political
agenda. The fact that *Black Teacher* came to be written and published in
1976 was very much a matter of its timeliness: that is, Gilroy's experience was deemed worthy of the attention of contemporary education professionals (and was thus marketable). It also relates to the conditions which
instigated the need for further legislation (the 1976 Race Relations Act)
to deal with indirect racial discrimination in the workplace.[26] It influenced a developing discourse of British anti-racist politics and is exem-
plary of writing which challenged the nation's perception of itself at
that time. In a recent article on this topic, Dave Gunning might have
considered *Black Teacher*'s contribution to anti-racist politics but he does
not; Gilroy's book could have illustrated his argument that black literature can only be understood when 'placed within the context of the
actual discursive practices of the state and civil society of the nation at
any given time'.[27]

Gilroy's perspective had already attracted the attention of the media:
in 1973, there had been an article on her work in the *Evening Standard*
with the headline: 'It's like a Mini UN at Beckford Infant's School.'[28]
Subsequently, she was asked to read a short piece on her experiences on
the BBC's *Woman's Hour*, and was immediately solicited by the publishers, Cassell, to write a full-length work. The autobiography was sought
out for its contribution to the debate on the way in which the British
education system was failing its multicultural intake. The mood of black
parents was increasingly one of resistance and anger, and by 1981 the
Rampton Committee had been forced to produce 81 recommendations
for action to be taken by schools to address the underachievement of black

children.[29] Gilroy's autobiography was an important document in evidencing the conditions which contributed to those recommendations and she later claimed to have written the work out of a growing sense of anger at them:

> My autobiography resulted from a fit of pique. After hearing the older generation of blacks in Britain being pilloried as 'Topsies and Toms', I decided to set the record straight. There had been Ted Braithwaite's *To Sir, With Love* and Don Hinds's *Journey to an Illusion*, but a woman's experiences had never been published. As I wrote, my anger mounted when I recalled the experiences of my contemporaries – false accusations by the police, innocent people being beaten up, black men being offered drinks of urine disguised as beer, and expulsion from clubs and public places were day-to-day occurrences in their lives. There were no race-relations apparatus, no pressure groups, no media to bring the news into drawing-rooms as it happened.[30]

A role in the history of British race relations also provided Gilroy with the opportunity to use her writing for its 'enormous therapeutic, restorative, and energising value'.[31] Her personal anger and quest for self-assertion coincided with a need for documentary evidence. Ironically, it is because of her experience of institutional racism that she was temporarily elevated by the media; yet her much publicized role as the first black head-teacher did little to assure her permanent value as a writer or commentator. In retrospect, her recognition as an important educationalist may simply be seen as a token gesture, which actually preserves the power of the dominant group. Psychologist Judith Long Laws explains how this dichotomy – of appearing to concede power to an oppressed group whilst still maintaining the social/racial binaries operates:

> Tokenism is ... found whenever a dominant group is under pressure to share privilege, power, or other desirable commodities with a group which is excluded ... Tokenism advises the promise of mobility which is severely restricted in quantity ... the Token does not become assimilated into the dominant group but is destined for permanent marginality.[32]

On its publication in 1976, the autobiography was reviewed in the education press but the reviewers were grudging with their praise. Whilst Gilroy's humour and fighting-spirit were generally celebrated, the reviewers found the book flawed by occasional moments of self-congratulation.

Edward Blishen, writing for the *Guardian*, is clearly troubled by the author's 'self-applause':

> About all this [the struggle to be treated decently] she writes in the face of the usual difficulty – that a teacher with a success to report can easily sound self-approving. But if one blushes for Mrs Gilroy (and maybe for oneself) when she says, 'slowly I built up in these children a need to achieve', et cetera, there's much more that makes the point with no suggestion of self-applause.[33]

But why does Gilroy's 'self applause' cause his discomfort? Is it because it simply 'isn't British' to brag about one's achievements, or is it because of the contradictions that such self-applause presents in the context of the author's accounts of subjection? It no doubt surprised and disturbed white male British critics in the mid-1970s who may have been reading *Black Teacher* for its 'token' multi-cultural value and yet who seem reluctant to name the 'usual difficulty' facing Gilroy as British racism.

I have always read this self-applause as the narrator's 'over-compensation'. The self-congratulatory voice is mobilized as a therapeutic-narrative strategy to reconstruct self-esteem under continual attack from British racism. Some evidence for this reading is in this quotation from *Black Teacher*:

> Prejudice showed by innuendo and implication and I reacted by over-compensation. My classroom became my obsession. I used it to prove to myself that I was once more the gifted teacher – the teacher who had been acclaimed in a faraway country.[34]

In her interview in 2002, Gilroy was still using this strategy to counter critical neglect. She tells the interviewer that *In Praise of Love and Children* is 'a very profound book, very profound'.[35] Such self-promotion, however therapeutic, is generally counter-productive for writers who want to be taken seriously. It is highly unusual for writers to make such statements about the value of their own work. But in the same interview Gilroy relates how a fellow Guyanese woman writer insisted that *Inkle and Yarico* 'is fantastic ... [and] better than [Caryl Phillips's award-winning] *Cambridge*'.[36] Towards the end of the interview, Bradshaw questions Gilroy's sense of importance and comments, 'It seems to me from what you tell me that you were raised with very high self-esteem', a judgement that Gilroy quickly affirms.[37] If that sense of self-esteem has been devastated by racial abuse and denials of her professional status, then Gilroy's over-investment in its preservation can be understood. The fact that Gilroy believed that publishers' readers missed the 'profundity' of *In Praise of Love and Children* when it was first submitted in the 1960s must have been yet another continual source of her 'pique'.

To return to the reviews of 1976, Roy Blatchford, a teacher of English at Stockwell Manor Comprehensive School, also wrote dismissively about *Black Teacher* for *The Times Educational Supplement*, describing it 'as Bess to Edward Braithwaite's Porgy'. Such a comparison which allows him to declare *Black Teacher* as surplus to requirements:

> This is, at times, a well-written, sensitive, often moving tale of school life, but the author can be embarrassingly over-sentimental and cloying in her repetition of anecdotes. Does she really remember all those inter-changes down to dropped Hs and 'Sucks and Knickers to you Miss'?
>
> We hear plenty of Nig-Nog, Nig-Pig and Wog hurled in her direction, about segregation in the loo, and her fight to be black and accepted. Her trials in the fifties were deplorably the common lot for the immigrant. None the less, is it worth yet another voicing? Can the publishers seriously ask that the book should be taken to heart by edu-cationalists and parents?[38]

Interestingly, his rhetorical '[I]s it worth yet another voicing?' buries racism in the 'trials [of] the fifties', precisely at a time (in the mid-1970s) when racial tensions were about to explode. If Blatchford appears reluctant to accept the book's analysis of a racist Britain, he certainly sublimates its relevance. There is little justification or evidence for his churlish sugges-tion that her rise to a headship was accomplished with much more ease than the book would lead us to believe:

> A few years off for her own mixed-marriage and private play groups, and the charismatic Mrs Gilroy swept back to the North London school where she is now head-mistress, denouncing licence, proclaiming class-room freedom, combating parental slings and arrows, suffering little kids, cuddling and comforting.[39]

Blatchford thus dismisses Gilroy's personal achievements, attributing them to a 'charismatic' personality rather than to professional skill or a genuinely pioneering approach. His review trivialized the importance of *Black Teacher*. The book went out of print after 1976.

Prior to the writing of *Black Teacher*, Gilroy, like George Lamming and Samuel Selvon, wrote a novel of migration: *In Praise of Love and Children*. This was submitted unsuccessfully to a publisher in the 1960s. If Gilroy objected to how '[West Indian] men-writers, became experts and publishers' advisors after the publication of their novels',[40] she would later write explicitly about her 'anomalousness' in the blossoming corpus of West Indian prose and poetry in an essay for *Leaves in the Wind: Collected Writings* (1998):

> I still wrote poetry and was asked to submit one to James Berry for a collection, his first [*Bluefoot Traveller* published the same year as *Black Teacher* in 1976]. He told me it was excellent but pulled it as it would have been the only one by a woman. This brings me to a crucial point which I want to make with considerable force. The sixties were a reaction to the historical and generalised oppression of women during the previous decades, whether we were wives, mistresses, courtesans, concubines, field or favourite slaves, we were controlled by men who ran the world.[41]

Although her poetry and fiction was rejected, on the grounds that it was atypical and therefore not marketable, Gilroy had no problem publishing *Black Teacher*. In a sense, then, it was the easily published autobiography that enabled her to explore many of the features which we might now associate with her later fiction. In *Black Teacher*, Gilroy was experimenting with an intermediary form of fiction and autobiography, with structure and dialogue to find an imaginative voice that would finally be accepted with the publication of her novels in the late-1980s. In terms of its structure, *Black Teacher* is unconventional autobiography. Unless you are Roland Barthes, autobiographies are usually linear, beginning in childhood and progressing through the formative stages of the author's life, but *Black Teacher* departs from this convention. Gilroy introduces the main character (herself) by beginning her story from the perspective of the present – a point at which she (the 'heroine') has already conquered the difficulties she is about to relate, and then shifts the narrative back to her expectations on leaving university.

The text thereafter moves forward from 1953, through 13 short chapters depicting battles to get work as a teacher, until we finally see her promoted to a headship. If we were to attend to the absences in the text, we might question why there is no sustained account of her childhood, or of the early formative experiences that life writing usually replays. Similar absences may be seen in Braithwaite's two autobiographies, *To Sir, With Love* (1959) and in *Paid Servant* (1962). He begins *Paid Servant* with the line 'As the Underground train rocked gently on its way …', immediately locating the writer's experience in the metropolis.[42] This textual strategy was likely to appeal to a British metropolitan readership with little interest in faraway British Guiana. However, accounts of Gilroy's childhood are found in *Sunlight on Sweet Water* (written before *Black Teacher* was commissioned) and in several interviews.

As an imaginative and aesthetic response to the feelings of alienation produced by the metropolis, the structure of *Black Teacher* allows Gilroy to replay a cultural schizophrenia. As part of a privileged elite of commonwealth students, she 'had a wonderful time', but her identity was splintered through contact with the majority of British subjects who assume she was an 'illiterate savage'[43] and that she is 'lecherous, incontinent and depraved'.[44] After finishing university, she should have easily found work as a gifted teacher but was forced to survive through menial jobs such as dishwashing at Joe Lyon's Cafe. In the context of the 1970s, and given the didactic tone of *Black Teacher*, it is easy to imagine how she might easily be cast as the instructor in the training manual for dealing with racism. But the burden of black tokenism is an unbearable one; as she writes: 'I always had to think of West Indians who were to come to be teachers in the future. I was a pioneer, an ambassador ... I was always being watched, assessed, measured and compared.'[45]

From the outset, Gilroy's autobiography is self-consciously concerned with a need to cast herself as a gifted multi-racial teacher and as a British citizen. An overwhelming desire for recognition underlies the numerous examples given of her teaching methods and the 'repetition of anecdotes' which must have provoked Blatchford's critical disdain. Gilroy's estranged narrator frequently intervenes to provide some item of instruction: 'Children who are socially handicapped and who lack close contact with adults – adults who will listen to them – need the opportunity to express grouses or confidences.'[46] Cultural schizophrenia is signalled by the instability of the narrative voice. A third-person 'pedantic' narrator alternates with an autobiographical 'I' that is characterisatically more provisional and self-doubting. For example, she describes the contingencies needed to protect her young family from being damaged by the racism prevalent in her own school and the wider society:

> My own children were now nine and six years old, and it became an economic necessity that I should seek promotion. The children attended private schools in my area because they were accepted there, with tolerance and humanity. They never had to defend their colour or their hair, or bother about identity. Nor were the traditional names of affection, like Sambo, Topsy or Fuzzy, ever used to them.[47]

Sending her own children to private schools was a pragmatic response to enable them to grow into human beings free from the institutional inequalities that Gilroy battled with on a daily basis.

It was much more difficult to protect herself from attacks, but in her responses, she exemplifies quick-thinking resilience and creativity. Gilroy interrogates the unquestioned superiority of 'Englishness', to silence a group of jeering men:

> The men were still standing there – still grinning and shouting nonsense. I walked over to them and said, 'Are you English-men? If you are, you are a peculiar kind. English-men don't stare and shout at women. I've never known them to. Who are you? Do you really know?' Their surprise gave way to embarrassment.[48]

This sketch of Gilroy's encounter with British racism may account for the sociological response to *Black Teacher* as indicative of a general phenomenon. But what is of interest here is the fact that, as a creative writer, Gilroy chose to write and publish an autobiography which, by its very genre, evaded the general experience. Indeed, *Black Teacher* articulates her unique perspective as a professional black woman in Britain, and this separates her writing from that of others. The telling of this tale reveals her uniqueness.

Like the men in the above incident, it is likely that some male critics of the 1970s would also have been squeamish about the text's explicit engagement with the physicality of a black woman's body.[49] Gilroy has often referred to the scarcity of black women on the streets of London in the 1950s. With few female black migrants in London, her presence caused a stir; journeying through London was particularly harrowing for a young woman's colour and 'exotic' beauty could provoke racial abuse and sexual harassment:

> Our women's concerns were with getting from A to B safely, without being assaulted by the Teddy Boys or chased by the grandparents of the National Front, the members of the League of Empire Loyalists.[50]

Gilroy was often seen as no more than her 'strange' black body. In *Black Teacher*, however, her descriptions of her own body challenge this fear and fetishization by revealing her humanity. In the 1970s, any acknowledgement of bodily functions such as urination or menstruation was highly unusual, and Gilroy deliberately discusses these elements in relation to perceptions of her 'difference'. In one particular account of an encounter while working as a filing clerk at a mail-order store, she points out the absurdity of the factory workers' ignorance:

> When I came out, [of the toilet] Sue eyed me with a look of prurient curiosity.
> 'Not bein' rude', she said, 'just bein' inquisitive. What do natives do when they ...'

'Go to bed?' I asked.

'You know', she said, self-consciously gesturing, 'your monthlies'.

'You mean when we menstruate?' I asked.

She nodded,

'Well Sue', I replied with mock seriousness, 'we swim! We jump into the nearest river and swim and swim for miles. Some of us swim for three days and some for four, but that's what we do.'[51]

Gilroy's discussion of the 'vulgar' reality of the body challenges the cerebral notion of art with its carefully cultivated sense of aesthetic distance. The distinction maintained by high art between the sacred and the profane overlaps with the cultural divide between classes and races. As Bourdieu writes:

The denial of the lower, coarse, vulgar, venal, servile, – in a word, natural – enjoyment, which constitutes the sacred sphere of culture, implies an affirmation of the superiority of those who can be satisfied with the sublimated, refined, disinterested, gratuitous, distinguished pleasures forever closed to the profane. That is why art and cultural consumption are predisposed, consciously and deliberately or not, to fulfil a social function of legitimating social differences.[52]

Gilroy's repetitive insistence on the humanity and physicality of the female black body, historically positioned under the sign of pollution, impurity and sexual deviance, is therefore an important theme. In the following scene from Black Teacher, Mrs Burleigh, a colleague, accuses Gilroy of contaminating the sacrosanct space of the female teachers' toilet with dribbles of urine:

'Did you notice that speck of wet on the floor in the loo, Mrs Ril?' she would begin. 'Did you notice? Dribs and drabs all over the place!'

Poor Mrs Rilson would reply by accelerating her knitting speed.

'There never used to be specks of wet on the floor in the loo. Now we've started to having specks of wetness like polka dots on a summer frock all over the place. Disgusting I say it is. There must be gremlins with foreign habits in this school.'[53]

Mrs Burleigh is not only concerned about 'gremlins with foreign' lavatory habits, but she is also convinced that black people carry life-threatening diseases and insists on a 'crockery' apartheid, in other words, a separation of food utensils. Gilroy withdraws from this painful situation by taking her break outside of the school: 'I wasn't involved in the appearance of specks in the lavatory. I couldn't be. I walked each lunch-break to the Tube station with my penny, whatever the weather.'[54]

In the text, blackness is presented stereotypically as malevolent and demonic; one of the children insists that 'black 'ands like yours leave black marks'.[55] In a more extreme example, when Gilroy attempts to remove a wasp from a child, the young girl screams out in terror: 'Don't ever touch me. Keep your hands off me!' When the wasp is removed by a passing tramp, the effect is devastating:

> The message rang out loud and clear. Rather the tramp and his filth, rather the wasp, rather even the sting of the wasp, than the slightest touch from me.
>
>   When we got back to our classrooms I began looking at my hands, almost as if I were seeing them for the first time. That night when I went out to dinner, it was an intelligent gathering but I took this new consciousness with me. At every introduction a handshake became a challenge. I dared not dance although I loved to dance in case some partner by look or gesture should reject my hands.[56]

These 'colonial encounters' forced Gilroy to perceive her own body as estranged. As Fanon's 'sociodiagnostic' in *Black Skin, White Masks*, would explain it, a fear of the white 'gaze' renders her body as a site of pain.[57] But the act of writing stories of psychological 'violation' is therapeutic and enables Gilroy to explore the dialectic between body and the world. Janice Williamson, writing about sexual abuse and life-writing questions the possible connection between a desire to write and the 'splitting' which occurs as a result of trauma: 'Did her engagement and splitting in response to physical invasion lead not only to a survivor's amnesia but a life-long desire to write?' She concludes that '[T]he textualisation of her body is less objectification than an "objectifiction" which restores agency to her being.'[58] Gilroy confirms the tradition of black women's writing as survival strategy: '[in] the tradition of Black women who write to come to terms with their trauma, or alternatively to understand the nature of their elemental oppression, I wrote to redefine myself and put the record straight.'[59]

As with most tales of survival, *Black Teacher* is full of humour and subterfuge. Gilroy's willingness to place herself in the employment of Lady Anne, where she is cast as a 'coloured' maid, subject to the philanthropic and idiosyncratic whims of 'her ladyship', is surprising. However, what is not unforeseen for those who knew the author, is the way in which she subverts the re-enactment of this slave/mistress scenario. She is positively Ortonesque in her dealings with Lady Anne. Telling her 'mistress', for example, that she is vegetarian because: 'One of my ancestors choked on someone's funny bone. My dislike of meat was the consequence'.[60] Undercover of employment, Gilroy learns at first hand to understand the historical relation of colonizer and colonized through an elaborate role play with Lady Anne for which she was paid wages. Gilroy's observations suggest the extent to which Lady Anne became *the* object of study. A mutual respect builds between the two women, but Gilroy has to learn about this too. When she receives a present from her employer, delivered from Harrods, her immediate response is one of deep suspicion:

> I knew whites ... I'd told Lady Anne I'd never seen or owned a golliwog before coming to this country. Perhaps she'd sent me one ...
>
> Tearing off the wrappings I dipped into the beautiful box and felt a delightful kittenish softness. Inside was a pale cream angora twin set. I was deeply touched by the thoughtfulness that had gone into the choice of such a splendid present.[61]

This, I believe, was Gilroy, the psychologist, at work in the field, confronting the mismatch between stereotype and individual. The text is enriched by psychological insights into the distorted social relations on which racism feeds, and into the way in which perception comes to 'mature only in a gnarled or distorted way'. Looking back, she writes: 'I learned to understand my own legitimate feelings of resentment and aggression and to understand theirs.'[62]

However, the difficulties associated with the fight to establish equitable social and professional relationships result in the occasional textual outburst which may leave 'the heroine' open to charges of inconsistency. Gilroy displaces her own feelings of rejection onto others. She also seems to regret the relatively easy passage of the new generation of immigrants into the profession; suggesting that this new generation may lack the fighting spirit of the pioneers:

> Occasionally there would be a coloured face among our scanty and short-lived contingent of supply teachers. I couldn't get over the fact that an immigrant now seemed able to walk into teaching almost within hours of getting off the boat. It seemed a far cry from my pioneer days and desperate attempts to get started ...[63]
>
> It was now the sixties, the age of the frenetic immigrant, whom many older immigrants see as the grabbers, the plum pickers, the protesters, the noisy people. The people who in some respects got off a boat into a virtual bed of roses and lost no time in trampling it.[64]

Yet it was 'the age of the frenetic immigrant' that created the challenges of the multi-lingual classroom. Equally worrying is the shorthand of racial stereotypes Gilroy uses to expound on the conflicting expectations presented by parents, when she herself has suffered from such perceptions:

> The French, West Indians and Greeks wanted to see their children handcuffed to their tasks. The Asians would have liked passive children chanting their lessons – preferably under palms. The Italian and Spanish mums thought school a kind of conspiracy to deprive them of their right to mother their children and in doing so occupy their own time at home.
>
> From the English there was a more subtle and varied reaction, as one would expect. The variations stretched from 'you're doing a jolly good job' to regarding us as highly-paid child-minders. Many had 'read a book' and knew all about teaching.[65]

There is a bitter tone to this passage that reminds us that Britain was undergoing a painful multi-racial transformation. Gilroy was on the frontline of new relationships that were stunted in a subsoil of historical ignorance and prejudice.

Conclusion

Gilroy's writing reveals how her remarkable personal skills, her charismatic courage and determination, enabled her to fight institutional racism. It was for these very qualities that *Black Teacher* was reprinted by Bogle-L'Ouverture in 1994. Reva Klein interviewed Gilroy for the *Times Educational Supplement* on its reissue, and concluded that it 'is as eye-opening and relevant today as it was first time around'.[66] By the time it was reissued, Klein found Gilroy more aggressive and pessimistic than in previous interviews:

> Today, 18 years on from when *Black Teacher* first appeared. Beryl Gilroy looks back in anger at the hardships she faced. 'I have struggled so much here for my identity as a healthy, competent, thinking black woman and have had difficulties with the expectations of the white world as a black woman. Sometimes people would patronise me. They would make a beeline for my secretary because black people aren't heads. They'd expect me to be the cleaner with a collapsible mop and bucket ... Sometimes I wonder why it is that more black people don't go mad.'[67]

The intervening years had done little to convince her that she had achieved equality – as a teacher, as an ethno-psychotherapist and as a writer. She was, in many ways, less well-known in 1994 than in 1976. The reissue of *Black Teacher* in 1994 served only to highlight how little progress had been made in the area of racial (and sexual) equality.

Even though *Black Teacher* came back into print in 1994, it has yet to be reclaimed as black British – let alone Caribbean – biography or *literature*.[68] Morgan Dalphinis' excellent 'Preface' to the 1994 edition highlights Gilroy's accomplishments. However, the blurb on the back cover asserts that the book is 'essential reading not only for the teaching profession, but also for social workers and educationalists'.[69] The 1994 reprint still advertises its usefulness for 'the teaching professions'. Even Carol Boyce Davis, in her celebratory tribute to Beryl Gilroy in 2001, writes, '*Black Teacher* should become staple reading in the education of black teachers',[70] as if the book is forever destined to remain known as a text book. This type of appropriation is not confined to Gilroy's life-writing. Russ claims it is just one of the many strategies of belittlement which maintain women writers' anomalousness: Among her list, the following would apply directly to *Black Teacher*:

> She wrote it, but look what she wrote about.
>
> She wrote it but 'she' isn't really an artist and 'it' isn't really serious, of the right genre – i.e. really art.
>
> She wrote it but she wrote only one of it.
>
> She wrote it but there are very few of her.[71]

Black Teacher's 'usefulness' as an educational/sociological text will therefore occlude its contributions to a wider discourse on a black British literary history and its agents of change. Yet, in 'Uses of History', Rena Jeneja explains, in general terms, what Gilroy's autobiography endorses specifically:

> Total hegemony is never achieved because subversion and resistance are ever-present counter forces, and even in the most oppressive circumstances human beings continue to exercise choices and actions that have the potency to alter social order. History in these texts is not merely to be suffered but also to be shaped, made, recreated and redirected.[72]

As a postcolonial text, *Black Teacher* is obviously an important part of the historiography of British race relations, but it might also now be reconsidered as a work which 'shaped, made, recreated and redirected' black British and Caribbean women's claim to a literary space too.

At least in the latter part of her life, Gilroy was formally recognized as the gifted teacher that she was intent on describing in *Black Teacher*. In 1995 she was awarded an honorary doctorate from the University of North London for her services to education. However, as an author who writes out of a literary tradition of Caribbean and black British literature, she is only now beginning to be more widely recognized, and then only for her novels of the 1980s and 1990s. Her entry in the *Bloomsbury Guide to Women's Literature* states: 'There has been little criticism of her writing to date.'[73] This critical silence has meant that Gilroy has been *the* major critic and theorizer of her own work. There are numerous essays and interviews in which she analyses her own creative practice, and many of her thoughts were collected together and published as *Leaves in the Wind: Collected Writings* in 1998.

I can still only speculate as to *Black Teacher*'s critical neglect: is it passed over because, as Guptara asserts about Ted Braithwaite's *To Sir With Love*, it 'is not considered angry enough by today's Black Briton?'[74] Yet, Peter Fraser commented in his *Guardian* obituary that, 'fearing for its sales, it was softened by its publisher'. Is it *Black Teacher*'s explicitness about the duplicity of a colonial identity that invokes a problematic narratorial voice? Is part of the problem its use of a literary form, autobiography, which critics are not often trained to read or value, even since the reevaluation of life writing by feminist theorists? Part of the 'problem' for literary critics may lie in the hybrid quality exemplified in *Black Teacher*, namely to what extent is it fictional, autobiographical and/or instructional? Gilroy's writing is loaded with inconsistencies, resisting the possibility of casting her as a 'representative' black feminist or black-nationalist voice. This makes for uncomfortable reading for both black and white readers; as Guptara ventures to suggest, her portrayals 'provide reading that must chasten, and this is no doubt one reason why the book has not been a roaring success'.[75] Her work refuses simple generic, racial or sexual political readings.[76] Accordingly, she remains an outsider and an anomaly in the established literary-critical practice or tradition. We cannot know what sort of writer she might have become had she been given the type of encouragement and networking that some of her male contemporaries thrived on in the 1950s. Her isolation affected her ability to write; creativity and identity, she writes, 'arrive from a nurtured and nourished in-scape. Mine had been damaged and left for dead.'[77]

Will she remain marginal to a literary-critical canon that otherwise would have strong reasons to include *Black Teacher* as a postcolonial text? Braithwaite's work will survive in popular memory, at least as the book which inspired the film of *To Sir, With Love*. Gilroy's autobiography, however, may not survive at all if it remains wedded to its utility for sociologists and educationalists alone.

Notes

1 H.J. Massingham, 'Introduction', in Flora Thompson, *Lark Rise to Candleford* (Oxford: Oxford University Press, 1944, first published in 1939), p. v.
2. Joanna Russ, *How to Suppress Women's Writing* (London: Women's Press, 1983), back cover blurb.
3. Russ, *op. cit.* p. 5.
4. Cited in E.A. Markham (ed.), *The Penguin Book of Caribbean Short Stories* (London: Penguin, 1996), p. xi.
5. John McLeod, 'Some Problems with "British" in a "Black British Canon"', *Wasafiri*, 36 (2002), p. 56.
6. Carol Boyce Davies and Meridith Gadsby, 'Remembering Beryl Gilroy August 20, 1924–April 4, 2001', *Macomere*, 4 (2001), p. 7.
7. Russ, *op. cit.* p. 84.
8. Mike Phillips, Review of James Procter's *Writing Black Britain 1948–1998*, in *Wasafiri*, 36 (2002), p. 63.
9. There were of course other published women writers from the Caribbean but she is unlikely to have read much of their work with the possible exception of Sylvia Wynter with whom she was friendly as a student and Una Marson and Louise Bennett. See Sandra Courtman, ' "Unnatural Silences" and the Making of a Bibliography of Anglophone West Indian Women Publishing in Post-War Britain', *Wadabagei: A Journal of the Caribbean and its Diaspora*, 2 (1999), pp. 55–85.
10. Cited in McLeod, *op. cit.* p. 56.
11. See Sandra Courtman, 'Lost Years: West Indian Women Writing and Publishing in Britain, c. 1960–1979', unpublished PhD, University of Bristol (1999).
12. Peter Fraser, 'Beryl Gilroy', *Guardian Unlimited Archive*, http//www.guardian. co.uk/Archive/Article/0,4273,4171552,00.html accessed 19 April 2001.
13. Now published as *In Praise of Love and Children* (Leeds: Peepal Tree, 1996) and *Sunlight on Sweet Water* (Leeds: Peepal Tree, 1994).
14. For example, a short extract from *Black Teacher* is provided in James Procter's *Writing Black Britain: An Interdisciplinary Anthology* (Manchester: Manchester University Press, 2000). More usually her novels are anthologized.
15. http://www.caribvoice.org/A&E/guyanesewriters.html accessed 10 August 2004.
16. Roxann Bradshaw, 'Beryl Gilroy's "Fact-Fiction" Through the Lens of the "Quiet Old Lady" ', *Callaloo*, 25.2 (2002), pp. 381–400, and 391.
17. This was my rationale for proposing a reprint of Jamaican writer Joyce Gladwell's 1969 'lost' autobiography *Brown Face, Big Master* (London: Palgrave Macmillan, 2003). Reprinted as a Macmillan Caribbean Classic in 2003.
18. Roger Sale, *On Not Being Good Enough: Writings of a Working Critic* (Oxford University Press, 1979).
19. Pierre Bourdieu, *Distinction: A Social Critique of the Judgement of Taste* (London: Routledge, 1986), p. 4.
20. Bourdieu, *op. cit.* p. 4.
21. Beryl Gilroy, *Leaves in the Wind: Collected Writings*, ed. Joan Anim-Addo (London: Mango Publishing, 1998), p. 211.

22. Gilroy, *op. cit.* (1998), p. 213.
23. Leela Gandhi, *Postcolonial Theory: A Critical Introduction* (Edinburgh: Edinburgh University Press, 1998).
24. E.R. Braithwaite, *To Sir, With Love*, 9th edn (London: Coronet, 1993; first published Bodley Head, 1959), back cover blurb.
25. Prabhbu Guptara, *Black British Literature: An Annotated Bibliography* (London: Dangaroo, 1986) p. 23.
26. The 1965 Act had already legislated against racial discrimination in the community, such as the discriminatory exclusions that regularly operated in pubs, clubs, restaurants, on buses and in parks. The 1965 Act also made illegal the charge of 'Deliberate incitement to racial hatred'. Signs that were common in the 1960s – for example 'Vacancy. No blacks need apply' – were legislated against in 1968. The 1976 Race Relations Act outlawed indirect discrimination, such as the setting of conditions of employment that were, in effect, discriminatory.
27. Dave Gunning, 'Anti-Racism, the Nation-State and Contemporary Black British Literature', *Journal of Contemporary Literature*, 39 (2) (2004), p. 29.
28. Lionel Morrison, 'It's like a mini UN at Beckford Infants' School', *Evening Standard*, 5 October 1973.
29. The main recommendations were summarized in the *Times Educational Supplement*, 29 May 1981. See 'Racism and Schooling', in *Racism in the Workplace and Community* (Milton Keynes: The Open University, 1984).
30. Selwyn Cudjoe (ed.), *Caribbean Women Writers: Essays from the First International Conference* (Wellesley: Calaloux, 1990) p. 199.
31. Renu Jeneja, 'Uses of History' in *Caribbean Transactions: West Indian Culture and Literature* (London: Palgrave Macmillan, 1996), p. 119.
32. Cited in Russ, *op. cit.* p. 84.
33. Edward Blishen, 'A Hard School', *The Guardian*, 22 July 1976, p. 16.
34. Beryl Gilroy, *Black Teacher* (London: Bogle L'Ouverture Press, 1994), p. 95.
35. Bradshaw, *op. cit.* p. 385.
36. *Ibid.*, p. 394.
37. *Ibid.*, p. 396.
38. Roy Blatchford,' To Miss ... with love', *The Times Educational Supplement*, 27 August 1976, p. 16.
39. *Ibid.*, p. 16.
40. Gilroy, *op. cit.* (1998), p. 211.
41. *Ibid.*, p. 206.
42. E.R. Braithwaite, *Paid Servant* (London: Four Square Books, 1965, first published in 1962), p. 5.
43. Beryl Gilroy, telephone interview, 22 February 1996.
44. Cudjoe, *op. cit.* p. 199.
45. See Mary Douglas, *Purity and Danger* (London: Routledge, 1978) and Mary Douglas, *Implicit Meanings* (London: Routledge, 1975).
46. Gilroy, *op. cit.* (1994), p. 95.
47. *Ibid.*, p. 144.
48. *Ibid.*, p. 160.
49. *Ibid.*, p. 68.
50. Beryl Gilroy, 'I write because ...', in Cudjoe, *op. cit.*, pp. 195–201 (p. 199).
51. Gilroy, *op. cit.* (1994), p. 23.

52. Bourdieu, *op. cit.* p. 47.
53. Gilroy, *op. cit.* (1994), p. 52.
54. *Ibid.*, p. 52.
55. *Ibid.*, p. 64.
56. *Ibid.*, p. 63.
57. Frantz Fanon, *Black Skin, White Masks* (London: Pluto, 1986) p. 111.
58. Janice Williamson, 'I Peel Myself Out of My Own Skin,' in Marlene Kadar (ed.), *Essays on Life Writing: From Genre to Critical Practice* (University of Toronto Press, 1992), p. 145.
59. Beryl Gilroy, *op. cit.* (1998), p. 209.
60. Gilroy, *op. cit.* (1994), p. 37.
61. *Ibid.*, p. 42.
62. Cudjoe, *op. cit.* p. 196.
63. Gilroy, *op. cit.* (1994), p. 150.
64. *Ibid.*, p. 121.
65. *Ibid.*, p. 189.
66. Reva Klein, 'No Grey Areas', *The Times Educational Supplement*, 29 July 1994, p. 15.
67. Klein, *op. cit.* p. 15.
68. It is not as if autobiography is unpopular. As I prepared the paper, which eventually was rewritten as this essay, Lorna Sage's *Bad Blood* (London: Fourth Estate, 2000) tops the paperback bestseller lists.
69. Beryl Gilroy, *op. cit.* (1994).
70. Carol Boyce Davies and Meridith Gadsby, *op. cit.* p. 7.
71. Russ, *op. cit.* p. 76.
72. Jeneja, *op. cit.* p. 118.
73. Claire Buck (ed.), *Bloomsbury Guide to Women's Literature* (London: Bloomsbury, 1992) p. 578.
74. Guptara, *op. cit.* p. 24.
75. *Ibid.*, p. 25.
76. Guptara's appraisal of the relative obscurity of Braithwaite's and Gilroy's autobiographies is generational. Guptara questions the justification of Braithwaite's dismissal: 'Braithwaite's name seems to be mud among black people today. The book is not thought to be angry enough by today's black Briton, and it is accused of telling the success story of one black, in apparent isolation from the struggles of other blacks. However, nearly ten years after publication, *To Sir, With Love* was banned from schools in Jamaica' (*op. cit.* p. 24).
77. Beryl Gilroy, *op. cit.* (1998), p. 211.

4

In the Eyes of the Beholder: Diversity and Cultural Politics of Canon Reformation in Britain

Femi Folorunso in conversation with Gail Low and Marion Wynne-Davies (9 December 2004)*

[GL and MWD] We thought we would start by contextualizing this discussion and ask you about your relationship with the Scottish Arts Council. Can you say something about what you do and the role that you presently occupy?

[FF] I started in the Scottish Arts Council three years ago and was employed specifically as a black and ethnic minority arts development officer. Although I was interested in the job, initially I was somewhat sceptical about its title and remit, and about what exactly the Arts Council was trying to do by labelling an area, 'black and ethnic minority arts'. As I expected, the job entails developing new areas and activities in the arts, fostering new audiences for these creative developments and spreading the benefits of the Arts Council's funding and expertise. These are, of course, all traditional concerns of the Art Council and ones to which every member of staff is committed by virtue of the fact that we earn our living there. However, the remit of my job is made both complicated and challenging because it contains a racialized dimension to it. I say 'race' because, I believe that in the final analysis, what is meant by 'minority ethnic' in the UK context today relates specifically to non-white immigration and immigrants. In Scotland, migration and integration seems to me to be contained within a policy of social inclusion. It is no accident that those who profit most from social inclusion are people often described as 'community leaders' of immigrant communities. They are the authors of ethnic-bounded practices, many of which do no more than to entrench misguided

---

* The views expressed by Dr Folorunso in the following interview are his personal views as an academic and do not represent official Scottish Arts Council policy.

anthropological representations of the non-white immigrants that petrify around what passes as ethnic cultures. These so-called community leaders latch themselves on to social inclusion in order to form personal networks, rather than engage with being a citizen, and of extending the rights and obligations of citizenship to others. There have been interesting, but somewhat muted debates, over the past five years about the place of non-white immigrants within the nation state. These have arisen mostly from policy initiatives, but even these debates still have a general tendency to adopt mechanistic terms suggesting that non-white immigrant groups wear an identikit badge, and that their desires are formed purely in relation to their skin colour – and exclusive of the politics of gender, class, skills and education within those communities.

When we speak about 'minority arts' in Scotland, we do so against the backdrop of, what some describe, as a more vibrant arts scene in England. Well, there is a bigger minority ethnic population in England. In some English regions, the minority ethnic population actually constitutes the majority, and hence tend to produce their own forms of engagement with and against statutory institutions. You could say that these contexts have made the emergence of a better organized response to a state induced policy of 'cultural diversity' easier. I was quite aware of all this and much else besides when I accepted the job.

I felt that one of my main tasks would be to increase the legitimacy of the Arts Council within the growing communities of non-white immigrants in Scotland by engaging directly with issues of social inclusion, but also not taking for granted issues of language, identity, gender and class.

To put it in more broadly intellectual terms, you could say that I am trying to return to the ideals of the enlightenment (this is of course a major issue for many postcolonial scholars and multicultural field workers). A return to the enlightenment's ideal of citizenship – equality and liberty – is vital to how the presence of the non-white immigrants should be understood. It is my job to make sure that the gains of citizenship are acquired equally by non-white immigrants and this is what we, in the Arts Council, try to project when we speak about cultural diversity.

[GL and MWD] In order to understand the way in which the need for a diversity officer developed, we want to take you back to the history of the Arts Council and to its ethos and founding charter. The Arts Council was born out of war-time legacy of the state encouragement of music and the arts, though much of such activity was initially directed at maintaining the standards, and national traditions, of the arts. After the war, the government wanted a national body of this kind to encourage knowledge, understanding and practice of the arts in the broader sense of the term. Accordingly, the Arts Council of Great Britain came into being. Its Royal Charter of 1967 outlined three specific aims: to develop and improve the knowledge and understanding of the practice of the arts, to increase the public accessibility, and to advise and cooperate with governmental, local authorities and other bodies on matters associated with the arts. Given this particular history and remit, could you discuss the Arts Council's role as an institution and as a funding body in relation to the promotion, shaping and the dissemination of arts, including its function in relation to non-white immigrants?

[FF] The Arts Council is one of the great postwar creations, as you rightly say, but I think we will be stretching imagination and kindness too far to suggest that the presence of non-white immigrants featured in its agenda in those early days. And why should it have anyway, when the historical context was totally different? However, we need to look at another circumstance – the moment of the Arts Council's birth – in order to understand how its relationship to non-white immigrant groups has had to evolve, that is, to incorporate these groups into the *national* culture. The Arts Council was part of the intellectual reconstruction, which I think was meant to run concurrent with the physical reconstruction of Britain in the postwar period. We can put the NHS at the apex of that intellectual reconstruction, but both are visible links between the intellectual and material. Some have argued that these institutions, from the NHS to the Arts Council, were also part of the remobilization of a British national identity in the wake of imperial decline. But here we are talking about internal struggles. During the war people made enormous sacrifices, as Angus Calder's book, *The People's War*, among other works on the period, outlines.[1] It seems to me, therefore, that the major political question after the war also became a cultural one, namely, how to utilize the already mobilized 'identity', in both economic and cultural terms? I would argue that the resultant welfare state and the cultural renewal were part of the same complex identity, namely a postwar settlement between the people and the ruling elite. Such a project would have to place culture (and the arts are very good at offering themselves up to fulfil such a need) at the centre of a re-creation of national identity, thereby sowing the seeds of the future. Some commentators have argued that, based on the immediate postwar context, what the Arts Council inherited was a 'top-down social mission', and that the Arts Council was created as an institution to teach and possibly legislate on culture. This is the extreme view of those who mistakenly regard the Arts Council as undermining the arts.

As you know, there are other views, not least Raymond Williams's, with which I entirely agree. In *The Long Revolution*, Williams situated this postwar modernism and management of the arts within a political framework, and identified the way in which culture could no longer be determined solely in aesthetic terms.[2] 'Art' should be looked at as an ongoing process, rather than a finished product and the Arts Council should offer infra-structure support for such a developmental process. These postwar influ-ences – cultural reconstruction, politicization and a commitment to growth – served to define an innocuous role for the Arts Council, which was to *sponsor* a national culture against the backdrop of the 'national identity' that had been forged during the war. The postwar framework took it for granted that there was a simple correspondence between 'culture and nation'; furthermore, that the English language, its variations notwith-standing, cemented that correspondence.

But it is interesting that this was also the time that non-white immigra-tion into the UK grew with the drives to recruit labour. If the moment of 'cultural diversity' began with those drives, I would also argue that such recruitment drives would themselves not have been possible without the history and legacy of Empire. These connections are very important for the understanding cultural diversity in Britain. 'Cultural diversity' was present from the moment of postwar reconstruction, but it was defined exclusively in relation to economic concerns and confined to the sphere of labour relations. To a large extent, diversity has been lived, ever since the postwar period, as a distorted relationship between the state and the citizens on one hand, and between the non-white immigrants and the mainly white mainstream on the other hand.

At that point in time, it was simply a case of getting non-white immi-grants to come in, not to settle in large numbers, but to work in Britain. Nobody considered that 15 or 20 years down the line, the presence of these immigrants would affect the terms and parameters of 'national cul-ture'. By the time this was realised in the sixties, it was already too late to turn back the clock. This led to tensions, such as Enoch Powell's infam-ous 'rivers of blood' speech, which was a pernicious diatribe about how Britain and British culture were being undermined by the immigrant population, and this, in turn, precipitated a legacy of incitement to racial hatred that we still have to contend with today.[3] But you cannot separate cultural processes from economic ones. There is a tradition of radical critique of 'national culture' dating back to the 1960s and, in particular, to the work of the Birmingham School, including Raymond Williams' contributions. Yet it was not until relatively recently that this critique began to take any notice of non-white immigrants. Even then, much of the highly interesting and original efforts so far have emerged mainly from popular culture rather than from anywhere else. The UK has had a significant tradition of diverse literature and art, but national culture was channelled towards an uncomplicated identity – almost a kind of 'heritage industry'. In the aftermath of the war, this produced a heritage-cum-arts dynamic which cultural institutions were supposed to support and maintain.

The modern Arts Council has in my view learned a lot, not necessarily because it was forced to do so, as is sometimes unfairly claimed, but because it is self-evident that the grounds for an all-white national culture was changing rapidly. As a result, many cultural institutions in the UK, including the Arts Council, are now trying to unpick some of the themes which they inherited from the postwar years. This is where we need to situate what we call 'cultural diversity'.

One of the fundamental changes the Scottish Arts Council faces, for example, is how to reconcile, in a post-devolution Scotland, the idea of a national culture with the new status of the country and its aspirations to be heard all over the world. Devolution has made it more apparent that Scotland cannot *be* the UK, just as England is not the UK.

[GL and MWD] We'd like to press you on the idea of national culture because there is obviously very little consensus over how it is currently constituted. Even if there was agreement in the 'top-down' approach to national culture in the early days of the Arts Council of Great Britain, we have yet to see a debate within the Scottish Arts Council policy documentation about what constitutes national Scottish culture. Using Scotland as an example, what are the strengths and limitations of not having this debate?

[FF] Let's deal with the limitations first. If one continues to do things the way they have always been done, then the Arts Council's role is merely one of managing the infrastructure and dealing with problems as they arise. This reactive role must be the major limitation in not engaging in critical debate about national culture. On the other hand, the advantage would be that national institutions do not dictate the terms of dynamic debates. In the Scottish context, we have to think about where the country should be in modern terms: what is going to be the role of Scotland in the UK context and internationally? What sort of Scottish cultural identity do we want to see in 20, 50 or 100 years from now? These questions would be fore-grounded by a debate about national culture and would help us to clarify where we're going. But in terms of the immediate, in terms of the here and now, we need to ask what the strengths and weaknesses of the country are, enabling us to identify the areas we need to develop and nurture. Above all, we must be wary of accepting a concept of national culture simply in terms of cultural artefacts, since this isn't, on the whole, productive.

What we need to consider are the dynamics of, and the things that, define Scotland. Central to this is, of course, the link between economic and cultural development in relation to the diverse strands of the population. For example, in parts of Scotland there are areas that are as economically desperate as those in Third World nations, and the health statistics in some parts of Scotland are similar to what one would find in some parts of Latin America or Africa. So how do we in the Arts Council respond to that in our day-to-day work? I honestly don't have an answer, but I am one of the believers in the idea that a national culture must be tied to human development, that is, national development.

Since devolution, it is heartening to be able to say that the Scottish Arts Council is trying to reverse these negative trends by saying things like, we would wish every child (every person!) in Scotland to be literate and numerate, learn and participate in the arts and cultural activities. The challenge is how to avoid this becoming simply a number-crunching mechanistic activity. We need to respond to everyday realities as an intrinsic part of a national-cultural framework. Cultural institutions, including the Arts Council, cannot ignore the market and should also be mindful of how far we are constructed by our own definitions of national culture. Any formulaic conclusions are inevitably open to corrosion.

[GL and MWD] You seem to be saying that one does not define national culture because if you define what national culture is you can exclude certain groups. Doesn't this preclude a debate?

[FF] I don't think it precludes a debate. If you pin things down, you run the risk of shutting the door against everything else. Perhaps the real reason for a debate is because you don't want mythologies to pass for facts or, put differently, the hagiography of the nation to overthrow the nation's verifiable history.

[GL and MWD] But, on the other hand, you also implied that, in terms of state funding mechanisms and institutional policies, one has to be able to think about a national strategy. Is this a contradiction?

[FF] I don't think so because we need to be concerned about citizenship. By this, I mean the right of belonging enjoyed by every citizen. I think it is the primary duty of national institutions to deliver the gains of citizenship, and this should be evident in the strategies and policies they put forward. I am old-fashioned enough to say without any fear that it is only the state that can confer and protect the gains of citizenship. That would be what national culture might properly entail. If you specify exactly what national culture is, then anything that does not relate to your definition is ruled out and you run the risk of excluding your citizens. I know this is problematic for some people, but it is essential to see the definition of national culture in terms of how institutions perform in the conferment and protection of citizenship.

[GL and MWD] We have talked about citizenship, diversity policy and diversity aesthetics, but we also want to backtrack a little and get you to talk specifically about the language of cultural diversity, and the imagining of a national culture (or citizenship) of Scotland. The Arts Council often discusses diversity in terms of recent immigration, promulgating a post-empire immigration that brought an influx of people into Britain, and that makes Britain in general, and Scotland in particular, a more diverse and vibrant place. At the same time, this emphasis on diversity and (recent) immigration is problematic, since it sets up an opposition between the indigenous population and 'outsiders'. But in Scotland, as in the rest of the UK, there are long-settled communities which are non-white. Do you think that it is problematic to see diversity as coming from outside, contributing a 'leavening' effect on national culture?

[FF] Yes, it is problematic. Every nation – every country – in the world experiences migration, whether recently or in the past. In Scotland, as in other countries, amnesia develops about non-white immigration; put more simply, it is always the other person, who does not look like me on the basis of colour, who is considered the strange *other*. At the *New Voices, Hidden Histories* conference hosted by the Arts Council in Dundee in 2004, Tom Devine characterized Scotland as a nation of immigrants, both white and non-white.[4] A lot of people said afterwards that they did not realize that this was the case. Well, at least the conference helped them to understand the meaning of immigration differently. It is characteristic of this amnesia that only non-white people tend to be categorized automatically as economic migrants, or, as nowadays, as refugee or asylum-seekers. What I think is important, is to recognize that there is not much said about the 'positive contributions' of immigrants, and that non-white migration into Scotland would be significantly reduced if Scotland had had no historical connection with empire. But there is very little debate about empire in Scotland. Very few people talk about the involvement of the Scots in building the British Empire, identifying it instead with English national identity. Such amnesia glosses over some horrendous histories *and* undermines the good achieved by some Scots abroad.

[**GL and MWD**] Indeed, black peoples, as well as Asian and Chinese populations have long been settled in particular areas of Scotland, following the migration patterns dominated by the history of empire and by the global trade that followed in its wake. So, for example, what about all the black people who have lived in parts of Glasgow for generations? They are also Scottish and yet there remain very recent problems associated with constructing their identity within a policy of diversity.

[**FF**] I am sympathetic to the idea that we should see such people as 'human beings' and then move on. Why does that sound post-modern to me? But, while it is true that some black people have settled here for many years – some going back to the end of the First World War – and that their children and grandchildren have lived in, say Glasgow, all their lives, many of these people are likely to be excluded, as individuals, from citizenship on the basis of the colour of their skin. This in turn breeds alienation and reverse rejection (on the part of the victims) of what is, effectively, their own society. The way this alienation usually functions is that you are alright in your street – everyone knows you in your street or neighbourhood – but once you step outside, once you go three or four blocks down the road, suddenly you are seen as a stranger. Moreover, when you look around our statutory institutions, how many of such people do you see there? One is not asking these people to construct their identity within a policy of diversity. On the contrary, the idea is that people do not have to internalize a bad situation so that their *racial* identity becomes the first principle in everything they do. That can debar people from participation in a collective citizenship. I have a feeling that there are many people out there who would have preferred that an anti-racist vocabulary or strategy was adopted instead of terms like cultural diversity. I sometimes have sympathy for this view, but for a variety of reasons that must now be deemed passé in the cultural environment.

What we have done, therefore, is to home in on migration. We are saying that migration is a continuum. It throws up different groups or communities at different times. This is a verifiable truth. However, at no time has there been so much and so regular non-white migration into the UK as has occurred since the 1950s. While this is a fact, it is also what has given migration a racial twist, which makes participation in a common culture difficult, but not impossible. An acknowledgement of these simple details will go a long way towards demystifying many of the ridiculous claims being made around ethnic identity today. The saying that identity is complex and has to be carefully negotiated pours out of every mouth so easily. But it is not enough to use this formulation to deny that the state has a role to play in the matter of citizenship and that this role should be exercized by institutions. There is a cultural struggle going on in Scotland at the point where the fertilization of popular culture develops a political edge. This is coming largely from the activities, or daring, of the young people across all racial barriers. As long as this is not hijacked by the corporatist ethos, it is something to which we all should look forward.

[GL and MWD] How, then, does Scottish culture ever get re-defined so that it isn't simply Braveheart/Highland culture, but also includes the particular histories of the communities and citizens you've mentioned? If diversity is constructed as a product of recent migrations, and the 'indigenous' population identified as long-settled, organic communities, then the idea of what constitutes Scottishness will never be redefined.

[FF] Speaking personally, I will argue that it is not the business of the Arts Council to define national culture, except perhaps in instrumental terms that commit it to the protection of citizenship in all its complexity. As we all know, the debates surrounding national cultures continue, and will continue, to be affected by many factors and forces. This is more so in the age of trans-border capital flow and movement. If the Scots of 500 years ago were to come back today, they would not recognize their own country. All I am saying is that what we need to be clear about is citizenship in every sense of the word. Secondly, I share your concern that diversity tends to conjure the image of two communities existing in parallel. This does not need to be as it is. We need to be clear – and perhaps emphatic – that the main objective is to make the rights of citizenship the end product of diversity.

My own experience so far is that many indigenous non-white Scottish people see the cultural industry as an occupation which never goes beyond certain 'legwork' in community activities. This results in a sense of disempowerment. It is also the case that there are so many people wanting to do so many things for/with the minority ethnic communities, thus creating a huge industry of helpers out there. Why is it that the best employment route for minority ethnic people, irrespective of their qualifications, is to work in diversity or diversity-bounded activities? The question we need to ask is how did these phenomena develop? This is not a rhetorical question but one directly connected to the purpose of diversity, national culture and the rights of citizenship. This also applies to the arts. For reasons which are not difficult to understand, diversity is often taken for an ethnic-bounded parade of festivals, with little or no potential for arts development. It is such interpretations that place a question mark on the value of cultural diversity policy and not necessarily the need for the policy in the first place.

Another, although very different, complication is the fact that there is a lot of activity at the level of popular culture. We should ask ourselves, why are there more activities and more diverse participation here than in what is conventionally regarded as high culture? Some have argued that it is because popular culture is more democratic that we see so much diverse participation. But this is not entirely true. Popular culture is, arguably, also the most market-friendly and market-driven arena; also, the market sometimes uses popular culture to enforce segregation. We must, therefore, be careful about how we represent the vibrancy and democratic credentials of popular culture forms. My argument here is that, yes, we need to have a sense of what constitutes Scottishness, but the primary qualification for Scottishness, or for any identity for that matter, is citizenship and its outward projection and protection. To return to my original point, I define citizenship in a liberal enlightenment agenda.

[GL and MWD] Yet, when Scotland is promoted internationally, the image sold ignores the hidden histories, community groups and popular culture groups that you have been talking about. This seems to pander to the image of Scotland as one long continuous narrative of settlement, and the story of diversity is relegated to being a modern product of immigration.

[FF] I think we should be fairly relaxed about that, because it very much depends upon what market you are targeting. The tourist board promotes Scotland in order to keep tourists coming. Quite frankly, we have to be aware that the market has its own way of packaging things. But the marketing of 'heritage' culture, at the expense of diversity, is not peculiar to Scotland. For example, television advertisements for some products allegedly based on Chinese or Indian origin employ historical images that sometimes look like sixteenth-century anthropological pictures! Very entertaining, but how many people will go beyond the images paraded before them in order to explore current diversity? Such cultivation of markets goes on in all parts of the world and at all levels. It is one of the inevitable products of what is now termed 'globalization'. What is crucial from my point of view is the quality of internal mobilisation against the institutionalization of such images.

[GL and MWD] In terms of this national representation on an international level, do you think there is a difference here between Scotland and England? In relation to Scotland we talked about how ethnic minorities were forgotten within the hidden history of empire, whereas, if you look at England, empire and imperialism are central to the notion of Englishness; they even bring tourists over!

[FF] That may well be the case, but don't forget that the histories of Scotland and England are closely bound in the matter of both empire and imperialism. Yes, there is more discussion about empire in England, but that was because England had to confront, rather early, the crisis of identity in the post-empire period and the extent of non-white immigration. It is very easy either to overlook these important points or to take them for granted. It is precisely because of the differences between England and Scotland in the post-mortem response to empire and imperialism that it becomes crucial to negotiate national distinctions in terms of black British identity. Sometimes, when I listen to radio broadcasts of some very high-minded English intellectuals, I find that they still have a difficulty in separating England from Britain; to them England is Britain, and Britain is England. There is no acknowledgement, let alone recognition, that there needs to be a separation.

I am deeply sympathetic to the idea that, in as much as Scotland is also deeply implicated in the British Empire, there was a good deal to suggest that the empire was controlled and managed along England's aspirations and prejudices. For Scotland, the impetus for participation in empire was more a question of economics. This is not to say that Scotland can be exculpated, but it is also important to look at the disparate economics of empire. From the eighteenth to the early twenty-first centuries, empire was the main outlet for jobs for educated Scots. This resulted in a huge Scottish representation in the workforce of empire at that time: around two out of every five bureaucrats in the empire were from Scotland. But the cultural and political impact remained overwhelmingly English. Take, for example, the construction and administration of the colonial legal systems. Despite the role of Scots within these developments, it was the English legal system, and not the Scottish one, that was universally adopted. How did that come about and what was the impact on the outward labour movement on development of Scotland itself? That most reviled of Scottish genres, the *kailyard* novel, seems to me to represent reportage of the economic and cultural changes that began to take place across Scotland in the shadows of the 'modernization' process that had been set in motion by the incoming profits from colonialist enterprises.[5]

Also, the empire provided other opportunities and outlets, and the Scots became mercantilists, travelling for trade and profiting from slavery. Involvement in these imperial projects was often the only outlets for Scottish people and, understandably, they seized these employment opportunities. Yes, empire was a sordid business, but rather than ignoring Scotland's role in it, we also need to explore what empire meant for Scottish national culture. In so doing, I am fairly certain that we would uncover further hidden histories of migration.

[GL and MWD] In some respects, don't you think that the absence of debate about Scotland's relation to empire has been because of a kind of victim mentality, a special pleading because Scotland was colonised by the English?

[FF] Scotland, of course, adopts a victim mentality. This is a complex subject and I certainly reject that simple 'we-were-also-colonized-by-the-English', rationale for the amnesia about our country's role in empire business (I say this because, as a naturalized British citizen, I am a black Scot). But things began to change at the end of the Second World War, when Scottish nationalism took on a totally different character, adjusting its strategies and language in the light of the postwar anti-colonial struggles. The conditions were, of course, different, but the rhetorical strategy adopted by the postwar Scottish nationalists was similar to those in many parts of the empire. This is what I describe as Scotland's postcolonial awakening and it can only be understood by paying close attention to the cultural and social fall-outs from the empire business. There is an intellectual movement in Scotland that likes to pride itself as the authority on an alleged Scottish inferiority complex. With all respect, I think the origin of what this school calls 'inferiority complex' is none other than one of the social outcomes of Scotland's total immersion in the business of empire and of the ruthless exploitation of the capital accumulation opportunities provided by that business.

That history apart, the victim psychosis has done nothing to discourage the recent contradictory response in Scotland to refugees and immigrants.

[GL and MWD] We would like to return now to the question of a national culture and the way in which the Arts Council and other arts institutions engage with diversity issues. Your comments earlier about citizenship and using an arts agenda to promote social inclusion dovetail with Scottish Arts Council literature, which states that the organization actively seeks opportunities to support artists in communities and to develop high professional standards. Given that this dialectic is a key focus for the debate about black British culture, we'd like you to comment on the potential conflict or contradiction between the policy of social inclusion and that of aesthetic excellence. How do you negotiate the two agendas?

[FF] There are two elements to be considered here: the diversity of practitioners, as well as the diversity of practice. As such, the notion of diversity must be allowed to engage with aesthetic standards and claims to excellence. Diversity, then, is not simply about promoting artists on the grounds of their ethnic or racial or sexual orientation or background. It is about ensuring that there are no barriers, which may be produced by fixed concepts of excellence, to entering the cultural arena. For example, if your parents or grandparents were Chinese immigrants and you grew up in Glasgow or Dundee, and then decided you would like to pursue a career as a Scottish artist in the Chinese or Japanese tradition of say pottery, you are no less a Scottish artist. The Arts Council would consider supporting the artist, but at the same time, he/she would have to be a good potter within their chosen 'cultural' field.

[GL and MWD] Nevertheless, there *may* be a conflict in relation to arts funding if one emphasizes social inclusion strategies and community arts practice in addition to being a standard bearer of sorts.

[FF] The Scottish Arts Council has a charter that describes itself as an agency for developing, supporting and sustaining the arts in Scotland. The 'arts' should be interpreted broadly, not just in terms of the product, but also in terms of the infrastructure. For example, few people realize how much money we give every year to certain venues; these are capital grants which may go into millions of pounds to support and maintain buildings and facilities. Issues such as geographical considerations, the urban and rural divide, as well as equality and equity cannot be ignored by the Arts Council. As a national body distributing public funds, the Arts Council must transcend the narrowness of concepts such as diversity as well as being part of it.

[GL and MWD] In your own role, as a diversity officer, how do you balance social inclusion with aesthetic excellence, and how does such juggling impact on both the cultural mainstream and its creation and maintenance of a canon?

[FF] It is reasonable to assume that, like all individuals, I and my colleagues make value judgements. However, the Arts Council has drawn up a set of criteria on which we base our decisions. These criteria vary from fund to fund. Actually, judging social inclusion along the lines of aesthetic excellence is not as difficult as is often thought because there are different funds which address different aspects of social policies in the context of arts development. On the question of juggling, I think we are fortunate in Scotland in that we are still at the developmental stage of spreading the equity of citizenship to non-white arts practitioners. To that extent, there is nothing to juggle in real terms. We are just opening up the national cultural space. Of course, a lot of people, not least many of those within the arts institutions don't seem to want to understand the Arts Council's concept of cultural diversity in the terms that I have described here. Social inclusion in the arts is when you can get about five kids out of twenty to say about a sponsored event, 'I like that, I want to do that, I would like to know more about that in the future.' These kids should be drawn from all groups and communities; for only then would the Arts Council have succeeded in implanting the seeds of future citizenship.

The existence or status of what you call a black British canon is, in my opinion, something that cannot be detached from the overall politics of culture in the UK today. To that extent, it is also connected to the subject of diversity. As a black immigrant from a country that once had a well-developed intellectual framework for managing and circulating knowledge – Nigeria – my own intellectual formation was to question canonicity. When I went to the university as an undergraduate, my generation was about the last to be educated in the contexts of both decolonization and Nigeria's oil-boom opulence. As I think was the case in a number of the English-speaking African countries with a well-developed system of higher education, we did not have the anomalous institution called 'English Literature'. Instead, what was in place was 'Literatures in English', and the idea was that this would expose us to varieties of literatures from all over the world, without de-contextualizing them. Although I am told that things have changed dramatically over the past few years, the essence of this was to make us aware of the world. This was a great gift of higher education in some of the post-colonial countries, particularly those which, for some time, were very serious about higher education. Coming from such a background, I was surprised when I arrived at Edinburgh University as a post-graduate student to discover that, despite the presence of the late Paul Edwards on the academic staff of the university, there was very little of black writing being taught at the university, let alone African writing. As anyone who is familiar with Equiano's work will remember, Paul Edwards was an important figure in the development of scholarly study of modern African writing.[6] I was saddened by the whimsical 'it is not part of our world' response that my enquiries about the exclusion of black writings from the teaching syllabus drew. Well, as I was no longer in Africa, I interpreted the absence in terms of what might be missing here, namely the denial of the black presence. It was then that I started to follow the debates about black British and the black canon in British writing. Since that time, I have come across African writing taught in a number of anthropological and history courses.

However, the wider Scottish cultural scene provides scope for optimism. Although not many people recognize this, the notion of the canon is very fluid in Scotland. This is for all sorts of reasons, some of which I had mentioned earlier. You will perhaps recall that Tom Nairn in his famous book, *The Break-Up of Britain,* led a vexatious attack on Scottish culture, the essence of which was to deny the existence of a coherent and lofty canon.[7] While some of Nairn's evidence can be said to have been partial, his overall strategy of distinguishing between an ever-optimistic canon that keeps within its own celebratory boundary and one that is born directly from the nation's own struggle for self-definition cannot be dismissed. For some of the sociological reasons which Nairn used and sometimes misused in his book, the canon is constantly a work in progress in Scotland, and I have no doubt in my mind that some of the existing developmental work will naturally grow into that process.

It is essential to recognize that cultural and art institutions play as much a part in the shaping of our notions of canon, our ideas of literature, and our sense of aesthetics, as do universities. It is for this reason that their interpretation of citizenship should be a valid subject of constant analysis. For example, approximately 13 per cent of the annual literature budget of the Scottish Arts Council goes to the publishing industry to support the publication of books. But the Arts Council cannot monitor what is chosen for publication without becoming entangled in accusations of Soviet-like intrusions. It has to leave that task to the publishers themselves. To that extent, it is the publishers who decide what is aesthetically valuable, and the money provided by the Arts Council is meant to support work which would otherwise not have been published without financial assistance. But, how do publishers decide what title they are going to support? Given the cultural and economic climate, it is unlikely that they will support any book which exists outside their notion of a *defined* cultural mainstream.

What this tells us is that canon formation is, more often that not, mired in the complexities of everyday language, of cultural transaction, of economics, and of the possible one-dimensional construction of national identity. Without becoming self-contradictory, I am suggesting that the *canon* does exist, but that we must be very careful to distinguish the differences between what the canon is for a cultural worker, and what it is for an academic. The canon may be fluid within academia, allowing a consideration of a diverse range of literatures in English, but the canon, and the black British canon in particular, is, from cultural institutions' point of view, only one element of a much wider infrastructure of cultural production. There is no automatic or easy answer to the question about whether aesthetic value and social inclusion are contradictory. My own approach is to try to remain even-handed; at a certain level I do know what needs to be done, but at another level I have limitations.

[GL and MWD] Continuing to focus on your role as a diversity officer, can you talk a little but about mainstreaming and marginality? One of the criticisms of cultural diversity and multiculturalism is that it can be a strategy of creating 'cultural bantustans', where funds may be used to maintain cultural ghettos that will never be mainstream, where what is labelled 'diversity' is always marginal and supplementary to the artistic and cultural centre ground.

[FF] The question seems to concur with the widely-held approach that the real problem occurs at the margins themselves, because those people situated there do not want to break into the mainstream. But such assumptions are continually undermined by a range of issues, not least, the refusal to extend the equity of citizenship to the non-white margin. There might be a lack of self-reflexive practices or an over-commitment to production values that offer practitioners a comfort zone. As a bureaucrat, I am not going to be rigid on the distinction between margin and mainstream, but use it instrumentally. Mainstream activities and venues may include the margins in their programming, and marginal sites can incorporate and welcome mainstream practitioners. The Arts Council works with both 'marginal' and 'mainstream' organizations, not only to support them financially, but also to help them overcome cultural preconceptions. It is inevitable that some of my work will involve targeting specific groups at a particular time with a view to helping develop new tastes and new audiences for the arts generally. Sometimes arts organizations express uncertainty about the practicalities of such innovation, but it is as simple as supermarket shopping. In supermarkets you don't see an aisle with special shelves marked, 'minority ethnic' or 'African immigrants', since such communities simply want the same as everyone else – good food of whatever national origin! In terms of cultural activities, therefore, mainstream and marginal groups simply want quality arts.

Notes

1. Angus Calder, *The People's War* (London: Cape, 1969).
2. Raymond Williams, *The Long Revolution* (London: Chatto & Windus, 1961).
3. Enoch Powell, 'Rivers of Blood' (April 1964) may be found at www. sterlingtimes.org/powell_speech.doc.
4. *New Voices. Hidden Histories. A Conference Report* (Edinburgh: Scottish Arts Council, 2004).
5. The Kailyard novel was popular in Scotland at the end of the nineteenth and beginning of the twentieth centuries. The genre expressed nostalgia for a rural past and explored concerns about industrialization and empire in a sentimental fashion.
6. Olaudah Equiano, *Equiano's Travels His Autobiography. The Interesting Narrative of Olaudah Equiano, or, Gustavus Vassa, the African*, ed. Paul Edwards (Oxford: Heinemann, 1996).
7. Tom Nairn, *The Break-up of Britain* (London: Verso, 1977).

Part II
New Languages of Criticism

5

Fantasy Relationships: Black British Canons in a Transnational World*

John McLeod

In a recent essay on the vitality and variety of contemporary black British poetry, Lauri Ramey attempts to focus her discussion with recourse to the debate about the cultural visibility and impact of black British writing on British writing as a whole. It is a debate shaped by crucial recurring questions: 'Is there a canon of black British writing? What relationship does this brand of writing bear to British literature as it has been commonly studied? What might the special features *be* that identify black British writing?'[1] Canons, nations, characteristics – the terms are familiar and overlapping. They suggest the vocabulary through which black British writing has been frequently evaluated; yet, paradoxically, such writing has simultaneously prompted a crisis of exactly these evaluatory terms, revealing them as unwieldy and often problematic concepts in a black British literary context, raising uncomfortable questions about the process of evaluation. How can, and why should, a provocatively counter-canonical body of writing become organized into a new catalogue of achievement that threatens to blunt the disruptive and radical consequences of black writing for British literature? Is a national paradigm the best way of declaring the cultural specifics of literary texts? Is black writing constituted by a series of shared literary techniques or concerns which might parallel the allegedly racial or cultural connections between black people (presuming, of course, we can agree on who is black)?

Ramey's attempts to engage with these issues are admirable yet highly instructive of the impossible task of working happily with, and across, the terms of black, British, and canon. Rightly arguing against the 'tokenism' of an accepted canon of black British poetry, she nonetheless insists upon

---

* An earlier version of this essay appeared as 'Some Problems with "British" in "a Black British Canon"' in *Wasafiri*, 36 (2002), pp. 56–9.

the necessity of installing black British poetry in the British canon. This will not happen, it seems, 'until [black British poetry] is widely recognized as a legitimate and valuable body of poetry – filled with range, dissension, variety, diversity and a sophisticated cultural contribution: a poetry that carries special insight into the urgent global issues of race and nation, the individual and society'.[2] Leaving aside the problems of exactly who legitimates and evaluates, Ramey rejects a racially and nationally limiting notion of black British poetry in her attention to its diversity, heterogeneity and global relevance, while simultaneously (inadvertently?) enabling its reinstallation by naming the supposedly predominant themes of race and nation (black, British). Later in her essay she attempts to identify the specificity of black British poetry by suggesting that it extends beyond accepted categories, claiming that, 'the new black British poems are not wholly at first what they appear to be, but instead reflect the sly double voicing often associated African American poetry and the archetypal personae of the Carnival'; a couple of pages later she virtually dismisses the legitimacy of the phrase 'contemporary black British poetry' on the grounds that the poets 'demonstrate as many differences as they do similarities'.[3] In being pulled between the canon and the counter-canonical, the British and the African American, similarity and difference, Ramey's thoughtful and patient essay ultimately exemplifies the incapability of racial and especially national paradigms in engaging with the specific challenges of black British poetry as well as, to my mind, much black writing in Britain. It is the purpose of this essay to explore these challenges in order to resist the imposition of inappropriate evaluative terms and suggest alternative important paradigms which take their cue from the transnationality of black writing in Britain.

An important sense of what I am calling 'transnationality' is given in Bernardine Evaristo's novel-in-verse *Lara* (1997), which combines ancestral and historical knowledges with a contemporary globalized or transnational consciousness. In Evaristo's narrative of the travails of Lara – London-born child of Nigerian, British, Irish and Brazilian histories – the book performs its own 'three-point turn' by shuttling between Europe, Africa and the Americas.[4] It is a work which emphasizes the cat's-cradle of historical threads that bind distant times and places securely to each other, and challenges the pedagogical protocols and border-controls of nationalist historiography by exposing the transnationality at the heart of London, Lagos and Rio, each its own 'rainbow metropolis'.[5] The novel occupies a space between 'massive floating continents', looking both within and beyond national borders to a transnational consciousness of how the world turns – to discover the sound of Catholic hymns hybridized by drums in the Amazon, Yoruba carvings in London base-ments, the West Indian diaspora in Lagos.[6]

As I have argued elsewhere, *Lara* cheerfully fragments the homogenizing fictions of race and nation with recourse to a transformative transcultural consciousness; so to describe it as black British text seems to do a dis-service to its achievement.[7] The insertion of Evaristo into an historical narrative of black British writing comes dangerously close to 're-covering' *Lara*, packaging it with recourse to the very rhetoric the book actively contests. Nonetheless, Kwame Dawes has discussed Evaristo's work as part of a distinctly black British body of contemporary writing, while Onyekachi Wambu includes an extract from *Lara* in *Empire Windrush: Fifty Years of Writing About Black Britain* (1998).[8] For Mark Stein, a subtle reader of *Lara*, the book remains a 'black British novel of transformation'.[9] In seeming keen to position Evaristo as part of a black British canon, there is always the danger of committing violence to the historical sensibility and trans-national fertility of her work.

This argument, of course, is not particularly new. In 1988, Fred D'Aguiar complained about the phrase 'black British literature' in his essay 'Against Black British Literature'. In contesting the unhappy and unhelpful alliance of the terms 'black' and 'British' as a way of labelling the work of 'three generations' of black authors in Britain, D'Aguiar argued that the phrase perpetuated the division of blacks from Britons, each conceived of as a racially-different homogeneous group. In addition, the phrase misrepre-sented the caprice of the creative imagination: 'Creativity itself cannot be contained for long in any fashion or vice-hold which the process of naming and compartmentalizing seeks to promote.'[10] D'Aguiar describes a model of creativity which is unsurprising: it is very difficult to think of a writer, past or present, who has not borrowed from or engaged with cultures or traditions different to the ones they consider their own. On the other hand, his remark bears witness to a certain frustration on the part of black writers in Britain, especially since the 1980s, who have become increasingly unhappy with 'black British' as naming a certain kind of artist and common literary tradition.

It will soon become clear that I, like D'Aguiar, find the notion of a dis-tinctly black British literature problematic for reasons I will explain. Yet, we must beware of rushing too quickly to D'Aguiar's side and consider first the construction of a black British canon as a significant achieve-ment within postwar British culture as a whole. Identitarian labels, liter-ary traditions, canons of a common culture – each is certainly a fabrication which excludes more than it includes and depicts stability and coher-ence where there is contingency by drawing borders of convenience.

Yet, the social and historical *necessity* to invest in these concepts may not be so quickly condemned. On 12 September 2004, 50 black writers in Britain assembled on the steps of the British Library to pose for a photograph taken by Manuel Vason, titled 'A Great Day'. The event was organized by Melanie Abrahams, director of the artist management and production agency 'Renaissance One', which promotes several black writers.[11] Based on Art Kane's 1958 photograph of American jazz musicians, 'A Great Day in Harlem', Abrahams' intention was to mark the contribution to British culture of outstanding writers of African, Asian and Caribbean descent, as well as the 'movers and shakers' who had promoted them and their work. Reflecting on the event, the novelist Andrea Levy (who was included in the picture) regarded it as a positive gathering: 'the chance to eat, drink and chat with a roomful of novelists, poets, playwrights, journalists and literary "movers and shakers", gave me a feeling of connectedness that I don't have as I sit alone in front of the computer'.[12] Although sensitive to the inevitable inclusiveness of the gathering (a total of 80 people had received an invitation), she argued that 'however temporary, shifting or partial our club may be, right at this moment it seemed worth recording – celebrating even'.[13] In a nation in which racism is still very much prevalent at the levels of street and state, despite the initiatives of many different people to re-imagine and redefine Britain in terms of meaningful multiculturalism, a gathering such as Abrahams' 'A Great Day' may be regarded as a political and politicizing act: a show of force which risks the pitfalls of canonicity in order to challenge the prevailing sense (regardless of the Booker Prize) that black culture in Britain is a minority culture or appeals only to a minority of people.

It is worth recalling here a comment made by Raymond Williams in his closing remarks to *Culture and Society* (1958). In defending postwar television from those who dismissed it as evidence of the philistinism of the masses, Williams talked about the 'general tendency to confuse the techniques themselves with the uses to which, in a given society, they have been put'.[14] Such a judicious separation may well serve our discussions of black British canonicity: certainly the 'technique' of canon-making is, to my mind, inevitably problematic, but in constructing a black British canon under certain circumstances and in response to certain social and cultural conditions, the 'uses to which it can be put' may well beckon our support, as well as suggest a level of political urgency – as the example of 'A Great Day' perhaps suggests.

Another writer pictured in 'A Great Day', Linton Kwesi Johnson, has recently remarked that 'in those days' when he first started writing he was seen as 'a Caribbean poet, a West Indian Poet, a Jamaican. Nowadays [however], I'm being sponsored by the British Council to go abroad and do readings so I suppose that means something.'[15] He also speaks in the same interview about a recent radio broadcast which mentioned his work as a significant landmark in the development of British poetry. The shift from 'in those days' to 'nowadays' marks perhaps a passage, or a victory, for black writers in Britain (leading to 'A Great Day'), one which concerns the issue of inclusion and the rights of cultural tenure, where (in this instance) the Jamaican migrant is no longer fated to remain outside the narrative of national culture. Although the 'achievement' of being considered 'British' may well misrepresent Johnson's work – which takes issue with the nation and moves creatively across national, cultural and linguistic boundaries – his insertion into a national frame of reference is, on one front, a certain kind of victory against those who would keep the border between 'black' and 'British' firmly closed.

In a similar vein, the anthologies of black British culture, which appeared around the 50th anniversary of the arrival of the ship carrying West Indian migrants, *SS Empire Windrush*, seem to me valuable, if not vital, not least because they seek to establish some kind of tradition of black British writing that celebrates the multifariousness of black Britain as a fertile conjunction, while simultaneously attending closely to its stormy histories. Each of these anthologies inevitably engages in a process of canon-formation: by gathering together a finite group of writers, using (albeit self-consciously) identitarian markers of race and nation, and constructing a genealogy of black British writing which may imply a tradition or model of generational influence. I am thinking here of Kwesi Owusu's *Black British Culture and Society* (2000) with its titular nod to Raymond Williams, James Procter's commemorative anthology *Writing Black Britain 1948–1998* (2000) significantly dedicated to the late Stephen Lawrence, Onyekachi Wambu's aforementioned *Empire Windrush* anthology, and Courttia Newland and Kadija Sesay's anthology *IC3: The Penguin Book of New Black Writing in Britain* (2000). Procter's fine collection is arranged chronologically and constructs an historical account of the evolution of postwar black Britain. Kadija Sesay's introduction to *IC3* includes the following remark, which clearly implies a benign model of black British influence and tradition:

we [the editors] are confident that the established writers will see the progress that new writers are making and be proud in the knowledge that there are wonderful writers following in their footsteps, and that it is due to their advances that they are able to make their own footprints with surety.[16]

These texts bear valuable witness to a significant social and cultural presence of black writers within British institutions and culture – a presence which has been earned at some cost – and in the midst of an often hostile, racist nation. Canon building, whatever its conceptual failures, despite its unacceptable exclusions, assists in the priceless process of transforming (to quote again Raymond Williams) 'a given society'.

However, one principal problem with such anthologies concerns the ways in which they risk falsifying the mechanics of black British creativity and tradition, and look only at national, rather than transnational, fields of influence. Sesay's image of black writers in Britain pursuing each other's footsteps perhaps gives too tidy an impression of what Caryl Phillips has termed 'following on'.[17] In a black *British* canon, literary tradition becomes spatially constricted, with certain influential figures prioritized over others. National paradigms are always reductive perhaps, but particularly so when thinking about the fortunes of black writing in Britain. By locating selected writers and their work within a distinctly national paradigm, this national-canonical 'technique' (Williams again) has unhappy consequences for the ways in which certain writers are mapped, remembered and read. These consequences must be weighed against the merits in building canons and traditions for important transformative political purposes.

In his essay, 'Following On: The Legacy of Selvon and Lamming' (1998), Caryl Phillips makes a series of important remarks that expose some interesting spatial and temporal passages fundamental to his art. In reading Sam Selvon as a younger man, Phillips recognized a series of anxieties and uncertainties which spoke to him of his own struggles while living and writing in Britain. In Phillips' sense of indebtedness we indeed discover an important relationship of influence, a sense of a younger writer following on the heels of others whose work in the 1950s helped to enable Phillips' writing. But, as he also remembers, 'in the 1970s there was not what we might term a black British literary tradition'.[18] Phillips had to explore beyond Britain to discover writers who spoke about a reality almost commensurate with his own, leading to both an intellectual journey as well as a prolonged physical departure from Britain in the 1980s.[19] Of equal importance to the richness of Phillips' work are a series of transnational and multi-generic influences from which he fruitfully draws. Central here is the United States, a nation which Phillips first visited in 1978. On being exposed to black American theatre in New York City, he noted that there was still 'something missing': black American writing could not speak to the landscape and the experiences he had encountered in Leeds as a boy.[20] But the USA was also the place where he was fired

[handwritten note: ff. note one of problem of Black British]

with the ambition to write. In his book of 1987, *The European Tribe*, Phillips remembers reading Richard Wright on a beach in Los Angeles:

> If I had to point to any one moment that seemed crucial in my desire to be a writer, it was then, as the Pacific surf began to wash up around the deck chair ... [*Native Son*] provided not so much a model but a possibility of how I might be able to express the conundrum of my own existence.[21]

Indeed, for many black writers in Britain the importance of black American writing to their work seems just as much a major part of their sense of 'following on' as do older black British counterparts, not least because it assists in demarcating exactly what is peculiar to British contexts. Phillips's writing draws productively upon a variety of literary sources, not just American and British of course. The extent to which one can separate these out into national threads or distinct areas seems futile and oddly against the spirit of his work, which is perpetually performing its own kind of 'three-point turn'. What kind of voice do we hear in the closing pages of *Crossing the River* (1993), for example, with its myriad echoes of American, Caribbean, European and British fiction, music, political rhetoric and nomenclature? What is gained, and lost, in declaring this voice as black British? In following the footsteps of black British writing, strictly national canons cannot bear adequate witness to the transnational pathways which, like Evaristo's heroine Lara, ultimately cross water. As Phillips suggests, to see black writing in Britain as 'following on' in the footsteps of Selvon, Lamming and others, is to detach only one important part of a much wider and complicated story. Richard Wright may be just as important as Sam Selvon to Phillips's writing, but only Selvon's footsteps will be visible in mapping the terrain of a black British canon.

Black British writers may have self-consciously followed on the heels of earlier black Britons, yet there is also a palpable sense that the previous generation did not provide the primary points of inspiration for later writers, nor did they necessarily face the same challenges – social and literary – as their children. In his memoir *The Rainbow Sign*, Hanif Kureishi talks of the importance of the Black Panthers, the Black Power Movement and James Baldwin to his emerging sense of political consciousness and locatedness in the London of the 1960s.[22] 'Writing black Britain' cannot be fully understood or appreciated without bringing into focus the influence of figures, like Baldwin, for so many younger writers of the period. More recently, Jackie Kay has spoken of her creative indebtedness to the USA, especially as regards popular music. Her novel *Trumpet* (1997) bears witness to the kinds of fertile British-American influences I am tracing, by translating into a postwar British context the 1930s story of the American musician Billy Tipton. A self-confessed fan of black American writing and music, and the author of a book about Bessie Smith, Kay places the influence of black American popular culture at the heart of her book's structure. As she explains, it was black America which spoke to her sense of not belonging to a palpable, recognizable black community in Edinburgh:

> I think that it is very important when you are black and you grow up in an environment that isn't, to find people that you can relate to imaginatively if you like. So I did have a number of different fantasy relationships with various black people from around the world, you know, Nelson Mandela, Angela Davis, Bessie Smith or Louis Armstrong or Ella Fitzgerald.[23]

Kay's novel is certainly structurally indebted to the patterns of American jazz music translated into a literary aesthetic. Her sense of the difficulty of 'following on' is particularly inflected by the facts of her adoption, but her remarks are not untypical of a certain generation's sense of cultural affiliations. Those 'fantasy relationships' have been absolutely central to the evolution of black writing in Britain for several decades. To what extent does the concept of a black British canon necessarily bear witness to these relationships? The 'following on' implied by the chronologically arranged black British anthologies is perhaps not the best way to render these relationships, not least because in privileging the national, a number of important transnational and translational circuits and axes cannot be mapped. This seems to do violence to much of the writing that has come to be known as black British.

In speaking of a vital transnationality at the heart of much of black writing in Britain, I am not joining with those such as Iain Chambers who privilege post-national paradigms in concepts such as globalization, cosmopolitanism or the 'Black Atlantic'. Nations are not so easily soluble, either imaginatively or materially. As Dave Gunning has warned, several recent discussions of black British writing have tended to ignore the materiality of national formations in their cheerful advocacy of diasporic aesthetics. Consequently, 'Britain becomes a signifier only in terms of its relationship to international allegiances and histories. There is a failure to locate the nation as simultaneously existing as a contained entity unto itself. "British" is then denied any explanatory power.'[24] This 'explanatory power' is vital to the conceptualization of transnationalism.

As Sallie Westwood and Annie Phizacklea understand it, the term stages a contradictory yet enduring state of affairs: 'On the one hand the continuing importance of the nation and the emotional attachments invested in it, and on the other hand those processes such as cross-border migration which are transnational in form.'[25] Those crossings – both actual and imaginative – can be discovered throughout twentieth-century black writing in Britain, certainly well before 22 June 1948. Rather than placing writers such as Sam Selvon and George Lamming at the beginning of a canonical tradition, which begins with the arrival of the *SS Empire Windrush*, what would happen if we were to think about the ways in which contemporary black British writers might be seen to be in part 'following on' (consciously or not) from black writers in Britain during the 1930s and 1940s: people like George Padmore, C.L.R. James and others. Although this generation's advocacy of different kinds of anti-colonial nationalism makes them distinct from the preoccupations of today's writers, their innovative attempt to draw upon a variety of national and cultural influences, as a means to intervening in British politics, colonial authority and nationalist projects abroad, has been too quickly forgotten when speaking of black writing in Britain. Making these figures 'canonical' might help expose an alternative genealogy of *transnational* black writing produced in Britain – forging a new and important 'explanatory power', if you like – as well as displace writers such as Selvon and Lamming from their position at the head of a black British canon.

Clearly, there are reductive consequences in confining, to the category 'black British', that postwar generation of authors about which Phillips writes – especially the talismanic figures of Sam Selvon and George Lamming. As James Procter has perceptively noted, 'despite the proliferation of black British writing in the late 1940s to the late 1960s, only one novel on this "subject", and from that period, Sam Selvon's *The Lonely Londoners* [1956], is currently available in Britain'.[26] Selvon is indeed fondly remembered, and certainly taught in institutions of higher education as the writer who created the quintessential novel of black Britain in 1950s. But to speak of Selvon primarily as a black British writer is to neglect his importance as a chronicler of his native Trinidad and as a central figure in the emergence, in the 1950s, of a literature which spoke to and about the Caribbean, not Britain. To put it crudely, in preferring the Selvon of the Moses novels and plays to the Selvon of the Tiger novels, the risk remains of trying to separate out two inseparable national contexts in his work which cannot be easily cleaved. Transnational fertile connections are filtered out of the national frame. If Selvon's London was altered by the language and presence of his migrant, mainly Caribbean arrivants, then his sojourn in Britain made possible the production of his Caribbean-centred work, which found, in migrant community experience, a creolising vision of pan-Caribbean identity, one both inspired by, and encouraging of, the dream of Caribbean federation. Britain and the Caribbean are two points upon a fruitful axis which created in Selvon's case a variety of different kinds of texts. But we cannot understand his vision of the Caribbean without embedding it in the materiality of postwar London; and whereas critical attention to Selvon's work has focused on the axis of migration from Trinidad to Britain, his diaspora-inflected enthusiasm for creolization in the *Caribbean*, which was nurtured in Britain, is neglected. So while it is easy to find *The Lonely Londoners* on the bookshop's shelves, the same cannot be said of *A Brighter Sun* (1952) or *Turn Again Tiger* (1958). The 'black British' Selvon seems an increasingly remote figure from Selvon as a black writer in Britain, writing across nations and between experiences. Half a life is remembered only.

To approach the work of writers such as Johnson, Phillips, Kay and Selvon in terms of a national paradigm ultimately fails to address to the transnational cultural influences and affiliations which impact upon their attempts to render the experience of black peoples in Britain. Rather than converting these figures into the representatives of a connected black British culture, where the paradigm of the nation is the primary platform for and the chief container of their work, I wonder if a transnational attention to black writing in Britain would have two significant, if urgent, consequences. The first would be to admit the influence of genres and texts from remote locations that have enabled black writing not just in Britain but *about* Britain. Phillips' American experiences helped him see the gap of black British specificity: those texts were absolutely vital to, as well as inadequate for, the task ahead. But, second, black writing in Britain also dares to expose, for all Britons, the criss-crossings, the comings and goings, the transnational influences, which arguably inform the construction of virtually all texts and canons that bear the signature of 'British'. This is not only a matter or reading texts contrapuntally, as Edward Said famously proposed, but of noticing the different streams of transnational influence which wash through many texts, each with its own politics.[27] Different versions of the transnational 'three point turn' experienced by Evarsito's Lara can be detected in the work of many British writers, not simply those labelled as black British, and their presence tells us much about the many different threads and histories which fuel cultural production in Britain. Just as one cannot read Kay without acknowledging the importance of Jazz, or approach Phillips without recognizing the influence of Richard Wright, we perhaps might need to think more about Angela Carter's indebtedness to Japanese popular culture of the 1970s, James Kelman's admiration for, and imitation of, Sam Selvon in novels like *The Busconducter Hines* (1984), or Adam Thorpe's international modernism that underwrites his critique of Englishness in *Ulverton* (1992) and *Still* (1995).[28] This, it seems to me, is one of the greatest gifts of black writing in Britain: the extent to which it revises the nationalist understanding of the islands we name as 'Britain' at the levels of both history and culture, and it points the way to re-conceptualizing the creation of British culture, if not British nationhood, in transnational terms.

Notes

1. Lauri Ramey, 'Contemporary Black British Poetry', in R. Victoria Arana and Lauri Ramey (eds), *Black British Writing* (New York and Basingstoke: Palgrave Macmillan, 2004), pp. 109–36; p. 111.
2. *Ibid.*
3. *Ibid.*, pp. 113, 115.
4. Bernardine Evaristo, *Lara* (Tunbridge Wells: Angela Royal Publishing, 1997), p. 108.
5. *Ibid.*, p. 137.
6. *Ibid.*, p. 140.
7. See John McLeod, *Postcolonial London: Rewriting the Metropolis* (London: Routledge, 2004), pp. 177–88.
8. See Kwame Dawes, 'Negotiating the Ship on the Head: Black British Fiction', *Wasafiri*, 29 (1999), pp. 18–24; Onyekachi Wambu (ed.), *Empire Windrush: Fifty Years of Writing about Black Britain* (London: Weidenfeld & Nicolson, 1998).
9. Mark Stein, *Black British Literature: Novels of Transformation* (Columbus: Ohio State University Press, 2004), p. 96.
10. Fred D'Aguiar, 'Against Black British Literature', in Maggie Butcher (ed.), *Tibisiri: Caribbean Writers and Critics* (Dangaroo: Coventry, 1989), pp. 106–14; p. 109.
11. For the photograph and to read about its genesis, see http://renaissanceone. com/agreatday/index.php (accessed 16 December 2004). I was employed briefly as an advisor to this project.
12. Andrea Levy, 'Made in Britain', *Guardian Review*, Saturday, 18 September 2004, pp. 34–5; p. 34.
13. *Ibid.*
14. Raymond Williams, *Culture and Society: Coleridge to Orwell* (1958; London: The Hogarth Press, 1982), p. 301.
15. 'Linton Kwesi Johnson in Conversation with John La Rose', in Roxy Harris and Sarah White (eds), *Changing Britannia: Life Experience With Britain* (London: New Beacon Books/George Padmore Institute: 1999), pp. 51–79; p. 70.
16. Kadija Sesay, 'Introduction', in Courttia Newland and Kadija Sesay (eds), *IC3: The Penguin Anthology of New Black Writing in Britain* (Penguin: London, 2000), pp. xii–xiv; p. xiii.
17. See Caryl Phillips 'Following On: The Legacy of Lamming and Selvon' (1998) in *A New World Order: Selected Essays* (London: Secker & Warburg, 2001), pp. 232–8.

18. *Ibid.*, p. 233.
19. See Caryl Phillips, 'Necessary Journeys', *Guardian Review*, Saturday, 11 December 2004, pp. 4–6.
20. Caryl Phillips, *op. cit.* (1998), p. 233.
21. Caryl Phillips, *The European Tribe* (Picador: London, 1987), pp. 7–8.
22. See Hanif Kureishi, 'The Rainbow Sign', in *My Beautiful Launderette and The Rainbow Sign* (Faber: London, 1986), pp. 8–38.
23. Maya Jaggi, 'Jackie Kay in Conversation', *Wasafiri*, 29 (1999), pp. 53–61; p. 55.
24. Dave Gunning, 'Anti-Racism, the Nation-State and Contemporary Black British Literature', *Journal of Commonwealth Literature*, 39(2) (2004), pp. 29–43; p. 31.
25. Sallie Westwood and Annie Phizacklea, *Trans-nationalism and the Politics of Belonging* (Routledge: London and New York, 2000), p. 2.
26. James Procter, 'General Introduction', in James Procter (ed.), *Writing Black Britain 1948–1998: An Interdisciplinary Anthology* (Manchester University Press: Manchester, 2000), pp. 1–12, p. 9.
27. Edward W. Said, *Culture and Imperialism* (London: Vintage, 1993), pp. 59–60.
28. Examples of Carter's non-fictional musings on 1970s Japanese culture can be found in her book *Nothing Sacred: Selected Writings* (London: Virago, 1982), pp. 29–57. Kelman speaks of his admiration for Selvon's use of 'dialect' in an interview with Maya Jaggi: 'I was struck by [Selvon's] The Lonely Londoners, and other Caribbean writers. I never met him – he was writer in residence at Dundee – but it would have been a short cut if I'd read him at 21'; see Maya Jaggi, 'Speaking in Tongues', *Guardian Weekend*, 18 July 1998, pp. 28–30, p. 30. For excellent discussions of Adam Thorpe's novels, see Ingrid Gunby, 'History in Rags: Adam Thorpe's reworking of England's national past', *Contemporary Literature*, 44(1) (2003), pp. 46–72, and ' "Dying of England": Melancholic Englishness in Adam Thorpe's *STILL*', in David Rogers and John McLeod (eds), *The Revision of Englishness* (Manchester: Manchester University Press, 2004), pp. 107–18.

6
'New Forms': Towards a Critical Dialogue with Black British 'Popular' Fictions

Andy Wood

> You're listening to the Streets
> Original pirate material
> Plucked down your ariel
>
> (The Streets, 'Has It Come To This?')[1]

The term 'street culture' has become shorthand for an urban, black or black influenced culture – raw, uncompromising and 'authentic'. That a white Brummie, Mike Skinner, could name his act The Streets and rap his way to critical acclaim and success in 2002 without being accused of wanting to be 'black' highlights the ways in which British youth culture has been so influenced by black styles and themes. Yet the terms 'urban' and 'street' are complex ones, often presented as simplistic shorthand for a 'black' culture that is debased, commercialized, unrealistic and compromised of themes and tropes, offering little more than a mythical, exaggerated view of life. Adrift from any significant engagement with mainstream culture or forms of political representation, street culture is seen as a marketing ploy, with a cynical eye cocked towards the success of the mainstream African-American forms derived from hip-hop culture. However, I would like to argue that street culture has a distinctly political role that can be traced back to the issues of representation, protest and identity politics that arose in the 1970s and 1980s. Rather than just a coded term denoting a form of popular culture or shorthand for 'black', the street is one of the most dynamic sites for the development, negotiation and contestation of a sense of black Britishness in the face of an often hostile reception from white Britons.

The street is also one of the key locations where black Britishness has been made visible, as the thoroughfares of Britain's inner-cities became a site for challenge, occupation and even celebration. Black British cultural forms, artists and texts have always engaged with the street, both as a site where non-white citizens go about their every day lives in Britain, and also as a place of communal and individual resistance. This bifurcated sense of the urban environment as simultaneously a location for 'home' and a site of conflict, runs through the works of many black British writers and artists. As this essay will show, the poetry of Linton Kwesi Johnson, a committed activist and writer, the violent world of Victor Headley's *Yardie* trilogy, the contemporary portrayals of inner-city life by authors such as Courttia Newland, Andrea Levy and Alex Wheatle, and the music of Dizzee Rascal and the 'grime' scene may be linked productively.[2] One common dominator occurring throughout all these seemingly disparate strands of black British creativity is that they are informed by, and feed into, a notion of street culture that has absorbed influences from the African diaspora in order to create styles and visions demonstrating that being black and being British are not mutually exclusive. The locations may be geographically specific or generic, but the texts portray them as complex sites, fraught with danger and conflict. Yet, equally, they are also communities, places of residence and, as such, territories worth negotiating, imagining, representing and defending.

Within a wider national context, black British popular culture has come to be portrayed as inextricably linked to street culture or style. Sometimes, this portrayal is negative and reductive. For example, the stylistic shorthand of gangster posturing and ostentatious display sometimes talked of as 'bling'[3] and more usually linked with US popular culture, is often employed to describe a wide and diverse range of black popular fiction and music. As such, in the eyes of many, street culture is not identified as a site of resistance or dwelling, but as a debased, homogenous style devoid of any meaningful political or social engagement. Moreover, critics have pointed to what they perceive to be the hegemonic influence of African-American culture upon black British forms. Part of the difficulty of discussing contemporary black British culture in the context of the street culture, thus stems from the way in which the term has become shorthand for a simplified generic and commodified form of black expression. Much of black music is described as urban, while black cultural styles are often simply labelled as 'street'. The majority of black people in Britain, and their attendant cultures, may be correctly described as hailing from a predominantly urban environment, however, problems arise when the specific British history of black settlement, political organization and its wide range of cultural expression is conflated uncritically with other black urban cultures from the United States or the Caribbean. For example, Kwame Dawes writes that 'in seeking to construct new myths for the British black world' authors such as Newland, Diran Adebayo and Q are working from a

> Fundamentally flawed premise: that black American experience is the same as the black British experience and that there is an interchangeability (which is really going in one direction) in the way that myth and style is approached in these two worlds.[4]

Dawes portrays black British fiction as a form dangerously in thrall to a pervasive, all-encompassing African-American aesthetic. Despite the 'strong foregrounding of blackness' that Dawes singles out for praise in novels such as *The Scholar*, *A Westside Story* and *Some Kind of Black*, he largely equates the world these novels portray with his view of African-American street culture. He argues that 'Newland's project [in *The Scholar*] is more fantasy than real because what he feeds [the readers] ... borrows so well from a mythic world of violence which is imported from another society'.[5]

But Dawes' critique relies upon a simplistic reading of black British cultures and their attendant productions. He asserts that many contemporary black British novelists and poets have largely chosen to adopt African-American culture as their model, as opposed to the 'reggae washed black British world of Linton Kwesi Johnson and Benjamin Zephaniah – an ethos that is quite coherent and quite well realised as a black British phenomenon'.[6] Dawes makes no mention of the fact that black music and culture has largely moved on from the earlier forms of reggae which inspired the work of Johnson and Zephaniah. He fails to note the ways that black British musical forms have mutated, a shift that is the result of a dialogue with black British diasporic styles, politics and forms, and not an imitative borrowing of the clothes of black America.

There is nothing new about this strand of Dawes argument. British reggae was often portrayed as inferior to Jamaican reggae while British forms of hip hop have been derided as poor imitations of the dominant American style. As with Dawes, such criticisms have been based upon the notion that black British forms have unthinkingly mimicked the 'authentic' original. Arguments, such as those outlined above, are often based upon an exceedingly limited and highly selective textual analysis. They offer flawed critical readings that ignore the multiple influences on, and dialogues between, different styles, forms and cultures, and show a lack of understanding of the diasporic and aesthetic modes of 'parental' musical forms. Both reggae and hip hop grew out of a number of influences. Reggae developed from the earlier Jamaican form ska, a musical style in itself which attempted to replicate and indigenize the African-American urban rhythm and blues music that was popular in the Caribbean. Hip-hop culture, Paul Gilroy notes, 'grew out of the cross-fertilisation of African-American vernacular cultures with their Caribbean equivalents rather than springing fully formed from the entrails of the blues'.[7] Asian and black British musical forms enter into a dialogue with a number of styles of music and do not simply borrow wholesale from a parent style or culture. In turn, such music has mutated and developed themes and styles that are distinctive to their locality. Black British forms, have documented and reflected upon what it means to be black and British in a society which often refuses to recognize that a number of its citizens can embrace both terms of identity. Indeed, black British music encompasses a diverse range of concerns, experiences and forms, from the politically engaged reggae of Linton Kwesi Johnson, Steel Pulse and Aswad, through the playful hip hop of the London Posse, Roots Manuva and Ty, to underground genres including jungle, garage and grime. That such work and artists had precursors and influences located elsewhere is, however, not to deny their specificity and locality, or their uniqueness and originality. Moreover, we should not underplay their ability to articulate a sense of black British identity, or fail to recognize the impact they have had on other mainstream cultural forms.

Recently, there has been some attempt to counter such reductive readings, notably, James Procter in *Dwelling Places*. Procter has sought to provide a complex and localized vision of representations of black British urban life in ways which focus upon the British context without ignoring wider transnational influences. Drawing on the works of Gilroy, Hall and Mercer, Procter acknowledges 'transatlantic correspondences' in styles, but argues that the subject 'need[s] also to be understood at a local level as part of a territorialized pedestrian culture ... a communal stance against "white oppression" on Britain's inner-city byways'.[8] As Procter suggests, any reading that takes seriously the sociology of street culture must challenge simplistic readings of black popular culture as culturally deviant. The blanket criminalization and vilification of black youths by sections of the state and media has a particularly long history, from the anxieties over the numbers of settlers and housing shortages in the 1950s and 1960s, to the racist stereotyping of blacks as criminals from the 1960s onwards.[9] Street culture and, by association, black culture has long been linked with criminality and used as a scapegoat for continuing failure in areas such as social provision (housing, education and employment), race relations legislation, and local and national political representation by the state. But when government ministers and newspaper columnists rail against what they perceive to be an amoral, nihilistic and violent black culture that promotes and glamorizes criminal activity,[10] they do so in terms that show how ill at ease modern Britain is with its non-white citizens, who are often second and third-generation children of migrant settlers.

In this essay, I want to explore the interface between literature and music, focusing on the representation, codification and narrating of street culture. While Asian and black British art, music, film and, to a lesser extent, television productions have achieved an increasing visibility and have been the focus of much critical attention and academic discourse, popular fiction has been less readily accepted, discussed or taught. Some individual authors have been critically acclaimed, yet many writers adopting popular forms of contemporary urban fiction have been excluded or marginalized. This has occurred despite the fact that their work often deals with important issues such as identity, representation, questions of race, class, gender and belonging. Paul Gilroy and Stuart Hall have made extensive use of art and music to develop a wider, more complex understanding of the development of the issues surrounding black British identities, but popular literature remains largely excluded from their analysis. This may be attributed to the authors' background in sociology and cultural studies, fields which tend to focus on audience and performativity, and not popular fiction. At this point, therefore, the task of engaging critically with popular writing by Asian and black British writers is both apt and urgent. The authors discussed in this essay, Linton Kwesi Johnson, Andrea Levy, Victor Headley, Courttia Newland and Alex Wheatle, all draw heavily on youth cultures and especially black musical forms. These street influences have a particular impact upon the writers' narrative techniques and, in this way, their works differ widely from those of novelists who simply employ youth cultural tropes to add authenticity or a sense of hipness to their work, without truly engaging in the multifaceted ways in which music operates as an organizing force in black British life.

Linton Kwesi Johnson (LKJ) has been a key influence, as writer, performer, journalist and record-label owner, in defining and developing a distinctly black British form of cultural production, which has its roots within the wider black diaspora. LKJ is a complex figure. He is a published poet who releases records and performs acapella or with a band; he attracts large audiences world-wide; and he is the second living poet to be anthologized by Penguin in the Penguin Classics imprint. Yet, he has also been derided as a polemicist who has wreaked havoc on the English language. LKJ's influence and connections are far flung: he has been involved with black power politics from the United States; developed an interest in theorists such as Aimé Césaire, Frantz Fanon and W.E.B. Du Bois; and employed in his own work the reggae music of Jamaica. LKJ brings to these diverse influences a particular perspective of black life in Britain. From the early 1970s onwards, his work has explicitly drawn upon his experiences of day-to-day life in Brixton and his role as a political activist.

LKJ began his writing career contributing journalism to *Race Today*, the in-house journal published by the radical Race Today Collective. In May 1973 he published his first poem, 'Five Nights Of Bleeding', in the same publication.[11] As an activist, journalist and London resident, LKJ had first-hand experience of the increasingly hostility that was and is directed at Britain's non-white citizens, and of the violence that fills their lives. 'Five Nights Of Bleeding' addresses both the racist violence experienced by, and internecine violence between, groups of black youths. The first verse gives a general account of the pressure building within black communities. Drawing from rasta-influenced reggae, the tone is ominous and full of dread:

> madness ... madness
> madness tight on the heads of the rebels

The subsequent five verses then list different outbreaks of violence in specific parts of London, mainly Brixton, as sites of recreation and leisure become scenes of violence. LKJ does not openly condemn such violence but the reader/audience is in no doubt of the foolishness and negativity of each event, as each verse culminates with the repeated refrain:

> it's war amongst the rebels
> madness ... madness ... war

Only in verse four does this refrain alter, as the source of the youths' anger is turned upon the real oppressor, the 'babylonian tyrants'. Thus, the community becomes enmeshed, not in civil war, but in a united attempt to defend and claim their own territory. With barely concealed satisfaction the narrator records that

> the song of blades was sounded
> the bile of oppression was vomited
> an two policemen wounded
> righteous righteous war[12]

In this refrain the pauses are omitted, so that the sense of dread and fore-boding are replaced with a feeling of satisfaction that the youths are fighting a common enemy in the form of the police. The flashpoint occurs when the police attempt to disperse the youths from outside the North London venue, where the African-American soul singer James Brown is performing. By moving outside of the immediate locale of Brixton, where the bulk of the violence occurs, the black youths are enabled to unite against a common foe, rather than expending their energies battling one another over small-scale territorial disputes. Beyond their individual communities the youths lose their false consciousness and take out their anger and frustration on the most visible agents of a racist and coercive state.

Given the range of themes and styles employed in LKJ's work over the past four decades this may seem a rather fleeting analysis. However, in looking at 'Five Nights of Bleeding', I wish to suggest a lineage between LKJ's 1970s work, itself connected to a longer tradition of diasporic black influences, and that of contemporary artists working in popular genres and styles. LKJ employs aspects of music and musical cultures, along with the street as a location, in his music and poetry, which is full of references to reggae artists, sound systems and record shops, together with quotes from lyrics. For LKJ music is central to much of his literary output, and such amalgamations may be seen in the works of younger writers and musicians, who similarly focus upon questions of identity and belong-ing. Other key themes developed by LJK, and adopted by more modern artists, are the complex issue of representation and the recording and documenting of a forgotten or ignored history of black British postwar life. Significantly, this does not preclude criticisms of aspects of black British life (particularly the internecine violence discussed by LKJ in the above poem) and white society. The texts discussed in this essay often refuse to accept the burden of representation, and reject the demand to portray the communities the authors 'belong' to in a positive light, no matter how fragmented or heterogeneous they may be.

These, then, are some of the themes that recur in black British musical forms and novels dealing with urban life. In discussing these issues, Mark Stein suggests that one of the main forms of black British fiction is the *Bildungsroman* or novel of transformation. Moreover, he argues that this transformation impacts not only upon individual characters and narrators, but also upon the concept of Britishness.[13] The fact that the transformations of individual characters are often incomplete or nega-tive, reflects the foreshortened and fragmented narrative of Britain as a truly multiracial society. For example, Courttia Newland's debut novel

The Scholar ends with the two main characters' lives shattered, as one ends up in prison and the other in enforced exile.[14] Newland, along with Diran Adebayo, have followed Mike Phillips in adopting the crime genre as a framework in which to explore a hidden narrative of race relations and racial politics, while reversing the dominant stereotype of the black male as criminal 'other'. Newland's *Snakeskin* portrays the story of a private investigator, Erwin James, as he traverses an often hostile England, isolated from his peers and community as he attempts to solve the brutal murder of a black politician's daughter.[15] In a different narrative form, Alex Wheatle and Andrea Levy also incorporate transformative elements as they excavate the recent histories of postwar black British life. They explore the lives of settlers and their British-born children in a range of contexts drawing upon youth culture, history and the conflicts involved in developing a sense of belonging in an often hostile environment.[16]

Black British 'pulp' fiction, a fairly new genre in itself, works in the same ways. Inaugurated with the publication of Victor Headley's debut novel *Yardie* by the small black British press The X Press in 1992, publishers and booksellers began to be aware of the potential demand for fiction written from the perspective of black Britons for a black audience.[17] At the same time, Headley's *Yardie* trilogy and The X Press has been the subject of much controversy. The debate surrounding the representation of a small segment of black life in Headley's novels often involve a misreading of the texts which are highly moralistic crime thrillers at heart. The novels also attempt to portray a diverse range of characters, many of them who are sympathetically drawn, and who struggle to improve the lives of the communities they live and work in. In Headley's narratives, crime, ultimately, does not pay. In the final analysis, the only result for many of the protagonists is death or incarceration. The trilogy engages in forms of culture and life that are often brutal and profane, but equally in ways that are tenderly and beautifully drawn. Music is also a life-affirming force, an important method of developing a sense of communal identity, as in the reggae festival organized in the final novel of the *Yardie* trilogy *Yush!*, and a way to assist youths in escaping crime, in developing a sense of their history and identity, as well as offering an outlet for creativity and a way to earn money.

In his book *London Calling. How Black and Asian Writers Imagined a City*, Sukhdev Sandhu describes an 'improper London'. By this he means a vision of the metropolis in direct opposition to the picture postcard London depicted by an earlier generation of Asian and black writers such as Sam Selvon, George Lamming and V.S. Naipaul. Improper London is a dangerous, previously unimagined or unrecorded environment, which is located not in the tourist sites, railway stations, bed-sits and basements of the city, but in the streets. Sandhu's exploration of the London of inner-city ghettoes, poverty, protest and strife suggests a uniquely masculine environment. Sandhu links the political poetry of LKJ to the violent world of Victor Headley's *Yardie* trilogy through the ways in which their works 'include a strident masculinity' and 'employ music as both a soundtrack and harbinger of metropolitan meltdown'.[18]

Sandhu's failure to concern himself with contemporary female voices dealing with street life appears to be a curious omission, although Procter does identify a lack of female voices directly writing about the street in the 1970s. For example, Sandhu writes that LKJ romanticizes 'a vision of London street culture – full of hustling, dread, strutting machismo – whose social manifestation he deplores',[19] while Headley falls 'into the trap of exalting the social deformation he claims to lament'.[20] But female authors, such as Levy, Leone Ross and Headley's female counterparts at the X Press, must be considered as they serve to complicate the masculine reading of urban fiction.

The lyrics of contemporary artists Est'elle, Ms. Dynamite and Shystie, and Andrea Levy's 1996 novel *Never Far From Nowhere* provide alternatives to the masculinized spaces of the street. These contemporary artists have been influenced, perhaps, by the earlier generation of writers, such as Buchi Emecheta, Beryl Gilroy and Joan Riley, who sought to represent feminised spaces in the home and the workplace. But in their works generational conflicts, poverty, schooling, class, gender and conflict are all dealt with in a manner that both emphasizes the joys of family and friendship, while simultaneously engaging directly with the tribulations of urban life. All of these texts draw heavily upon street culture, but in very different ways. The authors narrate and describe the streets of an improper London, whether in Shystie's east London (Hackney) or Levy's evocation of early 1970s north London (Finsbury Park). Each artist engages with notions of street culture in ways that negotiate, and even undermine some of the texts discussed elsewhere. They share a number of similar concerns with the male-authored texts described briefly above, but deal with them in ways that eschew the, at times, individualistic machismo of a Headley or a number of black British musicians. This is not to suggest that Newland or Wheatle, to give two examples, do not portray a range of emotions and characters – including female characters – sympathetically, but to posit that the female artists under discussion are confident in their dialogue with urban life and treat such themes in ways that are often more subtle and complex. They are unhappy with mere representation as well as with simply constructing feminized versions of male-authored

texts. Instead, they construct their own representations in direct negotiation with those by male writers. Similarly, they call upon the tradition
of *bildingsroman* drawing upon autobiographical details, youth cultures,
and the process of growing up in Britain, but they use humour to deal
with their immediate environment. For example, in *Never Far From
Nowhere*, Levy revisits the decades of the 1980s/1990s as well as early
1970s from a women's perspective. In doing so, these works help to create
alternative histories and stories of black Britain that are absent from
many published accounts.

The problematization of black British street culture by female artists
is more acute in the world of popular music than in that of urban fiction
publishing. Black musical forms rooted in street culture are often portrayed, as with Headley and LKJ's work, as celebrations of a hyper-
masculinity. In this world women are portrayed as trophies or as 'ho's'
(whores) and bitches. Rap lyrics abound with references to grasping and
scheming women who threaten to emasculate men, robbing them not
only of their wallets but also their credibility and manhood. Over the
last few years a number of successful female artists have emerged from
the predominantly boys-own clubs of UK garage, hip hop and 'grime', to
sign their own record contracts, top the charts and garner critical acclaim.
In doing so, these artists have developed a uniquely women's perspective
on the world they live in. They engage with a female audience, as well
as the male musical scene they have emerged from.[21] When Shystie
demands at the start of 'Woman's World', 'Boys sit down, ladies stand
up', it is difficult to imagine this as anything other than a form of empowerment in the context of a live performance or dancehall.[22] Ms. Dynamite is
probably the best known of the female performers, having won the
Mercury Music Prize for her debut album *A Little Deeper*.[23] She is also a
writer and performer who is firmly located within a black British urban
experience, but is spoken of positively by the establishment, having been
praised by critics and politicians for her outspoken stance against gun crime
in black communities. Before her successful solo career, Ms. Dynamite
was an MC, writing lyrics and performing in a largely male-dominated
underground scene at raves and on records such as 'Ramp'.

The lyrics of Ms. Dynamite's '1980' and 'Dy-na-mi-tee', along with
Est'elle's '1980', describe a childhood where the lack of money and
resources cast a long shadow over family life; yet they also affirm a sense
of community.[24] Despite the absence of male figures, these words detail
the positive influences of female family members and friends. Both sets
of lyrics contextualize the relatively impoverished backgrounds of their
authors in a manner that suggests they are speaking to a wider audience

who may have little understanding of the material world of the artist, seeing only the glamorous image portrayed by musicians. It is equally valid to suggest, however, that the lyrics also address another audience, one which clearly understands the black urban background of the artist:

> I grew up in the 1980s
> In a four bedroom house
> My family, my granma an' three or four aunties
> Uncles and brothers in an' out of prison daily
> Certain time when there was no heat we'd stay under covers
> There was life like you never seen
>
> Yo I'm that same little girl that grew up next 2 u
> Went through all the things a teenage girl goes through
> Hangin' out all night and breaking my curfew
> When my daddy hit the door I gave my mumma the blues
> Use 2 spend my time blazin' lazin' days away
> Thought I was grown left home at 15 didn't wanna obey
> Had 2 get my act together couldn't take the heat
> And now I'm makin' beats 4 the streets[25]

These lyrics chart a move from powerlessness to empowerment, and a major source of this empowerment is music, which fosters a sense of identity and belonging, giving pleasure and enriching the lives of those involved in listening to and performing the song.

Est'elle is a younger artist than Ms. Dynamite, having only risen to prominence in 2004 when she achieved chart success with her debut single '1980' and album *The 18th Day*.[26] Lyrically and musically both artists share similar styles and common ground, although Est'elle's background is in gospel and hip hop rather than the more underground garage scene. Est'elle also depicts a familial development, but her lyrics in '1980' additionally register a growing awareness of her historical position and a consequent identification with wider black culture:

> Me an' my cousin used to play Mel and Kim
> Practisin' dancing, coming down the stairs and sing
> I touched Africa an' came back darker
> Knowing myself and feeling my roots a little bit harder[27]

Although she recognizes the lack of material possessions, Est'elle's lyrics and music are upbeat, drawing on black musical forms such as hip hop, soul and gospel.

Significantly, both Ms. Dynamite and Est'elle are hostile towards those who would glamorize crime and the criminal lifestyle. In 'It Takes More' Ms. Dynamite is critical of the perpetrators of black-on-black violence stating 'U talkin' like a G but ur a killer killin' ur own/ur just a racist mans pussy.'[28] The culture of conspicuous consumption and the ostentatious display of wealth are also critiqued when Dynamite asks 'If it's not 2 complex/Tell me how many Africans died 4 the baguettes/on your Rolex?'[29] Both artists emphasize the importance of community and of the responsibility of being role models for women as successful female artists. While promoting an often positive message, neither artist shies away from dealing with the often harsh realities of urban life in Britain. Black music and musicians are seen to have an important role to play as a vehicle for both protest and communication. However, when drawn into the debate surrounding the culture minister Kim Howells' ill-judged attempt to lay the blame for gun crime on black artists who 'created a culture where killing is almost a fashion accessory', Ms. Dynamite responded that Howells was talking 'bullshit'.[30] In a genre where concepts of authenticity and 'keeping it real' are crucial in retaining the support of their core audience, Ms. Dynamite has managed successfully to negotiate the difficult task of maintaining the respect of an often highly critical black British audience, while at the same time criticizing aspects of black British urban life and some of her fellow artists who she perceives to be glamorizing internecine violence. Howells and the then Home Secretary David Blunkett's comments on 'idiotic rappers'[31] were seen to be highly charged and ill-thought out. Howells attempted to co-opt Ms. Dynamite as a representative of how he believed a black British artist should act, a role which she volubly declined. Ms. Dynamite has been careful to avoid both cooperation with the state apparatus and unqualified criticism, successfully retaining her role as an articulate and respected commentator on urban black British life. As Est'elle explains:

> [hip hop is] a way of speaking to people. It's brought people together; I feel that it's music and music, period, that moves people. It's the most popular art form right now ... if all these hip hop artists are down for it and they're so popular with the kids, maybe we should use it.[32]

Both Ms. Dynamite and Est'elle are able to address political issues because they draw upon a diverse range of black diasporic styles, from gospel, hip hop, soul and reggae, thereby ensuring that their music, performances, videos and lyrics are embedded within an urban black British cultural idiom. They eschew the bland Americanisms of an earlier generation of British rap artists, mixing a diverse array of musical styles with accents, words and images that locate them in specific urban locales. And their lyrics that talk of life in Britain rather than the Bronx. In so doing, they forge links with an earlier generation of those British reggae artists who developed styles that were as urban specific as they were diasporic – Steel Pulse's Handsworth, LKJ's Brixton and Aswad's Ladbroke Grove being but three examples.

The third female street artist to be considered here is Shystie, although her position is far more complex. Shystie began performing and recording as a member of the Roll Deep Crew, an east London collective which also consisted of Dizzee Rascal. Her debut album employs a more earthy, streetwise and often bawdy representation of contemporary urban life. For example, on her first single, a version of Dizzee's 'I Luv U', she portrays herself as a heartless gold-digger playing the 'bad bwoys' at their own games and winning easily – on her own terms.[33] The original version of 'I Luv U' whose vocals and perspectives are shared between vocalists of different sexes, explores modern gender relations in an unflinching, and satirical manner. In Shystie's version, it is her voice and viewpoint:

> Now bruv you're stupid
> You mean I thought? – There's no cupid
> You got played
> I'm a wild renegade
> I'm never gonna change
> It's just the way I'm made[34]

She employs satire, parody, wit and humour to undermine the casual and sometimes serious misogyny of those in the hip hop and 'grime' scenes. But, rather than countering misogyny with chauvinistic inverse or exchanging one form of abuse for another, she deconstructs the dominant discourse with humour. The gender role-reversal of 'Woman's World' starts out with such just such a portrait:

> Imagine if men lived in kennels like dogs
> And we only let them out to do the difficult jobs
> In the street, walk them around
> Leads around their neck
> Show him to my friend saying,
> 'He's my new pet'[35]

The song culminates in the hilarious portrait of men being forced to depilate and shave, and women walking around with beards and body hair, while a chorus of female voices respond with, 'ERGHHH!' Yet, there is a seriousness to the satire in 'Women's world'; as Shystie reminds her listeners, 'Yeah we crossed the line / but men do that shit all the time.'[36] Shystie stages a dystopian fantasy where women exact revenge on the worst aspects of male behaviour. However, her world is not merely a simplistic inversion, instead she asks her audience to make an imaginative leap: 'Now imagine if this whole globe was run by jus women / Jeeze gor blimme what a world we would live in.'[37] The second line suggests that, for Shystie, the humorous suggestion must be linked to serious intent. Other lyrics which negotiate with, and include, male voices and texts include, 'I Luv U' and 'One Wish'. In the latter, Shystie talks of how, from a young age, she ran with the local boys, not as a girlfriend or target of sexual attention but as an equal, learning from their mistakes and attempting to avoid the pitfalls that so many of her contemporaries have fallen into – prison, death, poverty.

As with Est'elle and Ms. Dynamite, childhood and youth are employed as central narrative themes. The opening verse of 'One Wish' resonates with '1980' and 'Dy-na-mi-tee':

> Yea, I can say my lifes been hard
> Six of us lived in a two bedroom yard
> So I keep this in mind
> Full well knowing
> I know where I've been
> So I know where I'm going.[38]

Shystie's environment (Hackney) is a complex terrain consisting not only of a sense of danger and threat but, in common with Courttia Newland's fictitious west London estate of Greenside and Alex Wheatle's early 1980s Brixton, diverse communities which offer a sense of belonging and identity. Shystie notes that the 'ghetto' is not just a war-zone, where the battle for survival and for a sense of identity must be fought on a daily basis, but also a location where people live, act and dream. In 'One Wish' she tells her audience that: 'The hood holds loyalty / the hood holds faith / The hood holds struggle / And the hood holds rage.'[39]

As with the other texts discussed in this essay, Shystie is interested in questions of representation: how she represents herself and her subjects, as well as the ways in which she is herself subject to representation. The song 'Questions' stages Shystie's appearance on a hip-hop styled chat show, 'The Nathan Never Show'.[40] The lyrics set up a dialogue between the laughably boorish host and Shystie. Nathan Never introduces Shystie as the woman he would, 'love to get between the sheets' before going on to ask her if she slept her way to fame.[41] Showing his complete lack of knowledge of British music, Never then goes on to talk about the relationships of multi-million selling African-American rap artists, before throwing open the floor for questions. The audience submit clichéd queries, such as did you have to sell crack 'to put clothes on your back', and they appear bemused when Shystie does not conform to their expectations as a working-class black rapper.[42] Cleverly, Shystie negotiates the questions with a mixture of humour and intelligence before directing her rage at the hapless host as the audience cheer her on. Shystie may claim that she is from the gutter, but she articulates the dangers of stereotyping and misrepresentation with a mixture of anger and humour.

In another politically laden song, 'One Wish', Shystie describes the problems facing black youths of both sexes from the impoverished ghettoes of London. Similarly, 'Bank Robbery' describes the act of committing crime in realistic and imaginative settings, the difference between fantasy and reality becoming obvious when the execution of the crime goes wrong.[43] As with Ms. Dynamite and Est'elle, Shystie's lyrics are written in the first person, a common feature in 'grime', rap and other black musical styles. As such, the songs might direct the listener to an autobiographical reading, yet to do so would be misleading. Songs such as 'I Luv U', 'Women's World' and 'Bank Robbery' are fantasies, responding to and playfully subverting existing texts, records and orthodoxies.

This essay began with an overview of black British street culture that covered both popular music and fiction, before dealing more specifically with male and female musicians. The undercutting of the masculinized versions of hip hop and reggae discussed in relation to the works of Ms. Dynamite, Est'elle and Shystie are, however, paralleled by female authors in the world of fiction. In the final section, I wish to turn to more detailed exploration of Andrea Levy's novels and discuss the way in which they contribute to new forms of street culture and black British writing.

*   *   *

Mark Stein has suggested that Andrea Levy's fiction are 'semi-autobiographical', a judgement echoed by Mike Phillips in his discussion with Andrea Levy following a reading at London Wall Museum in July 2004.[44] It is possible to read aspects of Levy's novel, *Never Far From Nowhere*, as autobiographical; for example, the story is set in the north London estates of Highbury and Finsbury Park in the early 1970s where Levy herself grew up.[45] However, the fact that the plot alternates between first-person narratives of two very different characters, Olive and her younger sister Vivien, both of whom experience London life very differently, demands that the work be read primarily as a work of fiction. Olive exists in a state of permanent conflict with her mother, a first-generation migrant from the Caribbean. Olive's darker skin marks her out as different; at an early age, she becomes aware of problems of being black in Britain. After becoming pregnant, Olive cuts herself off from her past life, leaving her employment and nights of clubbing behind her; but as a single mother she finds herself increasingly isolated and struggling to bring up her baby daughter. Vivien, unlike her older sister, negotiates the streets, youth clubs and pubs of north London with relative ease, making and casting off friends as it suits her with a degree of confidence that Olive does not possess. For most of the novel, Vivien also shifts between different social groups and classes with ease, and, when asked about her origins, she invariably identifies herself as a Londoner. Although both sisters experience racism, the lighter-skinned Vivien does not see herself as 'black'.

Like Shystie's east London, the north London of the 1970s is depicted as a violent and dangerous environment. But, unlike the other texts discussed in this essay, the urban milieu of *Never Far from Nowhere* is largely devoid of black faces. The girls' mother looks down on her fellow Jamaicans, whom she sees as being of a different class and, consequently, a cause of embarrassment to her. Despite the family's poverty and the fact that they live in a decaying housing estate, the girls' mother continues to believe that she is both respectable and accepted by the host community. Olive understands that this is not the case, but Vivien exhibits some of her mother's snobbery, telling her white boyfriend Eddie that her parents are from Mauritius rather than Jamaica.

As a result of her skin colour, Olive's experiences of racism are far more direct than Vivien's. At its harshest, Peter, Olive's white husband and the father of her daughter, leaves her for a white woman. While struggling to negotiate the bureaucratic labyrinth of the welfare state as a single mother, Olive witnesses first-hand the kind of racial politics that were becoming widespread in 1970s Britain:

> Then this big fat white man came in and stood at the back of my queue and started shouting. 'We're always queuing up 'cause of those fucking wogs over there.' Right at the top of his voice he shouted. People turned round to look at him. He pointed to two black people who were serving behind the counter, taking cards and getting people to sign things. 'What's a matter with everyone? People are fucking scared of

'em. Fucking coons. I wouldn't be here if it wasn't for those fucking wogs, and nobody does anything – they're fucking scared of 'em.'

Then people just turned back, uninterested. Nobody said anything to him, not even the people behind the counter, who looked up when he started but then carried on like they'd heard it all before.[46]

The complicit silence in the office is deafening. Because of this silence, which is shared by the two black co-employees who opt to ignore the man, and because she realizes that nothing she can say would psychologically wound the white man in the way his racist words have wounded, Olive remains silent. The belligerent white man's words predict a simplistic racism that would gain momentum as the 1970s unfolded. The man blames his lack of gainful employment on Asian and black people, whom he believes are displacing whites in the labour market. Despite evidence to the contrary, organizations such as the National Front would gather momentum in their campaigns to intimidate, verbally and physically abuse Asian and black peoples in the streets where they lived.

Vivien's encounters with racism are more indirect, as she is able to pass for white. Through her white friends Carol, Pam and Linda, and their involvement with local boys who define themselves as skinheads, she witnesses racist abuse directed at other black people and an assault upon a black youth who attempts to chat her up. This incident finally impels Vivien to distance herself from the group. Of greater significance to Vivien's characterization is the issue of class, as she traverses the different social strata associated with different groups of friends, struggling to keep abreast of changes in fashion and music. When she moves to Canterbury to attend art college, Vivien attempts to develop her own sense of identity. Here, among her more privileged upper-class art school colleagues, the issue of class looms large, as she is defined less by skin colour than by her apparent working-class background. A wealthy student remarks ironically that Vivien has 'a wonderful cockney accent that [she was] ... completely jealous of'.[47] In order to fit in, Vivien tells her fellow students that she is from Islington rather than Finsbury Park. Away from the streets of north London, one senses that she is out of her depth socially. Relating the interests of her new colleagues – 'horses, gym tournaments, violins, cellos, drama clubs'[48] – Vivien realizes she has nothing in common with any of her new peer group. Even though Vivien attempts to shed her urban black identity, the novel directs the reader back towards her origins, leaving an uncomfortable duality in which Vivien is neither a middle-class white woman, nor a working-class black woman heralding from the street culture of north London.

Olive does not experience the same geographical displacement as Vivien, yet her relationship to black street culture is equally as difficult. For Olive, the streets remain an increasingly dangerous location despite having gained a degree of self-confidence and independence, which living in her own flat and learning to drive has served to develop. This relative equilibrium is shattered when Olive is stopped by the police as she drives a borrowed van; the officers racially abuse her, plant cannabis in her bag and proceed to arrest her. Olive is charged with the possession of illegal drugs and her solicitor recommends that she plead guilty despite her constant protestations of innocence. Shortly after her sister's arrest, Vivien returns home for a brief visit. The two argue over Olive's plight. Vivien refuses to believe that the police can be the perpetrators of harassment and ill-treatment of black people on the streets of London. Olive, angered by what she believes to be Vivien's betrayal and her attempts to blend into a white, middle-class culture, attacks her sister, telling her, 'you'll never be accepted. It won't be all right for you – one day you'll see – it won't.'[49] In turn, Vivien accuses Olive of jealousy, telling her that she always has to blame someone else for her own problems. Olive's words and the novel's title convey succinctly the conflict inherent in questions of black identity and belonging in the early 1970s. At the end of the novel, Olive is on the brink of moving to Jamaica with her daughter, believing that she will be accepted there because they are 'black'. In opposition to her daughter's decision, her mother tells her: 'All this black colour stuff. I tell her "you're just you" and she belong here where she was born.'[50] For Olive's mother, returning to Jamaica is neither an option, nor is 'black' a point of identification. Politicized by her first-hand experiences of individual and institutional racism, though, Olive defines herself as black rather than British. Her family's stubborn approach to questions of race and identity has little efficacy in helping her face the realities of life in Britain, for a British-born child of migrants. Olive feels that she will be forever defined negatively by the white racists and by the silent majority who are complicit with such racism. Olive's story lends subtle support towards the politicization of black British citizens. Denied citizenship rights, harassed on the streets by racists and the police, demonized by the media, increasingly under- or unemployed, black communities set up a network of community support and organizations in order to raise political consciousness. Flight rather than fight may in Olive's case be no real solution, but in the absence of a visible black net-work to turn to for support, it has a strong appeal. Significantly, Levy does not give readers a sense of how things will work out for Olive. However, the final conversation between Vivien and a fellow passenger on a train hints that things might work out well for the younger sister. The woman asks:

> 'Where do you come from, dear?' I looked at my reflection in the train window – I've come a long way, I thought. Then I wondered what country she would want me to come from as I looked in her eyes. 'My family are from Jamaica', I told her. 'But I am English.'[51]

Thus, at the close of the novel, Levy posits two distinct endings. For Olive, a reassertion of her black identity takes the form of a return to Jamaica, although the success of national and racial reclamation is left undecided. Vivien, on the other hand, represents the way in which many young black people, while acknowledging their racial identity, sought to integrate themselves in British society. The geographical division of West Indies versus London, parallels the roles of the two characters, offering a bipartite resolution in which neither a return to the homeland or an embeddedness in the London urban scene can be seen as offering the equilibrium both sisters seek.

Vivien has indeed 'come a long way' in her search for a black British identity, as have the black communities, artists and writers discussed in this essay. While Levy's novel leaves the reader to contemplate different futures for the two sisters, its final paragraph resonates with LKJ's line in 'It Dread Inna Inglan', 'Come what may, we are here to stay.' More importantly, each of the texts discussed here represent a street culture that does not simply act as a commodity or genre, but functions as a complex site of protest, community and identity formation – a place where issues of representation and the right to be black and British are fought for in the face of seemingly insurmountable and intransigent opposition. There are clearly identifiable differences within this community of interests, for example the shifts between feminized and masculine street cultures. As such, street texts must be seen to represent a diverse and distinctive strand in contemporary Asian and black British expressive cultures, and therefore demand to be read against hegemonic and reductive readings of such cultures.

Finally, in suggesting the title 'New Forms' I should perhaps have added a question mark. As original as these texts may be, they are part of a longer lineage of black British culture, with roots in Britain, in the Caribbean and in North America. But at the same time these texts are integral to mainstream popular culture. The black street narratives thus penetrate into British history and political life in ways that suggest a complex community of interests, rather than a homogenous black British fiction that can be easily categorized or dismissed.

Notes

1. The Streets, *Original Pirate Material* (London: Locked On, 2002).
2. Linton Kwesi Johnson, *Mi Revolueshanary Fren: Selected Poems* (London: Penguin, 2002). Victor Headley, *Yardie* (London: The X Press, 1992) and *Yush* (London: The X press, 1994). Courttia Newland, *The Scholar. A West Side Story* (London: Abacus, 1998) and *Snakeskin* (London: Abacus, 2000). Andrea Levy, *Never Far From Nowhere* (London: Review, 1996). Alex Wheatle, *Brixton Rock* (London: Black Amber Books, 1999).

   'Grime' is a term used by musicians, producers, promoters and rappers including Dizzee Rascal, Wiley and the Mo Fire Crew. Drawing on a wide array of black musical styles, grime is an experimental, raw underground scene, which portrays life in specific 'ghetto' areas and disassociates itself from the 'bling' culture of the garage scene. To date, the scenes biggest success has been that of Dizzee Rascal, whose debut album *Boy In Da Corner* won the 2003 Mercury Music Prize. The scene remains defiantly unassailable and resolutely underground with those involved unable to reach agreement on the term 'grime'. It remains to be seen as to whether the mainstream will attempt to co-opt this scene or whether it will continue to mutate and develop on its own terms.

   This essay will also consider three female street artists: Ms. Dynamite, Est'elle and Shystie.
3. 'Bling', i.e. sparkling diamonds.
4. Kwame Dawes, 'Negotiating The Ship On The Head: Black British Fiction', *Wasafari*, 29 (1999).
5. Dawes, *op. cit.* p. 22.
6. *Ibid.*, p. 21.
7. Paul Gilroy, *The Black Atlantic. Modernity and Double Consciousness* (Harvard: Harvard University Press, 1993), p. 103. Gilroy also clearly elucidates the fact that as well as Caribbean influences on hip hop being marginalized in popular accounts of its history, the considerable Hispanic input into all aspects of hip-hop culture has largely been excluded.
8. James Procter, *Dwelling Places: Postwar Black British Writing* (Manchester: Manchester University Press, 2003) p. 72.
9. For a more in depth analysis of the radicalization of crime in Britain see Paul Gilroy, *There Ain't No Black in the Union Jack* (London: Routledge, 1987), and Procter *op. cit.* especially chapter 3.
10. For example see 'Minister labelled racist after attack on rap "idiots"', *Guardian,* 6 January 2003.
11. Reprinted in Johnson, *op. cit.*
12. Johnson, *op. cit.* pp. 6–8.
13. Mark Stein, *Black British Literature: Novels of Transformation* (Columbus: Ohio State University Press, 2004).
14. Newland, *op. cit.* (1998).
15. Newland, *op. cit.* (2000).
16. Wheatle, *op. cit.* Levy, *op. cit.*; a full discussion of Levy's novel may be found below, pp. 119–23.
17. Headley, *op. cit.* (1992).
18. Sukhdev Sandhu, *London Calling. How Black and Asian Writers Imagined a City* (London: HarperCollins), pp. 392, 342.

19. *Ibid.*, p. 364.
20. *Ibid.*, p. 384.
21. It is worth noting that one of the most successful British rap groups were the all-female South London group The Cookie Crew who enjoyed chart success in the late 1980s and collaborated with leading hip-hop producers while retaining a distinctly British viewpoint on songs such as 'From The South' and 'Born This Way'.
22. Shystie, 'Woman's World', *Diamond in the Dirt* (London: Polydor, 2004).
23. Ms. Dynamite, *A Little Deeper* (London: Polydor, 2002).
24. *Ibid.*
25. Est'elle, '1980,' *The 18th Day* (London: v2, 2004) and Ms. Dynamite, 'Dy-na-mi-tee' from the album *A Little Deeper* (London: Polydor, 2002).
26. Est'elle, *The 18th Day* (London: V2, 2004).
27. *Ibid.*
28. Ms. Dynamite, *op. cit.*
29. *Ibid.*
30. *The Guardian*, 6 January 2003.
31. *Ibid.*
32. Est'elle interviewed by Melissa Bradshaw, *Plan b magazine*, 5 (2004), p. 68.
33. Shystie, 'I Luv U' (London: white label, 2003).
34. *Ibid.*
35. Shystie, 'Woman's World,' *op. cit.*
36. *Ibid.*
37. *Ibid.*
38. *Ibid.*
39. *Ibid.*
40. *Ibid.*
41. *Ibid.*
42. *Ibid.*
43. *Ibid.*
44. Stein, *op. cit.* p. 192.
45. Levy, *op. cit.*
46. *Ibid.*, p. 178.
47. *Ibid.*, p. 247.
48. *Ibid.*, p. 247.
49. *Ibid.*, p. 279.
50. *Ibid.*, p. 281.
51. *Ibid.*, p. 282.

Part III
Genealogies and Interventions

7
Texts of Cultural Practice: Black Theatre and Performance in the UK

Michael McMillan

Introduction

> Burn the cork in a saucer with alcohol. Once completely burnt, mash to a fine paste. Then rub a cake of cocoa butter lightly over the face, ears, and neck, then apply a broad streak of carmine to the lips carrying it well beyond the corners of the mouth, then take a little of the prepared burnt cork, moisten it with water, and rub it carefully on the face, ears, neck, and hands being careful to avoid touching the lips. Put on the wig, wipe the palms of the hands clean, and the makeup is completed.[1]

The above quote taken from my new play, *Master Juba*, describes the makeup process white performers used to become a blackface minstrel and thus grotesquely caricature black culture. It was one of the most popular forms of entertainment during the nineteenth century, yet race was not allowed to be mixed on stage, until black performers blacked up and imitated white minstrels imitating them. Historically, black people in theatre were not writers or directors, but on-stage spectacles shoring up the colonial imagination of the other. Like Morgan Smith, Ira Aldridge came to Europe to escape racism in the United States during the nineteenth century and played a number of Shakespeare's leading male roles to popular acclaim. But he experienced similar discrimination in England and fled, eventually finding recognition and prominence in his tours of Western and Eastern Europe. His innovative contribution to the development of the Method School of Acting has still not been fully credited.[2]

It wasn't until the mid-1970s that the BBC, the bastion of 'balanced' broadcasting, decided it was time to take *The Black and White Minstrel Show* off the air. This programme, based on the first American theatre tradition, says more about the hegemony of a colonial fantasy constructed in the nineteenth century than about the black subject. In this Eurocentric discourse, black performers have been viewed more as strange exotic others, rather than skilled practitioners, reflecting the fear and desire of the black body as sexualized object. While black cultural practices have been appropriated, they are represented as inferior and marginal to the European canon and unsophisticated derivatives of Western forms and traditions.[3] *The Black and White Minstrel Show* in the late twentieth century suggests to us that race is not only inscribed in popular entertainment, but that the black body and culture as object and commodity are at the core of popular culture. It is against this hegemonic representation of the black performer that Amiri Baraka coined the phrase 'Black Theatre' during the late 1960s, when the Civil Rights Movements reflected a wider anti-colonial struggle globally.[4]

Much of the discourse around black theatre is in the context of the African diaspora. But diaspora has to be used metaphorically, as 'diaspora does not refer us to those scattered tribes whose identity can only be secured in relation to some sacred homeland to which they must at all costs return'. It is defined, 'not by essence or purity, but recognition of a necessary heterogeneity and diversity: by a conception of "identity" that lives with and through as process, the idea of difference, of hybridity'.[5] While diasporic transdialogues have sustained cultural practices in the UK over at least three generations, such temporal shifts are not smooth linear movements, but contested moments, as the next generation struggles over the meaning of their legacies. This is compounded, because black cultural practices, such as black theatre in the UK, have often suffered from fragmentation due to institutional and funding insecurities and lack of proper historical documentation and analysis, except for the odd hidden studies in the academy. In looking at cultural practices amongst black arts practitioners, the notion of generation has often been overlooked and/or overdetermined. If the notion of generation is historically inscribed, whose history is represented? Whose history becomes legitimized as the dominant version? If a canon is about legacy, and a legacy is what is enduring, my essay attempts to move beyond the notion of black theatre in Britain, towards black British theatre as a metaphor for identities in the process of becoming. Therefore, while I acknowledge and will refer to the antecedents of this diverse range of practices which constitute black theatre in a British context, my focus is on the intergenerational work beginning in the 1970s.

The front room

Black cultural practices in the UK are influenced by the wider black experience. Both my parents came from St Vincent in the 1960s and like many postwar black settlers looking for somewhere to live, they instead found in Elizabeth Regina's land signs saying, 'No Dogs, No Irish, No Coloured.' Many of these immigrants slept three to a bed in one room. Before the sun rose on cold winter mornings, they returned from the night shift, enduring the same coldness in the workplace as their children did in the classroom. With a growing family consisting of children born in the UK or sent for from back home, larger homes were necessary. Capital to make deposits on prospective properties was generated through the 'Partner Hand' and 'Susu' system of informal community banking.[6] Inscribed in the representation of the black experience on British television in sitcoms, such as *The Fosters*, *Empire Road* and *Desmonds*, was a narrative discourse about intergenerational conflict, shifting identities and desires. The site for this contestation was usually the front room, which became an emblematic motif embodying the 'West Indian' parent as 'speaky-spokey', conservative, upstanding, Jim Reeves-loving, turn the other cheek, god-fearing citizens in conflict with their children (read male and 'black youth') as problematic deviants. In a number of plays such as Edgar White's *The Nine Night*, the Front Room became a site of contested cultural identities and race politics.[7] The tone of Caryl Phillips's description of the main set in his play, *Strange Fruit*, suggests this ambivalent relationship:

> The action takes place in the front room of the Marshall's terraced house in one of England's inner city areas. Whilst the district is not a ghetto it is hardly suburbia. The room is cramped but comfortable and tidy ... a cabinet full of crockery that has never been, and never will be used ... In the centre of the display is a plate commemorating the Queen's Silver Jubilee. In the centre of the room is an imitation black leather settee with orange/yellow cushions ... As to the surroundings: the wallpaper is tasteless, and on the wall hang the usual trinkets ... As I said the room is cramped, even claustrophobic, but tidy.[8]

In my forthcoming exhibition/installation at the Geffrye Museum, I have been exploring the idea of the front room is a contradictory space. On one level, its opulent kitsch and consumer fetish, symbolizes the aspirations of an immigrant family striving for educational achievement, prosperity, moral cohesion and religious continuity. No matter how poor they were, if the front room looked good, then they were decent people. The representation of 'decency' and 'social respectability' are wrapped up with middle-class values, which in a colonial context the socially mobile would strive to emulate and imitate. This has been coded in the notion of 'good grooming', which, historically, is a transcendental response to the dehumanization of slavery and colonial oppression that ontologically reconstructed the self as whole. This is expressed, not only sartorially through the presentation of the body, but also through practices in the domestic domain. These desires find their expression through material culture, which can often be transient, in the practices of imitation, pastiche, innovation and hybridization. In the front room, ornaments such as plastic flowers are artificial and yet covered over by crochet doilies, as if cherished for the future of deferred dreams that never materialize. There is *Jesus Christ at The Last Supper* on the wall and the King James 1st version of the Bible on the sideboard. Christianity in the black communities is a form of both liberation and oppression. With its problematic authenticity, the front room became a symbolic space of contested and disavowed identities between generations.

Historically, 'West Indian' referred to those who owned slaves or had invested in plantations in the Caribbean. However, the term 'West Indian' (which refers to Christopher Columbus's mistake) became contested at a particular juncture in British history, signified by cultural political shifts brought about by anti-colonialist struggle and movements for independence, Civil Rights and Black Power. Postwar black settlers may have been represented as socially problematic 'others', but the de-colonizing process was already taking place through attempts at redefinition by sanitizing cultural and racial difference. Postwar immigrants from the Caribbean only began to call themselves 'West Indian' when they arrived in England and realized that they would fair better together, than apart, in the face of racism. The front room may have been dressed by the woman and mother of the home, but its master was the 'West Indian' father. He was from the Caribbean or Africa with values of those societies and cultures, which often found him at odds with his children, who were born in Britain and, in his eyes, English culturally. As a disempowered black man having to defer his dreams because of responsibilities placed upon his shoulders, he would project his alienation onto his family. This is the character of Hammond in Edgar White's play, *The Nine Night*, first directed by Rufus Collins, which portrayed a modern British family dealing with the opposing forces of, in the words of Caryl Phillips, 'dominoes and chic disco music, curry goat and fish and chip'.[9] Onye Wambu has argued that Edgar White is one of few dramatists to bridge the gap between the African, Caribbean and British experience in his work. White has lived in all of these places. His early play *Lament for Rastafari* is part ritual, part-panorama, the action moving from the Caribbean to London and finally to New York.[10] The play is episodic, the one narrative thread being the transformation of a character called Lindsey from prisoner in Jamaica to JuJu Man in a New York cemetery. His plays are, therefore, not peopled by characters in perpetual revolt, who by being elevated to the level of symbol, lose their human specificity. Rather, the characters, bewildered and yearning for an end to their exile, live on in our psyches, prodding and prompting us into re-examining the vision we formerly upheld.[11] And I will never forget the violence unleashed in the character of Hammond, played by T Bone Wilson, who knocks the door of his son Izak with a hammer. The act resonated with me forcefully, as it signified the generational conflict between upstanding black parents and their children, who were then represented as deviant black youths in the British media. Such an image eloquently expresses the tension between a black son and his father in Britain.

The conflict between father and son is a familiar plotline in much of black theatre's literary canon, but lately it has progressively taken a postmodern turn, evinced in Sol B. River's *48–98*. This play was produced in 1998, the 50th Anniversary of the arrival in England of the SS Windrush in 1948, which heralded the wave of post-second world war black settlers. The play looks beyond this moment of arrival to the future of black people in Britain, 'There was a time when I thought I was born too early and another time when I thought I was born too late.'[12] In Mustapha Matura's *Welcome Home Jacko*, produced in 1980, Jacko returns from prison to his old youth club and questions his peers' idealist following of Rastafari.[13] Consistent with the representation of contested cultural political identities at the time is the foregrounding of a struggle over masculinities. *Welcome Home Jacko* also tends to conflate the depiction of Rastafari as ideologically romantic with the stereotypical image of black youths, lounging on streets, smoking 'weed' and refusing to work in 'Babylon'. *Welcome Home Jacko* is an ideological contestation that reflects the generational conflict between parents born somewhere else and their children born and schooled in the UK. But the terms of its representation are limited; the play's focus on a cultural political opposition collapses the past and present, which leads it to gloss over some of the fears and desires of different generations in the black communities.

Language

For instance, as the cultural critic Errol Francis asks us, 'Can we accept the characterisation of our parents as virtually illiterate, save the Bible and correspondence courses?'[14] Francis wonders how, on the basis of this caricature, the younger 'second generation' were able to keep alive patois/creole traditions from the Caribbean if they were suppressed in England. Since this suppression also occurred in the Caribbean, the question is not whether, but how, where and by whom, this patois/creole – 'bad talking' – was suppressed, hidden and used. It is the 'Orientalist knowledge' to use Edward Said's concept, that is reflected in the cultural hegemony of colonialism that codes the Other's language as bastardized, pidgin and uncivilized.[15] And it is this psychic inferiorization of 'Nation Language', as noted by Frantz Fanon, which has provided a systematic framework for the political analysis of racial hegemonies at the level of black subjectivity.[16] This subjective is interrogated by Suzanne Scafe in her book, *Teaching Black Literature*, where she notes that black British students, weary of the stigma of being labelled as the 'race experts', claimed not to know how to speak creole while reading aloud black literary texts.[17] The performative survival strategy utilized by these students echoes the duality of generational race politics as a sobering lesson in the paradox of modernity: a means of freedom in expression, but also a means of suppression. It is the duality of the archetypal 'speaky spokey', who spoke or (attempted to use) the 'Queen's English', better than the Queen. As Kobena Mercer writes:

> Across a whole range of cultural forms there is a 'syncretic' dynamic which critically appropriates elements from the master-codes of the dominant culture and 'creolises' them, disarticulating given signs and re-articulating their symbolic meaning. The subversive force of this hybridising tendency is most apparent at the level of language itself where creoles, patois and black English decentre, destabilise and carnivalise the linguistic domination of 'English' – the nation a language of master-discourse – through strategic inflections, re-accentuations and other performative moves in semantic syntactic and lexical codes.[18]

Benjamin Zephaniah remarks, 'you cannot talk to a hurricane in standard English'.[19] Errol John's play *Moon on a Rainbow Shawl*, produced at the Royal Court in 1958, is said to be the first play to break the tradition of writing in the Queen's English by using Creole vernacular, or what Kamau Braithwaite has called 'Nation Language', though Una Marson had already done so in her play, *Pocomonia*, in 1938.[20] During the 1970s, Mustapha Matura's *Black Pieces* and subsequent plays such as, *As Times Goes By*, *The Coup*, *The Playboy of the West Indies*, employed a Trinidadian creole.[21]

Cultural renaissance

Black theatre and related artistic practices in the late 1970s and early 1980s emerged at a time of community resistance against ongoing racist immigration laws, police/state brutality, and marginalization in the labour market, housing and education. These struggles culminated in uprisings at the 1976 Notting Hill Carnival and inner-city revolts/uprisings/riots in 1981 and 1985. Kobena Mercer has argued that these uprisings encoded militant demands for black representation within public institutions as a basic right. Public institutions such as the Greater London Council (GLC) responded with 'benevolent' gestures, such as the redistribution of funds. New opportunities for black arts practitioners and organizations generated a cultural renaissance of black creativity. This moment marked a historical juncture, as second-generation blacks and Asians born and educated in Britain, demanded equal justice and civil rights, rejecting the second-class citizenship that their parents were made to accept.[22]

I want to mention Talawa Theatre here, not only because it is one of two black theatre companies left in London, the other being Nitro formerly Black Theatre Co-op, but because Talawa's first production in 1985, *The Black Jacobins* is part of the legacy. The play was written by C.L.R. James and is based on his classic groundbreaking history of the Haitian Revolution on San Domingo in the early nineteenth century – the first black revolution in the New World. The play was first produced in 1936, when facism was being legitimized in Europe, with Paul Robeson playing Toussaint L'Ouverture.[23] In 1985, when Talawa produced it again, it gained added relevance and power because of the miners' strikes, Thatcher's anti-trade union reforms, and the urban disturbances that were consequent from heavy-handed policing, unemployment and disenfranchisement in Britain's inner cities. Come the 1990s, Amani Napthali's play *Ragamuffin* connects the Haitian Revolution with the uprisings/riots/revolts; for example, Broadwater Farm of 1985, when Cynthia Jarrett was killed by the police, and PC Blakelock was murdered.[24] But the staging and performance was radical. The play takes the form of a mock trial, where the archetypal ragamuffin is charged, with prosecution and defence using the evidence of two revolts centuries apart to highlight choices faced by urban black youth. With deliberations presented in the form of DJ lyrics, a musical atmosphere provided by a sound system, and the audience as jury returning different verdicts every night, the play parodied the English criminal system, which black folks have never had much justice from. The audience became a church congregation and participated through call and response, to 'lick wood' and 'mek noise'. *Ragamuffin* broke the fourth wall in presenting a theatre of the people, about and with the people. It signified an emerging counter-culture in black performance in the 1980s, which subverted conventional theatre practice with more complex, fragmented subjectivities in a context that broke boundaries between drama, music, movement, dance and visual arts.

Black women and performance

By raising issues of racial and ethnic oppressions that cut across the power and powerlessness of women, the emergence of black women in a post-civil rights era as a distinct 'class' or group in politics has interrogated radical feminist notions of 'global sisterhood'. By the same token, black feminist/womanist positions disrupt complacent notions of a homogen-ous and self-identical black community. During the inner-city events of the 1980s, the representation of 'black youth' was coded as male, yet shifts in race politics also necessitated shifts in gender politics, as black women practitioners began to express the personal as political and polit-ical as personal in the cultural and artistic sphere. Sonia Boyce's painting *She's ain't holding them up, She's holding on* signifies this moment.[25] The family and the representation of family are central to black life and women, seen through their socially conventional expressions of care, love and labour, are intrinsic to it's nurturing and social mobility. Boyce's painting subverts the code of family respectability; her portrait, with its rich floral wallpaper, is also reminiscent of the décor of the front room. Her own over-sized self-portrait is either holding up or holding on to her family in a sofa above her head.[26] Black women are stereotyped as carers, but who cares for the carer? This idea is echoed in Winsome Pinnock's play *Leave Taking*, which returns to the theme of intergenerational con-flict, but from a feminine perspective.[27] Ntozake Shange's *for coloured girls who have considered suicide when the rainbow is enuf* was a seminal performance piece fusing poetry, dance and music in a choreopoem.[28] In the 1980 production of the piece, which involved the founders of Theatre of Black Women, the fusion of art forms and the foregrounding of the subjective seemed to symbolize a journey that had already begun, in the way that black performance was being made and practised, resonating in the work of the Theatre of Black Women's own performance pieces such as *Silhouette, Pyeyucca* and *Chiaroscuro*.[29] Munirah, a black women's per-formance collective, adopted this new aesthetic, and writers such as Barbara Burford and Jackie Kay explored abstract dramatic forms as a way of unpacking complex identities. In Jackie Kay's *Chiaroscuro*, there is a mix-ture of symbolism, stylized movement, visual imagery, poetic language and naturalism:

> I want to find the woman
> who in Dahomey in 1900
> loved another woman
> tell me what did they call her

did they know her name
in Ashanti, do they know it in
Yoruba do they know it in patois ...[30]

Identity

In their seminal book, *The Critical Decade: Black British Photography in the 1980s*, Stuart Hall and David. A Bailey suggest that, within a post-structuralist model, identity is not fixed, but positional, 'identities are floating, that meaning is not fixed and universally true at all times for all people, and that the subject is constructed through the unconscious desire, fantasy and memory'.[31] In other words, you weren't born black, you became black. To use Julie MacDougall's words, 'As a displaced person moving between cultures, I am viewing identity as a work-in-process, a disappearing act, a performance'.[32] The construction of identity is a performative process, constantly negotiated through, as Stuart Hall puts it, a 'complex historical process of appropriation, compromise, subversion, masking, invention and revival'; cultural identity is an 'articulation fostered in a complex structure of diverse and contradictory, yet connected relations'. Hall attempts to move beyond an identity based on the essentialising opposition between colonizer and colonized; in other words between colonialist and anti-colonialist. He posits cultural identity as dialectically continuous, disruptive, with unstable points of identification made within the discourse of history and culture. The idea that cultural identities can be dialectically continuous and disruptive, suggests a duality as double consciousness.[33] Hall's argument enables us to see black theatre as a process and a construct, and chimes with Shirley Tate's conception of black identity as a 'text of social practice'. They both support a conception of black theatre, paradigmatically, by situating it in a wider context of performance. This duality as 'double consciousness', enables us to see the performative taking place on stage and beyond the confines of the stage. Tate's conception of the 'text' can then be appropriated theoretically, seeing black theatre in the context of performance as 'texts of cultural practice', and thus enables us to speculate on its different meanings.[34]

It is within this articulation of identities as a negotiated process, which can be positional depending on the context, that much of black British theatre as an emerging discourse, practice and aesthetic needs to be repositioned. Tunde Ikoli, the son of a Cornish mother and a Nigerian father, examines these themes and issues in his play *Scrape off the Black*.[35] Through her writing, Winsome Pinnock describes a journey of exploring identities, which attempts to map the process of interculturalism and change. For instance, the urban vernacular of Britain's inner cities have been creolized with the mixing of a predominantly Jamaican dialect with regional English. This liminal zone of identity is also contested between Enid and her daughters, Dei and Viv, in Pinnock's *Leave Taking*, as they attempt to define for themselves what it means to be a black woman in Britain.[36]

Live arts

Much of the work emerging from live art practices in Britain has been conceptual in nature, focusing more on the expression of ideas than on the display of skills. More than conventional theatre, live art has been able to articulate the hybridized identities produced within the context of alienation, fragmentation and disenfranchisement experienced by black communities. Issac Julien adapted his film *Looking For Langston* as a site-specific piece in Camley Street near Kings Cross, 'a street that is notorious as a cruising ground for straights', in order to produce an 'investigation of sexual identity, inter-cultural conflict and dialogue, and the historical and contemporary assessment of black cultural expression'.[37] In parallel, Susan Lewis's work is personified by risk and expressive subjectivity, and her choice of form reflects the alienation and frustration she feels with conventional practice. In *Walking Tall* and *Ladies Falling*, Lewis investigates female oppression by using her own body to unpack historical and contemporary visual discourse around the black female body. *Walking Tall*, a movement-based performance piece, draws on the myth of Isis to explore the contemporary black female experience. Lewis's mixed-race background motivates her interest in cultural interweaving reflected in the double consciousness of being both African-Caribbean and English. Why does a black British person born and bred in the UK have to leave the country to be called English? At one stage during the performance, Lewis appears naked as she attempts to foreground the fetishistic sexualization of the black female body. Ironically, the gesture was more problematic for black members of the audience, than for white, perhaps because they readily identified with the fetishized body projected on stage. Another register Lewis called upon was her complexion and, as such, her identity as a woman of mixed-race heritage. As a residue of colonialism, light skin still has a social currency, and skin colour hierarchies persist within black communities. *Ladies Falling* uses tea, sugar and rum as metaphors to map out a counter-history, revealing the different values assigned to the same objects in different cultures. Movement, film, costume and performative gesture are combined to signify the alienation and fragmentation as experienced in the African diaspora and reflect the restricted and repressed nature of established value systems.[38]

Ronald Fraser Munroe reappropriates popular stereotypes and tropes in his performance pieces such as *Sir Arthur Stuffed Shirt and His Revolving Monocle*, and *L'Homme Blanc*, which have included such twisted characters as Cesare Cappuccino, Coco Chamelle and M.C. Kamelhead. Animal masks, uniforms and outlandish costumes contribute to a series of monologues, which are peppered with a hubristic polemic, producing witty, yet politically subversive, theatre. Fascinated and repelled by Nazis, and likening them to the Ku Klux Klan, Munroe places his central character on a pirate radio station broadcasting from outer space, admonishing and lecturing the listener whilst inhabiting his numerous characters, many of which make use of masks.[39]

Performance poets have gone through their own transformations. SuAndi's multimedia performance piece *This is all I have to Say* creates an intimacy, with her conversational style of poetry and poignant chat, enabling the audience to relax as if in her front room. Meanwhile, the audience tries to digest British Nazi Party (BNP) and Ku Klux Klan propaganda left on their seats, while images of black people's resistance to racism are projected overhead, and excerpts of BNP and KKK songs are played over the sound system. SuAndi's work is in the oral tradition of the African griot. In *The Story of M*, she explores the subject of interracial marriage and one woman's struggle to raise her children properly. The woman of her story loses one child to an oppressive social system; the other she manages to keep emotionally stable and focused.[40] Mimetically, we see a mixed-race black woman narrating the experience of a mixed-race black woman, yet she is, in fact, the voice of her white mother. The implications of this play is significant as it raises the question of representation: who is really being imitated in the mimesis of performance? Through what socially constructed filters do we perceive the performance? If we agree that performance can be viewed as 'texts of cultural practice', what are the moments of intertextuality ? This takes us back to the notion of imitation in the practice of the blackface minstrel. What or who is being imitated when we see a performance?

Conclusion

Bertolt Brecht has said that art is not truly revolutionary unless it is revolutionary in form.[41] In the work of the black live artists discussed here, we see both a subversion and fusion of art forms, a hybridized form of practice that reflects the polyphonic nature of black culture. These aesthetic representations signify a reinvention and re-imagining of the self in a cultural and political context, where identities are continually fragmented and hybridized. As Hall and Bailey point out:

> One day the world is going to wake up and discover that whole areas of life in Britain, in spite of Conservatism and Little Englandism, have been transformed. White hegemony is gradually being painted darker and darker. A kind of hybridization is happening to the English, whether they like it or not, and in this long process of the dismantling of the West, the new perspectives in Black cultural practice represented here may have to make this a real cultural and historical turning point.[42]

What does this say about an emergent black British theatre? The idea of identity as a work in progress is reflected in the process of challenging the critical orthodoxy surrounding black theatre, and complicates the term by bringing within its compass a heterogeneous range of practices and twenty-first century aesthetic desires. Much of the history and critical analysis of black performance in Britain is yet to be done, and a lot will be found not in university libraries, but on the lips of the pioneers, practitioners, and players. To conclude, I would quote the words performance artist Guillermo Gomez-Pena:

> The colonized cultures are sliding into the space of the colonizer, and in doing so, they are redefining its borders and culture. (A similar phenomenon is occurring in Europe with African Caribbean immigration.) We need to find a new terminology, a new iconography and a new set of categories and definitions. We need to rebaptise the world in our own terms.[43]

Notes

1. Michael McMillan, *Master Juba* (National Maritime Museum/Pursued by a Bear – commission – unpublished playtext, 2004).
2. Yvonne Brewster, 'Introduction', in *Black Plays: Two* (London: Methuen, 1989).
3. Frantz Fanon, *Black Skin, White Masks* (London: Pluto, 1986) and T. Golden (ed.), *Black Male: Representations of Masculinity in Contemporary American Art* (New York: Whitney Museum of American Art, 1994).
4. Kimberly W. Benston, *Performing Blackness: Enactments of African-American Modernism* (London: Routledge, 2000).
5. Stuart Hall, 'Cultural Identity and Diaspora', in Patrick Williams and Laura Chrisman (eds), *Colonial Discourse and Post-Colonial Theory: A Reader* (London: Harvester Wheatsheaf, 1993), p. 401.
6. The Partner Hand or Susu was an informal, yet organized system of saving, where, depending on the number of members, an individual's opportunity

to bank takings from each member would rotate. This system became the forerunner of the Credit Union.

7. Edgar White, *The Nine Night* (London: Bush, 1983).
8. Caryl Phillips, *Strange Fruit* (London: Amber Lane Press, 1981), p. 7.
9. Edgar White, *op. cit.* Caryl Phillips quoted in Kwesi Owusu, *The Struggle for Black Arts in Britain* (London: Comedia, 1986), p. 97.
10. Edgar White, *Lament for Rastafari and Other Plays* (London: Boyars, 1983).
11. Onye Wambu, 'Unholy Trinity', *Artrage*, 13 (1986), p. 21.
12. Sol B. River, *48–98* (Zebra Crossing, Lyric Studio Hammersmith, Talawa Theatre, 1998), unpublished.
13. Mustapha Matura, *Welcome Home Jacko* (London: Methuen, 1980).
14. Errol Francis, 'From Generation to Generation: "The Installation" Obaala Arts Collective' (Birmingham: Ten 8, no: 22, 1986), p. 41.
15. Edward Said, 'From Orientalism', in Williams and Chrisman, *op. cit*, pp. 132–49.
16. Frantz Fanon, 'On National Culture', in Williams and Williams, *op. cit.*, p. 37.
17. Suzanne Scafe, *Teaching Black Literature* (London: Virago Press, 1989).
18. Kobena Mercer, 'Diaspora culture and dialogic imagination,' in, M. Cham and C. Watkins (eds), *Blackframes: Critical perspectives on black independent cinema* (London: 1998), p. 57.
19. Benjamin Zephaniah, personal interview with Michael McMillan (London: July 1995).
20. Errol John, *Moon on a Rainbow Shawl* (London: Faber, 1958). Edward Kamau Braithwaite, *History of the Voice: The Development of Nation Language in Anglophone Caribbean Poetry* (London: New Beacon Books, 1984). For Una Marson, *Pocomonia* (1938), see D.Jarrett-Macauley, *The Life of Una Marson 1905–65* (Manchester: Manchester University Press, 1998).
21. Mustapha Matura, *Black Pieces* (London: Calder & Boyars, 1972), *As Times Goes By* (London: Calder & Boyars, 1972), *The Coup* (New York: American Theatre Magazine, 1993), *The Playboy of the West Indies* (New York: Broadway Play Publishing, 1996).
22. Kobena Mercer, *Welcome to the Jungle: New Positions in Black Cultural Studies* (London: Routledge, 1994), p. 79.
23. C.L.R. James, *The Black Jacobins*; first performed in 1936 and then in 1986, Riverside Theatre, London, unpublished in play form.
24. Amani Napthali, *Ragamuffin* (London: Oberon Books, 2002).
25. Sonia Boyce, *She's ain't holding them up, She's holding on*, cited in Stuart Hall and David A. Bailey (eds), *Critical Decade: Black British Photography in the 1980s* (Birmingham: Ten 8, Photo Paperback, 2.3., 1992).
26. *Ibid.*
27. Winsome Pinnock, *Leave Taking*, in *First Run* (London: Hern, 1989).
28. Ntozake Shange, *for coloured girls who have considered suicide when the rainbow is enuf* (London: Methuen, 1978).
29. For Theatre of Black Women, *Silhouette, Pyeyucca* and *Chiaroscuro* see Susan Croft, 'Black Women Playwrights in Britain', in Trevor R. Griffiths and Margaret Llewellyn-Jones (eds), *British and Irish Women Dramatists Since 1958: A Critical Handbook* (London: Open University Press, 1993), pp. 84–98; p. 79.
30. Jackie Kay, 'Chiaroscuro', in Jill Davis (ed.), *Lesbian Plays* (London: Methuen, 1987), p. 79.
31. Stuart Hall S. and David A. Bailey, 'The Vertigo of Displacement: Shifts within Black Documentary Practices', in stuart Hall and David A. Bailey, *op. cit.*

32. bell hooks, 'Performance Practice as a Site of Opposition', in Catherine Ugwu (ed.), *Let's Get it On: The Politics of Black Performance* (London: ICA/Bay Press, 1995), p. 221.
33. Stuart Hall, *op. cit.*, p. 401.
34. Shirley Tate, 'Colour Matters, "Race" Matters': African Caribbean Identity in the 20th Century', in Mark Christian (ed.), *Black Identities in the 20th Century: Expressions of the US and UK African Diaspora* (London: Hansib Publications, 2002), pp. 195–212.
35. Tunde Ikoli, 'Scrape off the Black', in Yvonne Brewster (ed.), *Black Plays: Three* (London: Methuen, 1995). Winsome Pinnock, personal interview with Michael McMillan, June 1995.
36. Winsome Pinnock, personal interview with Michael McMillan, June 1995. Pinnock, *Leave Taking, op. cit.*
37. Issac Julien quoted in Catherine Ugwu (ed.), *op. cit.* p. 58. See also David A. Bailey, Kobena Mercer and Catherine Ugwu (eds), *Mirage: Enigmas of Race, Difference, and Desire* (London: ICA, 1995).
38. For a description of Susan Lewis' performance pieces see Catherine Ugwu, *op. cit.* p. 68.
39. For a description of Munroe's performances see, Bailey, Mercer and Ugwu (eds), *op. cit.* p. 86.
40. Described in Catherine Ugwu, *op. cit.* p. 68.
41. For a discussion of Brecht and a translation of his writings on theatre see: John Willett (ed.), *Brecht on Theatre* (London: Methuen, 1964).
42. Stuart Hall and David A. Bailey, *op. cit.* p. 23.
43. Guillermo Gomez-Pena, 'The Multicultural Paradigm: An Open Letter to the National Arts Community High Performance', *High Performance Quarterly Magazine*, 47 (1989), p. 20.

8
Canon Questions: Art in 'Black Britain'

Leon Wainwright*

Any discussion relevant to art history, its canon and black identities in contemporary Britain has to begin by thinking at least as far back as the start of the 1980s. It was the time of the emergence and formal assemblage of artists of the first and second generations of migrants mainly from Britain's former colonies in the Caribbean, Africa and South Asia, but also from other places in South East Asia and the Middle East. They were not this country's first ever grouping of artists based, at root, on concerns with ethnicity,[1] but theirs was the largest show of affinity amongst artists of diaspora identities, in terms of the numbers involved and the breadth of their interests. Parading their commonalities and embracing a range of art forms – including filmmaking, photography, performance, painting and drawing, installation and combinations of these and other media – the group collaborated creatively, and organized together in exhibition curating, publishing, writing and criticism, archiving and promotion. Grouped ostensibly on the basis of common experiences of exclusion from Britain's art environment, its gallery network and spaces of promotion and criticism, the artistic activity, or 'arts activism'[2] of the 1980s, made for a distinctive period in our national cultural history. It was a special, often intense time of thought and action, and of enormous consequence.

Recognizing the importance of that decade depends largely on noting how these artists' collaborative interests were not confined to an assault on art spaces alone, but extended to art historiography and its canon: the recording of artistic achievements, and a key, yet never sole, means by which artistic values and a sense of the past are established and maintained. It is fair to say that when first assembling as a group most artists gave priority to an ebullient assertion of the right to be visible in art galleries and in documentation. This shaped a 'black' or 'diaspora' canon

143

which has since come to exemplify Britain's struggles around representation, ethnicity, authority, cultural value, heritage, community and art historical inscription. Subsequent changes, during the 1990s to the present, in the material circumstances artists have met with and the dissolution of any apparent group outlook and purpose (if ever there was such a plain consensus), have led to new perspectives on what the canon debate can deliver now that artists are no longer marginal or excluded in identical ways to how they once were. Nonetheless, as I suggest, these artists continue to struggle over the collection and display of their art and the terms of its reception, promotion and criticism, areas that are contingent with canonical issues. Based on such a narrative, this essay evaluates some of the formative ideas and practices giving rise to the present situation for the art of 'black Britain', and looks at the genealogy of the process of canon formation in its art history in order to suggest some possibilities for the future.

Whose canon?

In his 'The Fictions of Science' series,[3] Keith Piper enlarges his own face in the frame of a digital montage, putting a ruler to his cheek, clamped in place to measure the distance between his left nostril and ear (Figure 8.1). A traced outline in purple of a human skull is slipped beneath him, with a dictionary definition of 'craniology' trailing legibly above. This is a pictorial scheme of the body; a linear, monochrome diagram of the face, its features are ruled or crossed through with construction lines to rationalize its proportions. A self-portrait overlaid with measuring devices and subjected to an objectifying gaze, Piper's image is encumbered by the weight of external quantification, raising the question of scientific disinterest in racial typology. Part of a wider project of 'relocating the remains', as he called his Royal College of Art retrospective in 1997,[4] the series looks again at fragments from the time when Piper and his peers set out to define themselves in the face of alien standards of artistic value during the early 1980s. As he explained in 1984:

> You see, today what we are looking for is a Black visual aesthetic, a way of making works that is exclusive to us, in the same way as our musicians have invented many musical forms which are totally 'Black'. We need a Black visual aesthetic because as Black artists we still depend on forms and ideas about art borrowed from European art history. It is that history, and the dominance of its values over us, which we need to reject because they cannot serve us in our struggle.[5]

Figure 8.1   Keith Piper, 'The Fictions of Science' (1996)

Among the 'remains' Piper displayed were representations that have come to assault the art historical canon, to overcome the forced silence and invisibility of black subjecthood, and to assert Piper's creative, authorial presence.

It is common for documentation of Keith Piper's practice to interpolate him in a confrontation and struggle narrative,[6] foundational to the interventionist and 'critical decade'[7] of the 1980s.[8] With Eddie Chambers, Piper organized the first 'Black Art' exhibition at Wolverhampton Art Gallery in 1981,[9] and a year later used the 'First National Black Art Convention' at Wolverhampton Polytechnic to form the BLK Group, a collection of art students and recent graduates from the area of the West Midlands that staged exhibitions from 1982 to 1984.[10] They were followed by a run of largely group 'survey' exhibitions of topic- or issue-focused art works operating under the sign of 'Black Art', closely defined as art by black artists, that would speak to a black community and address 'black issues'.[11] Their curatorial purpose, betrayed by titles such as 'Plotting the Course', 'The Artpack: A history of Black artists in Britain', and 'The Essential Black Art', encompassed a drive for visibility and self-definition with the intention of naming, charting and documenting an artistic 'Black' presence, intended to highlight the institutional and political obstacles in the way of their wider and lasting recognition.[12]

The narrow prescription of 'Black Art' would translate initially into artistic references to racial violence, Thatcherite politics, issues of national belonging, a fervent black nationalist language of opposition, agitation and social uplift, and a nascent black feminism. Works characteristic of that emerging canon included Tam Joseph's 'UK School Report' of 1984,[13] addressed to the circumstances of young black Britons, quipping on the roots of disaffection and 'deviance' in the passage through school and college. Joseph's interest in othering and mistreatment at the hands of the British establishment developed into 'Spirit of the Carnival', 1988,[14] a look at 'frontline' clashes under the baton of police brutality, and a reminder of how annual celebrations in London's Notting Hill could dissolve into violence.[15] The photography of Vanley Burke, who has described his work as a sort of 'histograph', 'capturing the personal, social and economic life of black people as they arrived, settled and became established in British society',[16] brought attention to the workplace, to delicate portraits of children, worshippers and days at the fair, and to images of protest, such as an Afrikan Liberation Day march in a district of the West Midlands in the 1970s; all dimensions of 'black experience' drawn from everyday life in inner-city Britain.[17] Conveying the complicities of popular imaging with racism and stereotype became a signature concern in the multimedia work of Sonia Boyce, such as her 'From Someone Else's Fear Fantasy to Metamorphosis' of 1987,[18] a four-part self-portrait, with montage and sketched additions satirizing the fetishism of black people in film, advertising and photography, with a particular emphasis on femininity. Boyce's critical interests, coherent with her preference at that time for figurative pastel drawing, indicate how women artists would develop positions often remote from their male counterparts, yet still within the paradigm of a political emphasis on the primacy of their 'blackness'.[19]

From these examples alone, it is already clear that the varieties amongst participants in 'Black Art' production and display meant that any pursuit of an exclusive 'Black visual aesthetic', to quote Piper, was not propelled by a singular vision. Even so, despite their varieties, what may have made that early period distinctive were the adaptations and inclusions that the 'Black' concept could perform.[20] Whereas Piper and Chambers' 'activism' – expressed in the accompanying literature to their exhibitions, their other writings and Chambers' curatorial projects – had stridently rehearsed much US Black Arts Movement rhetoric and ideas about Pan-Africanism,[21] (simultaneously including reference to aspects of their British experience), many artists from a wider diasporic constituency would also espouse the 'Black Art' label. By 1988 it was possible for Rasheed Araeen to suggest that:

> The term 'black art' is now being commonly used by the black community as well as by people in Britain in general. But this common usage is often a misuse, as far as the work that might be called 'black art' is concerned. It may be a convenient term to refer to the work of black artists, but it also implies that their work is or should be different from the mainstream of modern culture ... 'Black art', if this term must be used, is in fact a specific historical development within contemporary art practices and has emerged directly from the joint struggle of Asian, African and the Caribbean people against racism, and the art work itself explicitly refers to that struggle.[22]

Some of the most significant support for exhibiting this jointly developed 'Black Art' came from artists of the South Asian[23] and other diasporas, including Sutapa Biswas, Zarina Bhimji, Chila Burman, Allan de Souza, Shaheen Merali and Sunil Gupta.[24] They added to the efforts begun in the late 1970s of Rasheed Araeen, a Pakistan-born member of the Black Panthers, confessed 'militant' artist and organizer, and founder of *Black Phoenix* magazine (later incorporated into the popular journal *Third Text*[25]), which published his rousing 'Black Art' manifesto,[26] who would go on to be the period's most prolific commentator.

This coming together of ethnic constituencies would help to establish the present-day currency of the term 'black British', and to distinguish race and representation debates in art history of the past two decades from more ethnically divided voices across the Atlantic.[27] For critics as well as artists, towards the end of the decade of the 1980s, that more pluralist conception of the black label had become impossible to ignore, even if it was not accepted by all. While Paul Gilroy conceded of the previous exclusionary uses of the black trope that 'none of us enjoys a monopoly on black authenticity',[28] he bemoaned the failure of the 'Black Arts Movement' in Britain and a collapse of 'black unity' due to 'an Asian retreat into much narrower notions of ethnicity than the "Movement" would allow'.[29] Gilroy's contribution to intellectual debate on the matter, within the academic discipline of Cultural Studies, led to his assertion of the idea, in 1988, of a 'diaspora aesthetic', which was developed further by Stuart Hall in 1989 in connection to Caribbean cinema,[30] and later by others such as Kobena Mercer and the curator, publisher and arts organizer Gilane Tawadros.[31] With their intervention, debate was lifted beyond the factional schisms[32] of creative individuals who were largely independent of institutions, in favour of academic criticism, widely circulating by the time of the decade's most public statement on British artists' supposed 'Afro-Asian' unity, *The Other Story* exhibition of 1989.[33]

Emphasizing less the trope of blackness than the more fluid category of a 'diaspora aesthetic', artists and critics shaped a structured critical debate on the canon. The key to seeing how this transcended some of the simplifications and contradictions of 'Black Art' depends on recognizing the ambivalent uses to which the concept was put; what Ien Ang has noted more generally of postcolonial intellectuals as their 'double focus'.[34] The first use of the diaspora aesthetic idea was as a fixed, easily identifiable definition for how black visual practices might be inherently typical of black and Asian people as a common group, distinguishing them as essentially connected and similar, regardless of their differing and changing circumstances. A second use was a more properly analytical motivation to elucidate the style of 'diaspora culture' in terms of 'dialogic strategies and hybrid forms',[35] or 'the hybrid, transitory and always historically specific forms in which questions of "race" and ethnicity are articulated'[36] both in black popular culture and popular culture in general.

Hall's use of the diaspora aesthetic term was tied to these two perspectives. On the one hand, he advocated critical work that 'allows us to see and recognise the different parts and histories of ourselves, to construct those points of identification, those positionalities we call a "cultural identity"',[37] and on the other he concurred with Mercer's observation that, 'across a whole range of cultural forms there is a "syncretic" dynamic which critically appropriates elements from the master-codes of the dominant culture and "creolises" them, disarticulating given signs and re-articulating their symbolic meaning ... [a] hybridising tendency'.[38] A point to note here is that the notion of aesthetics was being stretched, or at least tactically confused, to indicate modes of signification and communication – typical of the semiotic-like turn to representation in Cultural Studies – rather than aesthetic experience, perception or phenomenological 'sense' as such. This meant that the *aesthetic* in diaspora aesthetic operated as a blanket term for styles of visual meaning and how they are conveyed, that is in a hybrid, syncretic or creolizing way.

It is probably the case that the artists and works that audiences have most readily identified as canonically black are those that best elucidated critics' schemes for a diaspora aesthetic. One such is the concern with black women's experience, typical of Boyce, paralleled in the now iconic painting and collage by Indian-born Sutapa Biswas 'Housewives with Steakknives' of 1986 (Figure 8.2).[39] On a loose canvas, a modern day, multi-limbed *Kali* – amongst other things, a goddess of destruction – with henna-stained hands and protruding tongue threatens decapitation with kitchen utensils; a necklace of heads, including the rightwing extremist polit-ician Enoch Powell and other white males, marks out the targets of her aggression. Such a citation to the iconography of an ancient religion, made possible through contemporary figuration, shapes the sort of dis-ruptive femininity that women artists of this period would use to dissolve

Figure 8.2   Sutapa Biswas, 'Housewives with Steakknives' (1986)

'the fixed boundaries between past and present, public and private, personal and political'.[40] 'Untitled' of 1989 by South African-born artist and writer Gavin Jantjes made this syncretism overt, pointing to the entwined histories of Euro-American artistic modernism with a generalized African creativity, to reconfigure with parity the implicit hierarchy of modern art's Primitivism as a continuously reciprocal thread in a neutral starry night.

By the time works by less well-known artists such as Valerie Brown had appeared, with her 'Encounters' of 1991,[41] photographic 'evidence and confirmation' of the inevitability suggested in the racist fear of miscegenation,[42] the themes of national belonging, otherness and ethnic particularism typical of concerns in the 1980s, had all become codified and would firmly index issues being emphasized through wider critical debate.[43] Marcia Bennett's 'Between a Rock and a Hard Place' of 1992,[44] suggested an 'in-between' space or 'no-place', evidenced by a fantasy flag that flies for the hopes and promises of migration, despite their seemingly perpetually deferred fulfilment (Figure 8.3). This work has to be seen amongst a range of images and performances that present narratives trying to come to terms with the impossibility for migrant or diaspora subjects of a 'return to the beginning' to a 'homeland' and to 'origins'. Bennett's piece is a synecdoche for a widely enjoined critical elegy to the securities of belonging and a redemptive 'narrative of displacement'[45] that makes use of the symbolic and representation as an infinitely renewing reservoir of desire, memory, myth, search and discovery.[46]

At the same time as binding a programme of critical commentary onto a narrative of artistic developments, the diaspora aesthetic idea has furnished a situation in which, deliberately and productively, there has

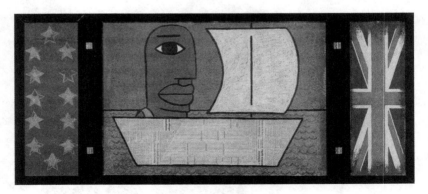

Figure 8.3   Marcia Bennett, 'Between a Rock and a Hard Place' (1992)

been little definition of such aesthetics with reference to actual works of art. This derives from a critical adoption of attitudes of ambivalence and 'postures of indiscernibility'[47] that have been useful in enabling critics and their black subjects to claim the foundation for a black politics of knowledge and representation. For Hall, it is a politics grounded in a new and potentially redemptive notion of 'ethnicity' and identity formation[48] intended to renew our sense of the importance of the 'diasporic' itself as an intellectual construct. As such, the common canonical ground for diaspora artists has been shaped by a politics of interpreting art-making as an ongoing activity of self-definition and identification. Formational for new cultural identities, the canon of black British art has figured as an artistic confrontation through the visual of the conventions and histories of picturing, display and documentation with wider implications for the symbolization of race, difference and nation.

Art and its institutions

The critical architecture for a canon of black British art would have amounted to little without the parallel activity of asserting its presence through institutions. The initiative summarized by Nanette Salomon that, 'as canons within academic disciplines go, the art historical canon is among the most virulent, the most virilent, and ultimately the most vulnerable',[49] had to be articulated with actual material change, so that to explode the hegemonic canon, and ensure the rise of a counter-canon, it was not enough simply to engage a novel genre of art criticism. The question of aesthetic discourses being tethered to institutional practices had been asked since the Caribbean artists who migrated to postwar Britain began to meditate on the issue of artistic 'sources', as in Ronald Moody's comment at a meeting of the Caribbean Artists Movement (CAM) in 1968 that 'Each one of us has to ... delve within himself and really begin to find out what he is ... And gradually a kind of inner fight had taken place, throwing away so much that I had learnt at school.'[50] With his CAM peers, Moody confronted the cultural capital of a colonial schooling and a Spivakian 'epistemic violence' in which forcefully manipulated representations of colonial cultural history, that 'remotely orchestrated, far-flung, and heterogeneous project to constitute the colonial subject as Other,'[51] had ensured Caribbean artists would remain exotic to the field and institutions of art history. Subsequent to their intervention, any radical illumination of the exclusionary and normalizing structures of the art historical canon, and in Salomon's phrase its 'sins of omission', has had to happen on many fronts.

The most significant among them is the patronage of artists and their public reception, where the effectiveness of critical movements for a black canon can be evaluated concretely. Initially the sort of gallery and exhibition spaces that 'Black Art' was given were mostly separate from mainstream commercial or prominent public galleries. As I have noted, for all the support they gave, these included spaces such as the Black Art Gallery and 198 Gallery which were less-known and little-accessed by a general art audience, and the Whitechapel Gallery, located in a part of London's East End which has traditionally been a place of sojourn and immigration. The situation was not improved by so-called 'community-based' initiatives such as the Greater London Council anti-racist mural project of 1985,[52] which attracted the common criticism that artists were being deliberately kept apart from the mainstream under the debilitating concept of 'ethnic arts' and 'ethnic minority arts'.[53] Until the impact of *The Other Story* in 1989, audiences would be relatively small and confined to narrow circles of those already attentive to how artists of a range of diasporas were articulating an emergent black cultural politics.

Replacing this situation during the 1990s was an alternative attitude to how best to support such artists. When I began interviewing arts programmers, curators, artists and critics in 1997, the official language of promotion had dispensed entirely with the notion of 'ethnic arts' in favour of a firmly multiculturalist emphasis on 'diversity' and recognition of 'difference',[54] similar to what had been around during the previous decade through the work of the Institute of Contemporary Arts.[55] This can still be seen in the recent priorities declared by the Arts Council England (ACE) that 'cultural diversity' with 'specific reference to ethnicity' ought to predominate among the funding and job opportunities for artists and curators. In May 2003, a national network of organizers was put in place to launch Decibel, an ACE initiative directed to 'ethnic diversity resulting from postwar immigration, with a focus on arts and artists from African, Asian and Caribbean backgrounds' promising 'to profile arts practice ... and to develop opportunities for increased access into the mainstream'.[56] But like the proposed ACE 'Year of Cultural Diversity', postponed from 2001 to 2002, re-branded as 'The Big Idea', and then subsequently scrapped, Decibel's agenda has already met with the criticism that it marks a 'current tendency towards a segregated visual arts sector'[57] and despite its declared aims to ensure that 'the landscape is changing',[58] 'has failed to spark debate about art world pathologies' typical of the 'institutional racism'[59] signalled in the 1999 MacPherson Report on the Stephen Lawrence Inquiry[60] and the Race Relations (Amendment) Act. The experience of organizations that try to work independently of ACE and its

Heritage Lottery-funded capital projects is perhaps best exemplified in the case of South Asian Diaspora Literature and Arts Archive (SALIDAA),[61] an online archive of 28 preserved collections relating to theatre, writing and art, including visual works by artists Samena Rana and Amal Ghosh. Once sources of funding run out, such as the three-year grant SALIDAA received from the New Opportunities Fund – drawn from £50 million of lottery money for digitization projects to produce online learning resources – the archive will again face a choice over how best to maintain its presence in the mainstream arts and heritage sector. If SALIDAA exemplifies wider 'efforts of ethnic-minority groups to preserve and interpret our own history',[62] achieving the requisite financial support to do so prompts careful thought about the gains and losses involved in resonating an 'accepted' language of cultural inclusion.

Since the 1980s, art institutions have obviously absorbed criticism about the exclusions they practice. Yet that this might be little more than the ability to construct and 'manage' cultural difference itself, is suggested by what Kobena Mercer has called 'multicultural managerialism' and 'multicultural normalization',[63] where ideas of diversity, heterogeneity and hybridity in the Western metropolis have largely become accommodated under conditions in which 'the subversive potential once invested in notions of hybridity has been subject to pre-millenial downsizing'.[64] Araeen has warned of how

> in the West, [multiculturalism] has been used as a cultural tool to ethnicise its non-white population in order to administer and control its aspirations for equality. It also serves as a smokescreen to hide the contradictions of a white society unable or unwilling to relinquish its imperial legacies. It is in this context that we should understand the fascination and celebration of cultural difference.[65]

Multiculturalist tokenism persists, it would seem, despite altering its appearance.

There is much to be said in favour of bringing Britain's diaspora artists into public visibility and establishing their presence in the historical record and imagination. Yet the canonizing project pursued to date has entailed a degree of circumscription and fixity that might actually narrow the possibility for understanding the experiences and concerns of such artists and their art, showering us with the 'mixed blessings' Lippard has noted of similar trends in the USA.[66] What gets overlooked in general are the differences among artists and their diverse histories, namely the range of ethnicities involved in struggles over representation. Hall wrote in 1988 that the 'black subject cannot be represented without reference to the divisions of class, gender, sexuality and ethnicity' and that we should make concerted efforts to see off any 'innocent notion of the essential black subject'.[67] Some commentators have suggested that the experience of racism is what all these artists have shared, and an experience of colonial history, or at least its after effects.[68] But is it fair to say that all of these individuals have been subject to racism in similar ways, and that their respective histories have been experienced identically? Gender aspects to any form of racism means it is unlikely that racism towards a British black woman will be the same as towards a British Asian man, and African and Caribbean ways of 'being black', of identifying with a community of black identities, can be strikingly at odds. Hierarchies have evolved whereby some artists are seen to be more disadvantaged (or more diasporic) than others, so that diaspora visuality has come to connote artists of the African and Afro-Caribbean diasporas, and occasionally those of South Asian descent, rather than their equally diasporic Chinese, Middle Eastern and Jewish peers.[69] Further decentring the presupposition of sharing are factors of sexuality, class, language, religion and beliefs. Finally, a simple generational division in which diaspora people in Britain are thought to belong either to the 'arrivant' group of the 1950s and 1960s, or their offspring, coming of age in the late 1970s, 1980s and 1990s, is not useful.[70] As many of the artists I have spoken with suggest, in simply erasing these differences, we can end up becoming essentialist without being necessarily strategic,[71] giving ground to the marginalizing forces and homogenizing tendencies of contemporary racism across the institutional, popular and critical landscape. It is worth noting that these issues were first raised during the growth of interest in inclusion and canonicity throughout the 1980s, but that arts policies have yet to confront even the most fundamental of these critical concerns. In arts policy and programming, institutional uses of the conclusions and polemics embedded in cultural criticism around the canon are still not a practised reality.

But cultural criticism itself cannot stand still. The common circumscriptions around the hetereogeneity of diaspora artists have not been halted by the albeit elastic nature of canonical terms like the diaspora aesthetic. The term is neither a term of description for an overall programme, a formal system of aesthetic evaluation, or a way of describing the reception of artists' works by a community of viewers. Rather, blind promotion of a canon of art thought to display a diaspora aesthetic has the effect of presupposing what kind of art is brought under discussion or on show in the first place, forcefully governing the sort of questions that may be asked about artists, and the histories proposed for their art. It is also no small irony that the political project of canonization, through commentary, display and promotion, has largely re-established the sort of narrative that it seeks to displace: a narrative unencumbered by 'ifs' and 'buts', by discontinuities, tensions and breaks, and not disturbed by exceptions to the rule. Indeed, the stability of any canon probably depends on making the commonalities among its selected artists outweigh their differences, glossing over their discrepancies to produce a persuasive uniformity. The result is an art history in the singular, a story without overlaps, loose ends, cross-currents or contradictions, which underscores a set of valued, valorized art works in a roll call of 'black' markers of heritage. It is the same sort of valorization that has historically ensured that diaspora artists remain marginal to national cultural narratives and that they are represented as a homogeneous, outsider mass.

There are artists who have chosen to distance, if not dissociate themselves, from any discussion of their art's relationship with talk of cultural or racial difference, concerns with ethnicity, 'blackness', diaspora and postcoloniality. An unfair reputation for making art solely around cultural identity debates, in the wake of a predominance during the 'Black Art' period of revisionism and opposition, has probably held back a more sophisticated reception. If there is pressure for artists to conform to patterns of cultural 'identification' whenever it is demanded of them by galleries and critics, they also face the threat of unpopularity whenever their assumed 'criticality' has been deemed undesirable or unfashionable. Like Marcia Bennett (Figure 8.3), many more artists have found themselves between a rock and a hard place. Writing about organizations specifically developed in the early 1990s 'to redress the balance created by the prevalent eurocentric attitudes in the visual arts', such as inIVA[72] and AAVAA,[73] the artist and curator Juginder Lamba has argued:

> The resultant elitism and inaccessibility have made them irrelevant to the majority of British artists with ancestral roots outside Europe. Much of the activity of these organizations focuses around a narrow band of artists whose work slots into their rationale, while the rest are ignored.[74]

Thinking of the selection and representation at work for artists from the African continent, John Picton has named the tokenism involved as 'the Jack-in-the-Box syndrome: the artist is thrust in a certain category, ready to jump out and dance only when the art historian springs the catch'.[75] As such, it had become increasingly rare by the mid-1990s for artists to feel comfortable with the implications suggested by the terms of the canon debate, especially since their entry into public recognition continued to be undervalued and vastly overshadowed by attention to their white contemporaries.[76] The general feeling about developments over the past two decades is that the ground of patronage and reception may indeed have shifted, but the core issues remain the same as artists are continually obliged to think about the ongoing terms of their representation.

Conclusions: a future canon?

Questioning the dominant, hegemonic canon continues to be a crucial project, widely enjoined by many thinkers and constituencies, and revealing of the still embattled beliefs invested in art practice as a critical site of transformation. The British case offers some distinct examples of the motivations and pressures for seizing the intellectual resources on offer to assemble canons, or counter-canons, and for contestation through art and its historiography. During the 1980s and early 1990s, these were much more conspicuous than they are at present; nowadays, exhibition organizers, curators and critical commentators are on the whole less inclined to name a stable corpus of art practices, and to describe any selection of artists as a coherent group sharing common outlooks and experiences. If artists of diverse backgrounds in Britain no longer focus their energies on 'becoming visible' as such, but more about the terms of their visibility – the manner in which they are promoted and received – this is some indication of the shifting, yet constant demands over representation in art and its histories.

The critical, institutional and historiographic project of canonizing the work of diaspora artists in Britain has not been without its mixed outcomes and discontents. The canon debate has happened without delivery of the guarantees of acceptance and understanding sought by the formation of artists and art works of recent decades, and we are left with some harrowing difficulties for writing a history of this art. Clearly canons have a troubling presence; living with and without a canon are equally as problematic, and never tenable for all of the time. The imperative to encapsulate a canon for a diverse community of identities has to be able to negotiate in a sustained way the double-bind of emphasizing ethnicity as the grounds for affinity. Since the canon debate is both enabling and yet so problematic, the advantage of knowing its history is about locating and learning from its problems: how to have a canon, but a self-reflexive one that is aware of its exclusions.

One such route to self-reflexivity has been opened up by the recent critique of how the discipline of cultural studies which has informed much black cultural criticism conceives of the art object and the artist. Regardless of claims that 'black cultural politics insists upon the ascendancy of a broader aesthetic and political project',[77] the weight of interest has rested unmistakably on the latter, as perhaps one might expect of a self-consciously, politically-led project to contest the dominant narratives of art history. Under these circumstances, however, alternative understandings of the histories of art remain very difficult to elucidate. So much so that, as artist Juginder Lamba has put it, simply: 'The work itself has become secondary',[78] or as Gabrielle Hezekiah suggests, commenting on a similar situation in the Caribbean, the outcome is 'the subsequent relegation of the work itself to relative obscurity and isolation in the midst of so much rhetorical fluff'.[79]

Despite its flexible usages, common to claims for a black British canon is that the art it names in some way communicates in the manner of (visual) texts and signs; indeed, much of the discussion around canonicity has taken place in the vocabulary of poststructuralist theory after its 'linguistic turn'. The linguistic and textuality paradigm would suppose that art objects have the ability to codify narratives, or to offer a didactic 'voice' in a wider political struggle, each of which requires the command of a visual language in which art does the work of a signifying cultural text. As Hal Foster recognized in his essay on 'The Artist as Ethnographer?', this renders the practitioner of art as 'a paragon of formal reflexivity, sensitive to difference and open to chance, a self-aware reader of culture understood as text'.[80] Yet for artist and critic Jean Fisher, thinking in this way tends to suggest that 'art is more a cultural product than a dynamic process or complex set of immanent and sensuous relations',[81] a complaint enlarged by Rasheed Araeen: 'As for the dominant discourse, it is so obsessed with cultural difference and identity, to the extent of suffering from an intellectual blockage, that it is unable to maintain its focus on the works of art themselves'.[82]

These criticisms presage a larger project of taking special issue with the implications of the prevailing theoretical attitude to art of Britain's diaspora communities, exemplified in the canonizing that has taken place, structured through the diaspora aesthetic idea. Seeking for the textuality of visual objects in the canon means that they have been made into signifiers, named as cultural products, transformed and translated into signs and representations. That this is an elaborate, circumambulatory way of skirting around the very art objects themselves becomes obvious when the constructed, discursive objects of art criticism (the objects of post-structuralist thinking) predominate at the expense of attention to the tactile and visually-apparent physical ones which emerge under the hands of artists: art objects with a material dimension, with textures and colours. Indeed, canonical claims have courted the risk of becoming complicit in what

Barbara Stafford sees as 'ruling metaphor of reading', 'the intellectual imperialism of collapsing diverse phenomenological performances, whether drawings, gestures, sounds or sense into interpretable texts without sensory diversity'.[83] And as the historian of philosophy Martin Dillon has remarked, 'One way not to see the world is to read it as text'.[84] In other words, the vitality and material presence of art in diaspora Britain remains undisclosed for as long as commentators allow debate on the art canon and theorization of the artist and art work to persist in the currently familiar ways.

Accordingly, any future assembling of a canon for black British art ought to be based on a high degree of reflection, not only about the institutions that would construct it, and their material effects, but on the intellectual architecture of art criticism – a place where the canon's structure is partly made yet still acutely felt. Granting value to the art of 'excluded' individuals or communities requires considerable energy to maintain in the face of the shifting hegemonic territory of art display, reception and commentary. There is perhaps a need to think less reactively about the supposedly urgent need for canonical practices in the first place, to ask why we ought to be burdened by perceptions of cultural marginality and exclusion. This is a question prompted by Zygmunt Bauman's suggestion about the recent history of interests in 'identity crisis', that 'Militant assertion of group identity will not remove the insecurity which prompted it'.[85] It oversteps the familiar territory of argument about what kind of canon might be most useful in constructing a secure cultural identity. Because the hegemonic terrain of representation is so unstable, one obvious measure is to keep firmly in view the alternatives for art writing if counter-canonization strategies should fall – or lead – into difficulties. Establishing the historical status of black British art practices might then depend on asking what other ways are there of 'writing art history' – of recording, dignifying, elevating, 'making visible', or 'making present' this art – which offer (at least provisional) political alternatives.

Certainly one possible route for future paths of art historiography and reception may be to explore more profoundly the interrelationships between cultural politics and cultural poetics, and to become receptive to how art practices have historically encompassed these intersections. Much can be gained, it seems, from treating concerns about art and aesthetics with insights about the limitations of canonization. They are insights that will help in fighting marginalization on several fronts: whether in terms of institutional practices of promotion, collection and display, or in the academic spaces of art criticism where the authorial agency of the artist is forced to vie for attention alongside semiotic-like readings of the social, cultural and political 'value' of the art work. I have

tried to show how these two areas are linked, how collapsing all types of
art production into a common pool of signifying, hybrid or ostensibly
'black' or 'diasporic' images makes for a counter-canon which has for
some time now ceased being critical and become an orthodoxy with dis-
appointing institutional consequences. One alternative, it seems, is to
reemphasize how it is that art objects offer a site at which language, signification and discourse actually intertwine with vision, touch and the
perceptual, and are objects in and of themselves before they are the means
and media of representation. Art works continue to refuse institutional
circumscription in their status as historical, physical deposits of a very
peculiar kind through being perceptually and aesthetically present, even
as they are culturally specific, discursive and contingent. Reflecting on the
work of artists at international art biennials, Jean Fisher has suggested
that 'what remains underdeveloped are transcultural studies of aesthetic
practice that would extend our understanding of the art of others beyond
ethnic typology'.[86] Perhaps much might be gained by exploring through
these terms the future directions for diverse artists in contemporary Britain
and the canons they will speak to and from.

Notes

* I thank the editors of this book for their kind assistance with this chapter during
my absence from the UK on fieldwork in the Caribbean. My thanks go once
again to Anne Walmsley for her continuing energies, encouragement and support, and for helping me to define and distinguish the focus of this chapter
alongside antecedent formations around CAM and its legacy. I am also grateful
to the University of Sussex and The Leverhulme Trust for the Early Career
Fellowship that enabled its completion, to Mary Turner and Kate Quinn of the
Institute of Commonwealth Studies, University of London, where I presented an
earlier draft of this chapter in February 2004, and to Anna Lora of the Institute
of Social and Cultural Anthropology, University of Oxford, for her constant support. Figures 8.1–8.3 are reproduced with the kind permissions of the artists.
 1. I am thinking not only of the artists who assembled to form the Caribbean
    Artists Movement (CAM), but other representations such as the showcasing
    of 'Commonwealth art' at the Commonwealth Institute, London, from the
    early 1960s, and the artists showing at Denis Bowen's New Vision Centre
    Gallery, who were mostly from the Commonwealth, even if they did not
    describe themselves as such. See A. Walmsley, *The Caribbean Artists Movement:
    1966–1972* (London: New Beacon Books, 1992), and my 'Francis Newton
    Souza and Aubrey Williams: Entwined Art Histories at the End of Empire' in
    S. Faulkner and A. Ramamurthy (eds), *Visual Culture in Britain at the End of
    Empire* (London: Ashgate, 2006).
 2. E. Chambers, *The Emergence and Development of Black Visual Arts Activity in
    England between 1981 and 1986: Press and Public Responses*, PhD thesis
    (Goldsmiths College, University of London, 1998).

3. Keith Piper, 'The Fictions of Science', 1996. Reproduced in D. Chandler (ed.), *Keith Piper: Relocating the Remains* (London: Institute of International Visual Arts and the Royal College of Art, London, 1997), p. 88.

4. See Chandler, 1997, *op. cit.*

5. Press release, Black Art Gallery, London 1984, unpaginated.

6. Again, see Chandler, 1997 *op. cit.*, and the artist's own writing: K. Piper, *A Ship Called Jesus* (Birmingham: Ikon Gallery, 1991); cf. Piper's collaged phototext works, K. Piper, 'Body and Text', *Third Text*, 2, Winter (1987/88) pp. 53–61.

7. See D. A. Bailey and S. Hall (eds), *Critical Decade: Black British Photography in the 1980s, Special Issue. Ten.8*, no. 3 (1992); and I. Julien and K. Mercer, 'De Margin and De Centre. The Last 'Special Issue' on Race?', *Screen*, 29, no. 4, (1988) pp. 2–11.

8. It was a decade that for some was disappointingly short-lived. Chambers for instance argues that the properly 'critical' period ended in 1986, after a spate of 'Black Art' exhibitions and 'arts activism'. See Chambers, 1998, *op. cit.*, and E. Chambers, 'The Black Art Group' *Artrage*, 14 Autumn (1986) pp. 28–29.

9. Wolverhampton Art Gallery, *Black Art an' Done: An Exhibition of Work by Young Black Artists* (Wolverhampton: Wolverhampton Art Gallery, 1981).

10. E. Chambers, *et al. The First National Black Art Convention to Discuss the Form, Functioning and Future of Black Art* (Wolverhampton: Wolverhampton Polytechnic, 1982).

11. See for example: P. Gilroy, 'Cruciality and the Frog's Perspective: An Agenda of Difficulties for the Black Arts Movement in Britain', *Third Text*, 5, Winter (1988/89) pp. 33–44.

12. See: Mappin Art Gallery, *Into the Open: New Painting, Prints and Sculpture by Contemporary Black Artists* (Mappin Art Gallery, Sheffield, 1984); Creation for Liberation *Creation for Liberation Open Exhibition: Art by Black Artists* (London: Creation for Liberation, 1985); L. Himid, *The Thin Black Line* (Hebden Bridge: Urban Fox Press, 1985); Institute of Contemporary Arts, *The Thin Black Line* (London: ICA, 1985); Black Art Gallery, *Some of Us Are Brave, All of Us Are Strong: An Exhibition by and about Black Women* (London: Black Art Gallery, 1986); Black Art Gallery, *From Generation to Generation (The Installation)* (London: Black Art Gallery, 1986); E. Chambers (ed.), *Black Art: Plotting the Course* (Oldham: Oldham Art Gallery; Wolverhampton: Wolverhampton Art Gallery, Liverpool: Bluecoat Gallery, 1988); E. Chambers, T. Joseph and J. Lamba (eds), *The Artpack: A History of Black Artists in Britain* (London: Haringey Arts Council, 1988); R. Araeen, *The Essential Black Art* (London: Kala Press, 1988); Stoke on Trent City Museum and Art Gallery *Black Art: New Directions* (Stoke on Trent: Stoke on Trent City Museum and Art Gallery, 1989); E. Chambers (ed.), *Let the Canvas Come to Life with Dark Faces* (Sheffield: Herbert Art Gallery and Museum, 1990).

13. Tam Joseph 'UK School Report', 1984, acrylic on canvas, 141 × 76 in. Collection of Sheffield City Art Galleries.

14. Tam Joseph, 'Spirit of the Carnival', 1988, reproduced in Chambers *et al.*, *op. cit.*, 1988, p. 30.

15. See E. Chambers (ed.), *Us an' Dem: A Critical Look at Relationships Between the Police, the Judiciary and the Black Community* (Lancashire: Lancashire Probation Service, 1994); K. Owusu, and J. Ross (eds), *Behind the Masquerade: The Story of the Notting Hill Carnival* (London: Arts Media Group, 1988); Arts Council of

Great Britain, *Masquerading: The Art of Notting Hill Carnival* (London: Arts Council, 1986).

16. M. Sealy (ed.), *Vanley Burke: A Retrospective* (London: Lawrence & Wishart, 1993), p. 12.

17. Vanley Burke, monochrome photograph, reproduced in Sealy, 1993 *op. cit.*, pp. 56–7.

18. Sonia Boyce 'From Someone Else's Fear Fantasy to Metamorphosis', 1987, mixed media on photograph, reproduced in G. Tawadros, *Sonia Boyce: Speaking in Tongues* (London: Kala Press, 1997), p. 43.

19. I am thinking of artists like Claudette Johnson, Joy Gregory, Veronica Ryan, Chila Burman, Ingrid Pollard, Lubaina Himid and others who led and helped to comprise many of the group 'Black Art' shows I have cited. Setting them apart from the Afrocentrism of those such as Piper and Chambers, with its inherent masculinist bias, were their concerns with by turns robust, counter-representations of femininity, themes of domesticity and intimacy, and an iconoclastic attitude to dominant configurations of British nationhood, enhanced by frequently collaborative practices that served to question the orthodoxy of the artist as an autonomous individual creator. For further elucidation, see Boyce's own views expressed at that time, in: J, Roberts, 'Sonia Boyce in conversation with John Roberts', *Third Text*, 1, Autumn (1987) pp. 55–64.

20. For contemporary sources that make note of this see: S. Dedi, 'Black Art in Britain Today' *Arts Review*, November, (1984) pp. 556–7, and N. Khan, 'Struggles for Black Arts in Britain' *Artrage*, 14 (1986).

21. Note, for example, what similarities the earlier quote from Piper bears to Larry Neal's writing of 1968:

> The Black Arts Movement is radically opposed to any concept of the artist that alienates him from his community. Black Art is the aesthetic and spiritual sister of the Black Power concept. As such, it envisions an art that speaks directly to the needs and aspirations of Black America. In order to perform this task, the Black Arts Movement proposes a radical re-ordering of the western cultural aesthetic. It proposes a separate symbolism, mythology, critique, and iconology. The Black Arts and the Black Power concept both relate broadly to the Afro-American's desire for self-determination and nationhood. Both concepts are nationalistic. One is concerned with the relationship between art and politics; the other with the art of politics. (L. Neal, 'Black Art' in W. L. Van Deburg (ed.), *Modern Black Nationalism: From Marcus Garvey to Louis Farrakhan* (London and New York: New York University Press, 1997))

For further parallels see E. Chambers, *Run Through the Jungle: Selected Writings by Eddie Chambers* (London: inIVA, 1999), and a concise review of that anthology: N. Ratnam, 'Run Through the Jungle: Selected Writings by Eddie Chambers', *Third Text*, 48 (1999) pp. 78–80.

22. R. Araeen, *The Essential Black Art* (London: Kala Press, 1988), p. 5. Araeen's definition compares to the larger pattern of political organization outside the art community, evident from an earlier statement by the Organization of Women of Asian and African Descent (OWAAD): 'When we use the term "black" we use it as a political term. It doesn't describe skin colour, it defines

our situation here in Britain. We're here as a result of British imperialism, and our continued oppression in Britain is the result of British racism', *Race and Class*, XXVII, no. 1 (1985) p. 32.

23. For an overview of this history see A. Ghosh and J. Lamba (eds), *Beyond Frontiers: Contemporary British Art by Artists of South Asian Descent* (London: Saffron Books, 2001).

24. See M. Keen and E. Ward, *Recordings: A Select Bibliography of Contemporary African, Afro-Caribbean and Asian British Art* (London: Institute of International Visual Arts and Chelsea College of Art and Design, 1996).

25. The relationship between the two publications is explained in R. Araeen, 'Why "Third Text"?', *Third Text*, 1 (1987) pp. 3–5.

26. R. Araeen, 'Preliminary Notes for a Black Manifesto', *Black Phoenix* 1 (1978) pp. 3–12; reprinted in R. Araeen, *Making Myself Visible* (London: Kala Press, 1984). For early evidence of campaigning by Asian diaspora artists, see R. Araeen and D. Medalla, 'Open Letter to the British Council', *Art Monthly* (1979) pp. 24–25; and B. Khanna, 'Obscure but Important', *Art Monthly*, 36 (1980) p. 25, sparking debate in a following issue: M. Rewcastle, 'The Place of "Ethnic" in Art', *Art Monthly*, 37 (1980) p. 17. Araeen and Medalla's letters partly respond to the official literature of the 1970s on public arts funding, such as N. Khan, *The Arts Britain Ignores: The Arts of Ethnic Minorities in Britain* (London: Arts Council of Great Britain, 1976).

27. That this aspect of the British context has yet to be understood properly abroad is obvious from misleading generalizations about the unquestioned collapsing in the UK of many diaspora identifications into a common black label, as expressed in the curator's essay in the exhibition catalogue: M.J. Beauchamp-Bird and M.F. Sirmans (eds), *Transforming the Crown: African, Asian and Caribbean Artists in Britain, 1966–1996* (New York: Caribbean Cultural Center, 1997). Understandably, it led one reviewer of the exhibition to state: 'Black Britain [is] a term that includes folk ranging from Bengalis to Zanzibaris and that most closely corresponds to our usage of "people of color" ', H. Chase, 'A New Take on an Old Kingdom: Black Artists Paint a Different Picture', *American Visions*, Dec.–Jan. (1997) pp. 18–22. This misreading is in no way compensated for by the narrowly defined Black paradigm of Powell's study, in which he cherry-picks for attention British artists such as Piper and Boyce, without treatment of their contingent history of identification with a wider range of ethnicities, see: R. Powell, *Black Art and Culture in the Twentieth Century* (London: Thames & Hudson, 1997). For another US authored publication that presents the cultural politics of difference in art history as a primarily 'white–black' binary, see K.N. Pinder, *Race-ing Art History: Critical Readings in Race and Art History* (London: Routledge, 2003). I enlarge on the detrimental implications this has for the discipline as a whole in my review of Pinder's book in: *Journal of Visual Culture in Britain*, V, no. 2. (2004), pp. 114–18.

28. P. Gilroy, 'Nothing But Sweat Inside my Hand': diaspora aesthetics and Black arts in Britain', in K. Mercer (ed.), *Black Film/British Cinema, ICA Documents 7* (London: Institute of Contemporary Arts, 1988), p. 44.

29. A. De Souza and S. Merali (eds), *Crossing Black Waters*, exhibition catalogue (Leicester City Art Gallery and Working Press, London, 1991), p. 7. Gilroy is quoted from Grey Art Gallery, *Interrogating Identity*, exhibition catalogue (New York: Grey Art Gallery, 1991).

30. A reprint of Hall's essay, 'Cultural Identity and Cinematic Representation', appears in Baker *et al.*, 1996, *op. cit.*, p. 220.

31. G. Tawadros, 'Beyond the Boundary: The Work of Three Black Women Artists', in Baker *et al.*, 1996, *op. cit.*, p. 240.

32. See for example the clash of priorities made plain in: R. Araeen and E. Chambers, 'Black Art: A Discussion', *Third Text* Winter (1988) pp. 51–62.

33. Presented as 'a story that has never been told' which would rewrite the 'official sequential or ideological' narratives of art history, the exhibition was initiated, researched and curated by Rasheed Araeen and organized by The South Bank Centre, London, after more than a decade of pressure from Araeen to have public money granted to a major retrospective of Britain's postwar artists of many diasporas. See: R. Araeen (ed.), *The Other Story: Afro-Asian Artists in Post-war Britain* (London: Hayward Gallery, 1989). The exhibition elicited a range of responses, from the constructively critical to the deeply harmful, see: B. Sewell, 'Pride or Prejudice', *The Sunday Times Magazine*, 26 November (1989) p. 8; and P. Fuller, 'Black Artists: Don't Forget Europe', *The Sunday Telegraph*, 10 December (1989) p. 10; H. Bhabha and S. Biswas, 'The Wrong Story', *New Statesman*, 15 December (1989) pp. 40–2; R. Keegan, 'The Story So Far', *Spare Rib*, February (1990) p. 36. Araeen's response to Sewell and Fuller and a look back at events of the previous decade is given in: 'The Other Immigrant: The Experience and Achievements of Afro-Asian Artists in the Metropolis', *Third Text*, 15 Summer (1991), pp. 17–28.

34. I. Ang 'Identity Blues' in P. Gilroy, L. Grossberg and A. McRobbie (eds), *Without Guarantees: In Honour of Stuart Hall*, (London: Verso, 2000), pp. 1–13.

35. S. Hall, 'What is this "Black" in Black Popular Culture?', in G. Dent (ed.), *Black Popular Culture: A Project by Michele Wallace* (Seattle: Bay Press, 1992), p. 29.

36. D. Morley and C. Kuan-Hsing (eds), *Stuart Hall: Critical Dialogues in Cultural Studies* (London: Routledge, 1996), p. 9; cf. S. Hall, 'New Ethnicities', in K. Mercer (ed.), *Black Film/British Cinema*, ICA Documents 7 (London: Institute of Contemporary Arts, 1988).

37. S. Hall, 'Cultural Identity and Diaspora', in J. Rutherford (ed.), *Identity: Community, Culture, Difference* (London: Lawrence & Wishart, 1990), p. 237.

38. Quoted in Hall (1996), *op. cit.*, p. 220.

39. Sutapa Biswas, 'Housewives with Steak Knives', 1985, oil, pastel and acrylic on paper and canvas, 96 × 108 in., Bradford Art Galleries and Museums, reproduced in Chambers *et al.*, *op. cit.*, 1988, p. 8; Beauchamp-Bird *et al.*, 1997, *op. cit.*, p. 29.

40. Tawadros, 1996, *op. cit.*

41. Valerie Brown 'Encounters' (from the series), 1991, colour photograph/montage, reproduced in *Four × 4: Installations By Sixteen Artists in Four Gallery Spaces* (Harris Museum and Art Gallery, Preston; Wolverhampton Art Gallery, Wolverhampton; The City Gallery, Leicester; Arnolfini, Bristol, 1991), p. 16.

42. Hall's comments on miscegenation should probably be quoted in full here. He writes:

> But I had forgotten how persistently in these early days at the centre of the problem – the problem of the problem, so to speak – was the core issue of sexuality: specifically, sexual relations between different ethnic or racial groups – or, to give it its proper name, the traumatic fantasy of miscegenation. It is as if, at the centre of this whole regime of representation, there

> was one unrepresentable [*sic*] image, which nevertheless cast a silent shadow across the visual field, driving those who sensed its absence-presence crazy: the image of black sexuality figured transgressively across the boundaries of race and ethnicity. In the mirror image of the imagery – screaming to be spoken – we find figured this 'unspeakable': the traumatic inscription of black and white people, together, making love – and having children, as the proof that, against God and Nature, *something worked*. (S. Hall, 'Reconstruction Work', in D. A. Bailey and S. Hall (1992), *op. cit.*, p. 112)

43. The continuing relevance of Brown's work, perhaps, is that those mainly unspoken fears of miscegenation and crude multiculturalist outlooks might in fact be of a piece, given their tendency to see ethnicity as an essentially-held difference, and Britain's national community as discrete partitions of difference and diversity to be kept apart and separately maintained.
44. Marcia Bennett 'Between a Rock and a Hard Place', 1992, mixed media 24 × 50 in., reproduced in Beauchamp-Bird *et al.*, 1997, *op. cit.*, p. 92.
45. Hall, 1996, *op. cit.*, p. 211.
46. For further discussion of these themes, and a thesis on the centrality of exile to artistic modernism, see: S. Maharaj, 'The Congo is Flooding the Acropolis: Art in Britain of the Immigrations', *Third Text*, 15, Summer (1991), pp. 77–90.
47. Tawadros (1996), *op. cit.*
48. S. Hall, 'On Postmodernism and Articulation: An Interview with Stuart Hall', in D. Morley *et al.*, 1996, *op. cit.*; cf. Hall, 1988, *op. cit.*
49. N. Salomon, 'The Art Historical Canon: Sins of Omission', in J.E. Hartman and E. Messer-Davidow (eds), *(En)gendering Knowledge: Feminists in Academe* (Tennessee: University of Tennessee Press, 1991).
50. Quoted in Walmsley, 1992, *op. cit.*, p. 181.
51. G. Spivak, 1991 'Can the subaltern speak?' in P. Williams and L. Chrisman (eds), *Colonial Discourse and Post-Colonial Theory* (Hemel Hempstead: Harvester Wheatsheaf, 1991), p. 76. See also P. Childs and P. Williams, *An Introduction to Post-Colonial Theory* (London: Prentice-Hall, 1997), pp. 164–6.
52. GLC, *Anti-Racist Mural Project* (London: GLC Race Equality Unit, Greater London Council, 1985); GLC, *New Horizons: Exhibition of Arts* (London: GLC Ethnic Arts Sub-Committee, 1985).
53. R. Araeen, *History of Black Artists in Britain*, unpublished papers (London: GLC Race Equality Unit, 1986); R. Araeen, 'From Primitivism to Ethnic Arts', *Third Text*, 1 (1987) pp. 6–25. These contributions from Araeen respond to as well as anticipate the prevailing official outlooks and practices typified during the period from Khan, 1976, *op. cit.*, until 1989. Some primary and secondary sources include: Arts Council, *The Arts and Ethnic Minorities: Action Plan* (London: Arts Council of Great Britain, 1985); K. Owusu, *The Struggle for Black Arts in Britain: What Can We Consider Better Than Freedom* (London: Comedia, 1986); Owusu 1988, *op. cit.*; R. Cork, B. Khanna and S. Read, *Art on the South Bank: An Independent Report* (London: Greater London Council, 1986); M. Fisher, 'Black Art: The Labour Party's Line', *Modern Painters*, 2 no. 4 (1989) pp. 77–8.
54. Arts Council of Great Britain, *The Arts and Cultural Diversity* (London: Arts Council of Great Britain, 1989); R. Lavrijsen (ed.), *Cultural Diversity in the Arts: Art, Art Policies and the Facelift of Europe* (The Netherlands: Royal Tropical

Institute, 1993); S. Walker, 'Black Cultural Museums in Britain', in E. Hooper Greenhill (ed.), *Cultural Diversity: Developing Museum Audiences in Britain* (Leicester: Leicester University Press, 1997); cf. Black Arts Alliance, *Black Arts Alliance Report* (Manchester, 1999); GLA, *Without Prejudice? Exploring Ethnic Differences in London* (London: Greater London Authority, 2000).

55. See for example: Institute of Contemporary Arts, *The Thin Black Line* (London: ICA, 1985); D.A. Bailey and K. Mercer (eds), *Mirage: Enigmas of Race, Difference and Desire* (London: ICA and inIVA, 1995); H. Bhabha (ed.), *Identity, ICA documents 6* (London: Institute of Contemporary Arts, 1987); K. Mercer (ed.), *Black Film/British Cinema, ICA Documents 7* (London: Institute of Contemporary Arts and the British Film Institute, 1988).

56. R. Hylton, 'The Politics of Cultural Diversity', *Art Monthly*, 274 March (2004), p. 20.

57. Hylton, 2004, *op. cit.*

58. http://www.decibel-db.org accessed 1 November 2004.

59. See Hylton, 2004, *op. cit.*, p. 21. Hylton writes: 'The notion that some people are more culturally diverse than others is as spurious as it is to consider some people as being more ethnic than others. ... "Ethnic minority" and "culturally diverse" are terms that privilege a limited notion of difference based on race. Such euphemisms are unhelpful because they presuppose normality to be white and everything else to be diverse'.

60. HMSO, *The Stephen Lawrence Inquiry: Report of an Inquiry by Sir William MacPherson of Cluny* (London, Home Office: February, 1999); Commission for Racial Equality, *The Stephen Lawrence Inquiry: Implications for Racial Equality* (Great Britain, 1999); Home Office, *Race Relations (Amendment) Act 2000: New Laws for a Successful Multi-Racial Britain* (London: Home Office: 2001).

61. http://www.salidaa.org.uk

62. S. Wajid, 'Resourceful Asian Seeks Partner with Money ...', *The Times Higher Education Supplement*, 10 September 2004.

63. Mercer writes: 'To the extent that the postcolonial vocabulary, characterized by such terms as "diaspora", "ethnicity" and "hybridity", has displaced an earlier discourse of assimilation, adaptation and integration, we have witnessed a massive social transformation which has generated, in the Western metropolis, what could now be called a condition of *multicultural normalization*', K. Mercer, 'A Sociography of Diaspora', in Gilroy *et al.*, 2000, *op. cit.*, p. 234; cf. S. Hall and S. Maharaj (2001), 'Modernity and Difference: A Conversation Between Stuart Hall and Sarat Maharaj', in S. Campbell and G. Tawadros (eds), *Stuart Hall and Sarat Maharaj: Modernity and Difference* (London: Institute for International Visual Arts, 2000), p. 46.

64. By 'downsizing' Mercer indicates the systematic absorption and circumscription of initiatives toward diversity by public and other institutions, a meaning given special inflection by this borrowing of vocabulary from a corporate ethos of productivity and efficiency. See Mercer, 2000, *op. cit.*, p. 235.

65. Araeen, 1994, *op. cit.*, p. 9.

66. L. Lippard, *Mixed Blessings: New Art in a Multicultural America* (New York: Pantheon Books, 1990).

67. This involves not only 'crossing the questions of racism irrevocably with questions of sexuality', destabilizing 'particular conceptions of black masculinity' and overcoming black politics' 'evasive silence with reference to

class', but more generally, 're-theorizing the concept of difference', so as to develop a 'non-coercive and more diverse concept of ethnicity'. Hall, 1988, *op. cit.*

68. See Gilroy, 1988, *op. cit.*; P. Gilroy, *Small Acts: Thoughts on the Politics of Black Cultures* (London: Serpent's Tail, 1993); Chambers, 1998, *op. cit.*

69. D. Yeh, 'Ethnicities on the move: "British-Chinese" Art – Identity, Subjectivity, Politics and Beyond', *Critical Quarterly*, 42, no. 2 (2000) pp. 65–91; F. Lloyd (ed.), *Contemporary Arab Women's Art: Dialogues of the Present* (London: I. B. Tauris, 1999); F. Lloyd (ed.), *Displacement and Difference: Contemporary Arab Visual Culture in the Diaspora* (London: Saffron Books, 2000); R. Garfield, 'Ali G: Just Who Does He Think He Is?', *Third Text*, 54 Spring (2001) pp. 63–70; R. Garfield, *Identity Politics and the Performative: Encounters with Recent Jewish Art* (London: Royal College of Art, unpublished PhD thesis, 2003); P. Skelton 'Restretching the Canvas', in R. Betterton (ed.), *Unframed: The Practices and Politics of Women Painting* (London: I.B. Tauris, 2003) pp. 162–183.

70. Many artists who featured in developments of the past three decades were in fact born abroad, yet share contemporaneity and peer group with those of immigrant parents. Some examples to note include: in the Caribbean case, Veronica Ryan who came here as a baby, and Denzil Forrester and Hew Locke as adolescents; from Africa, Yinka Shonibare and Sokari Douglas-Camp, who continue to move between Nigeria and Britain, Juginder Lamba and Zarina Bhimji from Uganda, and Johannes Phokela and Gavin Jantjes of South Africa; from South Asia, Rasheed Araeen of Pakistan, and Balraj Khanna of India; from the Middle East, Mona Hatoum of Palestine; and from elsewhere in Europe, Zineb Sedira of France. The differences between the experiences of the two generations has often been a matter of face-to-face debate, the earliest example is the seminar organized by Creation for Liberation in Brixton, 1987, when Aubrey Williams addressed younger, British-born artists of a range of ethnicities. See Walmsley, 1992, *op. cit.*, pp. 320, 340.

71. As Fisher puts it, 'Where art takes up an essentialist position – even if this is a masquerading tactic – it risks becoming excluded by the exclusionary politics it proffers, addressing a limited constituency which cannot alone sustain an adequate production or promotional support system'. J. Fisher, 'The syncretic turn: cross-cultural practices in the age of multiculturalism', in Kalinovska, Gangitano and Nelson (eds), *New Histories* (Boston: The Institute of Contemporary Art, 1996), p. 35.

72. In 1995, the Institute of International Visual Arts (inIVA), based in London, UK, largely funded by the Arts Council of Great Britain, was established under the rubric of 'internationalism' in art practice, with a continuing programme including publications, exhibitions, schools education, a web presence, commissions of art work, art writing, artists in residence and open lectures.

73. Artist Eddie Chambers began to assemble a small archive at his own home whilst still a student in the early 1980s, building the collection on documentation and visual examples of his own art and activities, those of collaborators, and of younger diaspora artists passing through Higher Education. In 1988 the Arts Council of England and the Gulbenkian Foundation gave Chambers enough support to establish the African and Asian Visual Artists Archive (AAVAA) in Bristol. In 1997 AAVAA was transferred to premises of the

University of East London, and Sonia Boyce and David A. Bailey were appointed as its co-directors.

74. S. Rizvi, 'Here and Now II: Juginder Lamba in Conversation', in A. Ghosh and J. Lamba (eds), *Beyond Frontiers: Contemporary British Art by Artists of South Asian Descent* (London: Saffron Books, 2001), p. 257.

75. J. Picton, 'In Vogue, or The Flavour of the Month: The New Way to Wear Black', *Third Text*, 23, Summer (1993) pp. 88–98. Similar implications have been noted for what this has come to mean for 'the relation between art from the black or non-European artist and the Western art system ... where the greater the work's visibility in terms of racial or ethnic context the less it is able to speak as an individual utterance. The galleries and museums have responded to the demand to end cultural marginality simply by exhibiting more non-European artists, albeit on a selective and representative basis, provided that they demonstrate appropriate signs of cultural difference': Fisher, 1996, *op. cit.*, p. 33.

76. K. Mercer, 'Ethnicity and Internationality: New British Art and Diaspora-Based Blackness', *Third Text*, 49, Winter (1999–2000), pp. 51–62.

77. Tawadros, 1996, *op cit.*, p. 274.

78. Lamba and Rizvi, 2001, *op. cit.*, p. 256.

79. G. Hezekiah, 'Conceptualising the Boundaries of Nation-Space: Some Thoughts on Art, Criticism and the Creation of a Canon', *Small Axe*, 6 September (1999) p. 81.

80. H. Foster, 'The Artist as Ethnographer?' in J. Fisher (ed.), *Global Visions: Towards a New Internationalism in the Visual Arts* (London: Kala Press, 1994). p. 14.

81. Fisher, 1996, *op. cit.*, p. 33.

82. R. Araeen, 'New Internationalism, or the Multiculturalism of Global Bantustans', in Fisher, 1994, *op. cit.*, p. 9.

83. B.M. Stafford, *Good Looking: Essays on the Virtues of Images* (Cambridge, Mass.: MIT Press, 1995), p. 8.

84. M.C. Dillon, *Semiological Reductionism: A Critique of the Deconstructionist Movement in Postmodern Thought* (New York: State University of New York Press, 1995) p. 104.

85. Z. Bauman, *In Search of Politics* (London: Polity Press, 1999), p. 197.

86. J. Fisher, 'The Work Between Us', in O. Enwezor (ed.), *Trade Routes: History and Geography* (Johannesburg, South Africa: Greater Johannesburg Metropolitan Council and the Prince Claus Fund for Culture and Development, 1997) pp. 20–2.

9
'Shaping Connections': From West Indian to Black British

*Gail Low**

Central to the debates surrounding the construction of black British expressive cultures are questions regarding nationality, canonicity and tradition. How 'black' modifies British (and vice versa) adds a layer of complexity: how to preserve the specificity of black history in Britain and yet also acknowledge its distinctive connections with black cultures within and outside the national polity. In his attempt to formulate a language of criticism that does justice to aesthetic and political contours of black British writing, John McLeod's essay in this collection, 'Fantasy Relationships' emphasizes their transnational interconnections. McLeod writes that to 'approach the work of writers such as [Linton Kwesi] Johnson, [Caryl] Phillips, [Jackie] Kay and [Sam] Selvon in terms of a national paradigm ultimately fails ... to render the experience of black peoples in Britain'.[1] Imagination cannot be bound by the borders of nation, and black writing from across the Atlantic has enabled black writing to occur 'in' and 'about' Britain. Black writing in Britain also dares to expose, for all Britons, the criss-crossings, the comings and goings, the transnational influences which arguably inform the construction of virtually all texts and canons which bear the signature of 'British'. Moreover, recent criticism has increasingly engaged with this emphasis upon a transnational, migratory and diasporic consciousness across cultures.[2]

A seemingly too easy emphasis on the 'post-national' aspects of black intellectual and aesthetic activity, however, may lead to a dangerous forgetting that citizenship, in the UK, and the right to belong, whether it be legally, or politically or culturally construed, are hard won. At times, the effortless internationalism of creative writing looks like an alarming suspension of critical faculties when set alongside a long history of black political struggles. Thus in 'Black British Writing – So what is it?',[3] Mike Phillips takes an opposing stance. He suggests that the ostensible reference

168

to skin colour in naming who and what 'black British' is may hinder, rather than help, clarify the situation. Phillips draws attention to Britishness in the equation, insisting on the distinctiveness of the black experience in Britain against a unproductive tendency to 'subsume the local and regional distinctiveness of black writers within a universalized rhetoric of "blackness" associated with the Caribbean, African and black America.' Similarly, Phillips' essay in this volume is also careful to insist on the specific circumstances, such as the 'historical crises' of the 'the Notting Hill riots', the struggle against the 'sus' laws and the murder of Stephen Lawrence, that have gone into the shaping of the 'concept of black Britishness'. He argues that what makes this narrative of private and public identity British, 'is that these things took place within specific geographical and cultural limits and are determined by the conditions and processes operating within the limits of these particular boundaries.'[4]

Yet, despite the deliberate polemical introduction, it is not my aim in this essay to construct a polarity of distinct and mutually exclusive positions; for this would be a deliberate misreading of the specific critical interventions. McLeod himself recognizes that 'nations are not so easily soluble', and Phillips' biography of black Britain describes a relentless traversing of cultures, peoples and places.[5] Rather, I will argue that there is a productive tension existing between the materiality of place and the spatiality of diasporic connections across borders and locations which should be acknowledged. So, instead of beginning with the obvious interrogative, 'what is black British?' and 'who does it name?', I want to ask a more troublesome question – 'black British for whom?' – in order to accentuate that the act of naming is not simply denotative, but also discursive. 'Black British for whom?' draws attention to who is speaking what, when, why and for whom, allowing us to historicize the discursive context of its utterance. It is thus essential to examine the usage to which such utterances are put to in diverse contexts. Crucially, it invites us to investigate how texts address their readership, and shows how reading communities are implicated in a textual process.[6] For the purposes of this essay, I want to offer three examples: the publication of the *West Indian Gazette*;[7] the appearance in print of James Berry's foundational anthologies of West Indian and black British writing, *Bluefoot Traveller* and *News from Babylon*;[8] and, finally, the launch of *Wasafiri* as an official journal of the pressure group for curriculum reform, the Association for the Teaching of Caribbean, African, Asian and Associated Literatures (ATCAL). My chapter will focus primarily on the *West Indian Gazette*, but I shall also look at prefaces and editorials in Berry's anthologies and in the pages of *Wasafiri*. The choice of these texts is deliberate, for they mark nodal points in the processes of migrancy and settlement, and in the historical transformation of West Indian and/or black in Britain to black British. These texts are also fascinating for their construction of the imaginary constituency of readers that people its pages: the sometimes public–and sometimes intimate – address to the constructed 'you' who reads the text. In discussing how these journals constitute and represent their reading communities, I will argue that they interpellate[9] a transnational reader who is attuned both to the Caribbean, African and (sometimes) Asian culture and history, via a life in Britain. In doing so, I shall contend that advocating transnationality does not mean that one forgoes the situatedness endemic upon an engagement with local political and artistic struggles.

The *West Indian Gazette and Afro-Asian Caribbean News* was conceived of as a popular campaigning newspaper directed at the West Indian community in Britain. It was published between 1958 and 1965 and edited for most of that time by the Trinidadian-born Claudia Jones, who came to Britain after having been deported from the USA for her political activities during the McCarthyite campaigns against communist and left-wing organizations. Jones became a member of the British Communist Party and was active in civil rights campaigns from within the West Indian community; she established an annual Notting Hill carnival, and founded and edited the *West Indian Gazette*. In many ways, Jones was a pivotal figure in the fostering of a West Indian identity, particularly in London, where she and the *Gazette* were based. Yet compared with her contemporaries, she seems to be a relatively neglected figure; to date there has been very few serious critical engagements with her life and work.[10] Yet, in founding the *Gazette*, Jones was responding to a political and cultural need created by the incursion and failure of early West Indian newspapers, and did so with remarkable professionalism. The *Gazette* was especially adroit at juggling both high and low culture, political reporting with more domestic and populist items. It took on the role of informing its readers not only about Caribbean history and politics, but also about major national and international news events of the day such as independence movements abroad, anti-apartheid campaigns, the Civil Rights movement in the United States, workers rights and immigration policy in Britain. It contained literary, cultural and art reviews, as well as fashion items, beauty tips, recipes, and gossip. In the 1950s, a small cluster of publications catered for a West Indian readership, notably, the *Gleaner, Caribbean News, Carib, Magnet, Link* and the *Anglo-Caribbean News*. The weekly *Gleaner* was the British edition of the conservative *Jamaican Daily Gleaner*, and was published to meet the demand for local news from the Caribbean from the migrant community. The *Caribbean News* was a left-wing, campaigning paper issued by the London branch of the Caribbean Labour Congress and ceased publication in June 1956.[11] *Link* survived a few issues after its launch, while the others did not outlast the *Gazette*.[12] In 1957, the West Indian Workers and Students Association set up a committee to explore the possibilities of establishing a more popular and accessible paper and the *Gazette* was launched as, in Jones' words, a 'progressive news-monthly'[13] priced at sixpence. Its circulation figures fluctuated between a peak of 30,000 and a low of 10,000.[14]

The *Gazette* seemed to be born out of a need for greater social cohesion arising from the problems that arose from living in Britain. It was aimed primarily, but not exclusively, at the West Indian community in Britain. An early editorial asserted that people canvassed prior to its creation wanted to have, 'an organization to represent their interests' and 'to further British – West Indian unity'.[15] The paper's inaugural editorial depicted the West Indian community as distinctive in its constituency and orientation, and its self-image continued to hinge on its ability to provide a voice for an identifiable community of readers whose needs were not being met by mainstream presses. Thus, the paper declared, the West Indian population 'form a community with its own special wants and problems' that it alone could meet.[16]

Many of these 'wants and problems' stem from difficulties of settlement, exacerbated by the hostility with which migrants was greeted. The paper encouraged its readers not to be defeated by racism and to take positive steps to counter discrimination. It carried information about specific civil rights campaigns, for example, the National Council for Civil Liberties' lobbying of Parliament for a bill against racial incitement. It canvassed support for particular marches or offered details about organizations that readers could join. It reported on Commons' debates on housing; about anxieties surrounding the creation of racialized ghettos; about statistics on migration and jobs; and, of course, the Commonwealth Immigration Act of 1962. In a leading article, 'No room at the Inn', which ironized the seasonal Christian goodwill that was absent in the reading of the Immigration Bill, the paper pointed out that such a Bill targeted, 'coloured Commonwealth citizens particularly West Indians, Indians and Pakistanis [and barred these groups] from entry into the United Kingdom'.[17] Monthly columns, which formed part of its campaign against the Bill, offered full accounts of arguments made by both its proponents and opponents. Features in the *Gazette* offered a rebuttal of misinformation about the numbers of immigrants arriving from the West Indies, immigrants' contributions (or lack of contributions) to the British economy, and their alleged stealing of 'British' jobs. The *Gazette* sought to place both immigration and racism in the context of colonial history:

> There would be no West Indian or Asian migrants to Britain if the British didn't go to our homelands in the first place. Already examples of racialist attacks and alleged police brutality involving references to this Bill have been reported ... If the coloured citizens in the United Kingdom are now compelled to unite together – so much the better.[18]

Editorials reflected an increasing communal solidarity and a bitter awareness that the Bill's effect was to heighten racial tension in Britain rather than lessen it. Yet at no time did the paper reach for a communal exclusivity. Its editorial spoke of 'allies' who 'recognize that they have an asset not only in the West Indian and Asian contribution to the British economy, but in deepening their fight against racialism and prejudice in their own self interest'.[19]

Issues of the *Gazette* also contained reports and offered advice about how to deal with the daily personal and institutional acts of racism experienced by its subscribers. They also contained specific discursive strategies to oppose the dehumanising of their subjects. For example, Jones's depiction of a community that had suffered together at the hands of racists in an editorial of November 1959 is instructive:

> In some respects it is amazing how short people's memories are ... much as we would like to forget unpleasant facts, we cannot fail to observe that the aftermath of Notting Hill is continuing in other ways ... Take the recent case of Joseph Dill Simon of Notting Hill, formerly of Portsmouth, Dominica, who was walking quietly with a friend to catch a breath of fresh air ... when he was summarily shot in the wrist, at the corner of Talbot Road. He said: 'I know the police do not believe me, but a white man fired at me, because I am coloured.'[20]

Jones's use of the inclusive pronoun 'we' works to galvanize a feeling of communal solidarity. Her reference to a named respondent personalizes and humanizes the recipients of abuse so that they are not rendered simple statistics in the fight against racism.

The *Gazette*'s news reporting was done in a serious manner but not with a dispassionate voice. The paper sought continually to cultivate a personal relationship with its readers, and often converted more abstract items, such as parliamentary bills and campaigns, into concrete information regarding their impact individual lives. Thus, the details of the Immigration Bill were put under the headline 'How The Bill Affects *Us*', and in 'New Immigration Rules: What *you* should know about the Commonwealth Immigrants Bill' (emphasis added), where the pernicious aspects of the Bill's different clauses and its effects on the community are set out in detail.[21] This translation of British laws and practices into specific effects on individuals also extended to concerns such as house purchasing or work injury claims. For example, a self-help question and answer column on 'learning the facts about securing [a house]' and another article on '6 steps to House purchase' offered helpful and practical advice about surveyor's valuation, solicitor's fees, sub-letting, mortgages and the like, to those unfamiliar with the whole process of home ownership in Britain. The paper also tried to mobilize its readers to participate in specific campaigns and marches. In a feature on the difficulties of finding decent accommodation, headlined 'Rent control concerns you!', the paper argued for the reintroduction of rent control and its editorial asserted, 'Every West Indian African and Asian has a stake in the success of the … campaign' to reintroduce rent controls and to force the Housing Minister to listen to the demands of tenant organizations.[22] Reporting details of demonstrations and public meetings, the editorial declared that such campaigns and marches 'deserve your support' and admonished its audience with the words 'Let us not be found wanting.'[23] Its concern about readers lives and its attentiveness to the specific problems *Gazette* readers faced, is acknowledged in readers' letters and bear out the newspaper's claims that it was providing the community with a space to air their collective anxieties. The newspaper's organization of local social events, like dances and carnivals, and its support by neighbourhood small businesses, such as grocers, hairdressers, haberdashery firms and cornershops, made the *Gazette* a paper firmly anchored in the West Indian community in Britain in general, and London in particular.

Yet the *Gazette* was not concerned simply with local issues. Donald Hinds, one of the staff reporters on the newspaper, reflected that one of the paper's functions was to 'bring news from back home', reporting on the many communities in the 'mother country'.[24] Accordingly, news items from the Caribbean were a staple for its readers. The paper was pro-Federation and reported on talks between the British government and the island politicians in the run-up to West Indian Federation. A regular column offered items of island news in brief, covering anything from elections and Independence Day celebrations, to more international items that have specific relevance to the Caribbean such as the US–Jamaica Military Assistance Pact, the meetings of West Indian Heads of State, and the disturbances in British Guiana. The newspaper also took on an educational role and produced features, such as 'Know your history' that cover topics from the history of the Carib peoples, the Morant Bay Rebellion of 1865 to more contemporary matters. Its factual column 'Did you know?' provided fact-sheets on a wide range of topics, from prominent figures of black history to lesser known items of black and Caribbean history and culture.

Caribbean politicians were profiled in the *Gazette* and eminent Caribbean writers, like George Lamming, Andrew Salkey and Jan Carew, contributed to the paper. The *Gazette* attempted to keep its readers in touch with the literary prizes and fellowships these writers were awarded, and offered details of their current writing projects. These authors were seen to be 'our' writers, and their successes were to be shared by all the *Gazette*'s readers. Poems also appeared within the pages of the paper. Yet despite the political and cultural seriousness of much of its subject matter, the *Gazette* also strove to maintain its popular appeal with local and domestic items concerning lifestyle and leisure activities, such as cooking, fashion, weddings, talent contests, dances and carnivals. Most of its monthly front pages carried Caribbean beauty contestants or black media personalities visiting from abroad. The *Gazette* kept faith both with its readers' desire to be informed about what was happening at home and in the Caribbean, and the newspaper's recognition of the diasporic ties of its distinctive readership can be seen in its charity work, for example, raising money for the hurricane-hit islands of the Caribbean.

Bill Schwarz has recently remarked that the paper's 'originality' is to 'found in its attempt to connect the local with the global' and 'the specific neighbourhood concerns of its readers ... to the wider global world of anti-colonialism and the Civil Rights movement'.[25] The *Gazette* was created at the time of decolonization and the paper saw the struggles of its diasporic community as an intrinsic part of a world-wide anti-colonial and independence struggle. There was, for example, a series titled, 'Colonial Peoples in the Fight for Liberation' and there was also widespread reporting on the independence movements in Africa, with Nigeria's Independence Day carried as front page news under the banner, 'And Now Nigeria – 35 MILLON AFRICANS FREE'. Features appeared on African leaders like Jomo Kenyetta, while updates on the state of British Guiana, Southern Rhodesia and South Africa were commonplace. The paper's opposition to racism in all its forms can be seen from its coverage of the plight of black peoples across the wider Atlantic world, where racism in Britain is compared to that of South African apartheid and segregation in the southern United States. Consequently, reporting of the resistance struggles against racism in Britain, anti-apartheid in South Africa and the Civil Rights marches in the USA were all linked.

In this retrospective overview of the pages of the *Gazette*, two things are particularly striking in relation to the paper's range and interests. The first relates to the transnational dimensions of the paper's readership. The *Gazette*'s specific interventions against structural and institutional racism in Britain grounds it firmly within a local context; as such the paper spoke from and was produced within a specifically geo-political British space, and was not simply a British version of a Caribbean paper. Yet, the *Gazette* promoted a transnational perspective in its desire to educate and politicise, to connect the political world of Britain with movements abroad. As Jones wrote in the American Civil Rights magazine, *Freedomways*, in 1964, the *Gazette*

> has campaigned vigorously on issues facing West Indians and other coloured peoples. Whether against numerous police frame-ups, to which West Indians and other coloured migrants are frequently subject, to opposing discrimination and to advocating support for trade unionism and the unity of coloured and white workers, West Indian news publications have attempted to emulate the paths of progressive 'Negro' (Afro-Asian, Latin-American and Afro-American) journals who uncompromisingly and fearlessly fight against imperialism outrages and indignities to our peoples. The West Indian Gazette and Afro-Asian-Caribbean News has served to launch solidarity campaigns with the nationals who advance with their liberation struggles in African and in Asia.[26]

As Procter and Schwarz have both remarked, the *Gazette*'s role in the creation of an imaginary community should not be underestimated; Benedict Anderson's study of the importance of news media in creating an imagined community of readers physically dispersed in space, yet simultaneously bounded into national body through the reading of print media transfers well to the contexts of the *Gazette*'s production and significance.[27] Yet, as Schwarz has argued, this imagined community's interpellation is not only local and national, but is resolutely connected with and part of wider transnational global political networks.

The *Gazette*'s hard work in maintaining a textual diasporic culture that sought to project a commonality of lives and preoccupations must be also imagined as a textual and interpellative process. This relates to the second of my two points. It is worth stressing that the *Gazette*'s representation of a community should be taken to be a performative act, not a passive reflection of the community's needs. In *Journey to an Illusion*, Hinds reminds his readers that the newspaper came into existence at a time when West Indian identity was in flux. Speaking of the racial conflicts in cities in 1958–59, he notes that the *Gazette* was 'repeatedly a best-seller' and that its campaigns and activities brought people together.[28] In *Freedomways*, Jones had characterized the resident West Indian community as at 'the stage of tentatively formulating their views', making the task of forming, organizing and uniting the community all the more urgent. She emphasized the paper's role as a catalyst in 'quickening ... awareness' for a Caribbean diaspora that would settle and make Britain their home, writing that 'steps should be taken to implement the recognition: that with permanency come the growth of new institutions with all its accompanying aspects'.[29] Through a combination of Jones's editorials, the paper's cultivation of a personal relationship with its readers, and its use of a personal voice, one can examine the discursive process by which the paper created an audience and readership that was predicated on the recognition of a specific British West Indian identity. The cultivation of a personal voice is deliberate stylistically; readers are addressed directly, using either the third-person inclusive, 'we', or the second-person interpellative, 'you'. Thus, in reporting on moves by the National Council for Civil Liberties campaign for anti-racial legislation, the reporter observed, 'we all know that legislation in itself is not the answer to the spread of discrimination. But neither, as has been argued is it a palliative. Legislation against incitement to racial, colour or religious discrimination is a very definite weapon to be used.'[30] In an editorial in September 1960, an appeal is made for more financial support based on the paper's legacy and what it sets out to achieve:

> Indeed every problem affecting West Indians and Afro-Asian Caribbean peoples, be it colour bar in housing, or employment, immigration, etc., have been reflected in the columns of W.I.G. Culturally too, through our annual Caribbean Carnivals, receptions, concerts, etc; our book reviews of West Indian novelists, and related themes, we have helped to fill a cultural gap existing among West Indians in England, we have brought to the English people some appreciation of our cultural heritage. Throughout we have constantly sought to show the contributions our people have made ... We are the only new journal of the kind in this country published and owned by and for coloured people. FOR A PRESS OF OUR OWN [*sic*].[31]

The refrain, 'for a press of our own', was used frequently during the life-time of the paper and is a leitmotiv in many of its editorials. Another editorial, for example, fashioned a similar declaration, 'We need WIG and Afro-Asian-Caribbean News to link nearly half million Africans, Asians and West Indians who face similar problems in the UK. *We need the WIG to know about ourselves* [my emphasis].'[32] In a later drive for more subscriptions, 'We claim the right to your aid', it is possible to ascertain a certain duality: the *Gazette* becomes the progressive voice of its readers but equally, its readers – West Indians and Afro-Asians – are constructed as signifiers of political representation:

> Who more than a progressive voice, has the right to claim support of its readers? Never was progressive voice more needed to champion West Indians and the Afro-Asian community in Britain than today ... Who can fail to be alarmed at the insinuations that the offspring of immigrant children should now be considered immigrants them-selves – the majority of whom were born here? What is this but an attempt to saddle second-class citizenship on these tots and to instil the racial prejudice in the minds of British children whom all the experts only yesterday held out as the hope of future better race relations?[33]

Such passages bring home the point that the interpellation is not a pas-sive process but an active one; it should not be taken for granted. The *Gazette*'s image held up for readerly self-recognition and affirmation is one that is politicized, grounded in a British geo-political space but trans-national in its orientation; in doing so the paper serves to call a specific local and diasporic identity into existence.

The *Gazette* closed soon after the death of its editor in 1965, although the paper had already experienced some financial difficulties, resulting in the absence of an occasional monthly issue. Hinds notes that the paper reached the height of its popularity during the years between 1958 and 1962, precisely the period that saw an initiation and fore-grounding of the campaigns over anti-racial legislation, the Immigration Act, the development of the West Indian Federation, and the start of the intense political activity over the process of decolonization.[34] The *Gazette*'s legacy demonstrates, therefore, that it is possible to remain resolutely local, while at the same time retaining an awareness of how individual subjectivities intersect with larger global narratives.

* * *

From one publishing milestone to another in the transition between West Indian and black British, I want to turn to James Berry's two foundational anthologies of West Indian–British poetry, both of which were concerned with establishing a place for Caribbean poets who were born or who had made their home in Britain. Berry's collection, *Bluefoot Traveller* was the first published anthology of poetry to argue for the distinctiveness of the West Indian settlement in Britain in creative terms and to look towards the emergence of a black British creativity. His hugely influential *News from Babylon*, published by the mainstream literary press Chatto & Windus, marked a shift from the cultural margins. For this anthology not only enabled a larger audience, but, crucially, made such verse available for use as a teaching text. Berry was himself a towering and tireless figure in the promotion of black British poetry; the award of a Cecil Day Lewis writing fellowship led to a career, that, in his own words combined writing with 'a taste for multicultural education and [the] tutoring of writers' workshops in classrooms and libraries'.[35] E.A. Markham has described Berry's legacy as poet and educationalist as particularly important for a younger generation of writers that succeeded the postwar Caribbean renaissance; Berry enabled unpublished writers an audience by creating opportunities for both in print and in performance.[36]

Berry's *Bluefoot Traveller* was first published by Limestone Publications, a poetry magazine edited by the poet Geoffrey Adkins. In 1976, Limestone also functioned as a small independent publishing outlet for the City Literary Institute workshop.[37] Other Caribbean verse anthologies preceded the appearance of *Bluefoot Traveller*, for example, Andrew Salkey's *Breaklight* (1971), George Lamming's *Cannon Shot and Glass Beads: Modern Black Writing* (1974), O.R. Dathorne's *Caribbean Verse* (1967), and John Figueroa's *Caribbean Voices* (1966 and 1970).[38] But the point was that many of these emphasized their Caribbean relation and orientation. As Prahbu Guptara remarks, such early anthologies were concerned with establishing the distinctive Caribbean quality of their creativity; some editors, like Figueroa, even defined 'nationality strictly' and excluding 'British-based poets'.[39] Seeking to position their work and the work of others of Caribbean ancestry within an evolving Caribbean literary tradition or within Commonwealth writing, they were not receptive to the possibility that by settling in Britain, they might 'become black British'.[40] Others, like Lamming, make a case for a broader black aesthetic. Lamming's introduction to *Canon Shot and Glass Beads* argues for a commonality of literary and social experiences that black

people can identify with that is the product of colonialism and its legacy
encompassing Africa, Europe and the Americas:

> It is fairly safe to assume that so long as this country lasts there will
> be substantial Black population in it, and that the overwhelming
> majority will, with time, be native to this land. Reading will therefore
> cease to be a participation in exclusively White experience. There will
> be an increasing demand by Black literacy for the imaginative render-
> ing of a social history with which Black people can easily identify.
> Such a population will, of course, create its own literature. This is
> inevitable. But there must remain the need to experience some spir-
> itual intimacy with its immediate as well as its ancestral past. This is
> one aspect of what this anthology is about.[41]

Lamming does not use the term 'black British'; yet he does, significantly,
allude to the possibility that such a moment may occur in the future
when settler populations 'create their own literature'.

Berry's 1976 anthology is careful to chart the distinctiveness of a life
lived in Britain. His careful biographical assembly of contributors' statements sketch out stories of their Atlantic crossings, and anchors their
consequence for the anthology firmly in their residency in Britain. The
problematic experience of settlement itself becomes a key theme in the
collection, in poems such as A.L. Hendriks's 'The Fringe of the Sea',
G.P.C. Durrante's 'Colours' and 'Frangments', Jimi Rand's 'Nock Nock
Oo Nock E Nock', Markham's satiric 'Compromise' and Berry's own
'Lucy's letter'. Yet like Lamming, Berry does not employ the term black
British, but uses 'Westindian in Britain' instead. Berry's introduction to
the 1976 edition speaks of the embattled state of West Indian settle-
ment, and crucially, against the conflation of black experiences in
Britain and the United States:

> These poems ... present something of the Westindians' response
> to life in British society. They show their incorporation into the
> society and their isolation within it. They reflect their settled
> and unsettled condition, their insecurity and, also, an underlying
> explosiveness ... There is no nourishing atmosphere for the develop-
> ment of black distinctiveness. Neither does Britain show any desire
> for cultural fusion. Westindians here are a long way away from the
> dynamic cultural activities of American blacks or their fellow
> Westindians at home.[42]

He goes on to assert that nationalism, decolonization and independence has had a profound impact on West Indian writing. In contrast, West Indians in Britain have 'missed out' and can only participate 'by proxy'. Yet Berry also asserts that 'something of the new relationship stimulates a new awareness and confidence which seeps through into the [new] poetry' in Britain.[43] Consequently, despite the gloom through which he views the given lot of the West Indian community in Britain, their transnational connections with Caribbean aesthetic life stimulates their creative output.

If the 1976 edition of *Bluefoot Traveller* fails to include any poet who was born or who had grown up in Britian, Linton Kwesi Johnson excepting, by the time of the publication of a revised and expanded edition in 1981 with the publisher Harrap, this lacunae is rectified and the volume includes poems by Denis Watson, Lorraine Flynn, Sandra Agard and Joan Davidson. The preface to the revised and expanded edition praises the liveliness of the West Indian literary community in Britain who, according to Berry, 'involves itself much more intensely with expressing its cultural background', not only writing, publishing and bookselling, but also engaging with the visual and performing arts.[44]

A new creative and energizing climate for the arts is also alluded to in Berry's introduction to *News from Babylon*, where he asserts that new '[d]evelopments and increased activity in this area of writing keep on demanding attention'.[45] Yet even in this volume, Berry does not use the term black British, but supplements his original categorization with, 'British Westindians' and 'Westindian-British literature'.[46] Poets chosen for the anthology 'all live in Britain or have lived here and made a significant contribution to the development of Westindian-British poetry'. The anthology is intended as 'another step towards the establishment of Westindian-British writing, generally, in its own right'.[47] A growing confidence in the maturity of poets and literary material enables Berry to make a specific case for cultural and aesthetic distinctiveness; while 'Caribbean life and culture will always be an importance source', functioning as 'background' to their verse', they do not 'substitute for a life lived in Britain'.[48] Berry does not stop here. Having carefully positioned the anthology not simply as yet another volume of Caribbean verse, he also makes a case for its difference from mainstream British writing:

> Westindian-British poetry has some distinctly different and unique qualities. Essentially, while other potent features are subdued, the poetry exposes a collective psyche laden with anguish and rage. And it

is expressed in standard English which it may use originally or combine, deliberately, with Creole language. Or it may be a poem composed entirely in Caribbean Creole. Like a new survival-challenge, Westindians have had to sort out their sources of identity.[49]

To begin, Berry notes that living in Britain has impacted on the Caribbean rhythms of speech, and the language used has not only been influenced by Caribbean Creole, but also by regional English. In parallel, he identifies a communal feeling between Caribbean and West Indian British poets, which has been created through a recognition of their mutual mistreatment by white communities, and he describes how a 'collective resistance developed [that is] deeply bound up with survival ... [and] a re-defining of the self and freedom'.[50] Significantly, life in Britain during the latter half of the twentieth century had triggered a collective West Indian memory of rage and hurt that was the legacy of slavery and colonial history. As such, the West Indian British community had to 'come into confrontation with unresolved historical black–white relationships'.[51] Here, Berry writes of a 'black aesthetics',[52] suggesting that living in Britain forces the poet to deal with – and express – not only the historical memory and experience of being black, but also the performative aspect of blackness as transnational and transatlantic. In Berry's representation, blackness is not only an external imposition, but also a modality by which one sees a continuum and connection with lives and histories from Africa, the Caribbean and the Americas. Such an Atlantic continuity may be, at heart, symbolic or metaphoric, but like Gilroy's notion of the black Atlantic, Berry identifies writers who, through performative processes, lay claim to connections across continents, and reading communities who sustain the relevance of those connections.[53] If Berry's move towards a black aesthetic reflects the influence of a Black Power movement crossing from the United States, its emphasis on the importance of Rastafarianism, its rhetorical invocation of Edward Brathwaite's 'nation language' and Caribbean Creoles preserve its Caribbean-British orientation.

Between the tentativeness of the 1976 introduction to *Bluefoot Traveller* and the more assertive *News from Babylon* in 1984, much had changed. By the time of the latter's publication, pressure towards multiculturalism in the arts and education created both a niche and a small but committed audience for such writing.[54] The late 1970s witnessed the publication of Naseem Khan's *The Arts Britain Ignores: The Arts of Ethnic Minorities in Britain* (1976), an investigation of the institutional racism in the arts that had been sponsored by the Commission for Racial Equality and the

Arts Council. Khan's report, for all its failings,[55] resulted in the creation of the Minorities' Arts Advisory Service (MAAS) and a flourishing of the black Arts movement. Magazines *Echo* and *Artrage* provided a valuable forum for intercultural visual arts, media and literary activity. A major British 'Conference on Ethnic Arts' was staged in 1982, sponsored by the Greater London Council (GLC). The GLC's commitment to multicultural-ism meant financial support for minority presses like Kala Press, specialist periodicals and black writers' workshops like Black Ink and the Asian Women Writers' Collective, and the first large-scale literary competition 'to be organized around black people in Britain'.[56] Furthermore, the Association for the Teaching of Caribbean, African and Asian Literatures (ATCAL), founded as a pressure group to 'advance the education of the British public in the works of authors of African, Caribbean and Asian origin' was formed in 1978.[57] ATCAL staged annual conferences, com-piled booklists for schools, submitted recommendations to Examination Boards, and organized meetings and workshops 'to increase awareness of the importance of the cultural diversity of British society in education at all levels.'[58] The organization's publicity pamphlet, produced around 1982, draws specific attention to what it terms 'Black British and allied literatures', stating that the organization', intention was to 'promote and encourage new writing by our own Black British artists',[59] and its 1985 conference theme was, 'Black British Experience in Literature', another milestone in the recognition of dissemination of black British writing. Equally significant was the Swann Report, 'Education for all', published in 1985 which endorsed the idea of an inclusive education that would serve, rather than disenfranchise, sections of the community. The Report argued that education should prepare students for a multiracial society, looked into ways that the underachievement among minority ethnic students could be redressed, and recommended an increased number of ethnic minority teachers and an expansion of multiculturalism in the school curriculum. ATCAL campaigned effectively in the 1980s to include African, Caribbean, Asian and black British writers in their curriculum, and was particularly effective in the London region.

* * *

It is in this context that the little magazine *Wasafiri* emerges, starting life in autumn 1984 as a publication of ATCAL, even though the organization continued to issue its own newsletter and bulletin, and surpassing the demise of its parent organization. The choice of title for the magazine, *Wasafiri* (travellers), emphasized the notion of moving between cultural boundaries and of enabling such cultural 'travelling' between writers, critics and reviewers interested in the particular world of African, Caribbean, Asian and associated literatures.[60] As Sushelia Nasta its founding editor remarks in a recent retrospective assessment:

> Our intention is to give serious literary coverage to the excellent writing that is being produced in this country and abroad and to provide a forum for debate. We really cover five main areas: criticism, prose, poetry, reviews, and interviews ... we support new writers from all over the world who want to get their work published .... We are looking to both establish a sense of authenticity and to promote cultural diversity.[61]

A biennial periodical, *Wasafiri*'s focused primarily on literature, providing criticism, interviews and creative writing; the magazine also provided a specific forum for black British writing, and includes this aspect of ATCAL's manifesto of encouraging 'new writing by our own Black British artists' as part of its founding editorial.[62] Unpublished writing, work-in-progress appeared within its covers. Forums on black writing appeared as early as the autumn of 1985, with Prahbu Guptara's editorial proclaiming the GLC's recent literary competition 'organized around black people in Britain' a 'triumph' against adversity.[63] Especially in its early years, *Wasafiri* kept up its engagement with pedagogic and institutional questions to do with the teaching of African, Caribbean, Asian and associated literatures. In addition to the special issues on education in 1987 or canon formation in 1990, *Wasafiri* included provocative pieces on censorship, publishing, approaches to instituting a multicultural curriculum, literatures and anti-racist teaching, and a column dedicated not only to conference listings but that contained information about resources and activities occurring in specific regions and universities across the United Kingdom. The funding for the first four issues of the magazine came from the GLC; later funding came from, among others, the Greater London Arts (GLA), the Arts Council Education department, and then the Arts Council of England, in recognition of the role that such a little magazine would play. As such, in these early years *Wasafiri* kept a predominant though not exclusive British focus. Yet what is also significant about the periodical is its relentless commitment to what it saw as a staging of a cultural travelling relevant to *all* local reading and educational communities in Britain. In an important early editorial by Susheila Nasta, a case was made for the dissemination of black and associated literatures in the school syllabus on two fronts. The editorial stressed the importance of these cultural expressions to the student communities in Britain that may have originated from the 'New Commonwealth'; these migrant and settler communities should have their chance to explore ancestral and cultural connections in imaginative writing. Secondly, the editorial also argued that relevance ought not be restricted to that of communal self-representation. To see black or Asian writing as of significance to black or Asian readers was unnecessarily limiting. True to the magazine's principle of cultural travelling, Nasta argued that educational and literary relevance also applies for other pupils, students and readers because they need to open 'their eyes to a [larger] world' outside:

> If Afro-Caribbean and Indian literature is to have a future in our academic institutions it must be presented as catering to the needs of every sector of the community, not simply to those most motivated to clamour for it ... As readers, teacher and scholars we must constantly keep in mind ... that this literature is born in one place, but for all people.[64]

Wasafiri's contribution to the debate surrounding place and space in situating black British writing is instructive; Nasta's editorial is particularly germane in the manner with which it moved beyond the cultural impasse of separate-but-equal development towards social and cultural inclusion, and a re-imagining of the representational contours of British life. Like Jones's *West Indian Gazette*, *Wasafiri*'s strength lies in its ability to imagine, especially in its early years, a diasporic and global significance for what remains a resolutely local constituency within a national polity.

*   *   *

In conclusion, what can be drawn from this eclectic and limited description of the important roles that the *West Indian Gazette*, James Berry's poetic anthologies and *Wasafiri* have played in the transition from West Indian to black British. Firstly, and the more obvious of the two points, is that any discussion of the transnational dimensions of black British writing should not be undertaken at the expense of a grounding in the specific histories of black British life. Equally, local histories of migration and settlement yield inevitable accounts of border crossings; Jones and Nasta's demands that such local cultures remain alive to the necessity and relevance of cultural travelling is a lesson worth insisting upon to keep sight of the myriad ways in which communities and histories are intertwined. Secondly, and this is perhaps the more contentious of my two points, discussions of texts should also be attentive to both the discursive contexts in which they signify, treating texts as rhetorical and performative speech acts. Such an approach should also take cognizance of institutional and publishing histories, for only then can we see not only why such writings matter, but how they matter. One should not take the name 'black British' and what it signifies for granted. Only an archival and discursive awareness that is sensitive to all these debates can offer us histories of a shaping of those discursive connections that have enabled such a name to have meaning.

Notes

* I am very grateful to the archivists at the Institute of Race Relations library in London who were extremely helpful in helping locate issues of the *West Indian Gazette*. The research for this chapter was undertaken with the help of a grant from the Leverhulme Foundation and the British Academy.
1. See p. 102.
2. See for example, Paul Gilroy, *The Black Atlantic* (London: Verso, 1993); C.L. Innes, *A History of Black and Asian Writing in Britain: 1700–2000* (Cambridge: Cambridge University Press, 2002); Sukhdev Sandhu, *London Calling: How Black and Asian Writers Imagined a City* (London: HarperCollins, 2003); and Mark Stein, *Black British Literature: Novels of Transformation* (Columbus: Ohio State University Press, 2004).
3. Mike Phillips, 'Black British Writing – So what is it?' in *London Crossings* (London and New York: Continuum, 2001), p. 146.
4. For Phillips' essay and the above quotations see p. 27.
5. See above p. 100.
6. The relationships between readers, reading and texts are complex as critical debates in book history have highlighted (for an indication of these debates see David Finkelstein and Alistair McCleery, *The Book History Reader* (London and New York: Routledge, 2002). But such questions raise the possibility of exploring how audiences are constituted through textual activity. They also raise the prospect that these identitarian labels (West Indian British, black British) refer to subjects in political representation rather than naming 'literal referents' in the real world. Gayatri Spivak has called these labels 'catachreses' in her attempt to focus on the signifier as political mobilization or representation; her deconstructive move is instructive for it draws attention to the 'imagined and negotiated constituencies' based on the (speech) act of political re-presentation. See Gayatri Spivak, *The Post-Colonial Critic* (New York and London: Routledge, 1990), p. 104.
7. A substantial but incomplete run of the *West Indian Gazette* is available in the library of the Institute of Race Relations. The Lambeth Library archives also hold a microfilm copy of what is available at the Institute.

8. James Berry (ed.), *Bluefoot Traveller: An Anthology of West Indian Poets in Britain* (London: Limestone, 1976) and *News For Babylon: The Chatto Book of Westindian-British Poetry* (London: Chatto & Windus, 1984).

9. I use 'interpellation' in the Althusserian sense of 'hailing', self-recognition and the staging of subjectivity. Althusser writes about the subject's recognition of him/herself in the ideological image formed of him/her as the constitution of their subjectivity:

> I shall then suggest that ideology 'acts' or 'functions' in such a way that it 'recruits' subjects among the individuals ... or 'transforms' the individuals into subjects ... by that very precise operation which I have called *interpellation* or hailing, and which can be imagined along the lines of the most commonplace everyday police (or other) hailing: 'Hey, you there!' Assuming that the theoretical scene I have imagined takes place in the street, the hailed individual will turn round. By this mere one-hundred and-eight-degree physical conversion, he becomes a *subject*. Why? Because he has recognized that the hail was 'really' addressed to him, and that 'it was *really* him who was hailed (and not someone else)'. (Louis Althusser, *Essays on Ideology* (London: Verso, 1984), p. 48)

This approach offers us a mode of analysis which is concerned with the textual production of a reading position, or how readers are implicated within and the framework and structures of the text and its mode of address. Such a mode of analysis does not, of course, give us the complete picture of the interaction between readers and texts; but it does sensitize us to the ways in which imagined communities might be produced via textual processes.

10. See Marika Sherwood, *Claudia Jones: A life in exile* (London: Lawrence & Wishart, 1999), part memoir and part biography; and Buzz Johnson, '*I think of my mother*': notes on the life and times of Claudia Jones (London: Karia Press, 1985), a short biography of Jones's life which includes some of her writing. For an excellent introduction to the *West Indian Gazette* and its achievements see Bill Schwarz, ' "Claudia Jones and the *West Indian Gazette*": Reflections of the Emergence of Post-colonial Britain', *Twentieth Century British History*, 14(3), 2003, pp. 264–85. For Donald Hinds' memoirs of his experiences as a reporter on the *West Indian Gazette* see Donald Hinds, *Journey to an Illusion: The West Indian in Britain* (London: Bogle-L'Ouverture, 2001 (1966)).

11. Ionie Benjamin, *The Black Press in Britain* (Stoke on Trent: Trentham Books, 1995), pp. 37–9. Also see Donald Hinds, *op. cit.*, pp. 125–6 and Buzz Johnson, *op. cit.*, pp. 75–6.

12. See Donald Hinds, *op. cit.*, p. 149, and Ruth Glass, *Newcomers: West Indians in London* (London: Centre for Urban Studies and George Allen & Unwin, 1960), p. 209.

13. Quoted in Buzz Johnson, *op. cit.*, p. 152.

14. Donald Hinds, *op. cit.*, p. 134.

15. Quoted in Ruth Glass, *op. cit.*, p. 209.

16. *Ibid.*

17. Unsigned article, 'No room at the Inn', *West Indian Gazette*, 12 December 1961, p. 1.

18. Editorial, *West Indian Gazette*, 12 December 1961, p. 4.

19. *Ibid.*
20. Quoted in Sherwood, *op. cit.*, p. 143.
21. See unsigned articles, 'How The Bill Affects Us', *West Indian Gazette*, 12 December 1961, p. 9 and 'New Immigration Rules' *West Indian Gazette*, July 1962, p. 5.
22. Editorial, 'RENT CONTROLS CONCERN YOU!', *West Indian Gazette*, August 1960, p. 4.
23. *Ibid.*
24. Hinds, *op. cit.*, p. 149.
25. Schwarz, *op. cit.*, p. 270.
26. Claudia Jones, 'The Caribbean Community in Britain', in Johnson, *op. cit.*, p. 152.
27. Following Benedict Anderson's analysis of the role of newspapers in creating imagined communities, Schwarz remarks that the *Gazette* created 'the possibility for imagining a larger collectivity as a community as – in some manner – knowable', while Procter speaks of the *Gazette* playing a 'key role in the dissemination and construction of a black British imagined community'. See Benedict Anderson, *Imagined Communities* (London: Verso, 1983), Schwarz, *op. cit.* and James Procter, *Writing Black Britain 1948–1998* (Manchester: Manchester University Press, 2000), p. 15.
28. Hinds, *op. cit.*, pp. 150–1.
29. Claudia Jones, *op. cit.*
30. Claudia Jones, 'NEITHER A PALLIALTIVE, NOR THE ONLY ANSWER … BUT – ANTI-RACIAL LEGISLATION: A KEY NEED', *West Indian Gazette*, December 1959, p. 4.
31. Claudia Jones, 'FREEDOM – OUR CONCERN', *West Indian Gazette*, September, 1960, p. 4.
32. Editorial, *West Indian Gazette*, May 1962, p. 4.
33. Unsigned column, 'WE CLAIM THE RIGHT TO YOUR AID!', *West Indian Gazette*, 6(3), March, 1964, p. 4.
34. Hinds, *op. cit.*, p. 152.
35. James Berry, 'Signpost of the Bluefoot Man', in E.A. Markham, *Hinterland: Caribbean Poetry from the West Indies and Britain* (Newcastle: Bloodaxe Books. 1989), p. 176.
36. E.A. Markham, *op. cit.*, p. 32.
37. See James Berry, 'Ancestors I Carry', in Fedinand Dennis and Naseem Khan (eds), *Voices of the Crossing* (London: Serpant's Tail, 2000), p. 159.
38. Andrew Salkey, *Breaklight* (London: Hamish Hamilton, 1971), George Lamming, *Cannon Shot and Glass Beads: Modern Black Writing* (London: Picador, 1974), O.R. Dathorne's *Caribbean Verse* (London: Heinemann, 1967), John Figueroa's *Caribbean Voices* (London: Evans Brothers, 1966 and 1970).
39. Prahbu Guptara, *Black British Literature: An Annotated Bibliography* (Coventry, UK: Centre for Caribbean Studies, University of Warwick, 1986), p. 44.
40. *Ibid.*, pp. 44, 14.
41. Lamming, *op. cit.*, p. 11.
42. Berry, *op. cit.*, p. 9.
43. *Ibid.*
44. James Berry, *Bluefoot Traveller*, revised edition (London: Harrap, 1981), p. 6.
45. Berry, *News from Babylon*, p. xii.

46. *Ibid.*
47. *Ibid.*
48. *Ibid.*
49. *Ibid.*
50. *Ibid.*, pp. xix–xx.
51. *Ibid.*
52. *Ibid.*, p. xxv.
53. Paul Gilroy's *The Black Atlantic* has been criticized for over-aestheticizing history. See Laura Chrisman, 'Journeying to Death: A Critique of Paul Gilroy's *The Black Atlantic*', *Crossings*, 1(2), 1997, pp. 82–96.
54. When I gave a version of this talk at the 'Black British' conference at the University of Dundee in 2004, both E.A. Markham and Mike Phillips observed that the arrival of *News from Babylon* into the cultural and publishing mainstream coincided with a period in the eighties where multiculturalism and cultural diversity were fashionable, and many funding bodies such as the Arts Council and the GLC seemed willing to fund projects that were deemed 'ethnic'. Markham in particular is scathing about what he perceives as Chatto and Windus's opportunism in the assembling of the poetry that makes the collection, and comments that the anthology is 'a general round-up of what was available rather than an attempt to employ aesthetic criteria' (see Markham, *Hinterland, op. cit.*, p. 13). In my recent interview with James Berry, however, he resisted such an account of the production of the anthology, insisting on the integrity of the collection and the interest in his work beyond multicultural opportunism.
55. For an incisive critique of Khan's report, see Kwesi Owusu, *The Struggle for the Black Arts in Britain: What can we consider better than freedom* (London: Comedia, 1986), chapter 3.
56. Prahbu, Guptara, 'Editorial', *Wasafiri*, 3, Autumn 1985, p. 3.
57. ATCAL, undated 'draft proposal for possible funding organizations' in the possession of Professor Louis James.
58. *Ibid.*
59. Committee Notes, *ATCAL Newsletter*, 6, June 1982, p. 1.
60. See Susheila Nasta's memoir and analysis of her editorship of *Wasafiri* in '*Wasafiri*: History, Politics and Post-Colonial Literature', in Hena Maes-Jelinek, Gordon Collier and Geoffrey V. Davis (eds), *A Talent(ed) Digger: Creations, Cameos, and Essays in honour of Anna Rutherford, Cross/Cultures: Reading in the Post/Colonial Literatures in English*, 20 (Amsterdam: Rodopi, 1996), p. 128.
61. *Ibid.*, p. 129.
62. *Wasafiri*, 1, Autumn 1984, p. 2.
63. Prahbu Guptara, 'Editorial', *Wasafiri*, 3, Autumn 1985, pp. 3–4.
64. 'From the Editors', *Wasafiri*, 2, Spring 1985, p. 3.

10
Afterword: In Praise of a Black British Canon and the Possibilities of Representing the Nation 'Otherwise'

Alison Donnell

In this afterword I want to give thought to what might be at stake in discussing the idea of a black British canon in the cultural and political climate of Britain at the start of the twenty-first century. As noted in the Introduction, this essay does not, therefore, set out a genealogical account of canon formation, but concludes the volume with possible interventions into, and questions derived from, the key critical debates relevant to our understanding of a black British canon today.

In many ways, the papers collected in this volume offer a full discussion of how critics and readers might begin to construct and also deconstruct certain versions of a black British canon across a range of creative disciplines. They propose important figures and works to be seen and read in order to debate how our ways of reading these works set limits on our understandings of the links between the cultural and the political spheres. They issue a valuable and considered interrogation of the confined, even damaging, version of black Britishness that could be put into circulation by a canon that does not, as James Procter demands, undo the 'boundaries between Asian and black, working-class and middle-class, the avant-garde and the everyday, high and popular culture, that bisect black British canon formation'.[1]

However, while many of the contributors make strong arguments for particular texts and ways of reading as vital to our understanding of this rich and increasingly diverse archive, what can also be read through this collection as a whole is a shared hesitation, reluctance or suspicion concerning the very proposal of a canon. On one level, it is perhaps not surprising that nearly every contributor to this collection expresses some suspicion around the idea of a canon as, in many ways, the term itself sets limits on our expectations of inclusiveness, diversity and the possibilities for representing cultural change. In Britain 'canon' was the term used to designate the selection of approved books in the Bible, and the intertwining elements of judgement, law and education suggested by this discursive origin have remained important. An understanding of this initial ecclesiastical provenance is useful in that it offers a way of interpreting later writers' reworking of the term 'canon'. Indeed, in some ways, Matthew Arnold adopted 'canon' in the absence of, or crisis of, a religion of the spirit, and what begins to evolve through Arnold's thesis is a displacement from religious doctrine to literature, not only in terms of asserting what is culturally important but also what is of moral benefit. Arnold's understanding of a canon, was amplified and reworked by F.R. Leavis in *The Great Tradition*, where he put forward statements about aesthetic value that were profoundly connected to the idea of moral value and, more specifically and problematically, to the 'upkeep of civilisation'.[2] T.S. Eliot also engaged with Arnold's thesis in 'Tradition and the Individual Talent', although Eliot's concept of a literary tradition was more spatially and chronologically located, moving the idea of canon towards the possibility of intertextuality.[3] The extent to which the canon has been part of the colonial project, a version of the great and the good to be exported alongside law, religion and other doctrines as the foundation stones of Western cultural achievement (and superiority) cannot, therefore, be underestimated. Nevertheless, while adopting the nomenclature of the canon may mean that we enter into this highly-charged territory of overlayered value systems and Western cultural dominance, I want to argue that it does not mean that we are compelled to leave behind the same kind of footprints that we find from the past.

Given the complex network of value structures (aesthetic, cultural, political) that rightly interplay and often collide in our discussions and judgements about cultural representations, what is the value of re-writing a black British canon for our time? Do the hesitations asserted around the idea of a canon arise from this history or from the highly-charged fraught nexus created when we bring the terms black British and the canon alongside each other? How can such a canon avoid the problem of promoting canonicity and the affirmation of a single coherent body of cultural texts in the name of a single governing ideology? Much of this afterword will be concerned with responding to the first two of these questions, but in order to re-imagine the value of a black British canon, I first want to consider how we might conceive of it as an agent of cultural interrogation and dialogue rather than authority and closure.

In his now famous response to Fredrick Jameson's 'Third-World Literature in the Era of Multinational Capitalism', Aijaz Ahmad comes up with a new definition of a national literary canon,

I would define the term national literature … as the sum of local (traditional, 'Indian'), indigenous (mixed, perhaps 'ethnic'), and dominant literary productions within the territory of the given national formations. Any national literary canon, therefore, will be a selection from all the available texts of these various kinds, and it may thus be thought to stand as the heterodox, collective autobiography of any who would define themselves in relation to a particular national identity – literature as a kind of multivoiced record of the American, for example.[4]

This proposal of a canon that can find room for oppositional voices, generate difference, debate and even conflict, seems much more appealing. A diverse, contingent and renewable canon would acknowledge the fact that we do have to make decisions about which texts to read, teach and circulate, but it could also do so with alertness to the motivations behind each selection. Instead of suggesting that a certain text is simply or universally 'great', such a canon could foreground the particular values of a work in a certain context and at a certain time. It need not depoliticize or dehistoricize our individual and collective decisions about what is of significance, but rather make them, and their relation to ideas of national identity, explicit.

Ahmad's creative and inclusive national canon would be particularly interesting in a British context, where challenges to the canon historically have not always envisaged a more inclusive postcolonial version. The first concerns about the canon of English Literature were rightly expressed in terms of its cultural irrelevance and imposition in other parts of the world, mainly (former) British colonies. Interestingly, though, initiatives that came from within British academies, especially from the universities of Leeds and Kent, from Norman Jeffares, from William Walsh and John Press, who edited the collection *The Teaching of English Literature Overseas* (1963), and from the provenance of what was then termed 'Commonwealth Literature', were largely seeking to redefine the study of literature by establishing parallel national Anglophone canons.[5] In addition, Caribbean literature was launched in English via the works of C.L.R. James, V.S. Naipaul, George Lamming, Sam Selvon, Wilson Harris, and later Merle Collins and Jean Binta Breeze.[6] While the establishment of these Anglophone traditions has been central in terms of foregrounding particular regional archives of postcolonial writings, it has also – albeit unwittingly – facilitated a false separation between postcolonial and British writings. From James to Breeze, all of these writers spent a substantial amount of time studying, living, working and writing in Britain, and all of them have produced texts that could also be usefully identified within a black British tradition. Indeed, I would argue passionately for a canon in which Wilson Harris can be read alongside D.M. Thomas, Salman Rushdie alongside James Joyce and Bernadine Evaristo alongside Angela Carter. However, this does not mean that there is no longer an urgent need to address the particular dialogues and debates that discussion of a black British canon provokes.

The success of the 1980s and 1990s in creating a visible and talented body of writers, artists, playwrights and musicians has meant that black culture in Britain both demands and allows for more diverse and plural forms of representation. This success has arguably made the idea of a canon both more and less possible. More so, because there is unquestionably a literary history from Equiano and Mary Prince to Alex Wheatle and Monica Ali that offers a wonderful and compelling narration of Britain's 'collective autobiography'. Less so, because the prolific and divergent nature of this archive means that the links that hold together the identity chain, black–British–artist, are now less obvious.

There is already more than enough material for several black British literary canons, as well as for Ahmad's heterodox national canon. In fact, the range of voices, subjects and styles represented by some recent literary anthologies makes the point well. The comprehensive and controversial *IC3: The Penguin Book of New Black Writing* with over one hundred contributors, published in 2000; the 1999 *Afrobeat* anthology with its wide thematic range; the *Bittersweet* collection of women's poetry published in 1998; the urban black poetry of *The Fire People* also published in 1998; and the differing narratives of immigration represented in *Voices of the Crossing* (2000), are all, to some measure, canon-making projects.[7] Yet their agendas are centrally concerned with making visible new literary constellations and new critical conversations.

Many of the articles included in this volume productively engage with these conversations. Sandra Courtman's essay points up the particular exclusions of early black British canons that celebrated the male writers who had settled in Britain from the West Indies in the 1950s (Selvon, Lamming, Salkey, Naipaul and Braithwaite being the major figures) and yet were unable to accommodate women's narratives, particular Beryl Gilroy's 1976 autobiography *Black Teacher*. Her own attention to Gilroy's writing and her detailing of a critical context in which a black woman migrant's marginality has been confirmed by so many narratives of exclusion is a significant act of restitution.

Andy Wood's reading of the lyrics of contemporary artists Est'elle, Ms. Dynamite and Shystie alongside Andrea Levy's 1996 novel *Never Far From Nowhere* provokes more recent questions around the marginalization of black women's voices in relation to an authenticated version of black writing – this time the fictional and musical accounts of street culture in the 1990s. It also extends the canon's generic boundaries by giving equal academic attention to song lyrics.

However, any assumptions about the cultural pitch of the canon are unsettled here by the different, even competing versions of what is favoured and privileged in terms of cultural forms. While Wood is keen to bring the song lyrics of popular artists into the same intellectual orbit as literary works and thereby reinvent the genre and prejudices often associated with canons, James Procter's article discusses the way in which popular cultural forms and figures have been coded as complex and counter-cultural at the expense of seemingly elite and detached 'high-cultural' narratives in different contexts. Staging his argument in relation to Paul Gilroy's essay 'Frank Bruno or Salman Rushdie?', Procter comments that:

> Rushdie seems destined to share a decidedly uncertain relationship to the question of a black British canon. It would appear Rushdie is too posh, too abstractly aesthetic, too lofty and detached to be worthy of consideration within the provincial, popular context of black British everyday life. At best, he represents a partially acknowledged, shadowy figure in available black cultural criticism.[8]

Mike Phillips is similarly concerned with the way in which particular versions of black Britishness have eclipsed others, although his focus is on the pressure exerted on the black British archive by current critical preferences for the framing of black British subjects as 'travellers, exiles, migrants'. Commenting on the lack of attention to rooted, inside subjects in Sukhdev Sandhu's *London Calling*, Phillips notes:

> There is no consideration of the writers who experience London as part of family life or childhood. No Courttia Newland, or the rash of Brixton boys like Alex Wheatle, Anton Marks et al. No mention either of the black writers who create characters from inside the enclaves of English professional life, like Mike Gayle's (un)black London teacher, or Nicola Willams's black and female South London barrister.[9]

Reading these articles alongside each other enriches our understanding of how certain types of marginality may be a passport to centrality on some occasions, while other forms simply remain marginal. Indeed, the numerous versions of the canon circulating through this collection – the elite, the popular, the masculine, the narrowly national, the transnational – all go to prove that discussions of the canon provoke very valuable exchanges about the politics of cultural forms and the wider questions of inclusion and exclusion in relation to national culture. Such exchanges are particularly timely given Mike Phillips's observation that, '"Black British" was a contentious and highly contested ascription, until about halfway through the 90s... But over the last ten years, as the label took on new meanings, it started to become a useful way of commanding attention in the cultural marketplace.'[10]

In his article for this volume, John McLeod takes the strongest stand against the canon when he states quite plainly that he finds, 'the notion of a distinctly black British literature problematic.'[11] Acknowledging the fact that several recent anthologies of black British writing (Wambu, 1998; Newland and Sesay, 2000; Procter 2000) have made visible a body of work that deserves more critical attention, McLeod moves on to question the possible value of a national paradigm in promoting a positive and responsive model of cultural engagement:

> One principal problem with such anthologies concerns the ways in which they risk falsifying the mechanics of black British creativity and tradition, and look only at national, rather than transnational, fields of influence. Sesay's image of black writers in Britain pursuing each other's footsteps perhaps gives too tidy an impression of what Caryl Phillips has termed 'following on'. In a black British canon, literary tradition becomes spatially constricted, with certain influential figures prioritised over others. National paradigms are always reductive perhaps, but particularly so when thinking about the fortunes of black writing in Britain.[12]

McLeod may well be right in asserting that 'in following the footsteps of black British writing, strictly national canons cannot bear adequate witness to the transnational pathways'.[13] However, is it not equally true that, in persuading us to connect black writings to the 'outside' of Britain, transnational pathways cannot bear adequate witness to internal pathways? I agree with his argument that, 'black writing in Britain also dares to expose, for all Britons, the criss-crossings, the comings and goings, the transnational influences, which arguably inform the construction of virtually all texts and canons that bear the signature of "British"'.[14] Moreover, migrant metropolitan texts, such as Bernadine Evaristo's *Lara* that McLeod draws on here, are very explicitly involved in creatively undoing assumptions about the cultural boundedness associated with regressive and homogenous versions of nationalism. Like the plays and productions that Michael McMillan discusses in his illuminating contribution, such narratives endorse the argument that 'Black cultural practices in the UK are influenced by the wider black experience.'[15] I do not, however, see any innate incompatibility between the idea of a national canon and the presence of transnational works within that canon. As Gail Low points out in her contribution 'recent criticism has increasingly engaged with this emphasis upon a transnational, migratory and diasporic consciousness across cultures'.[16]

In the present context in which metro-migrant narratives have achieved a strong, if not dominating, presence within a postcolonial literary canon, reading within and across the national frame may be the more searching and challenging paradigm. To my mind, it is the really fascinating horizontal connections across the 'spatially constricted' terrain of Britain that have received far less attention, as our ideas of diasporic identity and transnationality have been persistently translated through the very critical paradigms that McLeod wants to dis-identify from.[17]

My own way of reading the anthologies McLeod mentions is, not as acts of denial or closure in terms of transnational connections, but as specific theatres of exchange through which more sustained conversations can take place between writers and writings that have very often not been considered alongside each other. For example, it would be immensely instructive to our ways of theorising black British identities and the connections, rather than separations, between nationality and transnationality to read Evaristo's *Lara* and its metropolitan 'three point turn' navigating between London, Lagos and Rio in conversation with Charlotte Williams' *Sugar and Slate* and its non-metropolitan 'three point turn' between Llandudno in North Wales, Georgetown, Guyana and Nigeria. Such a reading would also engage productively with Femi Folorunso's argument that we need to pay equal attention to what circulates under the sign of 'Britishness' in black British culture.[18]

This sense of what can be gained through reading within rather than 'without' the nation is differently foregrounded in James Procter's article in this collection. Returning our critical attention to the early 1980s, a crucial moment in terms of defining a new politics of black identity in Britain, and theorising this in relation to black cultural production, Procter restores a national British context through which to read the works of Salman Rushdie – arguably the archetypal hybrid, migrant, postmodern figure of the postcolonial literary canon. Reading *Midnight's Children* (1981) and *Shame* (1983) as texts emerging 'at time of community resistance against ongoing racist immigration laws, police/state

brutality, and marginalization in the labour market, housing, and education... [that] culminated in uprisings at the 1976 Notting Hill Carnival
and inner city revolts/uprisings/riots in 1981 and 1985' (as McMillan
describes it in his contribution) does not diminish their currency as
wonderfully hybrid, diasporic narratives, but, rather, restores the very
social conditions under which such literary styles and themes came into
being.[19] Procter's claim that 'black British is worth persisting with is precisely because it seems to disrupt rather than enshrine certain canonical
orthodoxies associated with transnational postcolonialism' is certainly
evident in his own work.[20]

Likewise, Gail Low's discussion of the 'productive tension existing
between the materiality of place and the spatiality of diasporic connections across borders and locations which should be acknowledged' does
not seek to resolve this tension by looking only in one direction.[21] Low
takes this tension as her framework for a fascinating history of negotiations between West Indian and black British identities dating back to the
1950s and Claudia Jones' *West Indian Gazette* (published between 1958
and 1965), through James Berry's ground-making anthologies *Bluefoot
Traveller* (1976) and *News from Babylon* (1984), to the pioneering literary
magazine *Wasafiri* that was founded by Susheila Nasta in 1984 and continues to shape the field of contemporary black and postcolonial writing
in Britain today.

At one level the tensions and discontinuities between these two models –
the transnational/diasporic paradigm and national paradigm – may simply be arguments about what to include or exclude from a national canon,
how to respond critically to writings that disrupt a seamless sense of
belonging to one place, and whether to disband with national canons
altogether? However, it is also important to consider whether the terms
on which we both comprehend and conduct the conversations about
who is in, who is out, and where and how we draw the lines between,
can themselves be read with the wider cultural-political discourses relating to black subjects in Britain.

Clearly all of these interventions concerning the question of a canon
are instructive and valuable in their own right, but taken as a whole the
articles collected here could also be read as marking out the acceptable
limits of the debate. In other words, they indicate that it is seemingly far
more attractive (and possibly safe) to point out the kinds of exclusions,
blind-spots and ideological pressures that have been and might still be
perpetrated under the sign of the canon, than it is to argue for its positive characteristics. It is, perhaps, by bringing the wider frame of British
culture and its various positions in relation to the politics of race into

play that we might move beyond the hesitant voicing of academic correctness.

One of the particularly striking feature of the essays collected here is the echoed recourse to Stuart Hall and Paul Gilroy's theorizations of black identity that were developed in the early 1990s in response to the burgeoning of black cultural productions in a whole range of disciplinary fields. Many of these works were centrally concerned with the demands of navigating between critical debates concerning artistic identities and those concerning the social meanings of race in Britain at that time. Leon Wainwright's contribution to this volume makes an excellent assessment of the significance of these theoretical discourses and in particular the development of a diaspora aesthetic. As Wainwright points out this 'aesthetic' served two vital roles:

> The first use of the diaspora aesthetic idea was as a fixed, easily identifiable definition for how black visual practices might be inherently typical of black and Asian people as a common group, distinguishing them as essentially connected and similar, regardless of their differing and changing circumstances. A second use was a more properly analytical motivation to elucidate the style of 'diaspora culture' in terms of 'dialogic strategies and hybrid forms', or 'the hybrid, transitory and always historically specific forms in which questions of "race" and ethnicity are articulated' both in black popular culture and popular culture in general.[22]

While many of the contributors to this volume cite Gilroy and Hall in order to discuss the politics of artistic style, discussions of Wainwright's 'first use' – the politics of solidarity – are notably absent. There is simply no contesting the fact that many of Gilroy's and Hall's (as well as Mercer's) influential essays from the early 1990s have a continued purchase today and will continue to be profoundly enabling to theorisations of black British culture for years to come.[23] However, the way in which their work is circulating now is interesting. Not only is there something of a potential time-warp developing between cultural practitioners and their critics, but the de-linking of these theories from the context of British society in the 1990s means that their political resonance is often left untranslated for our own time.

In 1997, the British Council organized a week-long gathering of cultural practitioners and critics to discuss 'the explosion if creative work in the arts, both serious and popular, especially from young practitioners from Asian, African, Afro-Caribbean and other so-called minority communities now living in Britain'.[24] They named this event 'Re-Inventing Britain'. Responding in part to Homi Bahbha's 'manifesto', this event became a forum for discussing and celebrating the artistic explosion and the ways in which cultural diversity was remapping Britain from the inside. Although there was much to celebrate at this moment and much optimism about the redefinition of British identities in a postcolonial age, Stuart Hall's closing remarks to the forum proved to be salutary:

> I myself do not take what is sometimes a very conventional view about globalisation namely that it has completely evaporated the space of national culture. What I think it has done is to profoundly dislocate and transform the space of national culture, but not to erode it, not to obscure it. It still constitutes a reality, a level of organisation, of forms of identification etc which are going to give us trouble in the years to come... Do not talk about Re-inventing Britain because Britain is of no consequence any longer; it's going to trouble us one way or another, for a good, long time to come.[25]

Although we might like to forget, it is important to remember that what may have seemed 'optimistically probable' in terms of transforming national culture in the 1990s when Gilroy and Hall published many of their seminal essays on conceptualizing black identity, has now been relegated to the realms of the 'hopefully possible'. It would seem that those years of trouble, which Hall predicted, have come. And, although it is still possible and illuminating to read cultural works through the lens of 1990s theory, perhaps as critics we also need to find a new theoretical vocabulary that can match the imagination of writers and artists whose works map the complex and changing dynamics between inclusion and exclusion and are so central to our understanding of both local and global, the cultural and the political.

In an article published in *Wasafiri* in 2002, I was concerned to try to re-animate the debates about how a politics of black representations played alongside the politics of black rights in a twenty-first century British context. At that point, the post-September 11th 2001 fall-out of insinuated Islamophobia and hysteria over refugees and asylum-seekers in the media, as well as the recent interventions in Afghanistan, had made the limits of shared national experience and the ways in which minority populations had been used to mark these out very clear. Writing about black British writing at that moment had alerted me to a troubling discrepancy in the discourses of rights and representations. There was much to be optimistic about in the cultural sphere. In addition to the decades of brilliant and challenging writings that I was centrally concerned with, there had been several recent and important cultural events. In the *Wasafiri* article I noted that:

Donald MacLellan's photographic exhibition 'Black Power' which showed at the National Gallery in 1998 offers new ethical models of representation by returning to the relationship of white photographer/ black subject with an awareness of its historical dimensions and a strategy of empowerment, allowing subjects to enunciate their own subject positions through statements which appear alongside the photographs and thereby initiating a politics of representation in which that self–other threshold is both foregrounded and negotiated. The phenomenal success of the Asian television comedy series *Goodness Gracious Me* which satirises both South Asian and white British cultural traits alongside each other speaks of a certain confidence to address the issues of cultural sensitivities and idiosyncrasies across, as well as within, cultural and ethnic communities. The British Council now sends Linton Kwesi Johnson, of 'Inglan is a Bitch' fame, around the globe as an envoy of Britishness.[26]

However, while these cross-cultural productions of Britishness demonstrated the possibilities for more a reciprocal, mature and educated sharing of the postcolonial nation, I was concerned that the issues around rights had made less progress. Moreover, I wanted to question whether the persuasions of certain cultural representations were encouraging us to invest prematurely in the fulfilment of a successfully completed 're-invention,' with Britain as the 'self-consciously post-colonial space in which the affirmation of difference points forward to a more pluralistic concept of nationality and perhaps beyond that to its transcendence', that Paul Gilroy had proposed in his influential 1993 article 'The peculiarities of the black English'.[27] At that time I argued that:

From the vantage point of the twenty-first century there is perhaps less reason to be optimistic about the national identity that is currently on offer. Do labels such as black British culture, writing, and canon encourage us to reproduce the nationalist idea in new ways that may be creative and radical in an institutional or pedagogic context but which nevertheless suggest a democracy of identity that is still very much fictional for most? Even if the cultural capital of being black in Britain has risen considerably in certain contexts, what does it say about the politics of representation that Zadie Smith can cash in on this but the people living in the North London suburbs whose lives she so carefully depicts cannot?[28]

Re-examining some of these questions now is not a pleasant experience. The Iraq war has shown in its terrifying and blatant spectacles of the misuse of Western power that imperialism is no longer a cloaked operation that postcolonial critics can unveil in cultural discourses. Thousands of uniformed soldiers and tanks fighting 'insurgents' and CIA agents making 'transnational' crossings to establish venues for torture and imprisonment without respect to the Geneva convention, show Empire in its old/new guise of military might. Since the 7 July 2005 bombings in London, there has been even more accelerated and depressing changes in the cultural and political landscape of Britain, with an even 'tougher' approach to immigration and the detainment of those considered a threat to the nation. There are clear indications that calls for renewed national solidarity, more pressure from the state for its citizens to declare particular measures of national attachment, and more threats of limited access to accepted universal rights, are all cut across by deep-seated racist constructions of 'outside threats' inside the nation. It is in this context that I want to propose the positive horizons that might be brought into view by a black British canon.

In his 2004 study, *After Empire*, Paul Gilroy addresses – albeit from afar in some ways – the subject of Britain in the twenty-first century. Gilroy's attempt to restore to our vision the horizon of a 'peaceful accommodation of otherness in relation to fundamental commonality', through his conception of conviviality and his attention to, 'the processes of cohabitation and interaction that have made multiculture an ordinary feature of social life in Britain's urban areas', seems particularly valuable post-7 July 2005.[29] All the same, at this moment, Gilroy's idea that, for young people in Britain's cities, 'a strong sense of racial difference [is] unthinkable to the point of absurdity' rings painfully through my head as I think of the racially motivated killing of Anthony Walker and others, and of the riots in October 2005 between young African-Caribbean and Asian men over the alleged sex attack on a 14-year-old Jamaican girl by Asian youths.[30] This conflict gives a terrible new dimension to Sivanadan's remarks about ethnic communities in Britain battling each other 'over position and power... [for] a place under the ethnic sun' that Gail Low and Marion Wynne-Davies discuss in their introduction to this volume.[31]

Gilroy's words on the state's attitude to young British subjects attracted to political Islam are, however, almost prescient. In response to those who argue that this attraction is, 'nothing whatsoever to do with domestic relations and domestic racism', Gilroy rejoins, 'I think that this alienation from Britain has different roots in home soil.'[32] The revelation that one of the suicide bombers behind the London bombings of July 7th 2005 was a very 'integrated' subject, according to most social indices, bears out Gilroy's sense that these young people are both 'among us' and 'of us' and that their 'intimate and decidedly postcolonial connections with black [British] life' demand even more urgent consideration.[33]

In terms of trying to move some of these considerations back into the orbit of debates on the canon, Gilroy's observation that

Because 'race' *ought* (according to the tenets of liberalism) to be nothing, it *is* prematurely pronounced to be of no consequence whatsoever[34]

may offer a timely warning to academics and critics who, myself included, are wary about discussing cultural forms in relation to a politics of race and hesitant about categories such as black British for fear that they may seemingly re-invest in race as a defining identity.

Gilroy points out that arriving at a point where we no longer believe in race as an identity should not mean losing sight of race as a politics. Racism and nationalism are still on intimate terms in Britain and, while it might be tempting to counter their intimacy by stressing the cosmopolitan and transnational dimensions of black British culture, this runs the risk of implying that blackness is somehow 'routed' but not 'rooted', and that its ties to elsewhereness are more compelling, even more real, than its claims on hereness. Texts, like citizens, have lives both contained within and exceeding the nation's boundaries, and it is to the material complexity of this situation that a black British canon both can and must speak. To return to Ahmad's definition, one of the most significant, but contested, values of a black British canon is that it allows for a shifting but intimate, inside version of black Britishness, which is not commonly acknowledged when works by writers, artists, musicians and filmmakers of Caribbean, African or South Asian ancestry are categorized according to their assumed originary or minority ethnicities.

I recognize that my advocacy of a heterodox canon of black British culture may be taken as a gesture which intensifies our awareness of difference rather than commonality and which promotes the idea of cultural enclaves – and, therefore, runs the risk of working against, rather than with, the flow of Gilroy's thoughts.[35] Moreover, a black British canon could be made to serve the purposes of a stagnant multiculturalism if it is both produced and received as a model through which to define, represent and even market black Britishness as a homogenous, fixed and bounded politics of identity that confirms the links between race and culture – rephrased a little. And yet, despite this risk, I want to argue that a black British canon may also be a tool through which to undo these very assumptions. More than this, I want to argue that, only by staging a bold and confident theatre for exchange, the black in British can be released from increasingly narrow ethnically-based criteria in all social contexts – criteria that generate anxiety, mistrust and a negative sense of difference in many British subjects.

As the essays included in this volume confirm, the proposal of a black British canon is not a means by which to resolve the enduring questions of whether 'black' cultural forms in Britain should focus on 'black' issues in Britain, or whether they have a special responsibility to a socially engaged model of representation, or whether they are obliged to offer new terms for the social understandings of race, gender and class within a British context. Rather, a provisional and contested canon can be the very instrument through which these questions, and the project of exploring subjectivity and agency as represented in disciplinary fields and social contexts, is kept alive and open. The selections here may also help to advance those critical agendas that have been notably slower and less challenging than the cultural works themselves. Instead of reasserting the prescriptive ideas of black British culture, I would argue that a heterodox canon would actually confirm that this category is no more stable or homogenous than a British canon, a woman's canon or a queer canon. More than this, it would show that there are no fixed borders to the nation state and that being black does not mean being defined by race. Finally, such heterodoxy allows for a positive focus on the dimensions of 'hereness' within national culture, and the possibility of a serious conversation about Britain's story of itself as a postcolonial nation.

Notes

1. James Procter, see above, p. 36.
2. F.R. Leavis, *The Great Tradition: George Eliot, Henry James, Joseph Conrad* (1948. rpt: Harmondsworth: Penguin Books, 1962).
3. T.S. Eliot, 'Tradition and the Individual Talent', *The Sacred Wood: Essays on Poetry and Criticism* (London: Methues, 1922).
4. Aijaz Ahmad, 'Jameson's Rhetoric of Otherness and the "National Allegory"', *Social Text*, 17 (1987), pp. 3–25; p. 25. Fredric Jameson, 'Third-World Literature in the Era of Multinational Capitalism', *Social Text*, 15 (1986), pp. 65–88.
5. For example, Norman Jeffares pioneered Commonwealth Studies at the University of Leeds. William Walsh, *Commonwealth Literature* (London: Macmillan, 1980). John Press (ed.), *The Teaching of English Literature Overseas*

(London: Methuen, 1963*)*. See also, Gerald Moore's pioneering work on African writing, *Seven African Writers* (London: Oxford University Press, 1962), edited with Ulli Beier, *Modern Poetry From Africa* (Harmondsworth: Penguin Books, 1963), and *African Literature and the Universities* (Ibadan: Ibadan University Press, 1965). At the University of Kent, Louis James produced one of the first book studies on the Caribbean, *The Islands In Between* (Oxford: Oxford University Press, 1968). Longstanding and continuing Anglophone regional and national bibliographies may be found in the *Journal of Commonwealth Literature*.

6. See Alison Donnell, *Twentieth-Century Caribbean Literature* (London: Routledge, 2004), for a discussion of how Caribbean literature is discoursed upon, how canons are created, and what ideological and historical pressures shape such discussions.

7. Courttia Newland and Kadija Sesay (eds), *IC3: The Penguin Anthology of New Black Writing in Britain* (Penguin: London, 2000), pp. xii–xiv; p. xiii.; Patsy Antoine and Courttia Newland (eds), *Afrobeat* (London: Pulp Books, 1999); Karen McCarthy (ed.), *Bittersweet: contemporary black women's poetry* (London: Women's Press, 1998); Lemn Sissay (ed.), *The Fire People: a collection of contemporary black British poets* (Edinburgh: Payback Press,1998); Ferdinand Dennis and Naseem Khan (eds), *Voices of the Crossing: the impact of Britain on writers from Asia, the Caribbean and Africa* (London: Serpents Tail, 2000).

8. Procter, see above, p. 36.

9. Phillips, see above, pp. 14, 15.

10. Phillips, see above, p. 14.

11. McLeod, see above, p. 95.

12. McLeod, see above, p. 98. For anthologies see: Onyekachi Wambu (ed.), *Empire Windrush* (London: Phoenix, 1999); Newland and Sesay, *op. cit.*; James Procter (ed.), *Writing black Britain 1948–1998* (Manchester: Manchester University Press, 2000).

13. McLeod, see above, p. 99.

14. McLeod, see above, p. 102.

15. McMillan, see above, p. 130.

16. Low, see above, p. 168.

17. McLeod, see above, p. 98.

18. Folorunso, see above, p. 84.

19. McMillan , see above, pp. 134–5.

20. Procter, see above, p. 44.

21. Low, see above, p. 169.

22. Wainwright, see above, p. 148.

23. For example: Paul Gilroy, 'The peculiarities of the black English', in *Small Acts: Thoughts on the Politics of Black Cultures* (London: Serpent's Tail, 1993); Stuart Hall, 'New Ethnicities', in *Black Film/British Cinema*, ICA Document 7 (London, Institute of Contemporary Arts, 1988), pp. 27–31, and 'Reinventing Britain: A Forum', *Wasafiri*, 29 (1999), pp. 37–44; Kobena Mercer, *Welcome to the Jungle: new positions in black cultural studies* (London: Routledge, 1994).

24. Hall, *op. cit.* (1999), p. 37.

25. *Ibid.*, p. 43.

26. Alison Donnell, 'Nation and Contestation: Black British Writing', *Wasafiri*, 36 (2002), pp. 11–17; p. 16.

27. Gilroy, *op. cit.* (1993), p. 62.
28. Donnell, *op. cit.*, p. 16.
29. Paul Gilroy, *After Empire: melancholia and convivial culture?* (Oxford: Routledge, 2004), p. 3 and xi.
30. *Ibid.*, p. 132.
31. Gail Low and Marion Wynne-Davies, see above, p. 4.
32. Gilroy, *op. cit.* (2004), p. 134.
33. *Ibid.*, p. 137.
34. *Ibid.*, p. 159.
35. The term 'heterodox', rather than 'heterogeneous', has been used consistently through this afterword in order to engage fully with Ahmad's definition and argument.

Index